Michelle R .... lges of Manchester, ... e lively children. Now she lives in the .... unty of Cheshire, with her busy executive husband and two grown-up daughters. She loves reading, the ballet, and playing tennis when she gets the chance. She hates cooking, cleaning, and despises ironing! Sleep she can do without and produces some of her best written work during the early hours of the morning.

Michelle Smart is a *Publishers Weekly* bestselling author with a slight-to-severe coffee addiction. A book worm since birth, Michelle can usually be found hiding behind a paperback, or if it's an author she really loves, a hardback. Michelle lives in rural Northamptonshire in England with her husband and two young Smarties. When not reading or pretending to do the housework she loves nothing more than creating worlds of her own. Preferably with lots of coffee on tap. Visit michelle-smart.com

Jennie Lucas' parents owned a bookstore and she grew up surrounded by books, dreaming about faraway lands. At twenty-two she met her future husband and after their marriage, she graduated from university with a degree in English. She started writing books a year later. Jennie won the Romance Writers of America's Golden Heart competition in 2005 and hasn't looked back since. Visit Jennie's website at jennielucas.com

Passionate Encounters

March 2022
Tempted by the Boss

April 2022
Second Chance Seduction

May 2022
Consequences of One Night

June 2022
Risking It All

July 2022
A Price Worth Paying

August 2022
Revenge is Sweet

Passionate Encounters
Second Chance
Seduction

MICHELLE REID

MICHELLE SMART

JENNIE LUCAS

MILLS & BOON

First Published in Great Britain 2022
by Mills & Boon, an imprint of HarperCollins*Publishers* Ltd,
1 London Bridge Street, London, SE1 9GF

www.harpercollins.co.uk

HarperCollins*Publishers*
1st Floor, Watermarque Building,
Ringsend Road, Dublin 4, Ireland

PASSIONATE ENCOUNTERS: SECOND CHANCE SEDUCTION
© 2022 Harlequin Enterprises ULC

A Passionate Marriage © 2002 Michelle Reid
A Passionate Reunion in Fiji © 2019 Michelle Smart
Dealing Her Final Card © 2013 Jennie Lucas

ISBN: 978-0-263-30455-8

MIX
Paper from
responsible sources
FSC™ C007454

A PASSIONATE MARRIAGE

MICHELLE REID

CHAPTER ONE

LEANDROS PETRONADES sat lazing on a sunbed on the deck of his yacht and looked out on the bay of San Estéban. Satisfaction toyed with his senses. The new Spanish resort had developed into something special and having enjoyed a very much hands-on experience during its development, he felt that sense of satisfaction was well deserved. Plus the fact that he had multiplied his original investment, he was business-orientated enough to add.

He had done a lot of that during the four years since he took over from his late father, he mused idly. Multiplying original investments had become an expectation for him.

Which was probably why he'd found this project just that bit different. It had always been more than just another investment. He had been in on it from the beginning when it had been only an idea in an old friend's head. Between them, he and Felipe Vazquez had carefully nurtured that idea until it had grown into the fashionable new resort he was seeing today.

The problem for him now was, where did he go from here? The resort was finished. The luxury villas dotted about the hillside had their new owners, the five-star hotel, golf and leisure complex was functioning like a dream. And San Estéban itself was positively bustling, its harbour basin filled with luxury sail crafts owned by the rich and famous looking for new places to hide out while they played. By next week even this yacht, which had been his home while he had been based here, would have slipped her moorings. She would sail to the Caribbean to await the

5

arrival of his brother Nikos, who planned to fly out with his new bride in three weeks.

It was time for him to move on, though he did not know what it was he wanted to move on to. Did he go back to Athens and lose himself in the old cut and thrust of the corporate jungle? His wide shoulders shifted against the sun bed's padded white cushion as an old restlessness began to stir deep within his bones.

'No, it is not possible to go over the top with this.' A soft female voice filtered through the open doors behind him. 'It is to be a celebration of San Estéban's rebirth, and a thanks and farewell to all who worked so hard to make the project happen. Let it be one of fireworks and merriment. We will call it—the Baptism of San Estéban, and it will become its annual day of carnival.'

A smile eased itself across his mouth as Leandros listened, and his shoulders relaxed as the restlessness drained away. The Baptism of San Estéban, he mused. He liked it.

He liked Diantha. He liked having her around because she was so calm and quiet and so terribly efficient. When he asked her to do something for him she did it without bothering him with the irritating details. She was good for him. She tuned in so perfectly to the way of his thinking.

He was almost sure that he was going to marry her.

He did not love her—he did not believe in love any more. But Diantha was beautiful, intelligent, exceedingly pleasant company, and she promised to be a good lover— though he had not got around to trying her out. She was also Greek, independently wealthy and was not too demanding of his time.

A busy man like him had to take these things into consideration when choosing a wife, he pondered complacently. For he must be allowed the freedom to do what was necessary to keep himself and the Petronades Group of companies streets ahead of their nearest rivals. Coming from a similar background to his own, Diantha Christophoros understood and accepted this. She would not nag and complain and make him feel guilty for working long hours, nor would she expect him to be at her beck and call every minute of the day.

She was, in other words, the perfect choice of wife for a man like him.

There was only one small obstacle. He already had a wife. Before he could begin to approach Diantha with murmurings of romance and marriage he must, in all honour, cut legal ties to his current spouse. Though the fact that they had not so much as laid eyes on each other in three years meant he did not envisage a quick divorce from Isobel being a problem.

Isobel...

'Damn,' he cursed softly as the restlessness returned with enough itchy tension to launch him to his feet. He should not have allowed himself to think her name. It never failed to make him uptight. As time had gone by, he had thought less and less of her and become a better person for it. But sometimes her name could still catch him out and sink its barbed teeth into him.

Going over to the refrigerated drinks trolley, he selected a can of beer, snapped the tab and went to rest his lean hips against the yacht rail, his dark eyes frowning at the view that had only made him smile minutes before.

That witch, the hellion, he thought grimly. She had left her mark on him and it still had not faded three years on.

He took a gulp of his beer. Behind him he could still hear Diantha's level tones as she planned San Estéban's celebration day with her usual efficiency. If he turned his head he would see her standing in his main stateroom, looking as if she belonged there with her dark hair and eyes and olive-toned skin, her elegant clothes chosen to enhance her beauty, not place it on blatant display like...

He took another pull of the beer can. Up above his head the hot Spanish sun was burning into his naked shoulders. It felt good enough to have him flexing deep-bedded muscles wrapped in rich brown skin.

Recalling Isobel, he felt a different kind of bite tug at his senses. This one hit him low down in his gut where the sex thing lurked. He grimaced, wondering if or when he would ever want another woman the way he'd wanted Isobel? And hoped he never had to suffer those primitive urges again.

They had gone into marriage like two randy teenagers, loving each other with a passion that had them tearing each other to pieces by the time they'd separated. He had been too young—she had been too young. They'd made love like animals and fought in the same ferocious way until— inevitably probably—it had all turned so nasty and bitter and bad that it had been easier to lock it all away and forget he had a wife than to risk allowing it all to break out again.

But, like his sojourn in San Estéban, it was over now— time to move on with his life. He was thirty-one years old and ready to settle down with a *proper* wife, maybe even a family...

'Why the frown?'

Diantha had come up beside him without him noticing. Turning his head, he looked down into warm brown eyes, saw the soft smile on her lips...and thought of a different smile. This mouth didn't smile, it pouted—provokingly. And those intense green eyes were never warm but just damned defiant.

'I am attempting to come to terms with the fact that it is time for me to leave here,' he answered her question.

'And you do not want to leave,' Diantha murmured understandingly.

Leandros sighed. 'I have come to love this place,' he confessed, looking outwards towards San Estéban again.

There followed a few moments of silence between them, the kind that allowed his mind to drift without intrusion across the empty years during which he had hidden away here, learning to be whole again. San Estéban had been his sanctuary in a time of misery and disillusionment. Isobel had—

It took the gentle touch of Diantha's fingers to his warm bicep to remind him that she was here. They rarely touched. It was not yet that kind of relationship. She was his sister Chloe's closest friend and he was honour-bound to treat her as such while she was here. But his senses stirred in response to those cool fingers—only to settle down again the moment they were removed.

'You know what I think, Leandros,' she said gently. 'I think you have been here for too long. Living the life of a lotus-eater has made you lazy—which makes it a good time for you to return to Athens and move on with your life, don't you think?'

'Ah, words of wisdom,' he smiled. It was truly uncanny how Diantha could tap in to his thinking. 'Don't worry,' he said. 'After the San Estéban celebration I have every intention of returning to Athens and…move on, as you call it,' he promised.

'Good,' she commended. 'Your mama will be pleased to hear it.'

And with that simple blessing she moved away again, walking gracefully back into the stateroom in her neat blue dress that suited her figure and with her glossy black hair coiled with classical Greek conservatism to the slender curve of her nape.

But she did so with no idea that she had left behind her a man wearing another frown because he was seeing long, straight, in-your-face red hair flowing down a narrow spine in a blazing defiance to everything Greek. Isobel would have rather died than wear that neat blue dress, he mused grimly. She preferred short skirts that showed her amazing legs off and skinny little tops that tantalised the eyes with the thrust of her beautiful, button-tipped breasts.

Isobel would rather have cut out her tongue than show concern for his mother's feelings, he mentally added as he turned away again and took another grim pull of his beer. Isobel and his family had not got on. They had rubbed each other up the wrong way from the very beginning, and both factions hadn't attempted to hide that from him.

Diantha, on the other hand, adored his mother and his mother adored her. Being such a close friend to his sister, Chloe, she had always hovered on the periphery of his life, though he had only truly taken notice of her since she had arrived here a week ago to step into the breach to help organise next week's celebration because Chloe, who should have been here helping him, had become deeply embroiled in Nikos's wedding preparations.

It had been good of Diantha in the circumstances. He appreciated the time she had placed at his disposal, particularly since she had only just returned to Athens, having spent the last four years with her family living in Washington, D.C. She was well bred and well liked—her advantages were adding up, he noted. And, other than for a brief romance with his brother Nikos to blot her copybook, she was most definitely much more suitable than that witch of a redhead with sharp barbs for teeth.

With that final thought on the subject he took a final pull of his beer can, saw a man across the quay taking photographs of the yacht and frowned at him. He had a distinct dislike of photographers, not only because they intruded on his privacy but also because it was what his dear wife did for a living. When they had first met she had been aiming a damned camera at him—or was it the red Ferrari he had been leaning against? No, it had been him. She had got him to pose then flirted like mad with him while the camera clicked. By the end of the same day they'd gone to bed, and after that—

He did not want to think about what had happened after that. He did not want to think of Isobel at all. She no longer belonged in his thoughts, and it was about time that he made that official.

The man with the camera turned away. So did Leandros, decisively. He suddenly felt a lot better about leaving here and went inside to…move on with his life.

Isobel's own thinking was moving very much along the same lines as she sat reading the letter that had just arrived from her estranged husband's lawyer giving her notice of Leandros's intention to begin divorce proceedings.

She was sitting alone at a small kitchen table. Her mother hadn't yet risen from her bed. She was glad about that because the letter had come as a shock, even though she agreed with its content. It was time, if not well overdue that one of them should take the bull by the horns and call an official end to a marriage that should have never been.

But the printed words on the page blurred for a moment at the realisation that this was it, the final chapter of a four-year mistake. If she agreed to Leandros's terms, then she knew she would be accepting that those years had been nothing but wasted in her life.

Did he feel the same? Was that why he had taken so long to get to this? It was hard to acknowledge that you could be so fallible, that you had once been stupid enough to let your heart rule your head.

Or was there more to it than a decision to put an end to their miserable marriage? Had he found someone with whom he felt he could spend the rest of his life?

The idea shouldn't hurt but it did. She had loved Leandros so badly at the beginning that she suspected she'd gone a little mad. They'd been young—too young— but oh, it had been so wildly passionate.

Then—no, don't think about the passion, she told herself firmly, and made herself read the letter again.

It was asking her if she would consider travelling to Athens to meet with her husband—in the presence of their respective lawyers, of course—so they could thrash out a settlement in an effort to make the divorce quick and trouble-free. A few days of her time should be enough, Takis Konstantindou was predicting. All expenses would be paid by Leandros for both herself and her lawyer as a goodwill gesture, because Mr Petronades couldn't travel to England at this time.

She paused to wonder why Leandros couldn't travel. For the man she remembered virtually lived out of a suitcase, so it was odd to think of him under some kind of restraint.

It was odd to think about him at all, she extended, and the letter lost its holding power as she sat back in the chair. They'd first met by accident right here in England at an annual car exhibition. She'd been there in her official capacity as photographer for a trendy new magazine—a bright and confident twenty-two-year-old who believed the whole world was at her feet. While he was dashing and twenty-seven years old, with the looks and the build of a genuine dark Apollo.

They'd flirted over the glossy bonnet of some prohibitively expensive sports car. With his looks and his charm and his immaculate clothing, she'd assumed he was one of the car's sales representatives, since they all looked and dressed like a million dollars. It had never occurred to her that far from selling the car they were flirting across he owned several of them. Realisation about just who Leandros was had come a lot later—much too late to do anything about it.

By then he'd already bowled her over with his dark good looks and easy charm and the way he looked at her that left her in no doubt as to what was going on behind his handsome façade. They'd made a date to share dinner and ended up falling into bed at the first opportunity they were handed. His finding out that he was her first lover had only made the passion burn all the more. He'd adored playing the role of tutor. He'd taught her to understand the pleasures of her own body and made sure that she understood what pleasured his. When it came time for him to go back to Greece he'd refused to go without her. They'd married in a hasty civil ceremony then rushed to the airport to catch their flight.

It was as he'd led her onto a private jet with the Petronades logo shining in gold on its side that she started to ask questions. He'd thought it absolutely hilarious that she didn't know she'd married the modern equivalent of Croesus, and had carried her off to the tiny private cabin, where he'd made love to her all the way to Athens. She had never been so happy in her entire life.

But that was it—the sum total of the happy side of their marriage was encapsulated in a single hop from England to Greece. By the time they'd arrived at his family home the whole, whirling wonder of their love was already turning stale. 'You can't wear that to meet my mother;' his first criticism of her could still ring antagonistic bells in her head.

'Why, what's wrong with it?'

'The skirt is too short; she will have a fit. And can you not tie your hair up or something, show a little respect for the people you are about to meet?'

She had not tied her hair up, nor had she changed her clothes. But she had soon learned the hard way that stubborn defiance was one thing when it was aimed at a man who virtually salivated with desire for you even as he criticised. But it was not the same as being boxed and tagged a cheap little floozy at first horrified glance.

Things had gone from bad to worse after that. And—yes, she reiterated as her gaze dipped back to the letter, it *was* time that one of them took the initiative and drew the final curtain across something that should never have been.

In fact, Isobel had only one problem with the details Takis Konstantindou had mapped out in the letter. She could not see how she could spend several days in Athens because she could not leave her mother on her own for that long.

'What time does her flight come in?'

Leandros was sitting at his desk in his plush Athens office. In the two weeks he had been back here he had changed into a different person. Gone was the laid-back man of San Estéban and in his place sat a sharp-edged, hard-headed Greek tycoon.

Was he happy with that? No, he was not happy to become this person again, but needs must when the devil drives, so they said. In this case the devil was the amount of importance other people placed on his time and knowledge. His desk was virtually groaning beneath the weight of paperwork that apparently needed his attention as a matter of urgency. He moved from important meeting to meeting with hardly a breath in between. His social life had gone from a lazy meal eaten in a restaurant on the San Estéban boulevard, to a constant round of social engagements that literally set his teeth on edge. If he lifted his eyes someone jumped to speak to him. If he closed those same eyes someone else would ensure that he opened them again. The wheels of power ground on and on for twenty-four hours of every day and the whole merry-go-round was made all the more intense because his younger brother Nikos was off limits while he prepared for his wedding day.

On his father's death Leandros had become the head of the Petronades family, therefore it was his duty to play host in his father's stead. His mother was becoming more neurotic the closer it came to Nikos's big day, and was likely to panic if she did not have an open line to her eldest son's ear. If he complained she told him not to spoil this for her then reminded him that he had denied her the opportunity to stand proud and watch him make his own disastrous union. And because thoughts of marriage were already on his mind, he was hard put not to snap at her that maybe Nikos could take a leaf out of his own book and run away to marry secretly. At least the day would belong only to him and Carlotta. If there was anything about his own marriage he could still look back on with total pleasure, it was that moment when Isobel had smiled up at him as he placed the ring upon her finger and whispered, 'I love you so much.' He had not needed five hundred witnesses to help prove that vow to be true.

His heart gave him a punishing twinge of regret for what he had once had and lost.

'This evening.' Takis Konstantindou pulled him back from where he had been in danger of visiting. 'But she insisted on making her own arrangements,' Takis informed him. 'She will be staying at the Apollo near Piraeus.'

Leandros frowned. 'But that is a mediocre place with a low star rating. Why should she want to stay there when she could have had a suite at the Athenaeum?'

Takis just shrugged his lack of an answer. 'All I know is that she refused our invitation to make arrangements for her and reserved three rooms, not two, at the Apollo, one of which must have wheelchair access.'

Wheelchair access? Leandros sat forward, his attention suddenly riveted. 'Why?' he demanded. 'What's wrong with her? Has she been hurt…is she ill?'

'I don't know if the special room *is* for her,' Takis answered. 'All I know is that she has reserved such a room.'

'Then find out!' he snapped. Suddenly the thought of his beautiful Isobel trapped in a wheelchair made him feel physically ill!

He must even have gone pale because Takis was looking at him oddly. 'It could change everything, do you not see that?' His tycoon persona jumped to his rescue. 'The whole structure on which we have based our proposals for a settlement may need to be revised to take into account a physical disability.'

'I think you have adequately covered for any such eventuality, Leandros.' The lawyer smiled cynically.

'*Adequate* is not good enough.' He was suddenly furious. 'Adequate is not what I was aiming towards! I am no skinflint! I have no wish to play games with this! Isobel is my wife.' Hearing that 'is' leaving his lips forced him to stop and take a breath. 'I will leave my marriage with no sense of triumph at its failure, Takis,' he informed the other man. 'But I will hopefully leave it with the knowledge that I treated her fairly in the end.'

Takis was looking surprised at his outburst. 'I'm sorry, Leandros, I never meant to—'

'I know what you meant,' he interrupted curtly. 'And I

know what you think.' Which was why that derisory comment about Isobel being *adequately* compensated had made him see red. He knew what his family thought about Isobel. He knew that they probably discussed her between themselves in that same derogatory way. He had even let them—if only by pretending it wasn't happening. But they were wrong if they believed his failed marriage was down to Isobel, because it wasn't. Not all of it anyway.

Takis was wrong about him if he believed that he was filing for divorce because he no longer cared about Isobel. He might not want her back to run riot through his life again, but... 'Whatever anyone else thinks about my marriage to Isobel, she deserves and *will* get my full honour and respect at all times. Do you understand that?'

'Of course.' For a man who was twice his own age and also his godfather, Takis Konstantindou suddenly looked very much the wary employer as he gave a nod of his silvered head. 'It never crossed my—'

'Find out what you can before we meet with her,' Leandros interrupted, glanced at his watch and was relieved to see he was due at a meeting elsewhere so could end this conversation.

He stood up. Takis took his cue without further comment and went off to do his bidding. Leandros waited until the door closed behind him, then threw himself back down into his chair. He knew he was behaving irrationally. He understood why Takis no longer understood just where it was he was coming from. Only two weeks ago Leandros had called up his godfather and informed him he wanted to file for divorce. It had been a brief and unemotional conversation to which Takis had responded in the same brisk, lawyer-like way.

But a few weeks ago, in his head, Isobel had been a witch and a hellion with barbs for teeth. Now, on the back

of one small comment she was the young and vulnerable
creature he had dragged by the scruff of her beautiful neck
out of sensual heaven into the hell of Athenian society.

On a thick oath he stood up again, paced around his
desk. What was going on here? he asked himself. What
was the matter with him? Did he have to come over all
macho and feel suddenly protective because there was a
chance that the Isobel he would meet tomorrow was going
to be a shadow of the one he once knew?

A wheelchair.

Another oath escaped him. The phone on his desk began
to ring. It was Diantha, gently reminding him that his
mother would prefer him not to be late for dinner tonight.
The tension eased out of his shoulders, her soft, slightly
amused tone showing sympathy with his present plight
where his mother was concerned. By the time the conversation ended he was feeling better—much more like his
gritty, calm self.

Yes, he confirmed. Diantha was good for him. She re-
focused his mind on those things that should matter, like
the meeting he should be attending right now.

'You're asking for trouble dressed like that,' Silvia
Cunningham announced in her usual blunt manner.

Isobel took a step back to view herself in the mirror.
'Why, what's wrong with it?' All she saw was a perfectly
acceptable brown tailored suit with a skirt that lightly
hugged her hips and thighs to finish at a respectable length
just below her slender knees. The plain-cut zip-up jacket
stopped at her waist and beneath it she wore a staunchly
conventional button-through cream blouse. Her hair was
neat, caught up in a twist and held in place by a tortoise-
shell comb. She was wearing an unremarkable flesh-

coloured lipstick, a light dusting of eye-shadow and some black mascara, but that was all.

In fact she could not look more conservative if she tried to be, she informed that hint of a defiant glint she could see burning in her green eyes.

'What's wrong with that suit is that it's an outright provocation,' her mother said. 'The wretched man never could keep his hands off you at the worst of times. What do you think he's going to want to do when you turn up wearing a suit with a definite slink about it?'

'I can't help my figure!' Isobel flashed back defensively. 'It's the one you gave to me, along with the hair and the eyes.'

'And the temper,' Silvia nodded. 'And the wilful desire to let him see what it is he's passing up.'

'Passing up?' Those green eyes flashed. 'Do I have to remind you that I was the one who left him three years ago?'

'And he was the one who did not bother to come and drag you back again.'

Rub it in, why don't you? Isobel thought. 'I haven't got time for this,' she said and began searching for her handbag. 'I have a meeting to go to.'

'You shouldn't be going to this meeting at all!'

'Please don't start again.' Isobel sighed. They had already been through this a hundred times.

'I agree that it is time to end your marriage, Isobel,' her mother persisted none the less, 'and I am even prepared to admit that the letter from Leandros's lawyer brought the best news I'd heard in two long years!'

Looking at the way her mother was struggling to stand with the aid of her walking frame, Isobel understood where she was coming from when she said that.

'But I still think you should have conducted this business through a third party,' she continued, 'and, looking at the way you've dressed yourself up, I am now absolutely positive that coming face to face with him is a mistake!'

'Sit down—please,' Isobel begged. 'Your arms are shaking. You know what they said about overdoing it.'

'I will sit when you stop being so pig-stubborn about this!'

A grin suddenly flashed across Isobel's face. 'Pot calling the kettle black,' she said.

Her mother's mouth twitched. If Isobel ever wanted to know where she got her stubbornness from then she only had to look at Silvia Cunningham. The hair, the eyes, even her strength of will came from this very determined woman. Though all of those features in her mother had taken a severe battering over the last two years since a dreadful car accident. Silvia was recovering slowly, but the damage to her spine had been devastating. Fortunately— and her mother was one for counting her blessings—her mind was still as bright as a polished button and unwaveringly determined to get her full mobility back.

But Sylvia had a tendency to overdo it. Only a few weeks ago she had taken a bad fall. She hadn't broken anything but she'd bruised herself and severely shaken her confidence. It had also shaken Isobel's confidence about leaving her alone throughout the day while she was at work. Then Leandros's letter had arrived to make life even more complicated. It had been easier to just bring Silvia with her than to leave her behind then worry sick for every minute she was away from her.

On a tut of impatience Isobel went to catch up the nearest chair and settled it behind her mother's legs. Silvia lowered herself into it without protest, which said a lot about how difficult she'd been finding it to stand. But that was her mother, Isobel thought as she bent to kiss her

smooth cheek. She was a fighter. The fact that she was
still of this world and able to hold her own in an argument
was proof of it.

'Look,' Isobel said, coming down to her mother's level
and moving the walking frame out of the way so that she
could claim her hands. 'All right, I confess that I've
dressed like this for a reason. But it has nothing to do with
trying to make Leandros regret this divorce.' It went much
deeper than that, and her darkened eyes showed it. 'He did
nothing but criticise my taste in clothes. When he did, I
was just too stubborn to make even one small concession
to his opinion of what his wife should look like, wear or
behave.'

'Quite right too.' Her beautiful, loyal mother nodded.
'Pretentious oaf.'

'Well, I mean to show him that when I have the freedom
to choose what the heck I want to wear, then I can be as
conventional as anyone.'

A pair of shrewd old eyes looked into their younger
matching pair, and saw cracks a mile wide in those excuses
just waiting for her daughter to fall right in.

A knock sounded at the door. It would be Lester Miles,
Isobel's lawyer. With a hurried smile, Isobel got up to
leave. But her mother refused to let go of her hand.

'Don't let him hurt you again,' she murmured urgently.

Isobel's sudden flash of annoyance took Silvia by surprise. 'Whatever else Leandros did to me, he *never* set out
to hurt me, Mother.' *Mother* said it all. For Silvia was *Mum*
or *sweetheart*, but only ever *Mother* when she was out of
line. 'We were in love, but were wrong for each other.
Learning to accept that was painful for us both.'

Silvia held her tongue in check and accepted a second
kiss on her cheek while Isobel wondered what the heck

she was doing defending a man whose treatment of her had been so indefensible!

What was the matter with her? Was it nerves? Was she more stressed about this meeting than she was prepared to admit? Hurt her? What else could Leandros do that could hurt her more than he'd already done three years ago?

Another knock at the door and she was turning towards it, her mind in a sudden hectic whirl. She tried to fight it, tried to stay calm. 'What are you going to do while I'm out?' she asked as she walked towards the door.

'Clive has hired a car. We are going to do some sight-seeing.'

Clive. Isobel's mouth tightened. There was another point of conflict she had not yet addressed. Clive Sanders was their neighbour and very good friend. He was also what Isobel supposed she could call the new man in her life. Or that was what he could be if Isobel gave Clive the green light.

Clive had somehow managed to invite himself along on this trip—aided and abetted by her mother, she was sure. The first she'd known about it was when she'd been in the hotel foyer last night and happened to see him arrive. Clive had just smiled at her burst of annoyance, touched a soothing hand to her angry cheek and said innocently, 'I am here for your mother. You're supposed to be pleased by the surprise, you ungrateful thing.'

But she had been far from pleased or grateful. Too many people seemed to believe they had a right to interfere in her life. Clive insisted the trip to Athens fitted in with his plans for a much-needed break. Her mother insisted it made her feel more secure to have a man like Clive around. Isobel thought there was a conspiracy between the two of them, which involved Clive keeping an eye on her in case she went totally off the rails when she met up with Leandros again.

But she knew differently. For all that she'd just defended Leandros, she knew there was not a single chance that seeing him was going to send her toppling back into the madness of their old love affair. She didn't hate him, but she despised him for the way he had treated her. He'd killed her confidence and her spirit and, finally, her love.

'Don't let him tire you out,' was her clipped comment to Silvia about Clive's presence here.

'He's a fully trained physiotherapist,' Silvia pointed out. 'Give him the benefit of some sense.' Which was her mother's way of making it known that she knew Isobel disapproved of him being here. 'And Isobel,' Silvia added as she was about to pull the door open, 'a brown leather suit is not conventional by any stretch of the imagination, so stop kidding yourself that you're out to do anything but make that man sit up and take note.'

Isobel left the room without bothering to answer, startling Lester Miles with the abruptness with which she appeared. His eyes widened then slid down over the leather suit before carefully hooding in a way that told her he thought her attire inappropriate too.

Maybe it was. Her chin went up. Suddenly she was fizzing like a simmering pot ready to explode because her mother was right—she was out to blow Leandros right out of his shoes.

'Shall we go?' she said.

Lester Miles just nodded and fell into step beside her. He was young and he was eager and she had picked him out at random from the Yellow Pages. Yes, she was dressed for battle, because she didn't think she needed a lawyer to fire her shots for her—though she was happy for him to come along and play the stooge.

For today was redemption day. Today she intended to take back all of those things that Leandros had wrenched from her and walk away a whole person again. She didn't want his money or to discuss *settlements*. She had nothing he could want from her, unless he planned to fight over a gold wedding ring and a few diamond trinkets that had made his mother stare in dismay when she'd found out that her son had given them to Isobel.

Family heirlooms, she recalled. 'A bit wasted on you, don't you think?' his sister Chloe had said. But then, dear Mama and Chloe had not been in the bedroom when the precious heirlooms had been her only attire. They'd not seen the way their precious boy had decked out his wife in every sparkle he could lay his hands on—before he enjoyed the pleasure they gave.

Those same heirlooms still lay languishing in a safety deposit box right here in Athens. Leandros was welcome to them as far as she was concerned. It was going to be interesting to discover just what he was willing to place on the table for their safe return—before she told him she wanted nothing from him, then gave him back his damned diamonds and left with her pride!

The journey across Athens in a taxi took an age in traffic that hardly seemed to move. Lester Miles kept on quizzing her as to what was required of him, but she answered in tight little sentences that gave him no clue at all.

'You are in such a powerful position, Mrs Petronades,' he pointed out. 'With no pre-nuptial agreement you are entitled to half of everything your husband owns.'

Isobel blinked. She hadn't given a single thought to a pre-nuptial agreement or the lack of one, come to that. Was this why Leandros wanted to see her personally? Was he out to charm her into seeing this settlement thing from his point of view? The stakes had quite suddenly risen. A few family heirlooms didn't seem to matter any more when you put them in the giant Petronades pot of gold.

'Negotiations will stand or fall on which of you wants this divorce more,' Lester Miles continued. 'As it was your husband who instigated proceedings, I think we can safely say that power is in your hands.'

'You've done your homework,' she murmured.

'Of course,' he said. 'It is what you hired me to do.'

'Does that mean you might know *why* my husband has suddenly decided he wants this divorce?' she enquired curiously.

'I have not been able to establish anything with outright proof,' the lawyer warned her, then looked so uncomfortable Isobel felt that fizz in her stomach start up again. 'But I do believe there is another woman involved. She goes by the name of Miss Diantha Christophoros. She is from one of the most respected families in Greece, my sources tell me…'

His sources couldn't be more right, Isobel agreed as she shifted restlessly in recognition of the Greek beauty's name. A union between the Petronades and Christophoros families would be the same as founding a dynasty. Mama Petronades must be so very pleased.

'She spent some time with your husband on his yacht recently,' her very efficient lawyer continued informatively. 'Also, your brother-in-law—Nicolas Petronades—will be marrying Carlotta Santorini next week. Rumour has it that once his brother is married your husband would like to follow suit. It could be an heir thing,' he suggested. 'Powerful families like the Petronades prefer to keep the line of succession clear cut.'

An heir thing, Isobel repeated. Felt tears sting the backs of her eyes and the fizz happening inside her turn to an angry ache.

To hell with you, Leandros, she thought bitterly.

CHAPTER TWO

TO HELL with you, Isobel repeated fifteen minutes later, when finally they came face to face in the elegant surroundings of Leondros's company boardroom with all its imposing wood panelling and fancy portraits of past masters.

Here stood the latest in a long line of masters, she observed coldly. Leandros Petronades, lean, dark and as arrogant as ever. A man built to break hearts, as she should know.

He stood six feet two inches tall and wore a grey suit, white shirt and a grey silk tie that drew a line down the length of a torso made up of tensile muscle wrapped in silk-like bronze skin. He hadn't changed, not so much as an inch of him; not the aura of leashed power beneath the designer clothing, or the sleek, handsome structure of his face. His hair was still that let-me-touch midnight-black colour, his eyes dark like the richest molasses ever produced, and his mouth smooth, slim, very masculine—the mouth of a born sensualist.

She wanted to reach out and slap his face. She wanted to leap on him and beat at his adulterous chest with her fists. The anger, the pain, the black, blinding pulse of emotional fury was literally throbbing along her veins. It was as if the last three years hadn't happened. It could have been yesterday that she had walked out of his life. Diantha Christophoros of all women, she was thinking. Diantha, the broken-hearted one who had had to be taken out of

Athens by her family when Leandros arrived there with his shocking new wife.

Did he think she didn't know about her? Did he really believe his awful sister would have passed up the opportunity to let her know what he had thrown away in the name of hot sex? Did he think Chloe would have kept silent about the trips he made to Washington D.C. to visit his broken-hearted ex?

I hate you, her eyes informed him while the anger sang in her blood. She didn't speak, she didn't want to. And as they stared at each other along half the length of his impressive boardroom table the silence screamed like a banshee in everyone's ears. His uncle Takis was there but she refused to look at him. Lester Miles stood somewhere behind her, watchful and silent as the grave. Leandros didn't make a single move to come and greet her, his dark eyes drifting over her as if they were looking at a snake.

Well, that just about says it all, she thought coldly. His family has finally managed to indoctrinate him into their speciality of recognising dross.

Having just watched his wife of four years walk into his boardroom—and scanned her sensational legs—Leandros was held paralysed by the force of anger which roared up inside him like a lion about to leap.

So much for killing himself by imagining her a mere shadow of her former self, he was thinking bitterly. So much for feeling that overwhelming sense of relief when he'd found out it was not Isobel who was confined to a wheelchair but her mother—then feeling the guilt of being relieved about something so painfully tragic, whoever the victim! Silvia Cunningham had been a beautiful woman, full of life and energy. To think of that fine spirit that she had passed on to her daughter now quashed into a wheelchair had touched him deeply.

He was in danger of laughing out loud at his latest plan to make sure that Isobel's mother was provided for within the settlement. Indeed that plan was not about to change because of what he now knew.

Only his plans for this beautiful, adulterous creature standing here in front of him, with her glossed-back hair, spitting green eyes and tight little mouth with its small upper lip and protruding bottom lip that made him want to leap on it and bite.

Where only hours ago he had been content to be unbelievably kind and gentle. He now wanted to tear her limb from limb.

Four years—for four long years this woman had lived inside him like a low, throbbing ache. He'd felt guilt, he'd felt sadness, he'd wanted to accord her the respect he'd believed she deserved from him by making no one aware of his plans to remarry until he had eased himself out of this marriage in the least hurtful way that he could.

But that was until he discovered that his wife was suffering from no such feelings of sensitivity on his behalf, for she had brought her lover with her to Athens! Could she not manage for two days without the oversized brute? Did he satisfy her, did he know her as intimately as he did? Could he make her tremble from her toes to her fingertips and cry out and grab for him as she reached her peak?

Cold fury sparked from his eyes as he looked her over. Bitterness raked its claws across his face. She was wearing leather. Why leather? What was it she was aiming to prove here, that she was brazen enough to wear such a fabric—bought with his money, no doubt—but worn to please another man?

'You're late,' he incised, flicking hard eyes up to a face that was even more treacherously perfect than he remembered it. The gentle hairline, the dark-framed eyes, the straight little nose and that provoking little mouth. A mouth that knew how to kiss a man senseless, how to latch on to his skin and drive him out of his mind. He'd seen the oversized blond brute with the affable smile, standing in the hotel foyer wearing cotton sweats and touching her as if he had every right.

He should not have gone there. He should not have been so anxious to find out the truth about the wheelchair, then he would not have had to witness that man touching his wife in full view of anyone who wanted to watch.

His wife! Touching *his* wife's exquisite, smooth white skin, making that skin flush when it only used to flush like that for him! She had not been wearing leather then, but tight jeans and a little white top that showed the fullness of her beautiful breasts!

Her wonderful hair had been flowing down her back, not pinned up as if she was some little prude. A lying prude, he extended.

'This meeting was due to begin fifteen minutes ago. Now we will have to keep it brief,' he finished his cutting comment.

Then watched as her witch's green eyes narrowed at his clipped, tight tone. 'The traffic was bad—'

'The traffic in Athens is always bad,' he inserted dismissively. 'You have not been away from this city for so long that you could have forgotten that. Please take a seat.'

He took a seat. He pulled out a chair at random and threw himself into it with a force that verged on insolence. Takis was frowning at him but he ignored this lawyer's expression. The other lawyer was trying not to show anything, though Leondros could see he was thoroughly engrossed.

Perhaps fascinated was a better word, he decided as he

studied his wife's lawyer through glassed-over eyes. The man was nothing but a young hawk, still wet behind the ears, he noted with contempt. What was Isobel thinking about, putting a guy like this up against himself and Takis? She knew of his godfather's brutal reputation, she knew of his own! The only thing that Lester Miles seemed to have going for him was the cut of his suit and his boyish good looks.

Maybe that was it, he then thought with a tightening of just about every nerve. Maybe the body-builder was not her only man. Maybe this guy held a different place in her busy private life.

Irritation with himself made him take out his silver pen and begin tapping it against the polished boardroom table while he waited for this meeting to begin. Takis was shaking hands with Lester Miles and trying to appear as if Isobel's husband always behaved like this. Isobel, on the other hand, was walking on those long legs down the length of the boardroom table on the opposing side to his. The leather suit stretched against her slender thighs as she moved and the jacket moulded to the thrust of her breasts. Was she wearing anything beneath it? Did she have the jacket zipped up to her throat simply to taunt him with that question?

Her chin was set, her flesh so white and smooth it didn't look real—but then it never had. She chose to take the seat right opposite him. As she pulled the chair out his gaze moved to the smooth length of her slender neck, then up to the perfect shell-like shape of her ear, and his teeth came together with a snap. One cat-like lick of that ear and all of that cool composure would melt like wax to her dainty feet, he mused lusciously. He knew her, he knew her likes and dislikes, he knew every single erogenous zone, had been the one to take her on that journey of glorious discovery. He knew how to make her beg, cling, cry out his name in a paroxysm of ecstasy. Give him two minutes alone with her and he could wipe away that icy exterior; give him another minute and he could have her naked and begging for him. Or maybe he should be the one to strip his clothes off, he mused grimly. Maybe he should take her on the ride of their lives up against the panelled wall, with her skirt hitched up just high enough for his flesh to enjoy the erotic slide against leather while other parts of him enjoyed a different kind of slide, inside the hot, moist core of her ever-eager body.

It was almost a shame that he wasn't into sexual enhancers, though it suddenly occurred to him that the bodybuilder looked the type. A new and blistering flash of his recently constructed fantasy now being enacted by the lover sent his eyes black with rage.

She sat down, bent to place her handbag on the floor by her chair, then sat up straight again—and looked him right in the eye. Hostility slammed into his face. His pulse quickened as the glinting green look lanced straight through him and war was declared. Though he wasn't sure which of them had done the declaring.

She had certainly arrived here ready for a battle, though why that was the case he had no idea. It was not as if *he* had done anything other than suggest this divorce. Since it was very clear that she had not spent the last three years pining for him, her hostility was, in his opinion, without cause.

Whereas his own hostility... His narrowed eyes shot warning sparks across the table. She lifted her chin to him and sent the sparks right back. His fingers began to tingle with an urge to do something—they began tapping the pen all the harder against the polished table-top.

What is it you think you are going to get out of this,

you faithless little hellion? he questioned silently as his lips parted to reveal the tight, warning glint of clenched white teeth. You had better be well prepared for this fight, because I am.

She placed her hands down on the table, long white fingers tipped with pink painted fingernails stroked the polished wood surface like a caress. His loins tightened, his chest began to burn. She saw it happen and her upper lip offered a derogatory curl.

Takis took the chair beside him. Lester Miles sat down beside Isobel. She turned to her lawyer and sent him a smile that would have made an iceberg melt. But Lester Miles was no iceberg. As he watched this little byplay, Leandros saw the young fool's cheekbones streak with colour as he sent an answering smile in return.

It's OK, I am here, that smile said to her. Leandros felt the lion inside him roar again. She turned to fix her gaze back on him. I am going to kill you, he told her silently. I am going to reach out and drag you across this table and spoil your little piece of foreplay with the kind of real play that shatters the mind.

'Shall we begin?' Takis opened a blue folder. Lester Miles had a black leather one, smooth, trendy and upwardly mobile. Isobel slid her hands to her lap.

Leandros continued to tap his pen against the desk.

'In the midst of all of this tension, may I begin by assuring you, Isobel, that we have every desire to keep this civil and fair?'

Leandros watched her shift her gaze from his face to Takis. He felt the loss deep in his gut. 'Hello, Uncle Takis,' she said.

It was a riveting moment. Takis froze, so did Lester Miles, glancing up sharply from his trendy black leather dossier to sniff the new tension suddenly eddying in the air. The deeply respected international lawyer of repute, Takis Konstantindou, actually blushed.

He came back to his feet. 'My sincere apologies, Isobel,' he murmured uncomfortably. 'How could I have been so crass as to forget my manners?'

'That's OK,' she replied and, as Takis was about to stretch across the table to offer her his hand, she returned her eyes back to Leandros, leaving Takis suffering the indignity of lowering his hand and returning to his seat.

So she could still twist a room upon its head without effort, Leandros noted. You bitch, he told her silently.

The mocking movement of a slender eyebrow said— Maybe I am, but at least I won't be your bitch for much longer.

The air began to crackle. 'As I was about to say...' clearing his throat, Takis tried again '...with due regard to the sensitivities of both parties, at my client's instruction I have drawn up a draft copy of proposals to help ease us through this awkward part.' Taking out a sheet of paper, he slid it across the table towards Isobel. She didn't even glance at it, but left Lester Miles to pick it up and begin to read. 'As I think you will agree, we have tried to be more than fair in our proposals. The financial settlement is most generous in the circumstances.'

'What circumstances?' her lawyer questioned.

Takis looked up. 'Our clients have not lived together for three years,' he explained.

Three years, one month and twenty-four days, Isobel amended silently, and wished Leandros would stop tapping that pen. He was looking at her as if she was his worst enemy. The tight mouth, the glinting teeth, the ice picks flicking out from stone-cold black eyes, all told her he could not get rid of her quick enough.

It hurt, though she knew it shouldn't. It hurt to see the

way he had been running those eyes over her as if he could not believe he'd ever desired someone like her. So much for dressing for the occasion, she mused bleakly. So much for wanting to blow him out of his handmade shoes.

Lester Miles nodded. 'Thank you,' he said and returned his attention to the list in front of him, and Takis returned to reading out loud the list of so-called provisions. Isobel wanted to be sick. Did they think that material goods were all she was here for? Did Leandros truly believe she was so mercenary?

'When,' she tossed at him, 'did I ever give you the impression that I was a greedy little gold-digger?'

Black lashes that were just too long for a man lifted away from his eyes. 'You are here, are you not?' he countered smoothly. 'What other purpose could you have in mind?'

Isobel stiffened as if he'd shot her. He was implying that she was either here for the money or to try to win him back.

'Both parties have stated that the breakdown in their marriage was due to—irreconcilable differences,' Takis put in swiftly. 'I see nothing to be gained from attempting to apportion blame now. Agreed?'

'Agreed,' Lester Miles said.

But Isobel didn't agree. She stared at the man she had married and thought about the twenty-three hours in any given day when he'd preferred to forget he had a wife. Then, during the twenty-fourth, he'd found it infuriating when she'd chosen to refuse to let him use it to assuage his flesh!

He'd met her, lusted after her, then married her in haste to keep her in his bed. The sex had been amazing, passionate and hot, but when he had discovered there was more to marriage than just sex, he had repented at his leisure *during* the year it had taken her to commit the ultimate sin in the eyes of everyone—by getting pregnant.

Leandros must be the only Greek man who could be horrified at this evidence of his prowess. How the hell did it happen? he'd raged. Don't you think we have enough problems without adding a baby to them? Two and a half months later she'd miscarried and he could not have been more relieved. She was too young. He wasn't ready. It was for the best.

She hated him. It was all coming back to her how much she did. She even felt tears threatening. Leandros saw them and the pen suddenly stopped its irritating tap.

'Your client left my client of her own volition,' Takis was continuing to explain to Lester Miles while the two of them became locked in an old agony. 'And there has been no attempt at contact since.'

Yes, you bastard, Isobel silently told Leandros. You couldn't even bother to come and find out if I was miserable. Not so much as a letter or a brief phone call to check that I was alive!

'By either party?' Lester Miles questioned.

The pen began to tap again, Leandros's lips pressing together in a hardening line. He didn't care, Isobel realised painfully. He did not want to remember those dark hours and days and weeks when she'd been inconsolable and he had been too busy with other things to deal with an over-emotional wife.

'Mr Petronades pays a respectable allowance into Mrs Petronades' account each month but I do not recall Mrs Petronades acknowledging it,' Takis said.

'I don't want your money,' Isobel sliced across the table at Leandros. 'I haven't touched a single penny of it.'

'Not my problem,' he returned with an indifferent shrug.

'Now we come to the house in Hampshire, England,'

Takis determinedly pushed on. 'In the interests of goodwill this will be signed over to Mrs Petronades as part of the—'

'I don't want your house, either,' she told Leandros.

'But—Mrs Petronades. I don't—'

'You will take the house,' Leandros stated without a single inflexion.

'As a conscience soother for yourself?'

His eyes narrowed. 'My conscience is clear,' he stated.

She sat back in her chair with a deriding scoff. He dropped the pen then snaked forward in his chair, his black eyes still fixed on her face. 'But why don't you tell me about your conscience?' he invited.

'Leandros, I don't think this is getting us—'

'Keep your house,' Isobel repeated. 'And keep whatever else you've put on that list.'

'You want nothing from me?'

'Nothing—' Isobel took the greatest pleasure in confirming.

'Nothing that is on this list!' Lester Miles quickly jumped in as a fresh load of tension erupted around them. Leandros was looking dangerous, and Isobel was urging him on. Takis was running a fingertip around the edge of his shirt collar because he knew what could happen when these two people began taking bites out of each other.

'Mrs Petronades did not sign a pre-nuptial agreement,' Lester Miles continued hurriedly. 'Which means that she is entitled to half of everything her husband owns. I see nothing like that amount listed here. I think we should...'

Leandros flashed Lester Miles a killing glance. If the young fool did not keep his mouth shut he would help him. 'I was not speaking to you,' he said and returned his gaze to Isobel. 'What is it is that you do want?' he prompted.

Like antagonists in a new cold war they faced each other

across the boardroom table. Anger fizzed in Isobel's brain, and bitterness—a blinding, stinging, biting hostility—had her trembling inside. He had taken her youth and optimism and crushed them. He had taken her love and shredded it before her eyes. He had taken her right to feel worthy as the mother of his child and laughed at it. Finally, he had taken what was left of her pride and been glad to see the back of her.

She'd believed there was nothing else he could do to hurt her. She'd actually come here to Athens ready to let go of the past and leave again hopefully feeling whole. But no. If just one name had the ability to crush her that bit more, then it would be that of Diantha Christophoros.

For that name alone, if she only could reach him she would scratch his eyes out; if she could wrestle him to the ground she would trample all over him in her spike heels.

But she had to make do with lancing him with words. 'I don't want your houses, and I don't want your money,' she informed him. 'I don't want your name or you, come to that. I don't even want your wedding ring...' Wrenching it off her finger, she slid it across the table towards him, then bent and with a snatch caught up her bag. 'And I certainly don't want your precious family heirlooms,' she added, holding her three witnesses silent as she took a sealed envelope out of the bag and launched it to land beside the ring. 'In there you will find the key to my safety deposit box, plus a letter authorising you to empty it for yourself,' she informed Leandros. 'Give them to your next wife,' she suggested. 'They might not be wasted on her.'

Leandros did not look anywhere but at her face while she spat her replies at him. 'So I repeat,' he persisted, 'what is it that you do want?'

'A divorce!' she lanced back through tear-burned eyes. 'See how much you are worth to me, Leandros? All I want is a nice quick divorce from you so that I can put you right out of my life!'

'Insult me one more time, and you might not like the consequences,' he warned very thinly.

'What could you do to me that you haven't already done?' she laughed.

Black eyes turned into twin lasers. 'Show you up for the tramp you are by bringing your muscle-building lover into this?'

For a moment Isobel did not know what he was talking about. Then she issued a stifled gasp. 'You've been having me watched!' she accused.

'Guilty as charged,' he admitted and sat back indolently, picked up the pen again and began weaving it between long brown fingers. 'Adultery is an ugly word,' he drawled icily. 'I could drag you, your pride and your lover through the courts if you wish to turn this into something nasty.'

Nasty. It had *always* been nasty since the day she'd married him. 'Do it, then,' she invited. 'I still won't accept a single Euro from you.'

With that she stood up and, to both lawyers' deepening bewilderment, snatched up her bag and turned to leave.

'Isobel, please—' It was Takis who tried to appeal to her.

'Mrs Petronades, please think about this—?' Lester Miles backed him up.

'Get out of here, the pair of you,' Leandros cut across the two other men. 'Take one more step towards that door, Isobel, and you know I will drag you back and pin you down if necessary.'

Her footsteps slowed to a reluctant standstill. She was trembling so badly now she actually felt sick. In the few seconds of silence that followed she actually wondered if the two lawyers were about to caution him.

But no, they weren't that brave. He was bigger than them in every way a man could be. Height, size—bloody ego. They both slunk past her with their heads down, like two rats deserting a sinking ship.

The door closed behind them. They were alone now. She spun on her slender heels, her eyes like glass. 'You are such a bully,' she said in disgust.

'Bully.' He pulled a face. 'And you, my sweet, are such an angelic soul.'

The *my sweet* stiffened her backbone. He had only ever used the endearment to mock or taunt. He was still flicking that wretched pen around in his fingers. His posture relaxed like a big cat taking its ease. But she wasn't fooled. His mouth was thin, his eyes glinting behind those carefully lowered eyelashes, his jaw rigid, teeth set. He was so angry he was literally pulsing with it beneath all of that idleness.

'Tell me about Clive Sanders.'

There was the reason for it.

She laughed, it was that surreal. He dared to demand an explanation from her after three years of nothing? Walking back to the table, she leaned against it, placed the flat of her palms on its top then looked him hard in the face. 'Sex,' she lied. 'I'm good at it, if you recall. Clive thinks so too. He...'

The table was no obstacle. He was around it before she could say another word. The cat-like analogy had not been conjured up out of nowhere; when he pounced he did it silently. In seconds she was lying flat on her back with him on top of her, and in no seconds at all she was experiencing a different kind of sensation.

This one involved his touch and his weight and his lean, dark features looming so close that her tongue actually moistened with an urge to taste. It was awful. Memories of never holding back whenever he was this close. Memories of passion and desire and need neither had bothered to hold in check.

'Say that again, from this position,' he gritted.

'Get off me.' In desperation she began pushing hard against his shoulders, but the only things that moved were her clenched fists slipping against the smooth cloth of his jacket. She could feel the heat of his body, its power and its promise.

'Say it!' he rasped.

Her eyes flashed like green lightning bolts filled with contempt for everything he stood for. His anger, his arrogance, his ability to make her feel like this. 'I don't have to *do* anything for you any more, *ever*,' she lashed at him.

He released a hard laugh that poured scorn onto her face. 'Sorry to disappoint you, angel, but you still do plenty for me,' and he gave a thrust of his hips so she would know and understand.

Shock brought the air from her lungs on a shaken whisper. 'You're disgusting,' she gasped.

But no more than she was, when the cradle of her own hips moved in response and that oh, so damning animal instinct to mate dragged a groan from her lungs.

He laughed again, huskily, then reached up to tug the comb from her hair. 'There,' he growled as red fire uncoiled across his fingers, 'now you look more like the little wanton I married. All we need to do now is see how wanton,' and his fingers moved down to deal with the jacket zip. The leather slid apart to reveal her neat cream blouse with its pearly buttons up to her throat. Whatever the blouse was supposed to say to him, she did not expect the flaming clash of her eyes with his, as if she'd committed some terrible sin.

'Why the sexy leather?' he demanded. 'Why the prim

hairstyle and a blouse my mother would refuse to wear? What are you trying to prove, Isobel?' he lanced down at her. 'That there are different kinds of sexual provocation? Or is this the way you've learned to dress for your new lover? Does he like to peel you, layer by exquisite layer, is that it?'

'Yes,' she hissed into his hard face. 'The more layers I have on the more I excite him! Whereas you lacked the finesse to notice me at all unless I was already naked in bed and thoroughly convenient for a quick lay!'

The *quick lay* struck right at his ego. Both saw the blistering flashback of his last urgent groping before she'd left him for good. Sparks flew, heat, pain then an anguish that coiled a sound inside his throat.

'You bitch.' The sound arrived in a hoarse whisper.

He'd gone pale and tears were suddenly threatening her again. On a thick whimper she tried to dislodge him with the pushing thrust of her body, making leather squeak against polish wood and the heels of her shoes come close to scoring deep marks in the wood.

'Let me go!' she choked out helplessly. He caught the sound with his mouth and his tongue, and a full onslaught followed of someone who needed to assuage what she had just flung up into his face. Within seconds she had lost the will to fight this man who knew exactly how to kiss her senseless and make her cling with the hungry need for more.

One of his hands was in her hair while the other was sliding between their bodies, making her spine arch sensually as the backs of his knuckles skidded over her breasts. The blouse sprang free, he was that deft with buttons, long fingers slid beneath a final covering of flimsy brown lace and claimed her nipple. She groaned in dismay but was already threading her fingers into his hair as she did so, making sure that he didn't break away.

It was all so primitively, physically *basic*! The harried sound of their laboured breathing, the squeak of leather on polished wood. The heat of his lips and the lick of his tongue and the slow, deep, sinuous thrust of his hips against the eager thrust of her own, that even with the thickness of her skirt was pulling her deeper into a morass of desire. If he reached down and touched the naked flesh at her thighs she would be his for the taking; the tingling already happening there was so tight she could barely stop herself from begging for it.

Suddenly she was free. It happened so quickly that she wasn't expecting it. Dizzy, disorientated, she lay there gasping and blinking as he arrived lightly on his feet by the table and between two chairs. She'd forgotten the anger with which he'd started this. But now she remembered, felt tears of humiliation fill her eyes and didn't even bother to fight him when he took hold of her by the waist, lifted her up and swung her to her trembling feet.

He saw the tears, and a sigh rasped from him. 'I hate you,' she whispered shakily. 'You always were an animal.'

'You should not have brought your lover to Athens!' he ground out. 'You insulted me by doing so!'

She responded by instinct. A hand went up, caught him a hard, stinging slap to the side of his face, then she was grabbing up her bag and turning to walk away. Unsteady legs carried her forward, as her trembling fingers hurriedly tried to zip up her jacket—while her hair flowed down her spine like a red-hot flag that proclaimed what they had been doing.

He didn't stop her, which she took as a further insult. When she arrived in the next room the two lawyers stared at her tear-darkened eyes and dishevelled appearance in open dismay.

'Whatever he wants,' she instructed Lester Miles. 'Have him draw up the papers and I'll sign them.'

With that she just kept on walking.

Leandros had never been so angry with himself in a long time. He'd just treated her like a whore and for what reason?

He didn't have one. Not now that sanity had returned, anyway.

Three years.

He couldn't believe his own crassness! Three years apart and he had reacted to the sight of her with her lover as if he'd caught them red-handed in his own bed! She was young and normal and perfectly healthy. She was beautiful and desirable and she had a sex-drive like anyone else! If she had utilised her right to sleep with another man, then what did that have to do with him now?

It had a great deal to do with him, he grimly countered that question. On a dark and primitively sexual level she still belonged to him. Not once in the last three years had he thought about her taking other lovers. How stupid did that make him? Supremely, so he discovered, because from the moment she'd stepped into this room he'd tossed half a century out of the window to become the jealously possessive Greek male.

Then he remembered the expression in her eyes that had brought with it the memory of the last time they had been together. Something thick lurched in his gut and he reeled violently away from what it was trying to make him feel.

Guilty as charged. An animal lacking the finesse of which he was once so very proud. The boardroom door opened as he was splashing a shot of whisky into a glass.

It was Takis. 'She slapped your face,' the lawyer commented, noticing the finger marks standing out on his cheek. 'I suspect that you deserved it.'

Oh, yes, he'd deserved it, Leandros thought grimly and picked up the glass of whisky then stood staring at it. 'What did she say?' he asked grimly.

'Give him anything he wants,' Takis replied. 'I am to draw up the papers and she will sign them. So take my advice, Leandros, and do it now before she changes her mind. That woman is dangerous. Whatever you did to her here has made her dangerous.'

'She admitted it—to my face—that she's sleeping with that bastard,' he said as if it should explain away everything.

To another Greek male maybe it did in some small part. 'Did you tell her that you want this divorce because you already have her replacement picked out and waiting in the wings to become your wife?'

Shock spun him on his heel to stare at Takis. 'Who told you that?' he demanded furiously.

Takis suddenly looked wary. 'I believe it is common knowledge.'

Common knowledge, Leandros repeated silently. Common knowledge put about by whom? His hopeful mother? His matchmaking sister? Or Diantha herself?

Then, no, not Diantha, he told himself firmly. She is not the kind of woman to spread gossip about. 'Gossip is just that—gossip,' he muttered, more to himself than to Takis. 'Isobel will not be here long enough to hear it.'

Did that matter to him? he then had to ask himself, and sighed when he realised that yes, it mattered to him. What was wrong with him? Another sigh hissed from him. Why was he feeling like this about a woman he hadn't wanted in years?

He detected a pause, one of those telling ones that

grabbed your attention. He glanced at Takis; saw his expression. 'What?' he prompted sharply.

'She knows,' he told him. 'Her lawyer mentioned the Christophoros name before he went after Isobel.'

Leandros felt his mind go blank for a split-second. She cannot know, he tried to convince himself.

'The guy knew quite a lot as a matter of fact,' Takis went on and there was surprise and reluctant respect in the tough lawyer's voice. 'He knew that Diantha spent time alone with you on your yacht in Spain, for instance. He also mentioned conservative attitudes in Greece to extra-marital affairs, then suggested we review the kind of scandal it would cause if two big names such as Petronades and Christophoros were linked in this way in a court battle. He's a clever young man,' Takis concluded. 'He needs watching. I might even use him myself one day.'

Leandros was barely listening. His mind had gone off somewhere else. It was seeing Isobel's face when she'd walked in here, seeing the anger, the hate, the desire to tear him to shreds where he stood.

'Dear God,' he breathed. Where had his head been? Why had he not read the signs? When she hurt she came out fighting. Make her feel vulnerable and expendable and she unsheathed her claws. Let her know she wasn't good enough and she spat fire and brimstone over you then ran for cover as quickly as she could. Let her think she was being replaced with one of Athens' noblest, and you could not hurt her more deeply if you tried.

'The lack of a pre-nuptial is beginning to worry me.' Takis was still talking to a lost audience. 'She could take you to the cleaners if she decided she wanted to roll your name in the mud.'

Turning, Leandros looked at the table where the imprint of her body had dulled the polished wood surface. His stomach turned over—not with distaste for what he had done there but for other far more basic reasons. He could still feel the imprint of her down his front, could still taste her in his mouth.

Not far away, resting where it had landed when she tossed them at him, lay her wedding ring and the envelope containing access to the so-called family heirlooms.

What family heirlooms? he thought frowningly. It was not something his family possessed.

Until today she had still worn her wedding ring, even after three years of no contact with him, he mused on while absently twisting his own wedding ring between finger and thumb. Did a woman do that when she took herself a lover? Did she flout convention so openly?

Ah, the lover, he backtracked slightly. The muscle-building blond with the lover's light touch. His senses began to sizzle, his anger returned. Getting rid of the whisky glass, he walked up to the table and picked up the envelope and the ring.

'We need to start moving on this, Leandros,' Takis was prompting him.

'Later,' he said absently.

'Later is not good enough,' the lawyer protested. 'I am telling you as your lawyer that if you want a quick, clean divorce then you have to move now.'

But I don't want a divorce, was the reply that lit up like a halogen light bulb in his head. I want my wife back. *My wife!*

CHAPTER THREE

OUT in the street Isobel hailed a passing taxi, gave the driver the name of her hotel then sank back in her seat with a shaking sigh. Maybe she should have waited for Lester Miles to join her but at this precise moment she didn't want anyone witnessing the state she was in.

'You OK, *thespinis*?' the taxi driver questioned.

Glancing up, she saw the driver studying her through his rear-view mirror, his brown eyes clouded by concern.

Did she look that bad?

Yes, she looked that bad, she accepted. Inside she was a mass of shakes and tremors. Beneath her zipped-up jacket her blouse was still gaping open and there wasn't an inch of flesh that wasn't still wearing the hot imprint of a man's knowing touch. Her hair was hanging around her pale face and her mouth was hot, swollen and quivering from the kind of assault that should have set her screaming for help but instead she just—

'Yes—thank you,' she replied and lowered her eyes so he wouldn't see just how big a lie that was.

She felt like a whore. Her eyes filmed over. How could he do that to her? What had she ever done to him to make him believe he had the right to treat her that way?

You riled him into doing it is what happened, a deriding little voice in her head threw in. You went in there wanting to rip his unfaithful heart out and ended up with him ripping out yours!

She stared at the fingers of one hand as they rubbed anxiously at the empty place on another finger where her

47

wedding ring had used to be, and tried to decide if she hurt more because of the way he had just treated her, or because she was still flailing around in the rotten discovery that she was still in love with the over-sexed brute!

It had hit her the moment Lester Miles had mentioned a future wife and Diantha Christophoros in the same, soul-destroying breath. Couldn't he have come up with someone fresh instead of picking out his old love to replace her with?

He'd also been having her watched, she suddenly remembered. Had he been that desperate to find a solid reason to bring their marriage crashing down that he'd had to go to such extremes?

I hate him, she thought on a blistering wave of agony. And she did. The two opposing emotions of love and hatred were swilling around inside her in one gigantic, dizzying mix. The man was bad for her. He had always been bad for her. Three years on, she thought wretchedly, and her stupid heart had not learned anything!

The taxi pulled into the kerb outside her hotel. Fumbling in her purse, Isobel unearthed some money to pay the driver then climbed out into the heat of a midday sun. Within seconds she felt as if she was melting, which only made a further mockery of her sanity in coming here to Athens at all *and* wearing leather of all things in this city famous for the oppressive weight of its summer heat.

Her mother had been right; she'd been asking for trouble—and had certainly found it! Returning to her hotel room, she stripped off the wretched suit and walked into the bathroom to shower his touch from her skin.

Never again, she vowed as she scrubbed with a grim disregard for her skin's fragile layers. By the time she had finished drying herself she was tingling all over for a different reason and her mood had altered from feeling destroyed to mulish. If she'd ever needed to be reminded why she left Leandros in the first place then that little scene in his boardroom had done it.

She didn't need a man like him. Let him pour his money into his settlement, she invited, as she dressed in a pair of loose-fitting green cotton trousers and a matching T-shirt. Let him have his divorce so he can marry Diantha Christophoros and produce black-eyed, black-haired little thoroughbreds for his dynasty—

Was that it? Her head shot up, the brush she was using on her hair freezing as she struck at the heart of it. Had Leandros changed his mind about children and decided it was time he made an effort to produce the next Petronades heir?

What was it Lester Miles had said? She tried to remember as she brushed her hair into one long, thick, silken lock. Nikos was getting married. The lawyer called it an heir thing. Nikos might be three years younger than his brother but if Leandros wanted to keep the line of succession clear in his favour, then he needed to get in first with a son.

The tears came back. I would have given him a son. I would have given him a hundred babies if he'd only wanted them. But he didn't, not with me for a mother. He wanted a black-haired Greek beauty with a name exalted enough to match his own.

I'm going to be sick, she thought and had to stand there for a few minutes, fighting the urge as a three-year-old scar ripped open in her chest.

She had to get out of here. The need came with a sudden urgency that left her no room to think. Securing her hair into a simple pony-tail, she snatched up her camera case and slung the strap over her shoulder, slid a pair of sunglasses onto the top of her head then headed for the outer door.

It was only when she stepped out into the hotel corridor that she remembered her mother, and felt guilty because she didn't want to see her right now while she was in this emotional mess. But in all fairness she could not just walk out of here without checking Silvia was back. With a deep breath for courage, she knocked on the door next to her own room. There was no answer. Silvia must still be out with Clive. Relief flicked through her. In the next minute she was riding the lift to the foyer, so eager to escape now that she could barely contain the urge long enough to leave a message for her mother at Reception to let her know what she was doing.

As luck would have it, she was about to step outside when Lester Miles strode in.

'How quickly did they draw up the papers?' she questioned tartly.

'They didn't.' The lawyer frowned. 'Mr Petronades left just after you did.'

To dance attendance on his future bride? Isobel wondered, and felt another burst of bitterness rend a hole in her chest.

'So what happens now?' she asked.

'I am to wait further instruction,' Lester Miles informed her.

'Really?' she drawled. At whose command—Leandros's or Takis Konstantindou's? 'Well, since I am the one you are supposed to take instruction from, Mr Miles, take the afternoon off,' she invited. 'Enjoy a bit of sightseeing and forget about them.'

It was what she intended to do anyway.

'But, Mrs Petronades,' he protested, 'we are due to fly

home tomorrow evening. We really should discuss what it is you want from—'

'I don't want anything,' she interrupted. 'But if this thing can be finished by me accepting everything, then I will.' End of subject, her tight voice intimated. 'They will be back tomorrow with their proposed settlements,' she predicted. 'I'll sign and we will catch our flight home.'

Never to return again, she vowed as she left the poor lawyer standing there looking both puzzled and frustrated. He'd been looking forward to a good fight. He'd had a taste of it and liked it; she'd recognised that in the Petronades boardroom today.

As she stepped outside, the full heat of the sun beat down upon her head. She paused for a moment to get her bearings before deciding to revisit some of her old haunts that did not remind her of Leandros. There were plenty of them, she mused cynically, as she flopped her sunglasses down over her eyes then walked off down the street. While Leandros had played the busy tycoon during her year here in Athens, she had learned to amuse herself by getting to know the city from her own perspective rather than the one her privileged Greek in-laws preferred.

Leandros had just managed to park his car when he saw Isobel step into the street. About to climb out of the vehicle, he paused to watch as she stood for a moment frowning fiercely at everything before she reached up to pull her sunglasses over her eyes, then walked off.

Where was she going? he mused grimly. Why wasn't she sitting in her room sobbing her heart out—as he'd expected her to be?

A stupid notion, he then decided when he took in what she was wearing. It was what he had used to call her battle-dress. When the hair went up in a pony-tail and her camera swung from her shoulder, and those kinds of clothes came out of the closet, his aggravating wife was making a determined bid for escape. How many times had he watched the back of that fine, slender figure disappear into the distance without so much as a word to say where she was going or why she was going there?

His jaw clenched because he knew *why* she had used to disappear like this. It had usually occurred after a row, after she'd asked him for something and he'd snapped at her because he'd been too busy to listen properly, and thought the request petty in the extreme. Guilty conscience raked its sharp claws across his heart. He'd been hell to live with, he recognised that now. He'd done nothing but pick and gripe and shut her up with more satisfying methods. And had never seen how lonely she'd been as she had walked away.

Climbing out of his sleek red Ferrari, he paused long enough to remove his jacket and tie then lock them in the boot. Then he intended to go after her.

But Leandros remembered the lover, and stopped as a whole new set of emotions gripped. Was he still in the hotel? Had she just come from him? Was he receiving the same walk-away treatment because he hadn't listened to what she had been trying to say? Had they rowed about the disaster this morning's meeting had turned into? Had she told the lover that she'd almost made love with her husband on the boardroom table before she walked away? Had *they* made love just now, in there, in that shabby hotel that suited clandestine relationships?

His mind knew how to torment him, he noted, as he slammed the car boot shut.

Where was his mother-in-law while all of this was going on? Was she lying on her sickbed with no idea that her daughter was romping with the body-builder in the next room? Maybe he should go and talk to Silvia. Maybe he should tackle the lover while Isobel was out of the way.

But his mother-in-law was a dish best eaten cold, he recalled with a rueful half-grin at the memory of her blunt tongue. And he wasn't cold right now, he was hot with jealousy and a desire to beat someone to a pulp.

Isobel disappeared around a corner; the decision about whom he was going to tackle first was made there and then. To hell with everyone else, he thought. This was between him and his wife.

It was good to walk. It was good to feel the tension leave her body the deeper she became lost in the tourist crowds. Isobel caught the metro into Piraeus, drank a can of Coke as she walked along the harbour, pausing now and again to snap photos of the local fishermen and their brightly painted boats. She even found her old sense of fun returning when they tossed pithy comments at her, which she returned with a warm grasp of Greek that made them grin in shocked surprise. Most people hated the busy port of Piraeus but she'd always loved it for its rich and varied tapestry of life.

An hour later she had walked to Zea Marina where the private yachts were berthed and ended up getting out of the heat of the sun in Mikrolimano beneath the awning of one of her favourite restaurants that edged the pretty crescent-shaped waterfront. She couldn't eat. It seemed that her stomach was still plagued by a knot of tension even if the rest of her felt much more at peace. But she was content to sit there sipping the rich black Greek coffee while taking in the spectacular views across the Saronic Gulf to the scatter of tiny islands glinting in the sun.

Eventually Vassilou, the restaurant owner, came out to greet her with a warm cry of delight and a welcoming kiss to both cheeks. It was that time of the day when Athens was at its quietest because most people with any sense were taking a siesta. The restaurant had very few customers and Vassilou came to sit beside her with his coffee while he tested her Greek.

It seemed crazy now, that she'd learned the language down here with the real people of Athens and not up there in the rarefied air on Lykavittos Hill, or Kolonáki, where the wealthy Athenians lived in their luxury villas. No one up there had thought it worth coaching her in the Greek language. They spoke perfect English so where was the need?

The need was sitting right here beside her with his thick thatch of silver hair and craggy brown face and his gentle, caring eyes. Not many minutes later they were joined by a retired sea captain, who began telling her some of his old sea yarns. Soon the chairs at her small table had doubled along with the circle of men. The restaurant owner's son brought coffee for them all and sat down himself.

Isobel was relaxed; she was content to sit and be entertained by these warm-hearted people. Despite her nightmare marriage to Leandros, she'd loved Athens—*this* Athens—and she'd missed it when she returned to London.

Suddenly she sensed someone come to stand behind her chair. Assuming it was another local, drawn to the little coffee-drinking group, she didn't think to glance round. She simply continued to sit there on a rickety chair with her coffee-cup cradled between her fingers and her smile one of wicked amusement while she listened—until a hand settled on her shoulder.

His touch caused a jolt of instant recognition. Her body froze and she lost her smile. The old sea captain's voice trailed into silence, and as each set of eyes rose to look at Leandros she had to watch the warmth die.

Not into frozen shock, she noted, but into looks of respect, the kind men gave to another when they recognised a superior man come down into their midst.

They also understood the gentle claim of possession when they saw it. These shrewd men of Greece understood the light, *'Kalimera,'* when it was spoken with the smoothness of silk. 'I understand now why my wife goes missing,' Leandros drawled lazily. 'She has other suitors with whom she prefers to spend the siesta hours.'

The words were spoken in Greek with the aim to compliment, and Isobel was not surprised when the grins reappeared. Men were always first and foremost men, after all. She sat forward to put down her coffee-cup, though ostensibly the movement was supposed to dislodge his hand. It didn't happen; the long brown fingers merely shifted to curve her nape then he bent and she felt the warmth of his breath brush her jawbone just before the brush of his kiss on her cheek followed suit.

He must know that her expression did not welcome him, but he was trusting her not to reject him here in view of all of these interested eyes. And, oddly, she didn't. Which troubled and confused her as she watched the sudden genial shift of bodies and listened to the light banter that involved excuses as the others left the lovers to themselves while they made a mass chair-scraping exodus to another table.

It took only seconds for her to know she'd been deserted. The reason for that desertion chose one of the vacated chairs and sat down. He didn't look at her immediately but frowned slightly as he gazed into the distance with his mouth pressed into a sombre line and the length of his eyelashes hiding his thoughts. He had lost his jacket and tie, she noticed, and the top two buttons to his shirt had been tugged free. He looked different here in the humid weight of natural sunlight, less the hard-headed business tycoon and more the handsome golden-skinned man she had first fallen in love with.

Her heart gave an anxious little flutter. She converted the sensation into a sigh. 'How did you know where to find me?' she asked then added sardonically, 'Still having me watched, Leandros? How quaint.'

The sarcasm made his dark head turn. Their eyes connected, the flutter dropped to her abdomen and she sank back in her chair in an effort to stop herself from being caught in the swirling depths of what those dark eyes could do to her if she let them.

'You speak and understand my language,' he said quietly.

It was not what she had been expecting him to say. But she hid her surprise behind a slight smile. 'What's the matter?' she mocked. 'Did you think your little wife too stupid to learn a bit of Greek?'

'I have never thought you stupid.'

Her answering shrug dismissed his denial. 'Inept and uninterested, then,' which added up to the same thing.

He didn't answer. He was studying her so intently that in the end she shifted tensely and found herself answering the dark question she could see burning in his eyes. 'I have always had a natural aptitude for languages,' she explained. 'And this...' her hand gave a gesture to encompass Piraeus in general '...was my classroom three years ago, where I learned Greek from the kind of people you've just scared off in your polite but esoteric way.'

'Esoteric,' he repeated. 'You little hypocrite,' he denounced. 'I have yet to meet a more esoteric person than you, Isobel, and that is the truth. You lived right here in Athens as my wife for a year. You slept in my bed and ate at my table and circulated on a daily basis amongst my family and friends. Yet not once can I recall you ever mentioning your trips down here to your *classroom* or revealing to any one of those people who should have been important to you that you could understand them when they spoke in Greek.'

'Oh, but I heard so many interesting titbits I would never have otherwise, if they'd known I understood,' she drawled lightly.

'Like what?'

Light altered to hard cynicism. 'Like how much they disliked me and how deeply they wished poor Leandros would come to his senses and see the little hussy off.'

'You didn't want them to like you,' he denounced that also. And his eyes threw back the cynical glint. 'You made no attempt to integrate with anyone who mattered to me. You just got on with your own secret life, picking and choosing those people you condescended to like and holding in contempt those that you did not. If that isn't bloody esoteric then I misunderstand the word.'

'No, you just have a very selective memory,' she replied. 'Because I don't recall a moment when any of those people you mention cared enough to show an interest in anything I said or did.'

'Most of them were afraid of you.'

She laughed, that was so ridiculous. His expression hardened. The anger of this morning's confrontation had gone, she noticed, but what had taken its place was worse somehow. It was a mood with no name, she mused, that hovered somewhere between contempt and dismay. 'You slayed them with your fierce British independence,' he continued grimly. 'You sliced them up with your quick, sharp tongue. You mocked their conservative beliefs and attitudes and refused to make any concessions for the differences between your cultures and theirs. And you did it all from a lofty stance of stubborn superiority that only collapsed when you were in my bed and wrapped in my arms.'

Isobel just sat there and stared as each accusation was lanced at her. Did he really see her as he'd just described her? Did he truly believe everything he'd just said?

'No wonder our marriage barely lasted a year,' she murmured in shaken response to it all. 'You thought no better of me than they did!'

'I loved you,' he stated harshly.

'In that bed you just mentioned,' she agreed in an acid-tipped barb. 'Out of it? It's no darn wonder I came looking for my own world down here where I belonged!'

'I was about to add that unfortunately love is not always blind.' He got in his own sharp dig. 'I watched you cling to your desire to shock everyone. I watched you take on all-comers with the fierce flash of your eyes. But do you know what made all of that rather sad, Isobel? You were no more comfortable with your defiant stance than anyone else was.'

He was right; she'd hated every minute of it. Inside she had been miserable and frightened and terribly insecure. But if he thought that by telling her he knew all of this gave him some high moral stance over her then he was mistaken. Because all it did was prove how little he'd cared when he'd known and had done nothing to help make things easier for her!

Love? He didn't know the meaning of the word. She had loved. She had worshipped, adored and grown weaker with each small slight he'd paid to her, with his *I'm too busy for this* and *Can you not even attempt to take the hand of friendship offered to you?* What hand of friendship? Why had he always had something more important to do than to take some small notice of her? Hadn't he seen how unhappy she was? Had he even cared? Not that she could recall, unless the rows had taken place in their bed at night. Then he'd cared because it had messed with that other important thing in his life—his over-active desire for sex! If she'd sulked, he'd thrown deriding names at her. If she'd said no, he'd taught her how quickly no could be turned into a trembling, gasping yes!

'Talk, instead of sitting there just thinking it!' he rasped at her suddenly.

She looked at him, saw the glint of impatience, detected the pulsing desire to crawl inside her head. Well, too late, she thought bitterly. He should have tried crawling in there three years ago!

'What do you want, Leandros?' she demanded coldly. 'I presume you must have a specific reason for tracking me down—other than to slay my character, of course.'

'I was not trying to slay anything. I was attempting to...' He stopped, his mouth snapping shut over what he had been about to say. 'I wanted to apologise for this morning,' he said eventually.

'Apology accepted.' But as far as Isobel was concerned, that was it. He could go now and good riddance.

He surprised her with a short laugh, shook his dark head then relaxed into his chair. 'Bitch,' he murmured drily.

It was not meant to insult, and oddly she didn't try and turn the remark into one.

Maybe this was a good time for Vassilou to bring them both fresh cups of coffee. He smiled, murmured a few polite pass-the-time-of-day phrases to which Leandros replied. Then, as he was about to leave, he turned back to send Isobel a teasing look. 'You never mentioned your handsome husband to me. Shame on you, *pethi mou*,' he scolded. 'Now see what you have done to my son? His hopes are dashed!'

With that he walked away, leaving her alone to deal with Leandros's new expression. 'Never?' he quizzed.

'For what purpose?' She shrugged. 'Our relationship had no place here.'

'You mean I had no place here—other than to keep eager young waiters at bay, of course,' he added silkily.

Without thinking what she was about to do, Isobel lifted her left hand up with the intention of flashing her wedding ring, which to her made the statement he was looking for without the need of words.

Only the ring wasn't there. Tension sprang up, her ribcage suddenly felt too tight. No ring, no marriage soon, she thought and tugged the hand back onto her lap as an unwanted lump of tears tried to clog up her throat. Leandros looked on with his eyes faintly narrowed and his expression perfectly blank.

'Vassilou was making a joke.' Impatiently she tried to cover up the error.

'I know it was a joke,' he answered quietly.

'Then why have you narrowed your eyes like that?' she flashed back.

'Because the young waiter in question has been unable to take his eyes from you since you sat down at this table.'

'You've been watching for that long, have you? What did you do, hide behind a pillar and take snapshots every time he smiled at me?'

'He smiled a lot.'

She sat forward, suddenly too tense to sit still. She was beginning to fizz inside again, beginning to want to throw things at this super-controlled, super-slick swine! 'Why don't you just go now that you've made your apology?' she snapped, and picked up her coffee-cup.

Those luxurious lashes of his lowered to the cup; he knew what was going through her head. She'd done it before and thrown things at him when he'd driven her to it. Punishment usually followed in the shape of a bed.

But not this time, because she was not going to give him any more excuses to jump on her, she vowed, and took a sip at her coffee. It was hot and she'd forgotten to put the sachet of sugar in that she found necessary when drinking the thick, dark brew the Greeks so liked.

'Where is the lover?'

'What…?' Her head came up, green eyes ablaze because she was at war.

With herself. With him. She didn't know any more what was going on inside. She wished he would go. She didn't want to look at him. She did not want to soak in the way his head and shoulders were in a shaft of sunlight that seeped in through a gap in the striped awning above. She didn't want to see strength in those smooth golden features, or the leashed power in those wide shoulders.

He was gorgeous. A big, dark Latin-hot lover, with a tightly packed body lurking beneath his white shirt that could turn her senses to quivering dust. She could see a hint of black hair curling over the gap where he'd undone the top few buttons of the shirt. She knew how those crisp, curling hairs covered a major part of his lean torso. His rich brown skin was gleaming in the golden sunlight, and the sheen of sweat at his throat beneath the tough jut of his chin was making the juices flow across her tongue.

He was a man whom you wanted taste. To touch all over. A man whom you wanted to touch you. His hands were elegant, strong, long-fingered and aware of what they could do for you. Even now as they rested at ease between the spread of his thighs they were making a statement about his masculinity that sent desire coursing through her blood. His mouth could kiss, his eyes could seduce, his arms could support you while you flailed in the wash of rolling ecstasy the rest of him could give to you.

In other words he was a dark, sensual lover and she suspected one did not need personal experience of that to know it. A few weeks spent on his yacht in Spain and Diantha Christophoros must know it by osmosis. He was not the kind of man to hold back from something he wanted—as *she* knew from experience.

'The blond hunk with the lazy smile,' he prompted. 'Where is he?'

She blinked again and lowered her eyes. Oh, the temptation, she mused, as she stared at her coffee. Oh, the desire to say what was hovering right on the end of her tongue. 'His name is Clive and he's a physiotherapist.' She managed to control the urge to draw verbal pictures of Clive left sleeping off an hour's wild sex.

But her heart was still hammering out the temptation. She heard Leandros utter a soft, mocking little laugh. 'That cost you,' he taunted softly. 'But you had the sense to weigh up the odds of my response.'

'How is Diantha?' she could not resist that one.

Touché, his grimacing nod reflected. 'I have changed my mind about the divorce,' he hit back without warning.

'Well, I haven't!' she responded.

'I was not aware that I gave you a choice.'

'I don't think you have much control over my choice, Leandros,' she drawled witheringly. 'Why have you changed your mind?'

'Simple.' He shrugged, and with a bold lack of conscience lifted his hands enough for her to see what he was talking about. Pure shock sent a whole tidal wave of sensations washing through her.

'You should be ashamed of yourself!' she gasped in stunned reaction as heat poured into her cheeks.

He grimaced as if he agreed. 'I cannot seem to help it. I have been like this since you walked into my boardroom today. So, no divorce,' he explained. 'And definitely no other lovers until I get this problem sorted out.'

The problem being her and his desire for her, Isobel realised with a choke and incredulous disbelief that this was even happening.

'You are so excitingly beautiful,' he murmured as if that justified everything.

'But a bitch,' she reminded him.

'I like the bitch. I always did. It is part of your attraction I find such an irresistible challenge. Like the warning-red hair and the defy-me green eyes and the sulky little mouth that threatens to bite when I step out of line.'

His eyes were dark on her, his tone serious, the fact that he had already stepped out of line all part of what was beginning to burn between them. 'Everything about you I find an outright irresistible challenge,' he continued in a smooth, calm tone that could have been describing the weather, not what turned him on. 'When you walked into my boardroom this morning wearing leather, of all things, and it is thirty degrees out here, it was a challenge. When you sat there spitting hatred at me I don't know how I remained in my chair as long as I did before I leapt. I surprised myself,' he confessed. 'Now you sit here in military-style trousers and a T-shirt with your hair stuck in that pony-tail and you challenge me to crack the toughnut you are pretending to be.'

'It's no pretence. I am tough,' she declared.

'So am I. And you can leap on me and try scratching my eyes out if you want to, but what *I* want will be the end result.'

'You still haven't told me what you want!' Isobel sliced

back at him. 'I haven't the slightest idea where you think you are going with this!'

'I want you, right at this moment,' he answered without hesitation. 'I thought I had made that absolutely clear. I want to close my mouth around one of those tight button breasts I can see pushing against your tough-lady top and simply enjoy myself,' he informed her outrageously. 'Though I would not protest if you dropped to your knees, unzipped my trousers and enjoyed yourself by taking me into your mouth—only I don't think the setting is quite right for either fantasy.'

'I think you're right, and I've had enough of this.' She got to her feet. 'Go to hell with your fantasies, Leandros.' She turned to leave.

As he'd done once before today, he moved with a silent swiftness that gave her no room to react. His hand curled around her wrist and with the simplest tug he brought her toppling down onto his lap. Her stifled cry of surprise slithered through the humid air and had a table of interested witnesses turning their way.

To them it must look as if she'd dived on Leandros rather than been pulled there, she realised, even as his eyes told her what was coming next.

'Don't you dare,' she tried to say but it was already too late. His mouth crushed the refusal, then began offering an alternative to both his fantasies with the help of his tongue.

It lasted short seconds, yet still she was too lost to understand what was happening when he broke the kiss, then quite brutally sat her back on her own chair again. Dizzy and dazed, flushed and shaken, she watched as he climbed to his feet. For a horrible moment she thought it was him who was going to walk away now and leave her to the humiliating glances.

Was that why he'd come here, tracked her down like

this and said what he had just said, just to pay her back for the way she had walked out on him this morning?

His hand dipped into his trouser pocket then came out again. Something landed on the table with a metallic ping. Money. She began to feel as if she had walked into hell without realising it. Had he thrown money down on the table to pay for the pleasure of treating her like this?

Stinging eyes dropped to stare and took long seconds to comprehend what it was they were staring at. Leandros sat down again. She couldn't breathe or think. Lifting her eyes, she just stared at him, her mouth still pulsing from the pressure of his kiss and her heart beating thickly in her throat.

Yes, Leandros thought with a grim lack of humour as he watched her flounder somewhere between this stunning moment and the kiss. You might be in shock, and you might be unable to believe I've just done what I did in broad daylight and in public view of anyone wanting to watch. But just keep watching this space, my beautiful wife, because I haven't even begun to shock you.

I should have done it years ago. I should have taken you by the scruff of your beautiful, stubborn, *tough*, slender neck and dragged you back into my life.

He was angry. Why was he angry? he asked himself. And knew the answer even before he asked the question. Every time he touched her she fell apart at the very seams with her need for him. Each time their eyes clashed he could see the hurt burning in hers because she was still so in love with him.

Which all added up to three empty, wasted years. Because if he'd faced her with their problems three years ago they would not be sitting here like two damned fools fighting old battles with new words. They would be in a bed somewhere enjoying each other in the traditional

Greek way. There could even have been another child to replace the one they'd lost, sleeping safely in a room close by.

And she would certainly not have let another man touch her! How could she do that anyway? he extended furiously.

'Put it back on,' he instructed, even though he knew she was incapable of doing anything right now.

'I don't—'

'Not your choice.' He was back to choices. 'While you are married to me you will wear my ring.'

'We are about to end our marriage,' she protested. 'What use is a wedding ring in a divorce?'

But even as she made that bitter statement he could see his kiss still clinging to the swollen fullness of her lips. The tip of her tongue could not resist making a sensual swipe across them in an effort to cool their pulsing heat. He mimicked the action with his own tongue, saw her breath shorten and her throat move convulsively. The old vibrations came to dance between them. The air became filled with the heady promise of sex. They had been here before, felt this before. Only then they had been eager to follow where those senses led them.

Now…?

'It means nothing any more,' she said and broke eye contact.

Was she referring to the ring or the sexual pull? he mused, and decided to deal with the former because the latter, he knew, was going to take care of itself in the not too distant future.

Leaning forward, he brought his forearms to rest on the top of the small wooden table, forcing a wary glance from her because she wasn't sure what was coming next. Once he had her gaze, he drew it down with the slow lowering of his lashes and let her watch as he worked his own ring free from his finger then placed it next to hers.

She was so very still he knew she understood what he was doing. The pulse in his throat began to pound. The two rings lay side by side in the sunlight, one large, one small, both an exact match to the other, with their gloss smooth outer surface and the inner circle marked by an inscription that said *My heart is here*.

How could he have forgotten that when he'd stood upon the deck of his yacht in San Estéban complacently making plans to finish their marriage? How could she have forgotten it when she tossed her ring back at him with such contempt earlier today? They had done this together. They had chosen these rings with their arms around each other, and hadn't cared how soft and stupidly romantic they must have appeared as they'd made the decision to have those words inscribed in those inner circles so they would always rest next to their skins!

'Now tell me it means nothing.' He laid down the rasping challenge as he watched her face grow pale. 'If you can bear to walk away and leave your ring on this table, then I will do the same. If you cannot bear to do that, put it back on your finger and we will talk about where we can go from here.'

Her tongue made a foray of her lips again. His teeth came together with a snap to stop him from moving close enough so his own tongue could follow in its wake. She was his, and the sooner she came to accept that the sooner they could work out their problems.

'The divorce—'

'The ring,' he prompted firmly.

She swallowed tensely. The mood began to sizzle with the threat of his challenge and her defiant need to get up and walk away.

But she could not do it. In the end and with a lightning flash of fury, she reached out, snatched her ring up and pushed it back onto her finger.

It went on easily because it belonged there. The next lightning bolt came his way. 'Now what? Do we go back to your office and talk divorce settlements again?'

Her waspish tone didn't hide anything. She was shaking all over and almost on the point of tears. She wanted him. She could not let him go. His ring was back where it belonged and he'd never felt so good about anything in a long time. Picking up his own ring, he slid it back where *it* belonged then sat back with a sigh.

'No,' he answered her question. 'We go somewhere more private where we can talk.'

Her look poured scorn all over that lying suggestion. She knew what he was intending. She was no fool. 'Try again, Leandros,' she murmured bitterly.

'Dinner, then. Tonight,' he came back. 'We will drive out of the city to that place you like in the mountains. Eat good food, drink champagne and reminisce over the good points in our marriage.'

His mockery flicked her temper to life, and he was pleased to see it happen because it was just the mood he was pushing for. Put Isobel in a rage and you had yourself an easy target, because as one guard fell the others quickly followed. So he relaxed back and waited for the sarcastic, What good points? to come slashing back at him. But what he actually got threw him completely.

'Sorry, my darling,' she drawled. 'But I already have a date tonight.'

Just like that it was his own temper deserted him. The lion inside him roared. He retaliated with swift and cruelly cutting incision. 'And there I was about to break my date with Diantha for you. But—no matter, you may bring your lover; we will make it a foursome. Maybe we will go home with different partners. Who knows?' He added a casual shrug. 'Maybe I will ache like this for Diantha and all my problems will be solved.'

He knew the moment he had shut his mouth that he had made some terrible tactical mistake. She'd gone so white he thought she might be going to faint away on him and her eyes stood out like two deep green pits of pain. She was standing up, not in anger, but on legs that did not wish to support her.

'I was referring to my mother,' she breathed, and this time she did walk away.

CHAPTER FOUR

YOU little liar, Isobel accused as she made good her escape. You meant what he thought you meant. What you didn't expect was the counter-thrust that punched another hole in your stupid heart!

But he wasn't coming after her, which probably meant they were back to square one, she thought heavily. Why am I here? Why am I letting him get to me like this? A three-year long separation should have dulled these wretched emotions out of existence!

The hotel was only a short walk away but by the time she arrived there she had the beginnings of a headache, so the last thing she needed was to walk into the hotel foyer and straight into a bored and weary reception party. Her mother, Clive and Lester Miles were all sitting on the few comfortable chairs the dingy foyer possessed. On a low table in front of them lay the remains of an indifferent-looking afternoon tea.

'Where have you been?' her mother demanded the moment she saw her. 'I've been worrying myself sick about you.'

'But I left you a message at Reception,' she said frowningly as she walked towards them.

'I got your message, Isobel,' her mother said impatiently. ' "*I've gone out for while,*" does not really cover a three-hour disappearance, does it? Having dragged me all the way to Athens, I did think you would have spared a little time to be with me.'

'But I thought...' she began, then changed her mind.

70

Her mother was right and attempting to shift responsibility on to the fact that Clive was supposed to be taking her out for the day wasn't good enough. Especially when it only took a glance at Clive to know he was wishing he hadn't invited himself along on this trip.

'I'm sorry,' she murmured, and bent to press a contrite kiss on her mother's cheek. It felt warm and she looked flushed. It occurred to her that they all looked flushed. Clive was sweating and Lester Miles had lost his suit jacket and tie and was fanning himself with an ancient-looking magazine.

It was then that she realised the air-conditioning wasn't working, and that it was as warm inside as it was out.

'It's broken,' Clive offered, noticing the way she'd glanced up at the air-conditioning vents set in the walls.

Broken, Isobel echoed wearily. No wonder her mother was cross. She had promised her faithfully that the hotel would be cool when she'd bullied her into coming here with her. With a deep breath she braced herself. 'Look,' she said. 'Why don't we go upstairs and all take a nice shower, then we can find somewhere to—?'

'We can't go upstairs, either.' It was Lester Miles that spoke this time. 'The lift has broken down as well.'

'As well?' she gasped. 'You have to be joking.'

'Nope.' It was Clive again. 'We are in the middle of a power cut, in case you haven't noticed. No lights, no air-conditioning and no lift,' he pointed out. 'Apparently it happens all the time.'

'So you tell me, Isobel,' Silvia said crossly, 'how a wheelchair-bound, feeble woman climbs four flights of stairs to get her much-needed cool shower?'

I don't know, she thought, and wondered what they would do if she plonked herself down on the floor and had a good weep? Nothing had gone according to plan from

the moment she'd left here this morning. She wished she
hadn't come to Athens. She wished she was still at home
in rainy England, plodding away at her mundane photo-
imaging job! She certainly wished she hadn't had to set
eyes on Leandros again. He cut her up, he always had
done. She lost her calm and steady sense of proportion
whenever she was around him.

'You two men don't have to stay down here if you prefer to go and cool off in your rooms,' she murmured a
trifle unsteadily. 'I'll see if Mum and I can find—'

'Trust me, Isobel,' Clive put in deridingly, 'we are sitting in the coolest place right now.'

'This place is a dump,' her mother added.

'I'm sorry,' her daughter apologised once again, realizing she *was* going to cry. She placed a hand to her aching
head and tried to think. 'Just give me a few minutes—all
of you—and I'll see if I can find us another hotel to—'

'Is there a problem here?' another, deeper voice inserted.

If it was possible, Isobel's spirits sank even lower as she
turned with fatalistic slowness to face her nemesis.
Leandros didn't look hot, she noticed. He didn't look anything but cool and smooth, suave and handsome and...

'What are you doing here?' It was her mother who asked
the abrasive question.

'And good day to you, too, Silvia.' Leandros smiled,
but his eyes remained fixed on Isobel's pale face. 'What's
wrong?' he asked her gently.

Gentle did it. Her mouth began to wobble. The tears
bulged in her eyes. 'I...' She tried to think but found that
she couldn't. 'I...' She tried to speak again and couldn't
even do that. It wasn't fair. *He* wasn't fair. He'd spun her
round in circles until she didn't know what she was doing
any more.

Leandros's hand came out in front of him. She saw he was holding her camera case out by its strap. She must have left it at Vassilou's restaurant. Maybe she'd left her courage there too. She reached out to take the camera back, missed the strap and found herself clutching at a solid male wrist instead. He didn't even hesitate, but just used her grip to propel her towards him and the next moment her face was pressed into his shoulder and she stayed there, not even caring who watched her sink so easily into the enemy.

One of his hands was gently cupping her nape; the other just as gently curved her waist. The camera was knocking against the back of her leg and her fingers were clutching at a piece of his shirt. He felt strong and reassuringly familiar and, though she did not want to feel it, there was not another place that she would rather be right now.

Someone was talking, someone was tutting. Someone else was also sobbing quietly and she knew it was her. He didn't speak. He just stood there and held her and listened.

Then she heard her mother snap, 'This it is all your fault, Leandros.'

'Quite,' he agreed, the single word vibrating in his deep chest and against Isobel's hot forehead. 'Mr Miles,' he spoke to her lawyer, 'would you do me a great favour and go over to that excuse for a hotel receptionist and tell him that Leandros Petronades wishes to speak to him?'

This blatant bit of name-dropping brought Isobel's face out of his chest. 'What are you going to do?' she asked.

'What you once told me I am good at,' he replied. 'Which is solving other people's problems.'

It was an old gripe, and it stiffened her spine to be reminded of it. 'I can do that for myself.'

'Stay where you are.' The hand at her waist slid up her back to keep her still. 'This is turning out to be one of the best days of my life, and you are not going to spoil it by turning back into the tough-lady I know so well.'

Her worst day, his best day. That just about said it all for Isobel.

As you would have expected, when Leandros threw his weight around, the hotel manager came out of his hide-away at great speed to begin apologising profusely in Greek. Leandros answered him in equally profuse but incisive Greek. The conversation was so swift and tight that Isobel couldn't follow it all. By the time the little man had hurried away again, Leandros was letting her ease away from him, and she then had to brace herself to face their audience.

Which made it the third time in one day she'd had to do it. Well, they said that bad things always come in threes, so maybe her luck was about to change, she thought hopefully as she glanced from hot face to hot face.

Her mother was staring at her as if she couldn't quite believe that her daughter had just wept all over her estranged husband. Lester Miles had put his jacket back on and was looking invigorated because he had been given something to do. Clive had come to his feet and was weighing up the competition. If he had any sense, it was all he would do, Isobel thought, then took in a deep breath and decided it was time to introduce him to Leandros.

'Clive, this is my husband Lean—'

'Silvia, *thoes*! You do not look well.' Cutting her off with a brusque exclamation, Leandros didn't even glance at Clive as he went to lean over her mother. 'This has been too much for you,' he murmured concernedly and took possession of one of her hands. 'You must accept my sincere apologies on behalf of Athens. You will give me five minutes only and I will make your life more comfortable, *ee pethera,* I promise you. If the manager is doing as I instructed then a car is on its way here as I speak. It will carry you with air-conditioned swiftness away from this miserable place.'

As Isobel watched, her stubborn, tough, I-hate-this-man mother melted before her very eyes. 'This hotel was all we could afford,' she told him miserably. 'Isobel wouldn't listen to sense. She wouldn't let you pay. And she wouldn't let me stay in my own home where at least I could make myself a cup of tea if I pleased.'

'Away to where?' Isobel cut in on this very enlightning conversation.

'To our home, of course,' Leandros replied. 'Isobel is a very stubborn woman, is she not?' he conspired with her mother. 'Which she gets from you, of course,' he added with a grin.

'I don't cut my nose off to spite my face,' Silvia pointed out.

'What do you mean, to your home?' Isobel gasped in outrage.

'*Our* home,' he corrected. 'I am relieved to hear that, *ee meetera*. It is such a beautiful nose. Perhaps between us we could persuade Isobel to leave her nose where it is?'

'You always were an inveterate charmer, Leandros,' Silvia huffed, but her cheeks were now flushed with pleasure rather than heat.

'Leandros. We are not going to stay at your house,' Isobel protested. 'The power cut will be over in a minute or so, then everything here will be back to normal!'

'And if it happens again when your mother is in her room?' he challenged. 'Is it worth risking her being trapped up there?'

'Just what I'd been about to say before you arrived.' Her wretched mother nodded.

Isobel threw herself into one of the chairs and gave up

the fight. 'What about Clive and Mr Miles?' she tossed into the melting pot of calamities that were befalling her today. 'They will have to come too.'

There was a sudden and stunningly electric silence. Then Leandros rasped, 'Your lover can sleep where the hell he likes, so long as it is not in my house.'

Her mother stared at him. Clive looked as if he had turned to stone. Lester Miles just watched it all avidly, like a man watching some gripping drama unfold.

Isobel's heart stopped dead. Oh, dear God, she groaned silently and covered her eyes and wished the world would swallow her up. Too late, she remembered that she'd left Leandros with the impression that she and Clive were lovers.

She couldn't take any more. She stood up. 'I'm going to my room,' she breathed shakily, and headed for the stairwell on legs that shook.

By the time she'd climbed up four flights and felt her way down a dingy inner corridor to her room, she was out of breath and so fed up that she headed straight for the telephone and got Reception to connect her with the airport. If she could get them home tonight then they were going, she decided grimly. Even if that meant travelling in the cargo hold!

No such luck. When a day like this began it didn't give up on turning one's life into a living hell. No seats were available on any flight out of Athens. She was stuck. Her mother was stuck.

'I'm sorry,' a voice said behind her. 'My coming here seems to have made a lot of problems for you.'

'Why did you come, Clive?' She swung round on him. 'I don't understand what you aimed to gain!'

He was standing propping up the doorway. 'I thought I might be of some use.' His shrug was rueful. 'Your mother agreed. It didn't occur to me that your husband would view my presence here with such suspicion.'

He didn't just suspect—he *knew* because she had told him! Oh, heck, she thought and sighed heavily. 'He's been having me watched,' she explained. 'When he heard that you were here he automatically assumed the worst.'

'It's nothing to do with him any more what I am to you,' Clive responded curtly. 'You came here to agree a divorce, not ask his permission to take a lover.'

Isobel released a thick laugh. 'Leandros is a very powerful, very arrogant, and very territorial man. The moment he heard about you, the divorce thing was dropped. Now I'm stuck with a man who has decided to work on his marriage rather than give me up to someone else.'

'That's primitive!'

'That's Leandros,' she replied, then sighed and sat down on the end of the bed.

'You don't have to go with him.'

No? I wish, she thought. 'He's already sweet-talked my mother with promises of air-conditioning and I can't even begin to list the rest of the luxury she is now looking forward to.'

'She doesn't even like the man.'

'Don't you believe that front she puts up,' she said heavily. 'My mother used to think he was the best thing that ever happened to me.' Until it all went wrong; then she'd wished him in hell.

Clive slouched further into the room. He was built like a cannon. All iron with a sunbed-bronzed sheen. The women adored him and flocked after him in droves. He worked at a fitness club. He spent hours patiently helping broken people to mend. He was *nice*!

'You came to Athens hoping I would need putting back

together again after meeting Leandros, didn't you?' she suddenly realized.

The painful part of it was that he didn't deny it. 'A man can hope.'

And a woman could dream. Her dream was downstairs right now, taking over her life. 'I'm sorry,' she murmured huskily.

He came to sit beside her on the bed. 'What are you going to do?' he asked.

Cry my eyes out? 'Give it a chance.' She shrugged.

On a sigh, Clive put a big arm around her and gave her a sympathetic hug. It was a nice arm, strong and secure and safe. But it was the wrong arm and the wrong man, though she wished it wasn't.

'Well, this is nice,' a very sardonic voice drawled.

Isobel felt her heart sink to her toes. Clive gave her shoulder a final squeeze then stood up. As he walked towards Leandros she could feel the hostility bouncing between the two of them. It conjured up images of dangerous cats again, only these were two big male predators considering testing each other's weight. They didn't speak. It was all part of the test to keep silent. Clive didn't stop walking and Leandros didn't move so their shoulders brushed in one of those see-you-later confrontations you expected from a pair of strutting thugs.

The moment Clive had gone, the bedroom door closed with a violent thud. Isobel got up and went over to the small chest of drawers and pulled open the top drawer for some reason she couldn't recall.

'My car has arrived,' Leandros informed her levelly. 'Lester Miles and my driver are taking your mother on ahead.'

'You should have gone with them.' It was not meant nicely.

'And leave you alone with the body-builder? You must think I am mad.'

'Clive is a friend, not my lover.' There, she'd told him. Now he could relax and return to the issue of divorce.

'Too late for that, *agape mou*,' he said deridingly. 'Though *ex*-lover, he most definitely is.'

'He is not my lover!' she swung on him furiously.

His black eyes flared. He moved like lightning, making her heart pound as he pushed his angry face up to her. 'Don't lie to me!' he barked at her. 'I am not a fool! I can count as well as you can!'

'Count?' She frowned. 'What are you talking about?'

His breath left his lips through clenched white teeth. If he touched her she had a feeling he would end up strangling her, he was in such a rage. But he didn't touch. He brought up his hand and placed four long fingers in front of her face. 'Four people. Three rooms,' he breathed severely. 'You tell me how that adds up! You tell me where the extra person sleeps!'

'Why, you...' The words got lost in a strangled gasp as it sank in what he was getting at. 'Clive did not share this room with me!' she denied shrilly. 'He didn't come as one of my party. He came under his own steam. Booked in under his own name—and his room is not even on this floor!'

He didn't believe her, she could see it as the savagery locked into his face. Without another word she slapped his hand away then stalked across to the wardrobe, threw open the doors then stood back. 'My room. My clothes!' she said furiously. 'My single bed!'

Her hand flicked out, sending his angry gaze lashing across the utilitarian plainness of a three-foot divan set in the shoebox this hotel called a single room.

'You know what you are, Leandros? You're the original

chauvinist pig! You dare to come up here showing me your contempt for what you believe I've been doing with my sordid little life—while you shack up with Diantha Christophoros on your super-expensive bloody yacht!'

He spun to stare at her. 'What I said before about Di—'

'Talk about double standards,' she sliced over him. 'I really ought to go and confront her now, just to even things up a bit. Shall I do that, Leandros?' She threw out the challenge. 'Shall I strut the strut? Get all territorial and threaten to smack her in the face if she so much as looks at my man? Maybe I should.' She sucked in a fiery breath, breasts heaving, eyes flashing on the crest of a furious wave. 'Maybe I should just do that and let the whole upper echelons of this damn city know that Isobel, your scary slut, is back!'

She was gasping for breath by the time she had finished. He wasn't breathing at all and his face had gone pale. But the eyes were alive with a dangerous glitter. 'Slut,' he hissed out. 'You're no scary slut but just an angry woman on the defensive!'

'Defending what?' she asked blankly.

'Your blond Adonis.'

At which point she knew she was in trouble. He didn't believe her about Clive, and was coming towards her with the slow tread of a man about to stake his claim on what he believed belonged to him.

'Don't you dare,' she quavered, beginning to tremble as his arm came up. His hand purposefully outstretched and angled to take hold of her by the waist. If she backed up she would be inside the wardrobe; if she stayed where she was she was as good as dead meat for this predatory male.

'Andros—no,' she murmured shakily and tried a squirming shift of her body in an attempt to evade what was going to come.

His hand slid further around her waist and banded her to him. 'Say that again,' he gritted.

'Say what?' Too distracted by his closeness, she just looked blank.

'Andros,' he murmured in that low, deep, huskily sensual way that robbed her of her ability to breathe. Had she said his name like that? She couldn't remember. She hoped she hadn't because it gave too much away.

His other hand came up to coil around the thick silk lock of her pony-tail and began tugging with gentle relentlessness so he could gain access to the long column of her neck. She knew what was coming, her breath caught in her throat. If she let him put his tongue to that spot beneath her earlobe she was going to explode in a shower of electric delight.

'Say it,' he repeated, his eyes dark like molasses, his face locked in the taut mask of a man on the edge. His lips had parted, and were coming closer to her angled neck.

She released a stifled choke. *'Andros,'* she whispered.

His mouth diverted. It was so quick, so rewarding that she didn't stand a single chance. He claimed her mouth with devastating promise. He devoured it while she fought for breath. Her breasts heaved against his hard chest, her hips ground against the glorious power of his. Nothing went to waste, the kiss, touch, taste, scents, and even the sounds they made were collected in and used to enhance the whole experience.

It had always been like this. One second nothing, the next they were embroiled in a heady, sensuous feast. His fingers were in her hair. The next moment it was flowing over his hand and she quivered with pleasure because it always felt so very sexy when he set it free like this. Her T-shirt was easy; it disappeared without a trace. His shirt came next, revealing a torso that made her groan as she scraped her fingernails into the curling black mass of hair.

They kissed like maniacs; she nipped his lip, he bit back. Their tongues danced, their eyes locked together. She slid down his zip and covered him with the flat of her hand. He groaned something. He was hot and hard and out of control but then so was she. With one of his swift silent moves he picked her up and put her down on the divan bed then bent to rake the rest of her clothes down her legs.

'I'm going to eat you alive,' he said as he stripped himself naked. And he meant it. He began by bending his dark head and fastening on to one of her breasts. She squirmed with pleasure, her fingers clutching at his shoulders so she could pull him down next to her on the bed. He was magnificent, he was beautiful, his skin felt like oiled leather and she stroked and scored and kneaded it until he couldn't take any more and came to claim her mouth.

Every single inch of him was pumped up and hard with arousal. Every single inch of her was lost in a world of fine, hungry tremors that demanded to be quelled. They kissed, they touched, they rolled as a single sensual unit. When he reached between her legs, she cried out so keenly that he uttered a black oath and had to smother the sound with his mouth. The room shimmered in the golden light of the low afternoon sun. The heat was tremendous, their bodies bathed in sweat. His first plunge into her body brought forth another keening cry. He muffled this one with his hand. She turned her teeth on him, latching on to the side of his palm until he groaned in agonised pleasure, then pulled the hand away and finally buried his mouth in her neck.

Starbursts swirled in the steamy atmosphere. Her legs wrapped around his waist. With each thrust of his body she released another thickened cry and he groaned deep in his throat. It was a blistering, blinding coupling, incandescent and uncompromisingly indulgent in every sense. He brought her to the edge, then framed her face with his hands. His heart was pounding. His eyes were black, his beautiful mouth tight, his total commitment to what was about to happen holding his features drawn and tense.

The first flutters of orgasm took her breath away. He groaned, 'Oh, my God,' as her muscles rippled along the length of his shaft. His eyes closed, her eyes closed, and each flutter lengthened with each driving thrust until the whole experience became one long, tempestuous shower of sensation. It had always been like this for them; there wasn't a place where they could separate the sensuous storm at work inside each other.

Tenderness followed. It had to. They couldn't share something so deeply intimate and special then get up and walk away. Leandros rolled onto his back and took Isobel with him, curving her into his side with a possessive arm while he took deep breaths. Her cheek lay in the damp hollow of his shoulder; her arm lay heavy across his chest. She could feel the aftershocks at work inside him and turned her mouth to anoint him with a slow, moist kiss. It was one of those exquisite moments in time when nothing else mattered but what they were feeling for each other and through each other.

Then the lights flicked on. The small refrigerator in the corner began to whir. Muffled cheers sounded through the thin walls and reality returned with the electricity.

Leandros jerked into a sitting position then jackknifed off the bed. 'Tell me again that this bed is not big enough for two people,' he rasped and strode off to her tiny bathroom, slamming the door behind him in his wake.

He must be mad, he told himself as he turned on the poor excuse for a shower and attempted to wash the sweat from his flesh with tepid water that dribbled rather than sprayed.

Did he really want all of this back again? Did he want to feel so out of control all the time that he could barely think? She touched him and his skin was enlivened, she spat fury at him and it excited him out of all that was sane. She hated his family, she hated his lifestyle, she had learned his language but had not bothered to tell him so she could listen in like a sneaky spy on every conversation happening around her. She was already threatening to cause trouble and he would be a fool not to take her seriously.

He knew her. She was a witch and a hellion. Had he not reminded himself of these things only two weeks ago in Spain? Sluicing water down the flatness of his stomach, his hand brushed over the spot where she had laid her final kiss. Sensation quivered through him; hot and sweet, it caused a fresh eruption of flagrant passion to flow through his blood. Her barbs were not always sharp, he recognised grimly as he switched off the shower.

Grabbing one of the stiff hotel towels, he began to rub himself dry with it. It smelled of Isobel—her perfume was suddenly back on his skin and floating round his senses like a magic potion meant to keep him permanently bewitched. Did this dump of a hotel not even change the towels daily? Glancing around the tiny bathroom, he saw the signs of female occupation but no sign of a man's stamp anywhere.

No hint of a man's scent lay on the towels. Was she telling the truth? Ah, he would be a bigger fool to believe it, he told himself harshly. If the muscle-bound hulk did not know what it was like to fall apart in that woman's arms then he was no man, in his estimation.

Did he really want all of this back in his life?

It had been a day of madness, that was all; pure madness. He had seen and remembered and wanted and now had. It should be enough to let the rest of Isobel return to her other life so he could return to his.

But it wasn't, and he knew it the moment he stepped out of the bathroom with one of the towels wrapped round his hips. She was standing by the window in a blue towelling bathrobe, which looked familiar to him. Could it be the same one of his from his house in Athens that she used to pinch all the time because she liked to feel him close to her skin? Her hair lay down the back of it, her hands were lost in its cavernous pockets. He wanted to go over there and wind his arms around her but anger and frustration and outright damn *need* held him back from doing it.

Did he want to let her go again? Not in this lifetime. 'You can use the bathroom now,' he said as calmly as he could do and turned away from her.

'I will when you've gone,' she replied.

He was about to recover his scattered clothes when she said that but his movements froze on a sudden warning sting. 'In case you have forgotten,' he finished, bending to pick up his trousers, 'you are coming with me.'

'No, I'm not.'

His legs suddenly felt like lead beneath him. 'Of course you are,' he insisted. 'You cannot stay in this place, and your mother is…'

She turned to look at him then. His ribcage tightened in response. She looked so pale and fragile—ethereal, as if she could float away if the window were open.

'I would appreciate it if you could put my mother up for tonight,' she requested politely. 'You are right about this hotel; it isn't the place for her and I don't want to upset her further by moving her on again. But I'll stay here and collect her tomorrow in time for us to catch our flight home.'

'You come with me,' he insisted yet again and did not want to think about tomorrow.

But she shook her head. 'I think we've made enough mistakes for one day.'

'This is not a mistake.' Had he really just said that? While he had been locked away in the bathroom he had agreed with her. Now, when he could look at her again, he did not want it to be a mistake! 'We've just made love—'

'No,' she denied that, and what made it all the more frightening was that she did it so calmly. 'You've made your point.' A slight tilt of her head acknowledged his success at it. 'Two can lie in that narrow bed—I stand corrected. Now I would like you to leave.'

Leave, he repeated inwardly. She was dismissing him. 'So that the Adonis can get back in?'

Spark, he urged her silently. Say something like—Of course, he's waiting outside the door! Then I can retaliate swiftly. I can toss you back down on that blasted bed!

But she didn't say anything. She just turned and walked into the bathroom and left him standing there like a fool!

CHAPTER FIVE

LEANDROS turned to stare at the small hotel bedroom, with its scuffed grey marble flooring and the furniture that must have been there since the First World War. He stared at the bed with its coffee-coloured sheets covered with an orange spread made of cheap nylon, and thought of his own luxurious seven-foot bed set upon smooth white tiling and draped in cool mint-green silk over the finest white cotton sheets.

No effort was required to place Isobel's image on the mint-green coverlet, or to sit her cross-legged on the cool white floor while she sorted through a new set of photographs. Wherever he placed her in his bedroom, she created a glorious contrast to everything. He had missed that contrast in more ways than he had dared let himself know.

But he now had to ask himself if it was because he had missed her that he had gone to Spain and rarely returned to Athens for two years. Was it her ghost that had driven him out of his home and even now forced him to take a deep breath before he could walk back into it?

The sound of the shower being shut off had him moving out of his bleak stasis. By the time the bathroom door opened he knew what was going to happen next and that Isobel was going to have to accept it.

'What do you think you are doing?' Isobel came to a halt in surprised protest.

He was dressed and in the process of packing her suitcase. Beside the case, draped like a challenge on the bed, lay fresh underwear and the only dress she had brought with her to Greece.

'I believe that must be obvious,' he answered coolly.

'But I said…'

His glance flicked towards her. The way it slithered down her front made her heart give a shuddering thump. 'I recognise the robe,' he announced.

Without thought, her fingers went up to clutch the edges of her robe together across her throat. 'I…'

'You what?' he prompted, his dark eyebrows rising to challenge the guilty flush trying to mount her cheeks. 'You took it with you by mistake when you left me, then forgot to send it back to me? Or you stole it because you needed to take a part of me with you and have been hugging me next to your beautiful skin each time you have worn it since?'

'It's comfortable, that's all,' she snapped, shifting impatiently. 'If you want it back—'

'Yes, please.'

Without hesitation he walked towards her as if he was going to drag the stupid robe from her back! His dark eyes mocked the jerky step she took. They also saw the darkening swirl taking place in her eyes. He knew what that swirl meant. He knew everything about her.

Too much! she acknowledged helplessly as her senses began to clamour and he reached towards her with a hand. Prising her unwilling fingers free of the robe's collar, he then bent his dark head, buried his face in the soft towelling and inhaled.

'Wh-what are you doing?' she jerked out on a strangled breath.

'I am checking to see if you douse the robe with my aftershave,' he explained as he lifted his head. 'But no,' he sighed. 'It smells of you.' He took a step closer. 'And the promise of what awaits beneath.'

'I wish you would just stop this and leave,' she murmured crossly.

'Liar,' he drawled. 'What you want is for me to take the robe from you. You would love me to rip the thing from your body then throw you back on the bed and spend the next few minutes reminding you *why* I am still here!'

She was beginning to tremble. 'This is intimidation.'

'No,' he denied. 'It is a case of pandering to your preference for melodrama.' His fingers moved, releasing the towelling so he could brush a lazy fingertip across her pouting bottom lip. There was contempt in the small action but still her lip pulsed as the finger moved; it heated and quivered. 'You want me to *make* you surrender,' he said huskily. 'You would love me to use due force to make you come home with me so that you do not have to give up your precious stubbornness.'

Was he right? Yes, he was right, she conceded bleakly. Beneath the robe her body was already alive with anticipation, her breasts were tight, her abdomen making those soft, deep, pulsing movements that said fresh arousal was on its way.

With a toss of her head, she displaced his finger. 'It isn't home to me,' she denounced, utilising that stubbornness he spoke about. Then spoiled it all when her tongue slipped out to moisten the point where his finger had lingered.

Dark lashes lowered over even darker eyes as he watched the revealing little gesture. The power of his sexuality had never been a question for any woman who could witness that look. He was a dark golden figure with a dark, honeyed, sensual promise attached to everything he did.

'But it will be,' he assured, dragging her attention back

to the argument. 'Just as soon as you take off that robe and put on the clothes I have laid out for you, then we will drive *home*, together, as husbands and wives do—and find the nearest bed to finish what we have started here.'

With that, he turned and walked back to the suitcase, leaving her standing there having to deal with a sense of quivering frustration, which converted itself into a spitting cat. 'Will Diantha be joining us for a cosy little three-some?' she asked tartly. 'Or is this the point where I call up Clive and invite him along just in case we need the extra…?'

Her tongue cleaved itself to the roof of her mouth when he looked at her. Like the swinging gauge on a barometer, his mood had turned from tauntingly sexual to a cold contempt.

'There is no Diantha. There is no Adonis,' he clipped out with thin incision. 'This will be the last time either name will be mentioned in the context of our marriage again. Our marriage has just been re-consummated in this bed,' he added tightly. 'Here in Greece men still hold some authority over their women. Don't force me to impress upon you what that means, Isobel.'

He would, too, she realised as she stood staring at him while her mind absorbed his coldly angry expression. His willingness to be ruthless if she forced him into it was scoring lines of grim certainty into the lean cast of his face. Maybe she paled; she was certainly taken aback by his manner. They'd had many fights in their short-lived, highly volatile marriage, but she could not remember another time when he had used an outright threat.

Frissons sparked from one set of eyes to the other. Her fingers jerked up to clutch the robe again, closing the soft towelling across the pulse working in her throat. He watched it happen while he waited for a response from her. She saw a hard man, a tough man—much tougher than he had been three years ago. It was as if those years had taught him how to hone his strengths and use them to his own advantage. Four years ago he had been coming to terms with the knowledge that he no longer had a father to check every decision he made before it was put into action. Aristotle had been dead for only six months when Leandros and Isobel married. Leandros had been living with the stress of having to walk in a highly revered man's shoes. Advisors had hung around him like circling vultures, vying for a position of power in the new order of things that would eventually emerge from the melting pot of chaos into which his father's sudden death had thrown the Petronades empire. Leandros had lived in a permanent preoccupied state in which small things irritated the hell out of him because the big things totally obsessed his mind.

She had been a small thing. She had been a nagging irritant that he did not need during this dangerous cross-over period of his life. Oh, he had loved her to begin with. During that two-week sojourn in London, when most of the vultures had been left behind in Athens, he had been able to cast off his cloak of responsibility and become a carefree young man again for a while. So they met, fell in love, almost drowned in their happiness. Then they had come here to Athens, and he'd donned his heavy cloak again and become a stranger to her.

She hadn't understood then. She had been too young—only twenty-two herself. She had been too demanding, selfish and possessive and resentful of everything he placed higher on his list of priorities than her. Understanding had come slowly during the years they'd been separated, though the resentments had remained and hurts he'd inflicted upon her had refused to heal.

But she was now realising that Leandros had changed also. The circling vultures were no longer in evidence. The stress-packed frown of constant decision-making no longer creased his brow. He had grown into his father's shoes—had maybe even outgrown them to become a man who answered to no one, and was even prepared to be ruthless to get his own way.

'Why?' she breathed shakily. 'Why have you changed your mind about me?'

He did not even attempt to misunderstand the question. He knew they were back to divorce. 'I still want you,' he said. 'I thought that was obvious. All you need to do now is accept that you still want me and we can move on without all of this tedious arguing.'

'And if we make each other miserable again?'

He turned abruptly as if the question annoyed him. 'We will deal with that if or when it happens. Now, can we finish up here? Your mother's possessions still need to be packed and I would like to get away from here before the next power cut hits.'

He wasn't joking, she realised only half a second later, when there was a click, the lights went out and the fridge shuddered to a protesting halt. Problem solved, she mused bleakly. Stubborn desire to keep fighting him appeased.

Without another word she collected her clothes and returned to the bathroom, where it was pitch-black because there was no natural source of light in there. By the time she had fumbled into her clothes and knocked different joints against hard ceramic, she was more than ready to leave this hotel. Coming out of the bathroom, she found Leandros waiting for her by the open outer door.

'We are getting out of here while there is still enough light left to get down the stairs,' he said impatiently.

'But the bags—'

'The hotel will finish it and send your things on,' he announced with an arrogance that had always been there.

Before she knew it she was feeling her way down the dim corridor with her hand trapped securely in his.

'The city is being hit by lightning strikes due to a pay dispute,' he explained as they made it to the stairwell. 'The strikers are working on the principle that, because it is high season here in Athens, if they hit the tourist areas the government will sit up and take more notice, so the main residential areas are being left alone.'

'For how long, do you think?' She was feeling her way down the first flights of stairs while Leandros walked a few steps ahead of her.

'That depends on who is the most stubborn,' he replied, and turned his dark head to offer his first wide white grin. He was talking about them, she realised, not the strikers or the government.

Opening her mouth to make some tart reply, she missed her footing and let out a frightened gasp as she almost toppled. But he was right there to catch her. His hands closed around her slender waist and her body was suddenly crushed against his. Her stifled expression of fright brushed across his face and, on a soft oath, he trapped her up against the wall then lifted her up until their faces were level.

'I want you back in my life, my home and in my bed,' he declared with deep, dark, husky ferocity. 'I don't want us to fight or keep hurting each other. I want us to be how we used to be before life got in the way. I want it *all* back, *agape*. Every sweet, tight, glorious sensation that tells me that you are my woman. And I want to hear you say that you feel the same way about me.'

With her body crushed between the wall and the wonderful hardness of his body, and their eyes so close it was impossible not to see that he meant every passionate word, offering him anything but the truth seemed utterly futile. 'Yes,' she whispered. 'I want the same.'

In many ways it was a frighteningly naked moment. In other ways it was a relief. The truth was now out in the open and the only thing being held back were those three little words that would make exposure complete.

His dark eyes flared with the knowledge of that. She held her breath and refused to be the first one to say the words. 'Ruthless little witch,' he muttered thickly then his mouth found hers.

They actually shared, on that dim stairwell, the most honest kiss they had ever exchanged. It contained emotion, real emotion, the kind that rattled at the heart and dug its roots deep into that place where the soul lay hidden— along with those three small words.

When they were disturbed by the sound of someone else coming down the stairs, neither came out of the kiss breathing well. When Leandros levered his body away from her, he did so with a reluctance Isobel shared. She couldn't look at him, she was too busy trying to deal with the inner spread of those greedy roots of that oh-so-fickle thing called hope, that said yes, I want to take a risk on this. It is what's been missing for all of these years.

They continued their way downstairs into the foyer. The profusely apologetic manager listened as Leandros issued curt instructions about the packing of possessions and where to send them. The other man tried not to appear curious as to why the wife of Leandros Petronades had been staying in his hotel in the first place.

'He thinks we are very odd,' Isobel remarked as they stepped outside into a pink-glow sunlight.

'I feel very odd,' he came back drily—and caught hold of her hand.

Life suddenly felt so wonderful. Leandros's car was parked fifty feet away. It was low and sleek and statement-red and so much the car for a man of his ilk. Opening the door to the Ferrari, he guided her into the passenger seat, watched her coil her long legs inside, watched her tug her skirt down, filled her up with all of those sweet, tight sensations he had been talking about on the stairs, then closed the door to stride round the long bonnet and take the seat at her side.

The air was electric. He turned the key in the ignition and brought the car alive on a low, growling roar. The nerve-ends between her thighs flicked in tingling response to the car's deep vibration. The man, the car—it was like being bombarded by testosterone from every possible source, she thought breathlessly.

Did he know she was feeling like this?

Yes, he knew it. She could see his own tension in the way his long fingers gripped the squat gear stick, and the way his sensual mouth was parted and his breathing was tense as he looked over his shoulder so he could reverse the car in the few inches available to him to ease them out of the tight parking place. There was a hint of red striking along his cheekbones; his eyes glittered with that strange light that told her she was sitting beside a sexually aroused male. When he turned frontward again, she was showered with static. He changed gear, turned the steering wheel with one of those smooth fingertip flourishes that said the man controlled the car and not the other way around.

With a blaring of car horns he eased them out into the stream of traffic. The low sun shone on her face. She reached up to pull down the sun-visor and found her hand caught by another. The way he lifted it to his mouth and kissed the centre of her palm stifled her ability to breathe for long seconds. As he drove them through the busy streets of Athens, they communicated with their senses. He refused to release her hand, so when it became necessary to change gear it was her hand that felt the machine's power via the gear stick, with his hand holding it there.

It was exciting. She could feel sparks of excitement shooting from him, could feel the needle-sharp pinpricks attacking her flesh. Beneath the dress her breasts felt tight and heavy, between her thighs it was as if they were already having sex.

When they were forced to stop at a set of traffic lights he turned to look at her. His eyes filtered over her face then down her front. The dress was short, but not as short as she had used to wear three years ago, when glances like this used to be accompanied by a frown. This time her thighs were modestly covered but still he made her feel as if she were sitting there naked. The inner tingling turned into a pulsing. She tried pressing her thighs together in an effort to contain what was happening to her. His eyes flicked up, caught the anxiety in her eyes, the way she was biting down on her soft lower lip.

'Stop it,' she protested on a strangled choke of breathless laughter.

'Why?' was his devastatingly simplistic reply.

Because I am going to embarrass myself if you don't stop, she thought helplessly, but suspected that he already knew that.

The lights changed and he turned his glance back to the road again. She managed to win her hand back and tried to ignore what was passing between them. But the bright white of his shirt taunted her with what hid beneath it. If she reached out and touched him she knew she would feel the tension of muscles held under fierce control, and she could see a telling pulse beating in his strong brown neck that made her heart thump madly with the urge to lean across the gap separating them and lay her moist tongue against his throat. The way he moved his shoulder said he'd picked up on the thought and was responding to it.

They began to climb out of the city where the mishmash of buildings gave way to greener suburbs and breathtaking views over Athens to the sunkissed waters of the Saronic Gulf. Eventually they began to pass by the larger properties, set in their own extensive grounds and built to emulate classical Greece. Leandros's mother had a house here, though further up the hill. They drove past the Herakleides estate, where his Uncle Theron lived with his granddaughter Eve, who had been perhaps the only person in the family Isobel felt at ease with.

But then Eve was of a similar age and she was also half-English. She might be the very spoiled and the worshipped grandchild of a staunchly Greek man but she had always determinedly hung on to her British roots.

'Eve is married now,' Leandros broke their silence to inform her.

'Married?' Isobel turned disbelieving eyes on him. The girl she remembered had been a beautiful blonde-haired, blue-eyed handful of a creature who'd constantly foiled her grandfather's attempts to sell her into bondage—as Eve had called it.

'It's a long story,' he smiled, 'and one I think you will enjoy more if I let Eve tell it to you.'

The smile was rueful and turned her heart over because it reminded her of when he'd used to offer her sexily rueful smiles all the time. Rueful smiles which said, I want you. Rueful smiles which said, I know you want me but we will have to wait.

This smile was rueful because he knew what she was thinking about his precocious cousin Eve. But Isobel didn't smile back because she was remembering that, for all her staunch Englishness, Eve was adored by her Greek family. It was Eve's mother who had never made the grade. As Eve had once told her, 'They accept me because I do have their blood in my veins, even if I like to annoy them all by pretending I don't. But my poor mother was looked upon with suspicion from the moment she came here with my father. Thankfully, we spent the first ten years of my life living in London so the family didn't have a chance to put any spanners in the works of my parents' marriage. When they died and I was sent here to live with Grandpa they felt sorry for me so I got the sympathy vote. But that doesn't mean I don't know what they can be like, Isobel. Just do me one great favour and don't let them win.'

But they had won in the end. And, although Isobel remembered that Eve's grandfather had always been pleasant to her, she had never trusted his genial manner. Because like his much younger sister, Thea Petronades—Leandros's mother—Theron had no real wish to see the Herakleides blood-line further diluted with yet more English blood.

'Who did she marry?' she asked Leandros. 'Someone from a great Greek family no doubt?'

'Eve, meet Theron's expectations?' He grinned. 'No, she married a tough British bulldog called Ethan Hayes. And I don't think he is ever going to recover from the shock.'

'Who, Theron?' she prompted with just enough cynicism to wipe the grin from his face.

'No, Ethan Hayes,' he corrected. 'And your prejudice is showing, *agape*.'

Her prejudice? She opened her mouth to protest about that accusation then closed it again when she realised that he was right. She was prejudiced against these people. The knowledge did not sit comfortably as he turned the red car in through a pair of gates that led to the house that had once been her home.

This house was not as grand as the Herakleides mansion—or the Petronades mansion further up the hill. Leandros's mother still occupied the other home along with the rest of the Petronades family. But still, this building had its own proud sense of presence and made no secret of the fact that it belonged to a very wealthy man. Leandros had bought it just after they were married in an attempt to give them some private space of their own in which to work out the problems they were already having by then. His mother had taken offence, said it was not the Greek way, and if Isobel could not live with the family then maybe it should be Thea and the rest of the family who should move out, since the Petronades home had belonged to Leandros since his father's death.

Problems—there'd been problems whichever way she'd turned back then, Isobel recalled with a small sigh. Leandros heard the sigh, pulled the car to a stop in front of the neat entrance, switched off the engine then turned to look at her.

Her expression was sad again, the flush of sensual awareness wiped clean away. He wanted to sigh too, but with anger. Was the sight of their home so abhorrent to her? He glanced at the house and recalled when he'd bought it as a desperate measure in the hope that it would give them some time and space to seal up the cracks that had appeared in their relationship. He'd even got a friend in to refurbish the whole house before he'd brought Isobel down here to surprise her with his new purchase.

But all he had achieved was yet another layer of discontentment. For she'd walked in, looked around and basically that was all she could do. He had realised too late that to have the house decorated and furnished ready for occupation by some taste-sensitive interior designer had been yet another slight to Isobel's ability to turn this house into a home for them.

Home being an awkward word here, he acknowledged bleakly. For it had never become one—just a different venue for their rows without the extra pairs of ears listening in. He had still worked too many hours than were fair to her. She had still walked away from him down this sunny driveway each morning without a backward glance to see if he cared when he watched her go.

It was her one firm statement, he realised now, as they sat here remembering their own history of events. Because his working day had begun later than Isobel had been used to in England, she had left him each morning with her best friend, her camera, when really she knew he would much rather have been lingering over breakfast with her—or lingering somewhere else. If he came home at siesta time, she had rarely ever been here to greet him. After he'd burned the midnight oil working, she had been very firmly asleep when he'd eventually joined her in the bed. If he'd woken her she'd snapped at him and the whole circus act had begun all over again. Stubbornness was her most besetting sin but his had been gross insensitivity to the lonely and inadequate person she had become.

Strange, he mused now, how he did not move back into the big family house after she had left him for good. Strange how he'd preferred to leave Athens completely, having continued alone here for almost a year.

Hoping that she would return? he asked himself as he climbed out of the car and walked around its long, shiny red bonnet to help her alight.

Long legs swivelled out into the sunlight, cased in sheer silk; he caught the briefest glimpse of lacy stocking tops before the dress slid back into place. Classically styled and an elegant blue, the dress was not dissimilar to the one Diantha had been wearing the day he'd made his decision to break his marriage link to Isobel. But as she took his hand to help her to rise upright, there was nothing else about this woman or the dress that reminded him of any of those thoughts he'd had back then. In fact he could not believe his own thick-skinned arrogance in believing he could prefer Diantha's calming serenity to this invigorating sting of constant awareness that Isobel never failed to make him feel.

She was beautiful, stunningly so. As she came to stand in front of him he watched the loose fall of her shining hair as it slid silk-like across her slender shoulders, the curving shape of her body moving with innate sensuality beneath her dress. The length of her legs would make a monk take a second look but, for him, they made certain muscles tighten because he could imagine them wrapped tightly around his waist.

He was just contemplating that such a position might not be a bad idea with which to make the transition from here into the dreaded house, when he noticed a familiar car parked beneath the shade of a tree. His brows came together on a snap of irritation. Drawing Isobel towards him, he made do with dropping a kiss to the top of her head as he closed the door to the Ferrari and wondered how he was going to explain this away.

There was no explanation, he accepted heavily. He was in deep trouble and the only thing to do was to get it over with.

CHAPTER SIX

WALKING towards the house took more courage than Isobel had envisaged. The moment Leandros swung the front door open her stomach dipped on a lurching roll of dismay. The late-afternoon heat gave way to air-conditioned coolness in the large hallway, with its white glossed banister following the graceful curve of the stairs to the landing above. The walls were still painted that soft blue-grey colour; the tiles beneath her feet were the same cool blue and grey. To the left and the right of her stood doors which led into reception rooms decorated with the same classy neutral blend of colours and the kind of furniture you only usually saw in glossy magazines.

This house had never felt like home to her but instead it was just a showcase for this man and a bone of contention to everyone else. She had been miserable here, lonely and so completely out of her depth that sometimes she'd used to feel as if she was shrinking until she was in danger of becoming lost for good.

A strange woman dressed in black appeared from the direction of the kitchens. She was middle-aged, most definitely Greek, and she offered Isobel a nervous smile.

'This is Allise, our housekeeper,' Leandros explained, then introduced Isobel to Allise as *my wife*.

Wondering what had happened to Agnes, the cold fish his mother had placed here as housekeeper, Isobel smiled and said, '*Hérete*, Allise. It's nice to meet you.'

'Welcome, *kiria*,' the housekeeper answered politely.

102

'Your guests await you on the terrace. I shall bring out the English tea for everyone—yes?'

It felt odd to Isobel to be referred to for this decision while Leandros stood beside her. Agnes used to look to Leandros for every decision, even those simple ones regarding pots of coffee or tea. 'Yes—thank you,' she replied in a voice that annoyed her with its telling little tremor.

'What happened to Agnes?' she asked as Allise hurried back to her kitchen.

'She left not long after you did,' he replied, and there was something in his clipped tone that suggested it had not been a friendly parting of the waves.

But this was not the time to go into domestic issues. Isobel had a bigger concern looming forever closer. It came in the shape of her mother, and how Silvia was going to take the news that, having watched her daughter go off this morning ready to end her marriage, Isobel was now agreed to trying again.

Indeed, the marriage had again been consummated, as Leandros had so brutally put it.

They took the direct route to the terrace, treading across cool tiling to a pair of French doors at the rear of the house that stood open to the soft sunlight. They didn't speak. Isobel was too uptight to talk and she could feel Leandros's tension as he walked beside her. Was he worried about her mother's reaction? she wondered, and allowed herself a small, wry smile, because if she were in his shoes she would be more worried about his own mother's response when she found out about them.

The first person Isobel saw was her mother, sitting on one of the comfortable blue-covered cane chairs, looking a bit happier than she had done the last time she'd seen her. Lester Miles was there too, but he was wearing a brooding frown and he jumped to his feet the moment he saw them step outside.

Her mother glanced around; a welcome smile lit her face. 'Oh, there you are,' she greeted brightly. 'We were just wondering where you'd both got to!'

The *we* didn't register as meaning anything special until someone else began to rise from the depths of another chair. She was small, she was neat, she was dark-haired and beautiful. Even as she turned to them, Isobel knew who it was she was about to come face to face with. She had met her just once during a hastily put-together dinner party meant to celebrate Leandros's surprise marriage. The dinner party had been a complete disaster, mainly because everyone was so very shocked at the news, none less than Diantha Christophoros.

'I've just been explaining to Diantha how kind it was of you to put us up here after our dreadful experience at that awful hotel, Leandros,' Isobel's mother was saying with all the innocence of someone who had no idea whom it was she was giving this information to.

Leandros allowed himself a silent oath, and decided that if lightning could strike Silvia dumb right now, he would lift his eyes in thanks to the heavens. As it was, even the older woman had to feel Isobel stiffen and see the faintly curious expression Diantha sent him that had a worryingly amused and conspiratorial gleam about it.

He tried to neutralise it with an easy smile. 'Diantha,' he greeted mildly. 'This is a surprise. I don't think I recall that you were expected here today.'

Wrong choice of words, he realised the moment that Isobel took a tense step away from him.

'I know, and I am sorry for intruding like this,' Diantha replied contritely. 'Allise should have warned me that you had guests arriving unexpectedly, then I would not have made myself quite so at home.'

'Oh, you've been a great help,' Silvia assured in her innocence. Lester Miles was standing there looking distinctly ill at ease. 'We hope you don't mind, Leandros, but with stairs being a problem for me Diantha has arranged for your handyman to set up a bed in that nice little annexe you have attached to the main house. I think I will be very comfortable there until we catch our flight back to London.'

'It was my pleasure, Mrs Cunningham.' Diantha smiled a pleasant smile. 'I hope you will enjoy the rest of your stay in Athens. Leandros,' she turned back to Leandros without pause in her smooth, calm voice, 'I need a private word with you before dinner this evening. Your mother—'

His mother. 'Later,' he interrupted, feeling very edgy due to Isobel's silent stillness. What was more apparent was the way Diantha was ignoring Isobel. Did she believe she had a right to do that?

Had he allowed her to believe she had that right?

'Isobel, darling, you look very pale,' Silvia inserted. 'Are you feeling OK?'

No, Isobel was not OK, Leandros thought heavily. She believed Diantha was his lover. She had believed Diantha was the woman he had been about to put in her place. Her chin was up and her eyes were glinting. It was payback time for the way he had treated her Adonis and he did not for one moment expect Isobel to behave any better than he had done. But for all that he might deserve the payback, Diantha was innocent in all of this. He could not afford an ugly scene here, and turned urgently to face his statue of a wife.

'Isobel…' he began huskily.

'Oh, you do look pale!' Diantha exclaimed gently. Then

she was smiling warmly as she walked forward with a hand outstretched towards Isobel, and Leandros was at a loss as to how to stop what he knew was about to take place. The air began to sing with taut expectancy; he felt the sensation attack his loins. 'I don't suppose you remember me, Isobel,' Diantha was saying pleasantly. 'But we met once, at...'

Isobel turned and walked back into the house, leaving the horrified gasps echoing behind her and the sound of Leandros's urgent apologies to his mistress ringing in her head!

Striding back down the hall with the heels of her shoes tapping out a war tattoo against hard ceramic, she opened a door that led to one of the smaller sitting rooms at the front of the house. She stepped inside the room and slammed the door shut.

'Get out of here,' she lanced at Leandros when he managed to locate her several seething minutes later. 'I have nothing to say to you, you adulterous rat!'

'Back on form, I see,' he drawled lazily.

She turned her back to him and continued to glare out of the window that looked out on the front of the house. Her arms were folded beneath her heaving breasts and she could actually feel the fires of hell leaping inside.

The door closed with a silken click. A shiver chased down the rigid length of her spine. He hadn't gone. She could feel him standing there trying to decide how best to tackle the fact that his wife had just come face to face with his mistress!

'You were very rude.' He began with a criticism.

Typical, she thought. Attack instead of defence. 'I learned from an expert.'

'I suppose you are referring to me?'

Got it in one, she thought tightly. 'I hate this house.'

'As you hate me?'

'Yes.' Why bother denying it? She hated him and she could not believe she had let him seduce her into coming back here. She had to have gone temporarily insane. The whole day had been one of utter insanity, from the moment she'd got into that cab this morning with Lester Miles!

She heard his sigh whisper across the room, then felt the smooth, steady vibration of his tread as he began to walk towards her, her fingers curled into two tight fists. Suddenly she was having to fight a blockage in her throat.

'As soon as my luggage arrives I'm leaving,' she muttered.

He came to a stop an arm's reach away; she could feel his presence like a dark shadow wrapping itself around her shivering frame. If he touches me I won't be responsible for my actions! she told herself shrilly. If he dares make excuses I'll—

'Is that why you're staring out of the window?' He issued a soft, deriding laugh. 'It is just like you, Isobel, to cut and run in the face of trouble. I now have this great image of you walking up that driveway dragging your suitcase behind you. It looks so pathetically familiar that it makes me want to weep!'

His angry sigh hissed; she spun around to face him. She was shocked by how pale he looked in the deepening glow of the evening light. His clothes had lost their normal pristine smoothness and he needed a shave. Sinister was the word that leapt up to describe him. Sinister and frustrated and so angry it was pulsing out of every weary pore.

How could a man change so much in a few short minutes? It was this house, she decided. This hateful, horrible house. And that image of her that he had just conjured up was dragging on her chest and tugging out the tears.

'Don't you dare compare this with my life here before!' she cried.

'*Our* life!' he barked at her. 'Whatever happened here before happened to *both* of us! But we are not discussing the past.' His hand flicked out in an irritable gesture. 'We are discussing here and now, and your propensity to run instead of facing what threatens to hurt you!'

'I am not hurt, I'm angry!' she insisted. His mouth took on a deriding twist. The flames burning inside her leapt to her eyes.

'Diantha—'

'Is so comfortable here she instructs your staff on what to do!'

'She is a natural organiser,' he sighed out heavily.

He was daring to stand here defending his mistress? 'Just what you need, then,' she said. 'Because I can't even organise a pot of tea!'

He laughed; it was impossible not to. Isobel turned away again and managed to break free.

'I did not marry you for your organisational skills,' he murmured huskily.

Sex; they were back to the sex, she noted furiously.

'I married you because you are gorgeous and sexy and keeping my hands off you is like having an itch I cannot scratch.'

Her spine began to tingle because she knew her husband and he had just issued fair warning that he was going to touch.

'Get your mistress to scratch the itch,' she suggested.

'Diantha is not my mistress.'

Scornful disbelief shot from her throat. 'Liar,' she said.

The light touch of his fingers feathered her bare arms. Excitement shivered across every nerve-end. He was standing so close now her body was clenching in defence against that sensational first brush with his thighs.

'She is a close family friend, that is all.'

Isobel's second huff of scorn sent those fingers up to gently touch her hair. She was suddenly bathed in a shower of bright static.

'This conversation is developing a distinct echo to it,' he then tagged on ruefully.

He was comparing it with their row about Clive. 'The difference here being that I *know* about Diantha. You just jumped to conclusions about Clive because you have that kind of mind.'

'He was *raw* with desire for you,' he growled close to her earlobe.

'Whereas she only wants you for the prestige of your money and your exalted name.'

His low laugh of appreciation brought his lips into contact with her skin, at which point she was about to turn, deciding that braving eye contact had to be easier to deal with than the assault Leandros was waging on other parts. But a noise beyond the window caught her attention. Leandros straightened when he heard it too, and both of them watched a van come trundling down the drive bearing the name of the Apollo Hotel on its side.

Her luggage was about to arrive. Her heart began to thud. It was decision time. Did she stay or did she go?

'I stayed, *agape mou*,' Leandros said gruffly. 'Despite the suspicions I still have about you and the Adonis, I am still here and fighting for what I want. Don't you think it is about time that you stood still and fought for what you want?'

Fight the mistress? She did turn and look at him. 'Are you challenging me to go and throw her out of this house?'

A sleek black eyebrow arched in counter-challenge. 'Will it make you feel better about her if you did?'

No, it wouldn't, she thought bleakly, because throwing Diantha out of this house would not be to throw her far enough. 'You hurt her once before by marrying me in her place. Are you really prepared to do that to her again, Leandros?'

'I don't know what you're talking about.' He frowned.

Isobel's sigh of irritation was smothered by the sound of the van coming to a shuddering stop outside the window. 'I do know about your old romance with her,' she told him heavily. 'If an ordinary high-street lawyer like Lester Miles can find out about your present relationship, then we are talking about a serious breach of Greek family ethics here, of which—'

'Just a minute,' he cut in, and the frown had darkened. 'Back up a little, if you please. What old romance am I being accused of having with Diantha?'

He was going to make her spell it out. 'The way your sister Chloe told it, you virtually jilted Diantha at the altar when you married me.'

'Chloe?'

'Yes, Chloe,' she confirmed and could not stand still a moment longer looking into the clever face of confusion. Stepping round him, she put some distance between them. Outside a van door gave a rattling slam. 'Within days of you producing me as your wife, Diantha's family were shipping her off to Washington, DC and away from the humiliation you caused her.'

He was following her tense movements with increasingly glowering eyes. 'And my sister Chloe told you this?' he demanded. Her shrug confirmed it. 'When—when did she relay these things to you?'

'Does it matter?'

'Yes, it matters!' he snapped. 'Because it is not true! Nor is this—rumour, which seems to be everyone else's property but mine, that I am about to divorce you to marry her! I do not know who began it, and I can positively tell you that Diantha has received no encouragement from me—at either time—to believe that I have a marriage between her and me in mind!'

'Are you saying you have never considered marrying her?' Her challenge was etched in disbelief. But when he released a hard sigh then turned *his* back to *her*, Isobel knew the truth.

'Stop playing with people, Leandros,' she snapped and walked towards the door.

'I am likely to do a lot more than play, Isobel, if you try to walk through that door before we have finished this line of discussion.'

A threat. She stopped. Somewhere beyond these four sizzling walls a doorbell gave a couple of rings. She turned to face him. He was furious, she saw. Well, so was she! 'It was one thing playing the interloper here four years ago but to hell with you if you think I am going to go through all of that again!'

Her eyes were bright, her mouth trembling. If he dared to, he would go over there and...

And what? Leandros asked himself angrily. Force her to believe that which he could not deny outright? 'I had no such relationship with any other woman before I met you,' he announced thinly. 'Diantha did not leave Athens nursing a heart broken by me,' though he could tell who had broken her heart. 'Before Diantha arrived on my yacht in Spain as a hurried substitute for Chloe, who was needed here by my mother, I had not set eyes upon her in four years. During the two weeks Diantha stayed with me, we neither kissed nor slept together and very rarely touched.

But I did find her easy company to be with,' he admitted. 'And on an act of pure arrogance I made a decision that maybe—just maybe—she would eventually make a wife for me. The one I had did not, by that time, have much use for me, after all!'

'So it's my fault that you gave everyone the impression that you were divorcing me to marry her. Is that what you're saying?'

'No,' he sighed. 'I am saying that I was arrogant, but only within my own head!'

'But she uses this house as if she belongs here because *she* is arrogant.' If Isobel fizzed any more she was going to pop like a champagne cork, Leandros noted frustratedly.

'She is a friend—that is all,' he gritted. 'A *good* friend, who has been helping me out by liaising between myself and my mother, who is a neurotic mess because of Nikos's big wedding next week!'

'Liaising,' she scoffed. 'That's a good one, Leandros. Now I'm hearing repeated lies!'

Oh, to hell with it, he thought, and began striding towards her. Someone rattled the handle on the door. It flew inwards, forcing Isobel to leap out of its way and bringing him to a stop almost within reach of his aggravating target.

Isobel's mother appeared in the opening, propelling herself in her wheelchair. She looked cross—everyone was cross!

'Would you like to explain to me, young lady,' Silvia flicked sternly at her daughter, 'what happened to the good manners I taught you? How could you be so rude as to turn your back on that nice Miss Christophoros and walk away? I have just had to spend the last half an hour covering up for you!'

'That *nice* Miss Christophoros you have been happily *liaising* with happens to be *my* husband's mistress!'

Silvia's furious daughter replied, and, having silenced her mother, she then stalked away, hair flying like a warning flag, long legs carrying her out of the room and—

Leandros went to go after her…to stop her from leaving, then halted again when he saw her take to the stairs. A grin appeared. The minx might want to take his head off right now, but she was not going to leave him.

'What was she talking about?' Silvia demanded.

'She's jealous,' he murmured. 'She does not know what she's saying.'

'It sounded pretty clear-cut to me,' Silvia countered. 'Is that woman your current mistress?'

Current? He pondered on the word while he listened for that old familiar sound of a door slamming somewhere. Rear bedroom, not his, he calculated when, as predicted, the sound came.

Diantha, he noticed, had gone from being *that nice Miss Christophoros* to *that woman*. Silvia was nothing if not loyal to her own. Which brought forth another thought. 'Where is Diantha?' he asked sharply.

'She left just as the luggage arrived. Didn't you hear her car pull away?'

No, he had been too busy fighting with Silvia's witch of a daughter. 'Silvia,' he said, coming to a decision, 'you may not like what I am about to tell you, but I suggest you come to terms with it. Isobel and I are not getting a divorce,' he announced. 'We are, in fact, very much a re-united couple.'

He had to give it to his mother-in-law—she was not slow on the uptake. Her eyes went round. 'In just half a day?'

He smiled; it was impossible not to. 'It took less than half a day the first time we met,' he admitted candidly.

'That was before you broke Isobel's heart and sent her

home to me in little pieces,' Silvia said brutally. Eyes as fierce and contrarily vulnerable as her daughter's glared at him. 'I won't let you do it to her again.'

'I have no intention,' he assured. 'But I warn you again, Silvia,' he then added seriously, 'Isobel is still my wife and is staying that way.'

Isobel's mother studied his grimly determined expression. 'I think you should try telling her that,' she advised eventually.

'Oh, she knows it.' His eyes narrowed. 'She is afraid of what it is going to mean, that's all.'

'And the mistress?'

He mocked the question with a grimace. 'Is a mere friend.' The sooner certain other people recognised that the quicker he could settle down to convincing Isobel. 'Where is the lawyer?' he then asked thoughtfully.

'Still on the terrace looking slightly poleaxed by high-society living.'

Nodding, Leandros went to walk past her then paused and instead bent his dark head to place a kiss on her cheek. Her skin felt as smooth as her beautiful daughter's. But then Silvia was still a very attractive woman, even sitting here in this wheelchair. She had her daughter's eyes and beautiful mouth, and, though her hair might not be as red as Isobel's any more, it was still luxuriously silken.

'I am happy to see you back here again, *ee peteria*,' he told her huskily. 'But I am not happy to see you confined to this thing.'

'It won't be forever,' Silvia replied firmly. 'I am getting stronger by the day and don't usually spend so much time sitting here.'

'Would it be too much for you to explain to me what happened?'

Ten minutes later he was going to find Lester Miles,

with his head so filled with his new insight into Isobel and Silvia's last few years while they'd fought Silvia's battle together, that he didn't notice Isobel sitting on the top stair, where she'd listened in on the whole illuminating conversation.

When he'd gone she came down the stairs and brushed her mother's cheek with a silent salutation. She'd had no idea how tough her mother had found the last two years until she heard her confiding in Leandros.

'Come on,' she said softly. 'Let's go and check out your new accommodation.' And, taking charge of the wheelchair, she turned it round to face the hallway.

'You OK?' Silvia asked.

'Yes,' Isobel answered.

'You still love him don't you?'

'Yes,' she answered again; there was really nothing more either of them could add to it.

Together they checked over everything and found nothing to complain about. The rooms had used to be a fully self-contained study added on by a previous owner of the house who was a writer and liked his own space when he was working, so most of the necessary facilities had been built into the annexe. When the designers moved in they'd converted the whole thing into a state-of-the-art office for Leandros. But he'd rarely used it, preferring to use the conventional study in the main part of the house. Isobel had taken it over to use as a photo studio, where she'd developed her photographs and played around with them via the computer sitting in the corner on its state-of-the-art workstation.

With Diantha's famed organisational skills, a bed had been added along with a couple of armchairs and a huge TV set. Reluctant though Isobel was to admit it, the place looked great.

'I'll want for nothing here,' her mother announced with satisfaction. Even her luggage had been carefully unpacked and put away.

Now she must go and check on their other guest, she realised. 'Where's Lester Miles?' she asked her mother.

'Ask Leandros,' she suggested. 'He went looking for him a few minutes ago.'

But Lester Miles was being driven away from the house even as Isobel went to search him out. 'What have you done with my lawyer?' she demanded when she met Leandros in the hall.

'He's just left.'

Her very expressive eyes began to flash. 'Don't tell me you've sent him back to rough it at the Apollo!'

'No.' His mouth twitched. 'He had to go back to England with some urgency. My driver is taking him to the airport.'

'He won't get a flight,' Isobel stated confidently.

'Oh?' he murmured curiously. 'Why not?'

'Because all the flights to London are full—I already checked,' she drawled.

'How enterprising,' he commended. 'Were you hoping to escape *before* we made it to the bed or afterwards?'

Refusing to answer that, she turned and started up the stairs. Leandros arrived at her side.

'I am flying your lawyer home—along with the Adonis. There,' he smiled. 'Am I not a graciously accommodating man?'

Refusing to rise to that bit of baiting, she kept her gaze fixed directly ahead.

'Where are we going?' he enquired lightly.

She was on her way to find her own luggage; where he was going did not interest her one little bit.

He smiled at her again. She wanted to hit him. 'Is your mother comfortable?' he enquired.

'Perfectly, thank you,' she answered primly.

The sound of low laughter curled her insides up. They arrived on the upper landing, where six doors led to elegant bedroom suites. Isobel made for one door while Leandros made for another. With their hands on the door handles they paused to glance at each other, Isobel with the light of defiance in her eyes, because the room she was about to enter was not the one they'd used to share. Leandros simply smiled—again.

'Dinner,' he said, 'eight-thirty,' and disappeared from view, leaving her standing there seething with anger and a sense of frustration because, by refusing to comment on the fact that she was clearly not intending to share a bedroom, he had managed to grab the higher ground.

Dinner was a confusing affair. Silvia was tired and had decided to eat in her room then watch a video film before going to bed. Isobel came down, wearing the same dress— since it was her only dress. Though she had taken a shower, pinned up her hair and added some light make-up.

Leandros on the other hand was wearing full formal dinner dress. He looked handsome and dashing and her heart turned over. 'A bit over the top for an informal meal in, isn't it?' she remarked caustically.

'I have to go out later,' he explained. 'My mother is expecting me, and, since I have been strictly unavailable to anyone today, either I turn up or she will come here to find out what I am playing at.'

Isobel wished she knew what he was playing at. There were undercurrents at work here that made her feel out of control. Yet she didn't know why, because it wasn't as if she hadn't known about the dinner tonight. Diantha had mentioned it, being so efficient. What she had expected was that Leandros would make some concession for once in his important existence and have remained here with her.

Which was telling her what? she asked herself. She didn't like the answer that came back at her, and that revolved around dear Diantha and his preference for where he would rather be!

They walked into the smaller of the two dining rooms that the house had to offer, like two strangers on their first date. Leandros politely held out a chair for her. Allise, she saw, had pulled out all the stops for this cosy dinner for two and the table had been dressed with the best china and candles flickered softly instead of electric lights.

She sat down. Leandros helped her settle her chair. By the time he'd moved away without so much as touching her even by accident, she was feeling so incensed she felt she was living within her own personal battle zone.

He sat down opposite. Candlelight flickered over lean, dark features completely stripped of his thoughts. He was beautiful. It wasn't fair. The black of his jacket and the white of his shirt and the slender bow-tie gave sophistication a whole new slant. He reached for a napkin, shook it out then took a bottle of champagne out of its bucket of ice. The napkin was folded around the bottle. Long brown fingers deftly eased out the cork. It popped softly but did not dare to explode—not for this man who had learned how to open a bottle of champagne in his crib. Frothy gold liquid arrived in the crystal goblet in front of her without him so much as spilling a drop. He filled his own glass. She considered picking up hers and tossing the contents at him.

But the suspicion that he was already expecting her to do that held her hands tightly clenched on her lap. If he didn't say something to ease this tension, she was going to be the one to explode…like the champagne cork should have done.

'You can come with me, if you want.'

She sat there staring at him, unable to believe he had just said that—and as casually as he had done!

'Thank you,' she said coolly. 'But I am watching a film with my mother.'

His grimace said—fair enough. He picked up his fizzing crystal goblet and tipped it in a suave toast to her. 'Welcome home,' he said, then drank.

If Allise hadn't arrived with the food at that point, maybe—just maybe—Isobel would have reacted. But wars like this required nerves of steel and she had them, she told herself.

They ate in near silence. When she couldn't push her food around her plate any longer, Isobel drank some of the champagne, which instantly rushed to her head. Her mouth suddenly felt numb and slightly quivery. She put the goblet down. Leandros refilled it. Allise arrived with the second course. When the last course arrived, Isobel refused the delicious-looking honey-soaked pudding and asked for a cup of black coffee instead. She'd drunk two glasses of champagne like a woman with a death wish because she knew as well as Leandros knew that she had no head for the stuff.

When the dreadful meal was finally over, she got up on legs that weren't quite steady. Leandros didn't get up but lazed back in his chair, studying her without expression.

'Goodnight, then,' she said.

He gave a nod in acknowledgement. She walked out of the room. She suffered watching the film with her mother out of grim cussedness, then escaped to her self-allotted bedroom, got ready for bed, crawled beneath the crisp white sheets, pulled them over her head and cried her eyes out.

He was with her, she was sure of it. He was standing in some quiet corner of his mother's house, gently explaining the new situation. Would she beg, would she cry? Would he surrender to the liquid appeal in her dark eyes and stay with her tonight instead of coming home?

She drifted into sleep, only to be consumed by visions she did not want to see. It wasn't fair. She hated him. He was tying her in emotional knots just like the last time. A pair of arms scooped her off the bed and jolted her out of sleep.

CHAPTER SEVEN

'GET off me, you two-timing brute!' she spat at him.

'Well, that isn't very nice,' he drawled.

'Where do you think you are taking me?'

'You did not really think that I was going to let you sleep in any other bed than our own, did you? Foolish Isobel,' he mocked as he lifted up a knee then swung her down onto another bed.

The knee stayed where it was, the rest of him straightened so he could remove his robe, his eyes glinted dark promises down at her, and because she was too busy trying to cover her dignity by tugging her ridden nightshirt over the shadowy cluster of golden curls at her thighs she missed her only chance to escape. He came down beside her in a long, lithe stretch of male determination. One hand slid beneath the fall of her hair while the other made a gliding stroke down her side from breast to slender thigh. Then it came back up, bringing her nightshirt with it.

He stripped it from her with an ease that left her gasping. She aimed a clenched fist at him, he caught it in his own hand, then his mouth was coming down to cover her mouth. She groaned out some kind of protest but it wasn't enough to bring this to a halt. It was dark, it was warm and, as he subdued her, her senses were already beginning to fly. Seconds later she was lost in the hungry, driving intensity of the kiss.

Her fingers unclenched out of his grip on them, lifted then buried themselves in his hair. The kiss deepened. She could feel his heart pounding, felt the thick saturation of his laboured breath. Her body, her limbs, every sinew moved and stretched on wave after wave of desperate delight. He dragged his mouth away and looked down at her, no smile, no mockery, just heart-stunningly serious desire.

'Did you go to her?' she whispered painfully.

'No,' he replied.

'Was she there?'

His eyes darkened. 'Yes.'

Her fingers tugged at his hair until he winced. 'Did you speak to her—touch her?'

'No,' he grated. 'I had no reason to.'

The black ferocity of his gaze insisted that she had to believe that. Her mouth slackened into a wretched quiver. 'I imagined all sorts,' she shakily confessed to him.

'I am with the only woman who has *ever* done this for me,' he answered harshly. 'Why would I lust after less?'

'Three years, Leandros,' she reminded him painfully. 'Three years can make a man accept less.'

'Were you unfaithful?' He threw the pain right back at her.

'No—never.'

'Then why are we talking about this?'

They didn't talk any more, not after his mouth claimed hers again and his hands claimed the rest of her with a grim, dark, fierce concentration that robbed her of the will to do anything but feel with every single sense she possessed.

She was possessed, Isobel decided later, when she lay curled in the secure circle of his arms. Her cheek rested in the hollow of his shoulder, her fingers were toying with the whorls of hair on his chest. There wasn't another place she would rather be, but knowing it made her feel so very vulnerable. She didn't think she was any better equipped now than she had been three years ago to deal with what loving a man like Leandros meant.

She released a small sigh. The sigh aggravated the muscles controlling Leandros's steady heartbeat. She might be lying here in his arms but he knew she had problems with it. Did he take a leap of faith and force those problems out into the open so they could attempt to sort them out?

He trapped his own sigh before it happened. He didn't want to talk. His eyes were heavy, his body replete and content. Her hair lay spread across his shoulder, her soft breathing caressed his chest and the darkness soothed him towards sleep.

She moved just enough to place a kiss on his warm skin, then followed it up with another pensive sigh. Contentment flew out of the window. He moved onto his side and flipped her onto her back then came to lean over her with his head supported by his hand.

'What?' she said and she looked decidedly wary.

'Why the melancholy sighs?' he demanded.

'They were not melancholy.'

He arched an eyebrow to mock that little lie. She lowered dusky eyelashes until they brushed against skin like porcelain. Her mouth looked small and cute when he knew that the last thing you could ever call Isobel was *cute*.

'I have this urge to stand you up against the nearest wall and shine a bright light in your eyes,' he murmured drily. 'We have just made love. You cried out in my arms and clung to me as if I was the only thing stopping you from falling off the edge of the earth. You told me you loved me—'

'I did not!' The desire to deny that brought her lashes upwards.

'You thought it, then,' he amended with a shrug meant to convey a sublime indifference to semantics. Then he reached out to gently comb her hair from her face, and was suddenly serious. 'We need to talk, *agape mou*, about why we parted.'

Without the gentleness she might not have caught on to what he was actually daring to broach here. But he saw the light in her eyes change, saw them flood with horror then with tears. 'No,' she said, then was leaping out of the bed and racing from the room.

By the time he had grabbed his robe and gone after her she was standing in the other bedroom, huddled inside the blue robe. His chest ached at the sight of her, at the sight of that robe that said so many things about the real Isobel, like the look of pure anguish whitening her face.

'Will you stop running?' he ground at her. 'Just stop running from this,' he repeated almost pleadingly. 'If we do not face the past together, how are we supposed to move on?'

Isobel stood and shook and remembered why she hated him. If she could take back the last mad day then she would. Her heart hurt, her throat hurt; just seeing him standing there looking as if he was experiencing the same things made her want to wound him as he had once almost fatally wounded her. How could she have forgotten what he had done to her? How could she have lain in his arms and let herself ignore the kind of man she knew him to be?

'You didn't want our baby,' she breathed. 'Is that facing it?'

He winced as if the tip of a whip had just lashed him. 'That is not true…'

'Yes, it is,' she insisted. 'By the time I was pregnant I don't think you even wanted me!'

'No…' He denied that.

'I was the irritation you just didn't need, and you made

sure I knew it.' But he was right; she could not run from this! It had to be faced before they made the same mistakes a second time and turned lust into love, which then turned into regret filled with frustration and bitterness. 'You married me when you didn't need to, we both knew that—you'd already enjoyed what was on offer after all! You lifted me out of working-class drudgery into wealth and luxury beyond compare then expected me to show eternal gratitude. But how did I pay you back for this generosity and goodness? I refused to conform. I refused to smile weakly and say ''Yes, thank you, Mama,'' when your mother lectured me on how I should behave.'

'She was attempting to advise you.'

'She was cold and critical and so dismayed by me that I don't know how she managed to stay in the same room with me half the time!'

'So you played up to that criticism, is that it?' he bit out. 'Or should I say you played down to it just for the hell of watching her squirm?'

'I stayed *away* from it!' she corrected. 'Or didn't you notice?' She was aching and throbbing as it all came rushing back. 'I went out and found my own kind of people.' Her hand stretched out to encompass the view of Athens lying beyond the window.

'Like Vassilou.'

'Did your mouth flatten like that in distaste, Leandros?' she challenged the expression on his grim face. 'If you can't see the difference between *''Do you really need to wear those terrible trousers, Isobel?''* and *''Ah,* Kyria, *you look so cool and fresh today!''* well, I certainly can. Or—*some babies are ill-judged and ill-timed, Isobel.'* Her eyes began to sting. She swallowed thickly. 'Words like that when spoken by the mother of your husband rarely shore up an ailing marriage. They help to shatter it.'

'My mother could not have said such a thing to you,' he denied, but he'd gone pale. He knew she was telling the truth. 'She would not be so—'

'Cruel?' she finished for him when the word became glued to his tight upper lip. ' *"Maybe it was for the best."'* Hoarsely she quoted his own choice of words back at him. ' *"We were not ready for this."'*

He swung his back to her and walked over to stare out of the window. The desire to leap on that back and pummel it to the ground sang in her blood. If she shook any more fiercely she would have to sit down.He had lifted the lid on black memories, and now she was standing here being consumed by them.

'I was ashamed of myself when I said that,' he uttered.

'Good,' she commended. 'I was ashamed of you too.' With that she walked over to the chest of drawers and withdrew a fresh nightshirt then went into the bathroom. She didn't shut the door because she was *not* running away this time. Not from this—not from anything *ever* again.

He came to stand in the doorway. With her back firmly to him she dropped the robe and replaced it with the clean nightshirt. 'You were inconsolable and I did not know how to cope with your grief,' he said huskily.

'No, you were busy and had to be pulled out of an important meeting,' she gave her own version of events. 'And if it wasn't bad enough that you didn't want me to get pregnant in the first place, you then found yourself having to deal with an hysterical woman who didn't appreciate ' *"Maybe it is for the best."'*

'All right,' he rasped. 'So I did not want us to have a baby at that time!'

She swung round to look at his face as he dared to admit that! No wonder his skin looked grey!

'We were both too young. Our marriage was in a mess!

You were miserable; *I* was miserable! We had stopped communicating on any level—'

'Especially between the sheets.'

'Yes, between the bloody sheets!' he grated, and suddenly he was swinging away from the door and gripping her upper arms. 'I adored you. You fascinated me! You sparkled and sizzled and took on all-comers with a courage that took my breath away. When you were in my arms it was like holding something powerfully special. But our marriage had not had the time to grow beyond that all-consuming physical obsession before you were presenting me with a red stop light. I resented having to stop!'

'I didn't ask you to.'

'You did not need to.' His sigh took the anger out of him; dropping his hands, he moved away. 'You did not see how fragile you looked, as if you would shatter if I so much as touched you.'

He walked back into the bedroom. This time it was Isobel that followed him. 'Couldn't you have just told me that instead of turning cold on me?'

'Tell you that I was such a selfish swine that I did not want half a lover in my bed?' He released a self-derogatory laugh. 'Tell you that I did not want to share your body with anything?' An oath was thrust out from the cavernous depths of his chest. 'I despised myself. I did not know what was happening inside my own head! When you lost the baby I believed I had wished it to happen. I still believe that. My punishment was to lose you, and I was willing to take it. I was willing to take any punishment so long as I was not forced to face you with what I had done.'

'So you let me walk away.' She understood him now.

'You tied me in so many knots I was relieved to see you go.'

'And broke my heart all over again,' she said with painful honesty. 'Didn't it occur to you that I needed you to come for me?'

His shook his head; his shoulders were hunched, his gaze grimly fixed on his bare feet. 'I despised myself. It was easy, therefore, to convince myself that you despised me too.'

'I did.'

Silence fell. It came with a heavy thud. Isobel looked at the spacious bedroom with its cool floors and lavender walls and purple accessories, and wondered how silence could hurt so much.

'It wasn't your fault,' she murmured eventually. 'The baby, I mean,' she added, then had to swallow tears when he lifted his dark head to send her an agonisingly unprotected look. 'The statistics for losing a first baby in the first three months of pregnancy are high. It was simply bad luck.'

She tried a shrug to punctuate her absolute belief in that, but it didn't quite come off and she had to turn away in the end, wrapping her arms across her body and clutching at her shoulders with tense fingers that shook. A pair of arms arrived to cover her arms; long fingers threaded tensely with hers. It was so good to feel him hold her that she couldn't hold back the small sob.

'I had my own guilt to deal with,' she thickly confided. 'I felt I had failed in every way a woman could. I had to leave because I couldn't stand everyone's pitying expressions and the knowledge that they thought the loss of our baby more or less summed up our disaster of a marriage.'

He remained silent but his arms tightened, offering comfort instead of words. On a small whimper she broke the double arm-lock so she could turn and give back some comfort by placing her arms around his shoulders and pressing her face into the warm strength of his neck.

'Tomorrow we begin making a better job of this second chance we have given ourselves,' he ordained gruffly.

She nodded.

'We talk instead of fighting.'

She gave another nod.

'When people say things you do not like you tell me about it and I listen.'

She agreed with another nod.

He shifted his stance. 'Don't go too meek on me, *agape mou*,' he drawled lazily. 'It makes me nervous.'

'I'm not being meek,' she informed him softly. 'I'm just enjoying the feel of your voice vibrating against my cheek.'

With a growl, she was lifted up and kissed as punishment. The kiss led to other things, another room and a familiar bed. They slept in each other's arms and awoke still together, showered together and only separated when Isobel had to go back to the other bedroom to find something to wear.

They met up again on the terrace. The first cloud that blocked out her sunlight came when she saw Leandros was dressed for the office in a dark suit, blue shirt and dark tie. Handsome and dynamic he may look, but she needed him to stay here with her.

'For a few hours only,' he promised when he saw her expression, getting up to hold out a chair for her.

'It is reality, I suppose.' She smiled.

'And some unfortunate timing,' he added. 'I have been back in Athens for only a few weeks after a long stay abroad. Nikos's marriage is like a large juggernaught racing down a steep hill and taking everyone else along with it for the ride.'

Was he talking about his time in Spain as his long stay abroad? Isobel wondered. But didn't want to think about that right now when she was trying hard not to think of anything even vaguely contentious.

'So, when is the wedding?' she asked brightly.

'Next week.' He grimaced as he sat down again. 'In my father's stead I have been slotted into the role of host for the many pre-wedding dinners my mother has arranged, and also as to escort her to those that the Santorini family are having. Hence my having to leave you last night.' He paused to pour her a cup of coffee. 'Tonight I must do the same—unless I can talk you into coming with me?'

Body language was one hell of a way to communicate, Leandros mused as he watched her smile disappear and her eyes hide from him while she hunted for an acceptable excuse to refuse.

It came in the shape of Silvia Cunningham, who appeared on the terrace then. She was walking with the aid of a metal frame, and even to him it was a worthy diversion.

He stood up and smiled. 'What a delightful sight!' he exclaimed warmly. '*Ee pateria*, those beautiful legs look so much better when viewed upright.'

'Get away with you,' Silvia scolded, but her cheeks warmed with pleasure at the compliment. 'You know, I can't make up my mind if it is the fierce heat or the relentless sunshine, but I feel so much stronger today.'

Isobel got up to greet her mother with a kiss then pulled out a chair for her and waited patiently while Silvia eased herself into it. As he watched, Leandros saw the tender, loving care and attention Silvia's daughter paid to her comfort without making any kind of fuss.

He also noticed the look of relief on her face because their conversation had been interrupted. Stepping across the terrace to where the internal phone that gave a direct line to the kitchen sat, he ordered a pot of tea for Silvia then came to sit down again. He listened as mother and daughter discussed what kind of night Silvia had had while thoughts of his own began to form inside his head.

Allise arrived with the pot of tea. There was a small commotion as room was made on the table and an order for toast and orange juice was placed. Biding his time, he sipped at his coffee, watching narrowly as Isobel used every excuse she could so as not to look at him.

She was wearing the green trousers teamed with a white T-shirt today. The hair wasn't up in a pony-tail, which had to mean that she was not about to run. But, beautiful though she undoubtedly was, fierce and prickly and always ready for a fight, she was also a terrible coward. It had taken him a long time to realise that, he acknowledged, as he watched her bright hair gleam in the sunlight, her green eyes sparkle as they smiled at Silvia and her very kissable mouth curve around her coffee-cup.

He waited until both ladies had put their cups safely down on their saucers before he went for broke. 'Silvia,' he aimed his loaded bet directly at Isobel's weakest point, 'Isobel and I must attend a party tonight. We would be very honoured if you would accompany us.'

He had chosen his bet well, for he could remember Silvia before her accident. She might have spent her working hours stuck behind the window as a teller in a high-street bank but her social life had used to be full and fun.

'A party, you say?' Eyes so like her daughter's began to sparkle. 'Oh, what fun! And you really don't mind if I come along with you?'

From across the table, barbs began to impale him. He made eye contact with a brow-arching counter-challenge that gave no indication whatsoever to what was beginning to sizzle in his blood. This woman could excite him without trying to. She brought him alive.

'We didn't come to Athens equipped to attend parties,' Isobel reminded *both* of them.

Silvia's face dropped in disappointment. Isobel saw it happen and looked as if she had just whipped a sick cat.

'No problem,' he murmured smoothly. 'It is an oversight that can be remedied within the hour.'

'Of course!' Silvia exclaimed delightedly. 'We have time to shop, Isobel! It's about time we treated ourselves to something new!'

I hate you, the other pair of eyes informed him. The sulky mouth simply looked more kissable.

'Whose party is it?'

With the smoothness of a born gambler, he turned his attention to his mother-in-law and explained about his younger brother Nikos's wedding next week and how tonight's party was being held at Nikos's future in-laws' home, which was a half-hour's drive out of the city towards Corinth.

'You don't play fair,' Isobel told him in flat-toned Greek. 'You know I don't want to go.'

'What did you say?' her mother demanded.

'She said she didn't think it was fair to expect you to shop and spend the evening partying,' he lied smoothly. 'So we will solve the problem the rich man's way, and I will have a selection of evening gowns sent out here for you to peruse at your leisure.'

The *rich man* part was said to tease yet another smile from Silvia. The daughter didn't smile. But he did get a flashing vision of retribution to come. 'Try anything stupid just to get back at me, and I will retaliate,' he warned in Greek.

'What did *he* say?' Silvia wanted to know.

'He said choose something outrageously daring,' Isobel responded defiantly.

He laughed. What else could he do? He knew he had asked for that. It was fun having a wife that spoke his language, he decided.

But it was also time to cut and run, before she decided to corner him somewhere private and he did not get any work done today. Rising to his feet, he bid Silvia farewell and stepped round the table to kiss his wife's stiff cheek, then strode away, still feeling those wonderful barbs that had launched themselves at him.

'Don't you want to go to this party, Isobel?' her mother asked when she saw the way she glared at Leandros's retreating back.

Isobel turned her head to look at her mother, who had known about her problems with Leandros three years ago, but who had never been told about the problems Isobel had had with his family. 'I'm just a bit nervous about meeting people again,' she answered. 'It's too soon.'

'When you fall off a horse the best thing to do is get right back on it,' was her mother's blunt advice—while thoroughly ignoring the fact that mounting the dreaded horse had come about three years too late. 'And if I can see that you two looked so happy you have to be right for each other, then give other people the chance to make the same discovery,' she added sagely.

Isobel was about to open her mouth and tell her mother the hard facts about those other people, then changed her mind, because what was the use in stirring up trouble before it arrived? She was here—though she still wasn't sure how it had happened. She was staying—though she wished it didn't fill her with such a nagging ache of uncertainty.

Silvia sat back in her chair and released a happy sigh. 'Gosh, I feel reborn today,' she said. 'It makes me want to sing.'

She did sing—all morning. She loved every gown that

arrived—within the hour—complete with every accessory she could require. By the time Silvia went off for her afternoon siesta, Isobel was glad to escape to her room and wilt. But she couldn't wilt completely because she was expecting Leandros to walk in at any moment and she wanted to be ready for him.

However Leandros was running late. The few hours he had intended to spend at work had gone smoothly enough. Time began to get away from him when he went to the boot of his car to put away the briefcase he had left in his office the day before, and discovered that the jacket he had been wearing still lay where he had placed it before chasing after Isobel. He saw the edge of the envelope straight away. It was sticking out of one of the pockets but it was only when he reached down to slide it free that he remembered what it contained.

Two minutes later he was heading into the city, not out of it. A few minutes after that and he was striding into the bank with his wife's safety deposit box key and her letter authorising him to open the box. His curiosity was fully engaged as to what Isobel's idea of *family heirlooms* actually consisted of…

By the time he did eventually arrive home it was to find Isobel sitting cross-legged upon the bed, wearing what looked like one of his own white T-shirts—and nothing else from what he could see. She must have just come from the shower. Her hair was wet, and she was sitting with her head thrown forward while she combed the silken pelt with slow, smooth strokes, allowing the excess water to fall onto a white towel she had laid out in front of her.

'If you want a shower, I suggest you use a different bathroom,' she advised without lifting her head. 'Otherwise I might decide to murder you while you're naked and vulnerable in this one.'

He started to grin as he stood leaning in the doorway. In truth, after the trick he'd pulled this morning he had expected her to show her protest by refusing to come near this room.

'Not you, my sweet angel,' he denied lazily. 'You would see my quick death as being too kind to me.'

'Don't bank on it.'

'OK. I will live dangerously, then.' With that he levered away from the doorframe, came into the room and closed the door.

She still did not deign to lift her head as he walked across the room and placed two black velvet jewellery cases into the top drawer of a chest. Studying her as he removed his jacket and tie, he tried to decide whether to simply jump on her and give her no chance to defend herself, or whether to annoy her by ignoring her as she was ignoring him.

The former was tempting, but the latter should win since the shower seemed the best venue for the both of them. Her hair was wet already. The T-shirt belonged to him, and, having issued the threat, she would not, he knew, be able to remain sitting there passively without being drawn to carry out it out.

With a click and a scrape he undid his trousers and heeled off his shoes. Isobel's comb continued its smooth strokes while he removed his socks, then his under-shorts, which left only his shirt to conceal the fact that he was already very much aroused by this little game. He needed a shave so he strode into the danger-zone of the bathroom, paused long enough to reach in and spring the showerhead to life before he picked up his electric razor and began using it.

She arrived at the door as he had predicted, looked disconcerted to find him standing by the bathroom mirror, then mulish when she realised she had been outwitted by him.

'Choose your weapon,' he invited without allowing his eyes to leave the mirror, where his own reflection showed him a man who had changed a lot in the last twenty-four hours. Gone were the harsh lines of cynicism he had watched increase over the previous three years. Now he saw a pretty good-looking guy with a decent pair of shoulders and sexily provoking promise about him.

She did this for him, he acknowledged. This moody woman with the slicked-back wet hair and the sensationally smooth white skin.

She leapt without warning. Dropping the razor into the washbasin, he swung round in time to catch her against his chest. Green eyes glittered, her mouth quivered, her arms wrapped tightly around his neck.

'I don't want to go tonight!' she cried out plaintively.

She chose her weapon well. Anger he could deal with—a physical attack. But true tears and fear were different things entirely. 'Don't cry, *agape mou*. That isn't fair.'

'Can't we wait a few days before you toss me to the wolves again—please?' she begged.

The *please* almost unmanned him. He recovered while carrying her back to the bed. 'If anyone so much as glances at you wrongly I will strike them down, I promise you.'

'They can still think what they like about me, Andros!'

Andros; she was the only person to ever get away with calling him that, so when she did it, it turned his senses over, it tied possessive ropes around his heart. Vulnerable, cowardly, beautiful Isobel—the Isobel she let no one else ever see.

With grim intent he sat down on the bed then, as she still clung to him, he rolled them both backwards until they lay on their sides. 'Do you truly believe that we two are the only ones to regret what happened before?' he demanded. 'My mother had to watch me go to pieces. Within the year after you left I left here also and rarely ever came back again.'

'Where did you go?' She was diverted. He almost laughed at the irony. He revealed weakness and she suddenly became the strong one! 'To Spain,' he replied. 'To a place called San Estéban. I ran my companies from a stateroom on my yacht and learned to live with myself by pretending Athens didn't exist.'

'You should have come to me!' Her fist made contact with his shoulder. He trapped her beneath him on the bed. Her legs still clung though. She was not letting go of him and she was wearing nothing beneath the T-shirt.

'I did come to you,' he growled. 'Every night in my dreams!'

'Not good enough.'

'Then we have a lot of time to make up for,' he gritted and entered her—no preliminaries. Her cry was one of pleasure because she was ready to receive him. She clutched his head and brought his mouth crashing down onto hers. They rode the hot wind of raging passion. When it was over and he felt his strength return to him he got up as still she clung and walked them both beneath the shower, where he began the whole exhilarating ride all over again.

Getting ready to go out was not easy when he was feeling laid-back and slumberous. Fortunately, Isobel had wisely disappeared to the other bedroom so at least the temptation to forget tonight's party and remain lost in her was removed—in part. He was all too aware of that soft, pulsing sense of continued possession. He had only to think of her and he could imagine her crawling all over him in her desire to lay claim to every exquisitely receptive inch of his skin.

He grimaced as he retrieved the black jewellery cases from the chest of drawers, then went to find his red-haired tormentor. If she launched another attack on his defences, they would not be going anywhere, he promised his impatient senses.

CHAPTER EIGHT

HE ENTERED the room with a light tap to warn of his arrival. Isobel turned to the mirror to take one last look at herself and could not decide if she liked what she saw.

Nervous fingers fluttered down the short, close-fitting lined straight dress she had chosen to wear. It was made of a misty-jade silk-crêpe that clung sensually to her slender figure without being too obvious—she hoped. Her make-up was light and natural, her kitten-heeled lightweight mules matched the colour of the dress. But had she struck the note she had been striving for, in a different key to the old downright-provocative Isobel, without appearing as if she had conceded anything to the Greek idea of what was good taste?

'What do you think?' She begged his opinion while anxiety darkened her eyes and she wished to goodness that she'd worn her hair down—it had not occurred to her before that she liked to use her hair to hide behind and now she felt very exposed.

Leandros didn't reply, so she turned to gauge his expression, only to go breathlessly still when she found herself looking at a man from any warm-blooded woman's dreams. He'd discarded the conventional black dinner suit in favour of a white dinner jacket, black silk trousers and a black bow-tie. He looked smooth and dark and so sexually masculine that those tiny muscles inside her that were still gently pulsing from their last stimulation began to gather pace all over again.

His darkly hooded eyes moved over her in a way she

recognised only too well. Mine, the look said. 'Stunning,' he murmured. 'Nothing short of perfect.'

So are you, she was going to say, but as he walked towards her she noticed the black velvet jewellery cases in his hand and recognised them instantly.

Nervous fingers feathered the front of her dress again. 'S-so you got them back,' she said.

'The heirlooms?' His mouth twitched. 'As you see,' he confirmed easily.

With the neat flick of a finger he opened the flat case, gave her a few seconds to stare down at the platinum scrolls pierced with glowing emeralds and edged with sparkling diamonds that she had thought so beautiful when first she saw them. But that was before his sister's scornful, *'He's given you those old things? Mother always refused to wear them. Though they are definitely wasted on you,'* had taken their beauty away.

Now those same long fingers were lifting the necklace from its bed of velvet. 'Turn around,' he commanded.

'I...' Reluctance to so much as touch any of the pieces lying in that case was crawling across her skin. 'I gave you them back,' she pointed out edgily. 'I don't really want—'

'It has been a few eventful days filled with many second chances,' he replied in a light tone filled with sardonic dryness, 'for here I am, giving them back to you. They will be perfect with this lovely dress, don't you think?'

Maybe they would. 'But...' The necklace sparkled and glittered across the backs of his fingers. She lifted wary eyes to his and instantly felt as if she was drowning in a thick, dark sea of lazy indulgence. Let's go back to bed, she wanted to say. I feel safe there with you. 'Don't you think my wearing them tonight would be like slapping your family in the face with the fact that I am back? M-maybe I will wear them another time.'

'But you are back,' he pointed out with devastating simplicity. 'You are my beautiful wife. I gave these beautiful things to you and *I* want you to wear them. So turn around…'

She turned around, taking that sudden gleam of determination in his eyes with her. The necklace came to lie against her skin, circling the base of her throat as if it had been specially made to do so.

'A new beginning for you and I also mean a new beginning for everyone, *agape mou*,' he said deeply as she felt the warm press of his lips to her nape.

Then he was gently bringing her round to face him. With a neat flick the matching bracelet arrived around her slender wrist. Her stomach began to dance when he reached up to gently remove the tiny gold studs she was wearing in her ears. She could not believe there was another man alive who knew how to thread the fine hooks, from which there were suspended matching emerald-and-diamond-studded scrolls, into the piercing of a woman's ears without hurting.

He was standing so close—close enough for it to take only the slightest movement from her to close the gap. She stared at the sensual shape of his mouth and wanted badly to kiss it. Her breasts began to ache, her breathing shallowing out to hardly anything at all.

Flustered by her own crass lack of control around him, she turned away to stare into the mirror again. He was right about the jewellery looking perfect with the dress, she conceded reluctantly.

Her eyes flicked up to catch his in the mirror. He stood a head and the white-covered width of his shoulders taller than she did. She saw dark and light, frailty and strength.

They contrasted in every way there was, yet fitted together as if it had always meant to be this way.

'I still think that wearing these is like a slap in the face to your family,' she insisted.

Reaching up with a hand, he ran the gentle tip of a finger around the sparkling necklace. 'I think I am going to enjoy myself not too many hours from now.'

He was talking about sex on a bed draped with his wife wearing nothing but diamonds and emeralds. He was conjuring up enticing visions with which she didn't need any help to remember for herself. He laid a kiss upon her shoulder; she quivered, he sighed—then stepped away to pick up the other velvet box he had brought into the room with him.

She had forgotten all about it until he flicked up the lid. Her stomach was not the only thing to dance with fine flutters as he took a ring between finger and thumb. Ridding himself of the box, he slid the ring onto her finger until it came to rest against her wedding ring.

'This stays where it is,' he said very seriously.

The huge central stone seemed to issue a proclamation as he lifted it to his mouth. The diamonds framing the emerald almost blinded her beneath the overhead light. She might not know much about precious stones but she could recognise quality when she saw it.

'Who did these belong to—originally, I mean?' she asked curiously.

A mocking look appeared along with a lazy grin. 'The emeralds once belonged to a Venezuelan pirate who wore the one in the ring set into his front tooth.'

She laughed; it was irresistible not to at such an outrageous fairy tale. 'He would have had to have huge teeth!' she exclaimed.

'A swashbuckling, dark giant of a man with a black

velvet patch worn over one eye,' he embroidered shamelessly. Then, so unexpectedly it took her breath away, he bent to kiss her full on the mouth.

He stole her lipstick; she didn't care. He stole her every anxiety about tonight by reminding her of what really mattered. They left the bedroom hand in hand and walked down the stairs, meeting her mother, who was just making her way down the hallway, looking so lovely in her blue dress threaded with silver that her daughter stopped and sighed, 'Oh, Mum...'

The nerves returned when they turned into the driveway of a mansion house set in beautiful gardens lit to welcome its guests. Isobel's mother refused the use of her wheelchair, waving it away when their driver attempted to help her into it. Dignity and pride came before common sense tonight, though Silvia could not dismiss her need of her walking frame, no matter how independent she would prefer to be. However she was feeling buoyant and determined to enjoy herself.

Her daughter wished she could find the same motivation. Leandros's hand resting against her lower spine instilled some reassurance but the line-up of people waiting at the entrance was so daunting that Isobel was glad they were forced to take their time by matching their pace to her mother's slower steps.

She was introduced to Mr and Mrs Santorini and their daughter Carlotta, who was a lovely thing with dark hair and even darker liquid, smiling eyes. All three welcomed Isobel graciously but they were obviously curious about her, no matter how they tried to hide it. Nikos reminded her of Leandros when she had first met him, before life had got around to honing his handsome face. Nikos's smile was rueful as he greeted her with a lazy, 'Happy to see you here, Isobel.' As he bent to place a kiss on her cheek he added softly, 'And about time too.'

It was a nice thing for him to say, and helped to ease the next moment when Isobel had to face Leandros's mother. Thea looked stiff and awkward as she greeted the daughter-in-law who had been such a big disappointment to her. She was kind to Silvia, though, showed a genuine concern about her accident and promised to spend time with her later, catching up on what had happened.

'See, it wasn't so bad,' Leandros said quietly as they moved away.

'Only because you'd obviously primed them,' she countered.

The click of his tongue told her she had managed to annoy him. 'The chip on your shoulder must be very heavy, *agape*,' he drawled caustically, and the hand at her spine fell away. Feeling suddenly cast adrift as they stepped into a large reception room, Isobel then had to stand alone to deal with something like a hundred faces turning her way.

Some stared in open surprise, others glanced quickly down and away. Her skin began to prickle as the nerves she had been keeping under tight control broke free. Leandros could prime his family but he could not prime everyone, she noted painfully as the hiss of soft whispers suddenly attacked her burning ears.

It was awful. She felt that old familiar sensation as if she was beginning to shrink. With a lifting of her chin she stopped it from happening. Damn you all, her green eyes flashed.

Like the old times—like the old times, she chanted silently.

Her mother arrived at Leandros's other side, thankfully drawing some of the attention her way. Silvia, too, stopped to stare in surprise at what was taking place. 'Are we the star turn, Leandros?' she asked him. She wasn't a fool; her mother knew exactly what was going on here.

One of his hands went to cover one of Silvia's hands where it gripped the walking frame, the other arrived at Isobel's waist. Then he lifted his dark head to eye the room as a whole, and with a few economical movements he silenced whispers.

It came as a small shock to Isobel to see how much command he seemed to have over such an illustrious assembly. He had not warranted this much respect the last time she'd been here. Their three years apart had given him something extra she could only describe as presence. She had noticed it before in other ways but had not suspected that he could silence tongues with a single lift of his chiselled chin.

People went back to whatever they had been doing before they'd arrived to interrupt. Without uttering a word Leandros guided them towards a low sofa set against the nearest wall to them and quietly invited Silvia to sit. She shook her head. Like mother like daughter, Isobel mused ruefully. Neither of them was going to allow themselves to shrink here.

A waiter appeared to offer them tall flutes of champagne. Beginning to feel just a little bit nauseous, she allowed herself a tiny sip. 'OK?' Leandros murmured huskily.

'Yes,' she replied but they both knew she wasn't.

'I apologise for my earlier remark.' It was an acknowledgement that the chip-on-the-shoulder taunt had not been fair. 'I think I should have anticipated this. But, in truth, I did not expect them to be so...'

Rude, she finished for him. And—yes, he should have

expected it. But this was no time to jump into a row with him. That would come later, she promised herself.

'Isobel!' The call of her name brought her head up and the first genuine smile to widen her mouth. A diversion was coming in the shape of Eve Herakleides, who was bearing down upon them with her daunting giant of a grandfather and another man Isobel presumed must be Eve's new husband.

'Oh, this is just too good to be true!' Eve exclaimed as she arrived in front of them. Suddenly and intentionally, Isobel was sure, friendly, warm faces were surrounding them.

She and Eve shared kisses. Leandros was greeting Eve's grandfather—his uncle Theron—and introducing Theron to Silvia. Then Eve drew her husband forward and proudly presented him as her gorgeous Englishman. Ethan Hayes grimaced at being described in this way, but his eyes were smiling and his hand made its possessive declaration where it rested on Eve's slender waist.

Tensions began to ease as shifted they positions to complete introductions all round. Isobel found herself confronted by the great Theron Herakleides, who looked nothing like Leandros's mother. But then, they had been born several decades apart to different mothers. 'I am very happy to see you here,' he announced quite gravely, and bent to make the traditional two-kiss greeting.

Someone else arrived within their select little circle. It was Leandros's beautiful sister, Chloe, wearing an exquisite long and slinky gown of toreador red that set off her tall, dark, slender beauty to perfection. Her actions were stilted, the greeting she offered Isobel filled with the same awkward coolness as her mother's had been. Chloe was the youngest of the three Petronades children. All her life she had been adored and doted on by all the Petronades males, which in turn had made her spoiled and selfish, and she resented anyone who threatened to steal some of that adoration away from her.

She'd seen Isobel as one of those people. It still remained to be seen if Nikos's lovely Carlotta was going to be treated to the same petulant contempt. But, for now, Isobel was prepared to be polite and friendly—just in case Chloe had changed her attitude in the last three years.

Leandros saw his sister differently. Spoiled and selfish though she undoubtedly had been three years ago, she had gone through a very tough time after their father died. She'd worshipped him above all others, and losing him had left a huge gap in her heart that she'd looked to him and Nikos to fill. When he'd married Isobel, Chloe had taken this as yet another devastating loss and had fiercely resented Isobel for being the cause.

Chloe had changed over the last three years though. Grown up, he supposed, and was less of a spoiled little cat. Though he understood that Isobel didn't know that—which was why he felt her fingers searching for the secure comfort of his hand as Chloe levelled her dark eyes upon her and said, 'Welcome home, Isobel,' then concluded the greeting with a kiss to both of Isobel's cheeks with a very petulant mouth.

He was about to offer a wry smile at this bit of petulance, when something else happened to wipe out all hint of humour. As she drew away Chloe's gaze flickered down to the jewels flashing at Isobel's throat and a faint flush was suddenly staining her elegant cheekbones as she looked away in clear discomfort.

He had his culprit, he realised grimly.

The ever-sharp Eve also noticed Chloe's fleeting glance at Isobel's throat—and her ensuing discomfort. The little minx made a play of checking out Isobel's necklace. 'Oh, how lovely,' she declared. 'Are they old or are they new?'

'Most definitely new,' Leandros answered smoothly. 'I had them specially commissioned for Isobel just after we were married,' he explained. 'As far as I recall Isobel has only worn them once before—isn't that so, *agape mou*?'

'I… Yes.' He watched her fingers jerk up to touch the necklace. She was trying to hide her shock at what he had said, while his sister had turned to a block of stone.

'We like to call them the family heirlooms.' Oh, cruelty be mine, he thought with grim satisfaction as he soothed Isobel with the gentle squeeze of her hand and smiled glassily into his sister's unblinking eyes. Chloe realized that he now knew the kind of unkind rubbish she had fed to his wife. She also now realized that she was in deep trouble the next time he got her alone. He was looking forward to it, Chloe certainly wasn't.

The buffet dinner was announced. Maybe it was fortunate because it gave his darling sister the excuse to melt away. People shifted positions as the slow mass exodus to the adjoining room began. Eve strolled away with her husband. Theron was gallantly offering to escort Isobel's mother. They went off together, Theron matching his long strides to Silvia's smaller steps while talking away to her with an easy charm.

Which left them alone again. 'I think Theron has taken to your mother,' he observed lightly.

'Just don't speak,' his wife told him stiffly. 'I'm too angry to listen to you.'

He looked down into glinting eyes. 'Why, what have I done?' he asked innocently.

'You don't have to do anything to be a horrible person,' she answered. 'It must be in the genes.'

'Then you understand why my sister is the way that she

is,' he countered smoothly, and when she went to stalk away from him he stopped her by tightening his grip on her hand. 'We do not run away any more, *agape mou*,' he reminded her.

'Sometimes I can hate you.' Her chin was up. 'All the time you were dressing me up in these, you were laughing at me!'

He laughed now, low and huskily. She was beginning to sizzle. He loved it when she sizzled. 'The Venezuelan pirate was pure inspiration.' Another flash sparked from her eyes and he should have been slain where he stood. 'Now tell me the fairy tale Chloe fed to you.'

Her mouth snapped shut in refusal to answer. 'Loyalty from the witch for the cat?' he drawled quizzically. 'Now, that does surprise me.'

Isobel had surprised herself. She had a suspicion her silence had something to do with the pained look she'd seen on Chloe's face as Leandros taunted her, and the fact that Chloe had flicked her a glance of mute apology before she'd slipped away.

'I'm hungry,' she said, which could not be less true since she knew she would not be able to swallow a single thing tonight. But the claim served its purpose in letting him know that a discussion about his sister was not going to happen. Not until she understood where Chloe was coming from these days. It was Leandros who wanted her to give his family a chance, after all.

'Why Venezuelan?' she asked suddenly. 'Why not French or Spanish or—?'

His laughter sent his dark head back. People turned to stare as if they weren't used to hearing him laugh like this. He deigned not to notice their disconcerted glances, kissed her full on her mouth then led her to join the crush around the buffet table.

The evening moved on. With a quiet determination, Leandros took her from group to group and pulled her into conversation in a way that she could only describe as making a statement about the solidarity of their marriage. As he did this he also exposed yet another secret, by always making sure he made some remark to her in Greek. By the time a couple of hours had gone by there wasn't a person present who had known her before who did not know now that she understood their native tongue.

And he had done it with such ruthless intention. Leandros was making sure that people thought twice before discussing his wife in her presence. Some looked uncomfortable at the discovery; some simply accepted it with pleased surprise. The uncomfortable ones were logged in his memory; Isobel could almost see him compiling a list of those people who would not be included in their social circle in the future.

Other people made sure they kept their distance, which spoke even greater volumes about what they were thinking. Takis Konstantindou was one of those people. Chloe, of course, was another one. She could understand Chloe's reasons for steering clear of them but the lawyer's cool attitude puzzled her.

Then there was Diantha Christophoros. If Isobel glimpsed her at all it was usually within a group that contained either Chloe or Leandros's mother. In a way she could find it in herself to feel sorry for Diantha, because it couldn't have been easy for her to turn up here tonight knowing that everyone here was going to know by now that old rumours about Leandros wanting to divorce his wife to marry her had to be false.

'Don't you think we should go and speak to her?' she suggested when she caught Leandros glancing Diantha's way.

'For what purpose?' he questioned coolly.

'She has got to be feeling uncomfortable, Leandros. The rumours affect her as much as they do you.'

'The best way to kill a rumour is to starve it,' was his response. 'Diantha seems to have my sister and my mother to offer all the necessary comfort.'

Which said, more or less, what Isobel had been trying *not* to think. The family preference could not be more noticeable if they stuck signs on their backs saying 'Vote Isobel out and Diantha in'. It was Eve Herakleides who put it in an absolute nutshell when she came to join Isobel out on the terrace, where she'd slipped away to get some fresh air that did not contain curiosity and intrigue.

'Word of warning,' Eve began. 'Watch out for Diantha Christophoros. She may appear nice and quiet and amiable but she has hidden talents behind the bland smile. She has a way of manipulating people without them realising she's doing it. It was only a few weeks ago that she convinced Chloe that she should remain here to help her mother with Nikos's wedding arrangements, while Diantha went to Spain in Chloe's place to help Leandros with a big celebration party he threw in San Estéban. Chloe puzzled for ages afterwards as to how it had actually come about that she'd agreed, since she had been so looking forward to spending two weeks with her brother. Then, blow me if Diantha isn't back in Athens for less than a day when the rumours were suddenly flying about Leandros filing for divorce from you so that he could marry her. She wants your husband,' she announced sagely. 'And her uncle Takis wants her to have him.'

'Takis and Diantha are related?' It was news to Isobel.

Eve nodded. 'They're a tightly knit lot, these upper-crust Greeks,' she said candidly. 'Thank goodness for women

like you and my mother or they'd be so inbred they would
have wiped themselves out by now.'

'What a shocking thing to say!' Isobel gasped on a com-
pulsive giggle.

'And what shocking thing is this minx saying now?'
Leandros intruded.

A pair of hands arrived at Isobel's slender waistline, the
brush of his lips warmed her cheek—the lick of his tongue
against her earlobe as he pulled away again sent her
wretched knees weak.

'Woman-talk is for women only,' the minx answered
for herself. 'And you, dear cousin, have had a lucky escape
in my opinion.' With that provocatively cryptic remark,
she walked away.

They both turned to watch her go, an exquisite creature
dressed in slinky hot pink making a direct line for her
husband, who sensed her coming—his broad shoulders
gave a small shake just before he turned around and
grinned.

'She hooked him in against his will,' Leandros confided.
'I think he still finds it difficult to believe that he let her
do it.'

'Well, I think he's a very lucky man,' Isobel stated loy-
ally because she liked Eve and always had done.

'Mmm,' he murmured, 'so am I…'

'No—don't,' she breathed when he began to lower his
dark head again. 'Not here; you will ruin what bit of dignity I have managed to maintain.'

His warm laughter teased as he used his grip on her
waist to swing her round until her hips rested against the
heavy stone balustrade behind her. His superior bulk was
suddenly hiding her from view of everyone else. Eyes like
molasses began sending the kind of messages that forced
her to lower her gaze from him.

'I like you in this,' she murmured softly, running her fingers beneath the slender lapels of his white jacket.

'Tell me I look like a Greek waiter and I will probably toss you over this balustrade,' he warned.

Her smile appeared wrapped in rueful memories of the time she had once said that to him in an attempt to flatten his impossible ego. 'I was such a bitch,' she confessed.

'No,' Leandros denied that. 'You assured me at the time that you had a hot thing for Greek waiters. I think I was supposed to feel complimented,' he mused thoughtfully.

It was irresistible; she just had to lift her laughing eyes upwards again. It was a mistake. She just fell into those eyes filled with such warm, dark promises. Her breath began to feather, a new kind of tension began circling them like a sensual predator circling its two victims while inside the house, beyond the pair of open terrace doors, a party was taking place. Music was filtering out to them on the warm summer air along with laughter and the general hum of conversation.

'I love you,' she said. It came out of nowhere.

He responded with a sharp intake of breath. His shoulders tensed, his whole body stiffened, his grip tightened on her waist. 'Fine time to tell me that!' he snapped out thinly. But he wasn't angry, just—overwhelmed.

She began to tremble because it had been such a dangerous thing for her to say out loud. It committed her, totally and utterly. It stood her naked and exposed and so vulnerable to hurt again that her throat locked up on a bank of emotion which threatened to turn into tears.

He was faring no better. She could feel the struggle he was having with himself not to respond in some wildly passionate way. A verbal response would have been enough for Isobel. A simple, 'I love you too,' would have helped her through this.

'I'll take it back if you like,' she shot out a trifle wildly.

'No,' he rasped. 'Just don't speak again while I...'

Deal with this; she finished the sentence for him. It was silly; it was stupid. They were grown-ups who were supposed to have a bit more class than to put each other through torture in public. She couldn't stop herself from flicking a glance at his face. As she did so he looked down. A wave of feeling washed over both of them in a static-packed blowback from just three little words.

They could have been alone. They *should* have been alone. Her breasts heaved on a tense pull of air. His hands pulled her hard against him. 'Don't kiss me!' she shot out in a constrained choke.

'The balustrade is still very tempting,' he gritted. 'I thought Eve was the biggest minx around here but you knock her into a loop.'

Heat was coursing through her body; the shocking evidence that he was on fire for her was shutting down her brain. The music played, the laughter and hum of conversation swirled all around them. In a minute, she had a horrible suspicion, she was going to find herself flattened to the ground with this big, lean, suave and sophisticated man very much on top.

'All sweetness and light,' he continued, thrusting the words down at her from between clenched teeth. 'All smiles and quiet answers for everyone else. The hair is up, so neat and prim—since when did you ever give way to such convention? Everyone back there sees the beautifully refined version of Isobel but I have to get the tormenting witch!'

'Keep talking,' she encouraged. She was beginning to get angry now. 'If you do it for long enough maybe you will wear yourself out!'

'I am not wearing out.' He took her words literally. 'I

am just getting started. From the moment you strode back into my life on those two sensational legs of yours you've had me standing on pins like some love-lost fool with no idea what is happening to me.'

'Did you dare use the love word then?' she taunted glacially.

'I've *always* loved you!' he thrust out harshly. 'I loved you when we flirted across the top of a Ferrari. I still loved you when you left me pining for three damn years!'

'Three years of pining,' she mocked unsteadily. 'I didn't see any evidence of it.' But he'd said it. He had actually said it.

'We've been through that already,' he snapped out impatiently.

'You brought me back here to divorce me.'

'It was an excuse. Anyone with sense would have realised that.'

'You had your next wife all picked out and ready.'

'I am arrogant. You know I am arrogant. Can you not cut a man a bit of slack?'

'Which is why I had to say it first, I suppose.'

The air hissed from between his teeth. If an electric cable had been fitted to them, they could have lit up the night there was so much static stress.

'I think the *both* of us are about to go over this balustrade,' he gritted furiously.

'You will go first,' Isobel vowed. 'And I hope you break your arrogant neck!'

A sound behind them brought them swinging round in unison. Isobel's heart sank to her shoes when she saw her mother-in-law hovering a few yards away. What did they look like? What did she see? Two people locked in a row that probably brought back a hundred memories of similar rows like this? She looked wary and anxious, her black eyes flicking from one to the other. Oh, God, please help me, Isobel groaned silently.

'I am sorry to intrude,' Thea said stiffly, and her gaze finally settled upon Isobel's blushing face. 'But I am concerned about your mama, Isobel. Theron has her dancing with her walking frame and I am afraid his enthusiasm is tiring her out.'

A single glance through the doors into the house was all that was needed to confirm that Thea's concerns were real. The seventy-year-old Theron was indeed dancing with her mother, who was using the walking frame as a prop. The man was flirting outrageously. Silvia was laughing, enjoying herself hugely, but even from here Isobel could see the strain beginning to show on her face.

'I'll go and...' She went to move, but Leandros stopped her.

'No, let me. She will take the disappointment better if I do it,' he insisted. At Isobel's questioning glance, 'Two men fighting over her?' he explained quizzically, then dropped a kiss on her lips and strode off, pausing only long enough to drop a similar kiss on his mother's cheek.

Suddenly Isobel found herself alone with a woman who did not like her. Awkwardness became a tangible thing that held them both silent and tense.

'My son is very fond of your mother.' Thea broke the silence with that quiet observation.

'Yes.' Isobel's eyes warmed as she watched Leandros fall into a playful fight with Theron for Silvia's hand. 'My mother is fond of him, too.'

She hadn't meant it as a strike at their cold relationship but she realised that Thea had taken it that way as she stiffened and turned to leave. 'No, don't go, please,' she murmured impulsively.

Her mother-in-law paused. An ache took up residence

inside Isobel's chest. This was supposed to be a time for fresh starts and for Leandros's sake she knew she had to try to reach out with the hand of friendship.

'You were arguing again.' Once again it was Thea who took up the challenge by spinning to face her with the accusation.

'You misread what you saw,' Isobel replied, then offered up a rueful smile. 'We were actually making love.' Adding a shrug to the smile, she forced herself to go on. 'It has always been like this between us. We spark each other off. Sometimes I think we could light the whole world up with the power we can generate...' Her eyes glazed on a wistful float back to what Thea had interrupted. Then she blinked into focus. 'Though I understand why you might not have seen it like that,' she was willing to concede.

Her mother-in-law took a few moments to absorb all of this, then she sighed and some of the tension dropped out of her stiff shoulders. 'I understand that you learned Greek while you were here the last time.'

'Yes,' Isobel confirmed.

'I think, perhaps, that you therefore heard things said that should not have been said.'

Lowering her gaze. 'Yes,' she said again.

Another small silence followed. Then Thea came to stand by the balustrade. 'My son loves you,' she said quietly. 'And Leandros's happiness is all I really care about. But the fights...' She waved a delicately structured hand in a gesture of weariness. 'They used to tire me out.'

And me, Isobel thought, remembering back to when the sparks were not always so lovingly passionate.

'When you left here, I was relieved to see you go. But Leandros did not feel the same. He was so miserable here that he went to Spain on a business trip and did not come back again. He missed you.'

'I missed him too.'

'Yes…' Thea accepted that. 'Leandros wants us to be friends,' she went on. 'I would like that too, Isobel.'

Though Thea's tone warned that she was going to have to work at it. Isobel smiled; what else could she do? Her mother-in-law was a proud woman. She was making a climb-down here that took with it some of that pride.

Taking in a deep breath, she gave that pride back to her. 'I was too young four years ago. I was overwhelmed by your lifestyle, and too touchy and too rebellious by far to accept advice on how best to behave or cope.' Lifting her eyes to Leandros's mother's eyes, 'This time will be different,' she promised solemnly.

Her mother-in-law nodded and said nothing. They both knew they had reached some kind of wary compromise. As she turned to go back to the party Thea paused. 'I am sorry about the baby,' she said gravely. 'It was another part of your unhappiness here, because kindness was not used to help you through the grief of your loss.'

It was so very true that there really was no ideal answer to give to that. Her mother-in-law seemed to realise it, and after another hesitation she walked back into the house.

Leandros appeared seconds later and Isobel had to wonder if he had been leaving them alone to talk. He searched her face. 'OK?' he asked huskily.

She nodded, then had to step up to him and, sliding her arms inside his jacket and around his back, she pressed herself against his solid strength. 'Don't ever let me go again,' she told him.

'I won't.' It was a promise.

They left the party soon after that, making the journey home without speaking much. The talking was left to

Silvia, who chattered away about Theron and the plans he had to take her out tomorrow for the day.

'I can't believe it,' Isobel said to Leandros as they prepared for bed. 'My mother has caught the eye of the wealthiest man in Greece!'

'His roving eye,' Leandros extended lazily. 'My uncle Theron is an established rake.'

'But he's got to be seventy years old! Surely he can't be looking at my mother and seeing...'

Her voice trailed away in dismay as a dark eyebrow arched. 'I share the same blood.' He began to stalk her with a certain gleam in his eyes. She was wearing nothing but the family heirlooms. 'Do you think you will be able to keep up with me when I reach seventy and you will be...?'

'Don't you dare tell me how old I will be!' she protested.

But, as for the rest, well, she was more than able to keep up with him throughout the long, dark, silken night. This time it was different, like a renewal of vows they made to each other four distant years ago. There were no secrets left to hide, just love and trust and a desire to hold on to what they had found.

The morning brought more sunshine with it and breakfast laid out on the terrace for two. Silvia was taking breakfast in her room today before she got ready for her date. When it came time for Leandros to go and spend a few essential hours in his office, he left her with a reluctance that made her smile. Theron arrived. A big, silver-thatched, larger-than-life kind of man, he was polite to Isobel, flirtatious with her mother and somehow managed to convince Silvia that her wheelchair was required today, which earned him a grateful smile from Silvia's daughter.

Left to her own devices, Isobel asked Allise for a second

pot of tea, then sat back in her chair and tried to decide
what she wanted to do with the few hours she had going
spare while Leandros wasn't here.

She was wearing the green combat trousers and a yellow
T-shirt today. The sum total of the wardrobe she had
brought with her from England had now been exhausted
and she was considering going out to do a bit of shopping,
when Allise arrived with the promised pot of tea and an
envelope that she said had just been delivered by hand.

Maybe Isobel should have known before she even
touched it that it could only mean trouble. Everything was
just too wonderful, much too perfect to stay that way. But
the envelope did not come with WARNING printed on it,
just her name typed in its centre and the fizz of intrigue
because she could think of only one person who would do
this, and he had been gone only half an hour.

He was up to something—a surprise, she decided, and
was smiling as she split the seal.

But what fell into her hands had her smile dying. What
she found herself looking at had her fingers tossing the
photographs away from her as if she were holding a poi-
sonous snake and she lurched to her feet with enough violence to send crockery spilling to the ground. Her chair
toppled over with a clatter against the hard tile flooring,
her hand shot up to cover her shaking mouth. Her heart
was pounding, eyes that had been shining were now dark
with a horror that was curdling the blood.

She stepped back, banged her leg on the upturned chair.
She was going to be sick, she realised—and ran.

CHAPTER NINE

ALLISE found Isobel sitting on the floor of the bathroom which lay just off the terrace, her cheek resting against the white porcelain toilet bowl. On a cry of dismay the housekeeper hurried forward. '*Kyria,* you are ill!'

It was a gross understatement. Isobel was dying inside and she didn't think she was going to be able to stop it from happening.

'I get the doctor—the *kyrios.*'

'No!' Isobel exploded on a thrust of frail energy. 'No.' She tried to calm her voice when Allise stood back and stared at her. 'I'm all right,' she insisted. 'I just need to— lie down for a wh-while.'

Dragging herself to her feet, she had to steady herself at the washbasin before she could get her trembling legs to work. Stumbling out of the bathroom, she headed for the stairs, knew she would never make it up there and changed direction, making dizzily for the only sanctuary her instincts would offer up as an alternative—her mother's room.

Back to the womb, she likened it starkly as she felt the housekeeper's worried eyes watch her go. She was going to ring him; Isobel was sure of it. Allise would feel she had failed in her duty if she did not inform Leandros as to what she had seen.

But Leandros didn't need informing. At about the time that Isobel received her envelope, he was receiving one himself. As he stared down at the all-too-damning photographs the phone began to ring. It was Diantha's father;

he had received an envelope too. Hot on that call came one from his mother, then an Athens newspaper with a hungry reputation for juicy gossip about the jet set. It did not take a genius to know what was unfolding here.

Leandros was on his way home even as Isobel paused at the table where the photographs lay amongst the scattered crockery. His mobile phone was ringing its cover off. With an act of bloody, blinding frustration he switched it off and tossed it onto the passenger seat with the envelope of photos. Whoever else had received copies could go to hell because if he was certain about anything, then it was that Isobel had to be looking at the same ugly evidence.

His car screeched to a halt in the driveway, kicking up clouds of dust in its wake. He left the engine running as he strode into the house. Watching him go, the gardener went to switch off the engine for him, his eyes filled with frowning puzzlement. Allise was standing in the hall with her ear to the telephone.

'Where is my wife?' he demanded and was already making for the stairs when the housekeeper stopped him.

'Sh-she is in her mama's rooms, *kyrios*.'

Changing direction, he headed down the hallway. He lost his jacket as he hit the terrace. His tie went and he was about to stride past the debacle that was the breakfast table and chairs, when he saw the envelope and scatter of photographs, felt sickness erupt in his stomach and anger follow it with a thunderous roar.

Pausing only long enough to gather up the evidence, he continued down the terrace and into the rooms allotted to his mother-in-law. He had not been in here since Silvia took up residence and was surprised how comfortable she had managed to make it, despite the clutter of Isobel's photographic equipment still dotted around. Not that he cared about comfort right now, for across the room, lying curled on her mother's bed like a foetus, was his target.

His heart tipped sideways on a moment of agony—then it grimly righted again. Snapping the top button of his shirt free with angry fingers, he approached the bed with a look upon his face that promised retribution for someone very soon.

'Isobel.' He called her name.

She gave no indication that she had even heard him. Was she waiting for him to go down on his knees to beg for understanding and forgiveness? Well, not this man, he thought angrily and tossed the photographs down beside her on the bed.

'These are false,' he announced. 'And I expect you to believe it.'

It was a hard, tough, outright challenge. Still she did not even offer a deriding sob in response. It made him want to jump inside her skin so that she would *know* he could not have done this terrible thing.

'Isobel!' he rasped. 'This is no time for dramatics. You are the trained photographer. I need you to tell me how they did it so I can strangle the culprit with their lies.'

'Go away,' she mumbled.

On a snap of impatience, he bent and caught hold of her by her waist, then lifted her bodily off the bed before firmly resettling her sitting on its edge. Going down on his haunches, he pushed the tumble of silken hair back from her face. She was as white as a sheet and her eyes looked as if someone had reached in and hollowed them out.

'Now just listen,' he insisted.

Her response was to launch an attack on him. He supposed she had the right, he acknowledged as he grimly held on to her until she had finally worn herself out. Eventually she sobbed out some terrible insult then tried scrambling backwards in an effort to get away. Her fingers made contact with the photographs. On a sob she picked them up.

'You lied to me!' she choked out thickly. 'You said she meant nothing to you but—look—*look*!' The photographs shook as she brandished them in his grim face. 'You, standing on your yacht w-wearing nothing from what I can see, h-holding her in front of you while she's just about covered by th-that excuse for a slip!'

'It never—'

The photograph went lashing by his cheek, causing him to take avoiding action, and by the time he had recovered she was staring at the next one. 'Look at you,' she breathed in thick condemnation. 'How can you lie there with her, sleeping like an innocent? I will never forgive you—'

She was about to send the images the way of the other when he snaked out a hand and took the rest from her. 'You will believe me when I say these are not real!' he insisted harshly.

Not real? Isobel stared at him through tear-glossed eyes and wondered how he dared say that when each picture was now branded on her brain!

'I believed you when you said you hadn't—'

'Then continue to believe,' he cut in. 'And start thinking with your head instead of your heart.'

'I don't have a heart,' she responded. 'You ripped it out of my body and threw it away!'

'Melodrama is not helping here, *agape*,' he sighed, but she saw the hint of humour he was trying to keep from showing on his lips.

That humour was her complete undoing, and she began wriggling and squirming until he finally set her free to stand.

'I'm leaving here,' she told him as she swung to her feet.

'Running again?' he countered jeeringly. 'Take care,' he warned as he rose up also, 'because I might just let you do it. For I will *not* live my life fearing the next time you are going to take to your feet and flee!'

Isobel stared at him, saw the sheer black fury darkening his face. 'What are you angry with me for?' she demanded bewilderedly.

'I am not angry with you,' he denied. 'I am angry with—these.' He waved a hand at the photographs. 'You are not the only one to receive copies...' Then he told her who else had. 'This is serious, Isobel,' he imparted grimly. 'Someone is out to cause one hell of a scandal and I need your help here, not your contempt.'

With that he turned and began looking around the room with hard, impatient eyes. Spotting whatever it was he was searching for, he strode over to her old computer system and began checking that everything was plugged in. 'You know how to do this better than I do,' he said. 'Show me what I need to do to bring this thing to life.'

'It hasn't been used for three years. It has probably died from lack of use.'

'At least try!' he rasped.

It was beginning to get through to her that he was deadly serious. Moving on trembling legs and with an attitude that told him she was not prepared to drop her guard, she went to stand beside him. With a flick of a couple of switches she then stood back to wait. It was quite a surprise to watch a whole array of neglected equipment burst into life.

'Now what?' she asked stiffly.

'Scan those photographs into the relevant program,' he instructed. 'Blow them up—or whatever it is you do to them so we can study them in detail.'

'A reason would be helpful.'

'I have already told you once. They are fakes.'

'Sure?'

He swung on her furiously. 'Yes, I am sure! And I would appreciate a bit of trust around here!'

'If you shout at me once more I will walk,' she threatened fiercely.

'Then stop looking at me as if I am a snake; start using a bit of sense and believe me!' Striding off, he recovered the photographs—yet again. Coming back, he set them down next to the computer screen.

'Fakes, you say,' she murmured.

'Do your magic and prove me right or wrong.'

The outright challenge. Still without giving him the benefit of the doubt, she opened the lid on the flatbed scanner and prepared to work. Her mouth was tight, her eyes were cold, but with a few deft clicks of the mouse she began to carry out his instructions. If he was lying then he had to know she would find him out in a few minutes. If he was telling the truth then...

Her stomach began to churn. She was no longer sure which alternative she preferred. It was one thing believing that your estranged husband had been involved in an affair during your separation but it was something else entirely to know that someone was willing to go to such extremes to hurt other people.

'Why is this happening?' she questioned huskily. 'Who do you think it is that took these? It needs a third party involved to take photographs like these, Leandros. Someone close enough to you to be in a position to catch you on film like this.'

He was standing to one side of her and she felt him stiffen; glancing up, she caught a glimpse of his bleak expression before he turned away. 'Chloe, of course,' he answered gruffly.

Chloe? 'Oh, no.' She didn't want to believe that. Not Chloe, who adored her brother. 'She has nothing to gain by hurting both you and her best friend!'

'She gains what she's always wanted,' he countered tightly. 'Work—work!' he commanded as the first photograph appeared on the screen. Turning back, she clicked the mouse and the picture leapt to four times its original size. 'All her childhood she fantasised about one of her brothers marrying her best friend,' he continued darkly. 'Nikos and I have ruined those fantasies, so now she is out for revenge.'

'I don't want to believe it.'

'She has also been cleverer than I ever gave her credit for,' he added cynically. 'She damns me in your eyes. Damns both Diantha and me to Diantha's father, who honoured me with his trust when he allowed her to stay on my yacht with me. I saw a man taking photographs of the yacht from the quay. This one,' he flicked a finger at the screen, 'Shows exactly how I was dressed that day.'

'In nothing?'

'I have a pair of shorts on, you sarcastic witch!' He scowled. 'He had to have been paid by someone. Scheming Chloe is the logical person. Her ultimate aim is to see you walking off with a divorce and me being forced into marrying Diantha to save her reputation!'

'All of that is utterly nonsensical!' Isobel protested. 'No one goes to such drastic extremes on someone else's behalf.'

'Who else's behalf?' he challenged. 'Diantha's? She is being manipulated here just as ruthlessly as we are,' he insisted. 'Look at the evidence. Chloe sends Diantha in her stead to San Estéban. These photographs were taken there. I actually saw the guy taking this one!'

'And the one in your bedroom?' she prompted. 'How did he get in there?'

He paused to frown at the question. Then the frown cleared. 'He has to be a member of my crew,' he decided. 'He was too far away for me to recognise him.'

He thought he had an answer for everything. But Isobel was recalling a conversation with Eve Herakleides the night before, and suddenly she had a very different suspect to challenge Leandros's claims.

Flattening her lips and concentrating her attention on the screen, she took only seconds to spot the first discrepancy. Within a few minutes she had circled many—a finger missing, a point on the yacht's rail that did not quite fit. With the mouse flying busily, she copied then pasted each detail onto a separate frame, increased their size then sent them to print.

Through it all Leandros watched in silent fascination as the whole photograph was broken down and revealed for the fraud that it was. 'Do you want me to do the same to the rest of them?' she asked when she'd finished.

'Not unless you need to assure yourself that they are all fakes,' he responded coolly, gathering up his precious evidence.

It was a clean hit on her lack of trust. Isobel acknowledged it with a sigh. 'I suppose you want me to eat humble pie now.'

'Later,' he replied. 'Humble pie will not come cheap.'

But neither smiled as he said it. Fakes or not, the photographs had stolen something from them and Isobel had to ask herself if they were ever going to get it back again.

'Leandros…' He was striding for the door when she

stopped him. 'Chloe knows what I do for a living; remember that when you confront her.'

'Meaning what?' He glanced at her.

Isobel shrugged. 'Just go there with an open mind, that's all,' she advised. It wasn't up to her to shatter his faultless image of Diantha. And, anyway, she wasn't sure enough of her own suspicions to make an issue out of it.

But she was as determined as he was to find out.

He had been gone for less than two minutes before she was printing off her second lot of copies. His car was only just turning off the driveway when she was calling a taxi for herself. The Christophoros mansion was much the same as most of the houses up here on the hill. She was greeted by a maid who showed her into a small reception room, then hurried off to get the daughter of the house.

Diantha took her time. Needing something to do, Isobel reached into her bag to search out a hair-band and snapped her hair into a pony-tail. Leandros would see this as her donning her tough-lady persona, but she didn't feel tough. Her nerves were beginning to fray, her stomach dipping and diving on lingering nausea. She didn't know if she had done the right thing by coming here, wasn't even sure how she was going to tackle this—all she did know with any certainty was that Diantha had to be faced, whether guilty or innocent.

The door began to open and she swung round as Diantha appeared looking neat in a mid-blue dress and wearing a thoroughly bland expression that somehow did not suit the occasion, bearing in mind that Isobel could be a jealous wife come here to tear her limb from limb.

Indeed Diantha looked her over as if she were the marriage breaker in this room. 'We will have to make this brief.' There was a distinct chill to her tone. 'My father is on his way home and he will not like to find you here.'

Then she really took the wind out of Isobel's sails when she added smoothly, 'Now you have seen the truth about Leandros and myself, can we hope that you will get out of our lives for good?'

Isobel's fingers tightened on the shoulder strap to her bag. 'So it was you who sent the photographs?' she breathed.

Diantha's cool nod confirmed it. It seemed a bit of a let-down that she was admitting it so easily. 'Though I must add that anything I say to you here I will deny to anyone else,' she made clear. 'But you are in the way, and I am sick of being messed around by Leandros. Two weeks ago he was promising me he would divorce you and marry me, then I am being sidelined—for business reasons, of course; isn't it always?'

'Business reasons?' Isobel prompted curiously.

'The lack of a pre-nuptial agreement between the two of you put Leandros in an impossible situation.'

It was like being in the presence of some deadly force, Isobel thought with a shiver. Diantha was calm, her voice was level and Isobel could already feel herself being manipulated by the gentle insertion of the word pre-nuptial. Before she knew it Lester Miles' warnings about the power of her own position came back to haunt her. She was seeing Leandros's sudden change from a man ready to sever a marriage to a man eager to hang on to that marriage.

'I have to say that I am seriously displeased at being forced to lie about our relationship while he sorts out this mess,' Diantha continued. 'But a man with his wealth cannot allow himself to be ripped off by a greedy wife. Nor can he afford to risk our two family names being thrown into the public arena with a scandal you will cause if you wish to turn your divorce ugly. But you mark my words, Kyria Petronades, a contract will appear before very soon, mapping out the details of any settlements in the event of your marriage reaching a second impasse.'

'But you couldn't wait that long,' Isobel inserted. 'So you decided to cause the feared scandal and get it out of the way?'

'I am sick of having to lie to everyone,' she announced. 'It is time that people knew the truth.'

'About your affair in Spain with my husband,' Isobel prompted.

'A relationship that began long before you left him, if you must know the truth.' Her chin came up. 'He visited me in Washington, DC.'

Isobel remembered the Washington trips all too well.

'Our two weeks spent in Spain were not the first stolen weeks we managed to share together. I have no wish to hurt your feelings with this, but he was with me only yesterday, during siesta. We have an apartment in Athens where we meet most days of the week.'

'No photographic evidence of these meetings?' Isobel challenged.

'It can be arranged.'

'Oh, I am sure that it can.' And she removed the print-outs from her handbag and placed them down on the table that stood between them. Believing she knew exactly what she was being presented with, Diantha didn't even deign to look.

'You are nothing but a lying, conniving bitch, Diantha,' Isobel informed her. 'You manipulate people and *adore* doing it. Chloe was manipulated to get you to Spain. My mother-in-law has been beautifully manipulated by your ever-so-gentle eagerness to please and offer her up an easier alternative to me as the daughter-in-law from hell.'

'You said it,' Diantha responded, revealing the first hint that a steel-trap mind functioned behind the bland front.

Isobel laughed. 'Leandros extols you for your great organisational skills—not a very appetising compliment to the woman he loves, is it?' she added when Diantha's spine made a revealing shift. 'Apparently you know how to put together a great party.' She dug her claws in. 'As for me, well, I struggle to organise anything, but he calls me a witch and a hellion and claims I have barbs for teeth. When we make love he falls apart in my arms and afterwards he sleeps wrapped around me. Not like this.' She stabbed a finger at the photograph. 'Not with him occupying one side of the bed while I occupy the other.'

Black eyelashes flickered downwards, her face kept firmly under control. Now she had drawn her attention to the photographs, Isobel slid out the other one, and its enlarged partners in crime. 'Thankfully, Leandros still has *all* his fingers.' She stabbed one of her own fingers on the missing one splayed across Diantha's stomach. 'If he stood behind you like this, the top of your head would reach no higher than his chest, not his chin. You are short in stature, Diantha—let's call a spade a spade here, since you wish to talk bluntly. You are not quite this slim or this curvaceous. And when you cut, shave and paste with a computer mouse it is always advisable to make sure you fill in the gaps you make, like the yacht rail here, which seems to stop for no apparent reason. A good manipulator should always be sure of all her facts and you forgot to check one small detail. This is my job.' She stabbed at the printouts. 'I am a professional photographer. I dealt with computer photography almost every day of my working life. So I know without even bothering to enlarge the bedroom scene that the folds of the sheet don't quite follow a natural line.

The slight shrug of Diantha's shoulders and indifferent expression surprised Isobel because she should have been feeling the pinch of her own culpability by now. But she just smiled. 'You are such a fool, Isobel,' she told her. 'I have always known what you do for a living, and these photographs were always meant to be exposed as fakes. Indeed it is essential that I did so to allay a scandal. I merely intended to expose them myself for what they are, then suggest that you probably did these yourself as a way of increasing your power in a divorce settlement. For who else is better qualified?'

She believes she has everyone tied up in knots, Isobel realised in gaping incredulity. She is so supremely confident of her own powers of manipulation that she has stopped seeing the wood for the trees!

'There is only one small problem with your plan, Diantha,' Isobel said narrowly. 'These photographs may be fakes, but I have no reason to want a divorce.'

'But does he want you or is Leandros merely protecting his business interests?'

'Oh, yes, I want her,' a smooth, deep voice replied.

The two women glanced up, saw Leandros standing there and looking as if he had been for quite a long time.

'Every minute of every waking moment,' he added smoothly. 'Every minute of every moment I spend lost in my dreams. You have a serious problem with your dreams, Diantha,' he told her sombrely, then without waiting for a reply he looked at Isobel. 'Shall we go?'

She didn't even hesitate, walking towards this man who was her life, with her eyes loving him and his loving her by return.

But Diantha was not about to give up so easily. 'Just because these photographs are not real, it does not mean we did not sleep together,' she threaded in stealthily. 'Tell her, Leandros, how we spent the nights upon your yacht. Tell her how your mama thinks she is a tart and your sister Chloe despises every breath that she takes. Tell her,' she persisted, 'how your whole family knew she was having an affair with some man while she was here last, and how you tried to discover who he was and even believed the child she was carrying belonged to this other lover!'

Isobel's feet came to a shuddering standstill. Her eyes clouded as she searched his. She was looking for sorrow, for a weary shake of the head to deny what Diantha was saying! For goodness' sake, she begged him; give me anything to say that she's still manipulating me here!

But he'd gone as pale as she'd ever seen him. His fingers trembled as he lifted them up to run through his hair. Most damning of all, he lowered his eyes from her. 'Come on,' he said huskily. 'Let's get out of here.'

Someone else was standing just behind him, and as Leandros moved Isobel saw Chloe looking white-faced. 'Diantha, stop this,' Chloe pleaded unsteadily. 'I don't understand why you—'

'You don't understand.' Diantha turned on her scathingly. 'What has it got to do with you? Your brothers used me and I will not be used!'

Brothers? Each one of them looked at her when she said this. She was no longer calm and collected, Isobel noticed. The veils of control had been ripped away and suddenly Diantha was showing her true cold and bitter self.

'All my life I had to watch you, Chloe, being worshipped by your family of men. You have no idea what it is like to be unloved and rejected by anyone. My father rejected me because I was not a desired son. Your brother rejected me because I was not what he wanted any more.'

'Diantha, I never—'

'Not you,' she flashed at Leandros. 'Nikos! Nikos rejected me four years ago! He said we were too young to know what love was and he did not even want to know! But I knew love. I waited and waited in Washington for him to come for me. But he didn't,' she said bitterly. 'You came instead, offering me those pleasant messages from home and not one from Nikos! So I came back here to Athens to make him love me! But when I arrived he was planning to marry Carlotta. I was out in the cold and there you were, Leandros, hiding in Spain with your broken heart! Well, why should we not mend together? You were thinking about it, I know you were. You can lie to her all you like, but I know that it was for me that you told Uncle Takis to begin divorce proceedings with her!'

His eyes narrowed. 'So Takis has been talking out of line,' he murmured silkily.

'No!' she denied that. 'I have discussed this with no one.'

'Then how did you know there was no pre-nuptial agreement?' Isobel inserted sharply.

Diantha floundered, her mouth hovering on lies she could not find.

'I think this has gone far enough,' yet another voice intruded. It was Diantha's father. 'You have managed to stop the photographs being printed in the newspaper, Leandros?' he enquired. At Leandros's grim nod, he nodded also. 'Then please leave my house and take your family with you.'

Mr Christophoros had clearly decided that his daughter had hurt enough people for one day.

The journey away was completed in near silence. Chloe sat sharing the passenger seat in Leandros's Ferrari with Isobel, her face drawn with shock and dismay. Leandros took his sister home first, pulling up outside a house that was three times the size of his own. As she climbed out of the car, she turned back to Isobel.

'I'm sorry,' she whispered urgently. 'I never meant—'

'Later, Chloe,' her brother interrupted. 'We will all talk later but now Isobel and I have to go.'

'But most of this is my fault!' she cried out painfully. 'I encouraged her to believe that she was meant for one of my brothers—'

'Childhood stuff,' Leandros said dismissively.

'I let her know how much I disliked Isobel!'

Isobel's chin went down on her chest. Chloe released a choking sob. 'I confided everything to her and she took it all away and plotted with it. I can't tell you how bad that makes me feel.'

Isobel could see it all. The two girls sighing over Leandros's broken heart—as Diantha had called it. The two of them wishing that Isobel had never been born.

'But I never knew a thing about her and Nikos,' Chloe inserted in stifled disbelief.

'It was nothing,' her brother declared. 'They dated a couple of times while you were away at college, but Nikos was made wary by her tendency towards possessiveness. He told her so and she took it badly. He was relieved when her family went to live in Washington—and I would prefer you not to mention this to him, Chloe,' he then warned very seriously. 'He will not appreciate the reminder at this time.'

He was talking about Nikos's coming marriage. Chloe nodded then swallowed and tentatively touched Isobel's arm. 'Please,' she murmured, 'can you and I make a fresh start?'

A fresh start, Isobel repeated inwardly, and her eyes glazed over. Everyone wanted to make fresh starts, but how many more ugly skeletons were going to creep out of the dark cupboard before she felt safe enough to trust any one of them?

She lifted her face though, and smiled for Chloe. 'Of

course,' she agreed. But the way her voice shook had Leandros slamming the car into gear and gunning the engine. His sister stepped back, her face pale and anxious. Isobel barely managed to get the car door shut before he was speeding away with a hissing spin of gravel-flecked tyres.

'What's the matter with you?' she lashed out in reaction.

'If you are going to cry, then you will do it where I can damn well get at you,' he thrust back roughly.

'I am not going to cry.'

'Tell that to someone who cannot see beyond the tough outer layer.' He lanced her a look that almost seared off her skin. 'I did not sleep with her—*ever*!' he rasped, turned his eyes back to the road and rammed the car through its gears with a hand that resembled a white-knuckled fist. 'I *liked* her! But she has poison in her soul and now I can feel it poisoning me.' His voice suddenly turned hoarse. 'Did I give her reason to believe what she does about me? Did I offer encouragement without realising it?'

His hand left the wheel to run taut fingers through his hair. It was instinctive for Isobel to reach across and grab the wheel.

'You don't need to do that,' he gritted. 'I am not about to drive us into a wall.'

'Then stop acting like it.'

The car stopped with a screech of brakes. Isobel had not put on her seat belt because Chloe had been sharing her seat and the momentum took her head dangerously close to the windscreen before an arm shot out and halted the imminent clash with a fierce clenching of male muscle.

Emotions were flying about in all directions. Stress—distress! Anger—frustration. He threw open his door, climbed out and walked away a few long strides, leaving

Isobel sitting there in a state of blank bewilderment as to what it was that was the matter with him.

It was her place to be this upset, surely? She had been the one who'd had to place her trust on the line ever since she came back here! She got out of the car, turned and gave the beautiful, glossy red door a very expressive slam. He spun on his heel. She glared at him across the glossy red bonnet. They were within sight of their own driveway but neither seemed to care.

'Just who the hell do you think you are, Leandros?' she spat at him furiously. She was still responding to the shock of almost having her head smacked up against the windscreen; her insides were crawling with all kinds of throbs and flurries. He was pale—*she* was pale! The sun was beating down upon them and if she could have she would have reached up and grabbed it then thrown it at his bloody selfish head! 'What do you think her poison is doing to me? You want a divorce then you don't want a divorce. Rumour has it that you have your next wife already picked out and waiting in the wings. Pre-nuptial agreements are suddenly the all-important topic on everyone's lips! And I am expected to trust your word! Then I am expected to trust your word again when those photographs turn up. I even face the bitch with her so-called lies!'

'They are lies, you know that—'

'All I know for certain at this precise moment is that you have been working me like a puppet on a string!' she tossed at him furiously. 'I've been insulted in your board-room—*stalked* around Athens—which appears is not the first time! I've been seduced at every available opportunity, teased over family heirlooms, paraded out in front of Athens' finest like a trophy that was not much of a prize!'

He laughed, but it was thick and tense. She almost climbed over the car bonnet to get her claws into

him! 'Then I am forced to stare at those wr-wretched
ph-photographs.' Her throat began to work; grimly she
swallowed the threatening tears. 'Do you think because I
could prove them to be fakes that they lost the power to
hurt?'

'No.' He took a step towards the bonnet.

'I haven't finished!' she thrust at him thickly, and the
glinting green bolts coming from her eyes pinned him still.
'*I* faced the poison—while you went chasing off to the
wrong place!' she declared hotly. 'I listened to her say all
of those things about you and *still* believed in you. My
God,' she choked. 'Why was that, do you think, when we
only have to look back three years to see that we were
heading right down the same road again?'

'It is not the same!' he blasted at her.

'It has the same nasty taste!' she cried. 'Your mother is
prepared to *try* and like me for your sake and now your
sister is prepared to do the same. Do I care if they like
me?' Yes, I do, she thought painfully. 'No, I don't,' she
said out loud. 'I don't think I care for you any more,' she
whispered unsteadily.

'You don't mean that—'

She flicked his tight features a glance and wished to hell
that she did mean it. 'Tell me about the pre-nuptial thing,'
she challenged. 'Then go on to explain about this other
man I am supposed to have fathered my child to. And
then,' she continued when he opened his mouth to answer,
'explain to me why I have just had to listen to you be-
moaning the poison that wretched woman has fed into
you!'

Silence reigned. He looked totally stunned by the final
question. A silver Mercedes came down the road. It
stopped beside Isobel. 'Is something wrong?' a voice said.
'Can we be of assistance?'

Isobel turned to stare at Theron Herakleides. Beside him in the passenger seat, her mother was bending over to peer out curiously. 'Yes,' she said. 'You can give me a lift.' With that, she climbed into the back of the Mercedes.

'What about Leand—?'

'Just drive,' she snapped. Theron looked at her in blank astonishment. He had probably never been spoken to like this before in his life! Then she put a trembling hand up to cover her equally tremulous mouth. 'I'm sorry,' she apologised, and tears began to burn her eyes.

'Drive, Theron,' her mother murmured quietly. Without another word, Theron did as he was told, his glance shifting to his rear-view mirror, where he saw his nephew left standing by his car looking like a man who had just been hit by a car.

Watching his uncle Theron drive away with Isobel, Leandros was feeling as if he had been hit—by an absolute hellion with a torrent that poured from her mouth.

How had she done it? How had she managed to leave him standing here, feeling like the most selfish bastard alive on this planet?

Because you are, a voice in his head told him. Because there was not a word she'd said that did not ring true.

Ah. He spun around to stare blankly at his native city spread out beneath him and shimmering in a late-morning haze, and instead saw a jigsaw of words come to dance in front of his eyes. Words like, insulted, stalked, seduced—trophy. He uttered the same tense, half-amused laugh then wasn't laughing at all because she believed it to be the truth.

Just as she believed that he suspected their baby could have belonged to another man. His heart came to a stop, thudding as it landed at the base of his stomach as he joined that new belief with her old belief that he was glad when she miscarried. And what had he done? He'd sat beside her in his car and voiced concerns about his behaviour towards Diantha.

Was he mad? He turned around. Did she accuse him of possessing the sensitivity of a flea? Because if she did not then she should have done. Where the hell had his head been? he asked himself furiously.

What was he doing standing here when there was every chance she was packing to leave him right now?

Damn, he cursed, and climbed into his car. The engine fired; he pushed it in gear. If her suitcase was out then he was in deep trouble, he accepted as he covered the fifty yards to his driveway at breakneck speed.

Theron's car was already parked outside the front door and empty of its passengers. Striding into the house, he didn't think twice about where to look for her and took the stairs three at a time, arriving outside their bedroom before he paused then diverted to the room next door.

Thrusting the door open, he stepped inside. His instincts had not let him down. She was standing by the window, facing into the room with her arms folded.

Waiting for him, he noted with grim satisfaction, and closed the door. 'I did not believe you had been unfaithful to me,' he stated as he strode forward. 'The only marriage contract that you and I will ever have will have to be written in my blood on my deathbed since I have no intention of letting you go before I die. I do not think of you as a trophy, a puppet or a thing of mockery. And I don't *stalk* you, I *follow* you like some bloody faithful pet dog who does not want to be anywhere else but where you are.'

He came to a stop in front of her. Her eyes were dark, her mouth small and her hair was stuck in a pony-tail. She was wearing combat trousers and a tough-lady vest top but there were tears sliding down both smooth cheeks.

'If I loved you any more than I do already they would have to put me away because I would be dangerous,' he continued huskily. 'And if I sounded bloody insensitive back there then that is because I was hurt by those photographs too.'

She stifled a small sob. He refused to reach for her. He would answer all charges and *then* he would touch.

'Diantha has been a part of my family since she and Chloe were giggling schoolgirls. I believed Nikos had hurt her four years ago, I thought he had deliberately set out to turn her head and when she became serious left her flat. I even felt sorry for her so I visited whenever I was in Washington. But Nikos now tells me that he recognised her need to manipulate even then. I was wrong about her and now I am sorry—and don't think those tears are going to save you,' he added, 'because they are not.'

'Save me from what?'

'Retribution,' he answered. 'For daring to believe I could question the parentage of our child.'

'Your face—'

'My face was pained, I know,' he admitted. 'There is only one person who could have put such a filthy idea in her head and that is Takis. And how do I know that? Because he once dared to suggest such a thing to me.'

'Takis...?' Her eyelashes fluttered, tear-tipped and sparkling.

He rasped out a sigh that fell between anger and hurt. 'I was miserable, you were miserable,' he reminded her. 'We were living within a vacuum where we did not communicate. Takis was the closest thing I had to a father back then. He asked about our marriage, and when I stupidly said in a weak moment that I was worried about you because you were forever going missing he suggested that maybe I should find out where you go.'

He clamped his mouth shut over the rest of that conversation. What it contained did not matter here. What did was that his most trusted friend and employer had been passing on confidential information. 'Now I find he has been disclosing confidential information about pre-nuptial contracts and the lack of.'

'Did he set up the photographer too?'

He sighed and shook his head. 'I am hoping he did not. I am hoping that the photographs were all Diantha's idea. Has it occurred to you that she had taken those things before she knew that you and I would get back together? Which means she always planned to use them whether or not you were still on the scene. A safeguard,' he called it. 'In case I did not come through with the marriage proposal. How do you think it makes me feel to know I was open to such manipulation?'

'An idiot, I guess.' She offered him a shrug that said she believed he deserved it. Insolence did not begin to cover the expression on her beautiful face.

His eyes narrowed. Challenge was suddenly back in the air. Then without warning she issued a thick sob then fell into his arms—because she belonged there.

'I've had a h-horrible day,' she sobbed against him.

'I can change that,' he promised, picked her up and took her to the bed. They could make love—why not? It was the most effective cleanser of poison that he knew of.

Afterwards they went downstairs to find their home overrun by people who wanted to make amends for all the ugliness. His mother was there, his sister, Chloe, even Nikos had come with Carlotta pinned possessively to his side. Silvia and Theron were looking shell-shocked because someone had run the whole sequence of events by them.

No Takis Konstantindou though, he noticed, and felt a short wave of anger-cum-regret flood his mind. Takis was out, and he probably knew it by now. Diantha's father would have seen to it. He was a man of honour despite what his daughter was.

Eve arrived with Ethan Hayes, carrying a crate of champagne. 'To welcome Isobel back into the fold,' Eve announced, but they all knew that she'd heard about today's events too.

'You don't need jungle drums up here,' Isobel whispered to Leandros. 'The rumours get round on a current of air!'

But her cheeks were flushed and she was happy. The doorbell sounded and two minutes later another visitor stepped onto the sunny terrace. 'My God, I don't believe it,' Leandros gasped in warm surprise—while everyone else was thrown into silence by the sight of the dauntingly aloof Felipe Vazquez, while he appeared taken aback by so many curious faces. 'When did you get into town?'

'My apologies for the intrusion,' he murmured stiffly.

'No intrusion at all,' Leandros assured and took him to meet his beautiful wife, who stared up at his friend as if what she was seeing lit a vision in her head.

Leandros grinned as he watched it happen. 'No,' he bent to murmur close to her ear. 'Felipe is Spanish, not Venezuelan.'

'Oh,' she pouted up at him. 'What a terrible shame.'

The afternoon took on a festive quality. By the time everyone drifted away again, Isobel was looking just a little bewildered. 'We seem to have become very popular all of a sudden,' she said.

'Too popular,' he answered. 'After Nikos's wedding you

and I are flying to the Caribbean to gatecrash his honey-moon,' he said decisively.

'But we can't do that!' Isobel protested.

'Why not?' he countered. 'He intends to cruise on my yacht. I intend that we stay so stationary that it will be an effort to move from the bed to the terrace. But for now,' he began to stalk her, 'you owe me something I am about to collect.'

'Owe you what?' she demanded.

'Humble pie?' he softly reminded her.

A PASSIONATE REUNION IN FIJI

MICHELLE SMART

This is for Keanu Reeves,
my teenage object of lust,
who, like a fine wine,
grows only better with age.

CHAPTER ONE

LIVIA BRIATORE CLIMBED the metal steps to the sleek jet's cabin, her heart hammering so hard she felt the vibrations in the tips of her hair. The sun was setting, the growing darkness perfectly matching the darkness that had enveloped her these recent months.

The flight crew, the same crew from when she'd first boarded this plane over two years ago, greeted her warmly but with questions ringing from their eyes.

Livia responded with a smile but the effort was such the muscles of her mouth protested. She didn't think she'd smiled once these past four months.

Sick dread swirled in her stomach. Clamping her teeth together, she straightened her spine and raised her chin, then stepped into the luxurious cabin where she was destined to spend the next twenty-six hours flying to Fiji.

Immediately her senses were assailed by the familiar smell of expensive upholstery mingled with the musky yet citrusy scent of the man on the plush leather seat, a laptop open before him.

She almost doubled over with the strength of the pain that punched through her stomach.

The first time Livia had stepped on this plane her

heart had pounded with excitement and anticipation. Her body had run amok with brand-new feelings.

That first time in this plane, taking off from this very same airport in Rome, she had been filled with more happiness than she had known existed. The man whose attention was currently fixed on his laptop had hardly been able to wait for take-off before dragging her into the bedroom to make love to her.

All that was left of the flame of the passion that had seen them married within a month of meeting was ashes.

She blinked the painful memories away and forced her leaden legs forward.

She'd made a promise and she would keep it, however much it hurt.

The plane had four luxury window seats facing each other with the aisle between them. Massimo had raised his partition and when she took the seat diagonal to his, all she could see of him were his shoes. They were as buffed and polished as they always had been, a quirk she had thought adorable. Her husband was the least vain man she had ever met but he always took pride in his footwear.

She fastened her seat belt then laced her fingers tightly together to stop herself giving in to the need to bite her nails. She'd had an expensive gel treatment done on them the day before, masking that they were all bitten to the quick. She didn't want Massimo to see them like that. She couldn't bear for him to look at her and see the signs of her broken heart.

Livia had patched her heart back up. She'd licked her wounds and stitched herself back together. That was the only good thing about her childhood. It had taught her how to survive.

She would survive the next four days too. Four days and then she need never see him again.

The captain's voice came over the tannoy system, informing them they were cleared to take off. His words brought Massimo to life. The partition acting as a barrier came down as he closed his laptop and stored it away, then fastened his seat belt. Not once did he look at her but Livia was aware of every movement he made. Her heart bloomed to see the muscles of his tall, lean body flex beneath the expensive navy shirt with the sleeves carelessly rolled up, the buttons around his strong neck undone. No doubt he'd ripped the tie he would have worn to the conference from his neck the moment he'd left the venue. A maverick even by usual standards, Massimo conformed to rules only when *he* judged it necessary. She supposed the engineering conference in London he'd been guest of honour at had been an occasion he'd decided was worthy of bothering with an actual suit.

Livia only knew he'd been in London because his PA had casually mentioned it in her email when they'd been making the arrangements for today.

It wasn't until the plane taxied down the runway that the soulful caramel eyes she had once stared into with wonder finally met her gaze. It was the briefest of glances before he turned his attention to the window beside his head but it was enough for Livia's stomach to flip over and her throat to tighten.

Massimo's face was one she'd been familiar with long before they'd met. Employed as his grandfather's private nurse, she'd stared at the large Briatore family portrait that had hung in his grandfather's living room too many times to count. Her gaze had always been drawn to the only member whose smile appeared forced. It was a beautiful face. Slightly long with high cheekbones, a strong Roman nose and a wide firm mouth, it was a chameleon of a face, fitting for a construction worker, a banker or a poet. That it belonged to one of the richest self-made billionaires in the world was irrelevant. She would have been drawn to that face no matter who he was.

Seeing him in the flesh for the first time, in the church his sister was getting married in, had been like having all the oxygen sucked out of her.

The first time she'd seen him smile for real her insides had melted as if she'd been injected with liquid sunshine. *She* had brought that smile out in him. She couldn't even remember what she'd said, only that after hours of sidelong glances at each other throughout the wedding ceremony and the official photographs, she'd gone to the bar of the hotel the reception was being held in and suddenly the air around her had become electrified. She'd known before even turning her head that he'd come to stand beside her. Her tongue, usually so razor sharp, had tied itself in knots. Whatever she'd said in those first awkward moments had evoked that smile and in that instant all the awkwardness disappeared and it was as if they had known each other for ever.

And now he couldn't even bring himself to look at her.

She had no idea how they were going to get through a weekend with his family, celebrating his grandfather's ninetieth birthday, pretending to still be together.

Massimo watched an illuminated Rome disappear beneath the clouds and tried to clear the hot cloud that was the mess in his head.

When he'd agreed to speak at the engineering conference in London, it had made sense to fly to Rome afterwards and collect Livia en route. It had been logical.

He'd assumed that after four months apart, being with her again would be no big deal. He hadn't missed her in the slightest. Not that there had been time to miss her with all the hours he'd been putting in. Without the burden of a hot-tempered wife demanding his attention, he'd been able to devote himself to his multiple businesses just as he had before she'd collided into his life and torn it inside out. The day she'd left, he'd bought himself the bed for his office which the mere suggestion of had so angered her. He'd slept in it most nights since. It was far more comfortable than the blanket on the sofa he'd used the nights he'd worked late and decided it wasn't worth driving home.

He hadn't anticipated that his blood would become hot and sticky and his hands clammy just to land in his home city and be under the same sky as her again.

And now that she was here, in the cabin of his plane, every cell in his body, dormant all this time apart, had awoken.

He could curse his logical mind. Why hadn't he insisted she fly to Los Angeles, where he was scheduled to refuel, and board his plane there? He couldn't have her fly all the way to Fiji separately from him—that would defeat the whole purpose of her being there—but he could have engineered things so they only had to spend a minimal amount of time on his plane together, not the full twenty-six hours it would take to travel to the other side of the world.

For the return journey he would fly with her to Australia and charter a plane to fly her back to Italy.

He'd listed all the excuses he could have made to avoid bringing her with him but it had all boiled down to one thing. This was for his grandfather, Jimmy Seibua. His terminally ill grandfather, who'd taken a cruise from Rome to Fiji with his family and an army of medical personnel in attendance and had arrived on the island three days ago. This weekend was all that had been keeping his grandfather alive, this one last visit to the homeland he'd left as a twenty-two-year-old the spark giving him the fight needed to beat the odds. Jimmy would celebrate his ninetieth birthday on the Fijian island of his birth, now owned by Massimo, with the family he loved. His grandfather thought of Livia as part of his family. He loved her as a granddaughter. His only regret at Massimo marrying her was that it meant he lost the private nurse who had tended to him with such care during his first battle with cancer.

And, whatever his own feelings towards his estranged wife, Massimo knew Livia loved Jimmy too.

'Are you going to spend the entire flight ignoring me?'

Massimo clenched his jaw as Livia's direct husky tones penetrated his senses, speaking their native Italian.

That was the thing with his wife. She was always direct. If she wasn't happy about something she made damned sure you knew about it. For a long time the object of her unhappiness had been Massimo. Her declaration that she was leaving him had come as no surprise, only relief. Marriage to Livia had gone from being passionate and invigorating to being like a war zone. And she wondered why he'd spent so much time at work? The nights they had spent together those last few months had been with her cold back firmly turned to him. She'd even started wearing nightshirts.

He swallowed back the lump that had suddenly appeared in his throat and finally allowed his gaze to fall on her properly.

The lump he'd tried to shift grew but he opened his mouth and dragged the words through it. 'You've had your hair cut.'

Her beautiful thick, dark chestnut hair, which had fallen like a sheet down to her lower back, now fell in layers to rest on her shoulders in loose curls. It was lighter too, streaks of honey blonde carefully blending with her natural colour. Livia was not the most beautiful woman in the world but to his eyes she was stunning. It was the whole package. A sexy firecracker with a dirty laugh. He'd heard that laugh echo through the walls of the church while they'd waited for his sister, the bride, to arrive and when he'd spotted the woman behind it he'd felt the fabric of his existence shift. He'd grabbed the first available opportunity to speak to her and had been blown away to discover she had a thirsty, inquisitive mind. He'd been smitten. In Livia he'd found the woman he'd never known he'd been searching for. Or so he'd thought.

Her dark brown eyes, always so expressive, widened before a choked laugh flew from her mouth. 'That's all you can think to say?'

She didn't wait for a response; unbuckling her seat belt and springing to her feet.

She'd lost weight, he noted hazily.

Her kissable plump lips were tight as she stalked past him, the bathroom door closing sharply a moment later.

Massimo rubbed his jaw and struggled to get air into his closed lungs.

He hadn't expected this to be easy but it was a thousand times harder than he'd envisaged.

Livia sat on the closed toilet seat and hugged her arms across her chest, willing the threatening tears back. She hadn't expected this tumult of emotions to engulf her or for the ache in her chest to hurt so much.

She had shed enough tears for this man, so many she'd thought herself all cried out.

Massimo had never loved her. That was the truth she needed to keep reminding herself of.

But she had loved him. Truly, madly, deeply.

And in return he'd broken her.

The worst of it was he had no idea. For all his high intelligence, her husband had the emotional depth of an earthworm. She'd just been too blind to see it.

She closed her eyes and took three long inhalations.

There was no point in driving herself crazy with her thoughts. She had loved him once and while echoes of that love still beat in her heart they weren't real. She didn't love him any more. She was only there to honour the promise she'd made to him the day he'd let her go without a solitary word of fight to make her stay.

He'd wanted her gone. He'd been relieved. She'd seen it in his eyes.

Three more deep breaths and she got back to her feet and flushed the unused toilet.

She was Livia Briatore, formerly Livia Esposito, daughter of Pietro Esposito, Don Fortunato's most trusted clan member and henchman until her father's gangland murder when she'd been only eight. She'd been raised in the Secondigliano surrounded by drugs and brutal violence and she'd learned from an early age to show no fear. To show nothing.

Escaping Naples to study nursing in Rome had been like learning to breathe. Dropping her guard had not been easy—constantly checking over her shoulder when she walked a street was a habit it had taken many years to break—but she had forged a new life for herself and the joy it had given her had been worth the anxiety that had gnawed at her to be separated from her siblings. Life had gone from being a constant knot in her belly to being an adventure. She'd learned to laugh. With Massimo she had learned to love.

But her old protective barrier had never fully gone. It had sat patiently inside her waiting to be slipped back on.

To get through the next four days she needed that barrier. She needed to keep her guard up, not as protection against Massimo but as protection against her own foolish heart.

She took her seat and was not surprised to find Massimo working again on his laptop.

This time he raised his eyes from the screen to look at her. 'I've ordered us coffee. Did you want anything to eat?'

'I've eaten,' she answered with strained politeness, not adding that all she'd eaten that day had been half a slice of toast. Her stomach had been too tight and cramped to manage anything else. The countdown to seeing Massimo again had wrecked the little equilibrium she'd regained for herself.

It was hardly surprising that there was an awkwardness between them but they had a long flight ahead and she didn't want to spend it in uncomfortable silence. 'How have you been?'

He pulled a face and turned his attention back to his laptop. 'Busy.'

She dug her fake nails into her thighs. How she hated that word. It was the word he'd always used to justify never being there. 'Are you too busy to stop working for five minutes and talk?'

'I have data to interpret and an analysis to send.'

Two years ago he would have explained both the data and analysis to her, assuming rightly that she would find it interesting. The truth was she had found everything about Massimo interesting. Enthralling. The workings of his brain had never failed to astonish her. How could they not? This was the man who'd used his downtime from his computer engineering degree to create a web-based platform game that had taken the world by storm and which he'd sold upon his graduation for two hundred million US dollars. That money had been the linchpin for his move to America, where he'd formed his company, Briatore Technologies, whilst simultaneously studying for a PhD in energy physics, followed by a second PhD in applied physics and material sciences. His company, of which he was still the sole owner, now employed thousands worldwide, creating environmentally friendly solutions for many of the world's greatest carbon-related threats. He was on a one-man mission to save the planet one invention at a time. That he'd earned himself a fortune in the process was almost incidental. Only a month ago he'd been named in the top thirty of the world's most powerful people and in the top fifty of the world's richest.

It would have been so easy for him to make her feel stupid but he never had. Anything she didn't understand—which when it came to his work was most things—he would explain patiently but never patronisingly, his face lighting up when she grasped the finer details of something, like how a lithium ion battery worked and what carbon capture meant on a practical level.

She had been so thrilled that this man, clever, rich, successful and with a face and body to make the gods envious, had been as seemingly enthralled with her as she had been with him that she'd been blind to his emotional failings. Once the first flush of lust had worn off he'd retreated into the all-consuming world he'd created for himself, hiding himself away from the woman he'd married.

She wished she knew what she'd done to make him back away from her but every time she'd tried to get him to open up, the further into his shell he'd retreated.

The silence, filled intermittently by the sounds of Massimo tapping on the laptop's keyboard, grew more oppressive.

She watched him work. The familiar furrow of concentration was etched on his brow. How could he tune her out so effectively?

But as she watched him she noticed subtle changes. Flecks of white around the temples of his thick black hair that had never been there before. The full beard, as if he'd given up the bother of shaving altogether. Dark rings around his eyes as if he'd given up sleep along with shaving. Not that he had ever slept much. His brain was too busy for sleep.

Livia swallowed back the pang that had crept through her. Massimo was thirty-six years old; old enough to not look after himself if that was what he wanted.

He reached absently for the strong black coffee on the desk beside his laptop and took a large sip. His attention did not stray from the screen before him. He tapped something else onto the keyboard. The sound was akin to nails being dragged down a chalkboard.

Suddenly she could bear it no more. Jumping back to her feet, she took the three steps to him and slammed his laptop lid down.

CHAPTER TWO

MASSIMO CLENCHED HIS teeth together and placed a protective hand on his laptop to prevent Livia from snatching hold of it and throwing it onto the floor. 'What was that for?'

Diminutive though she was in height, in presence she was larger than life and right then, standing over him, she seemed magnified, the anger rippling from her in waves. 'We've been in the air for an hour and you've spared me only ten words.'

'Twenty-six,' he corrected through gritted teeth. 'I have spoken twenty-six words.'

'And now you're being pedantic as well as rude.' She pulled her hair together in a fist then released it. 'How are we supposed to convince your grandfather and the rest of your family that we're still together if you won't look at me or talk to me?'

'I'm not being rude. This is a very important time for me. On Monday we are running the prototypes on...'

'I don't *care*,' she interrupted with a cry. 'Whatever you're working on, I do not care. I'm here as a favour to you for your grandfather's benefit. The least you can do is treat me with some respect.'

'If I'm being disrespectful then I apologise,' he answered stiffly, biting back the retort of *what did you expect?* Livia had been the one to walk out on their marriage, not him. She had been the one to laugh in his face when he suggested they have a child. How did she expect him to be around her?

Damned if *he* knew how to act around her. Focusing his attention on the screen before him was the only tool he had to drive out the tumultuous emotions ripping through him. That these emotions were still there defied belief but Livia had always been able to induce feelings in him that had no place in his world, feelings that went far deeper than mere lust and friendship. She took up too much head space. She distracted him. That would have been easy to deal with if she'd only distracted his head when he'd been at home.

'I don't want your apologies. You don't mean it. You never do. Your apologies are meaningless.'

It was an accusation she had thrown at him many times and usually preceded an escalation of her temper, which only got wilder when he refused to engage. Massimo disliked meaningless confrontation, considered it a waste of energy, and would walk away when she refused to listen to reason.

Unfortunately, right now there was nowhere for him to walk away to. To escape to.

Keeping his own temper in check—keeping a cool head when all those around him lost theirs was something he took pride in—Massimo inhaled slowly through his nose and gazed at the angry face before him. 'What I'm working on is important. I'll be finished before we land in Los Angeles. We can spend the time between Los Angeles and Fiji talking if that's what you want.'

She laughed without any humour then flopped onto

the seat opposite his and glared at him. 'Great. You're going to do me the huge favour of talking to me if *I* want. Thank you. You're too kind.'

She'd folded her arms across her chest, slightly raising her breasts. He knew she hadn't done it deliberately—intimacy between them had died long before she'd called time on their marriage itself—but it distracted him enough for a sliver of awareness to pierce his armoury.

Livia had a body that could make a man weep. Even dressed as she was now, fully covered in tight faded jeans and a roll-neck black jumper, her feminine curves were undeniable. The first time he'd made love to her he'd thought he'd died and gone to heaven. Her virginity had surprised and delighted him. Surprised him because he would never have believed a twenty-four-year-old woman with such a dirty laugh and who carried herself with such confidence could be a virgin. Delighted him because it had marked her as his in a primal way he'd never experienced before.

Sex had never been a great need for him. When he'd shot up from a scrawny teenager into the frame he now inhabits, he'd suddenly found women throwing themselves at him, something that had only increased when he'd sold his web-based game after graduation and become worth a fortune. If he'd been in the mood he'd been happy to oblige, finding sex a satiating yet fleeting diversion from his work. Livia was the first woman he'd been truly intimate with. When they had first got together they'd been unable to keep their hands off each other. For the first time in his life Massimo had found himself consumed by lust.

The loss of that intimacy had not been his choice. Their marriage had disintegrated to such an extent that the nights he had made it home, they'd slept back to back. A man could take only so much rejection from his own wife before he stopped bothering.

Had she taken a lover? It was a thought that sent a stabbing motion plunging into his chest and for a moment he closed his eyes and breathed the pain away.

It was none of his business if she'd taken a lover and it would be unreasonable to expect her to have remained celibate during their separation. If not for his grandfather they would already be divorced.

'When did you last see your grandfather?' she asked suddenly, cutting through his attempts to concentrate on the screen in front of him rather than the bombshell opposite.

Livia felt only fleeting satisfaction to see the caramel eyes raise to meet hers.

'Why do you ask?'

'Because when I saw him the day before he set sail for Fiji he complained that you hadn't been in touch. I emailed Lindy about it.'

Lindy was Massimo's PA, a dragon of a woman who ran his business life. She was the only person in the world who knew their marriage was over in all but name. As far as their respective families were concerned, they were still together.

When they'd married, Livia had hoped Massimo's new status would encourage him to see more of his family but it hadn't worked that way. In their two years of shared life they had spent one Christmas with his family and that had been it. Livia had made numerous visits from their house in Los Angeles to Italy alone, visiting her youngest brother and dropping in on Massimo's family, all of whom she adored.

Since they'd gone their separate ways, her frequent visits had continued. They were used to her visiting alone so Massimo's absence had gone unremarked. Only Madeline, Massimo's sister, had the perception to see that anything was wrong but as she had a newborn child to take care of, her perception skills were less honed than usual. The ache that formed in Livia's heart as she held Madeline's baby only added to the ache already there but she would have been helpless to resist cradling the tiny bundle in her arms even if she didn't have a show to perform.

None of the Briatores or Espositos had any idea she was back on Italian soil permanently. Whenever she was asked about Massimo—who rarely bothered to message his family and had never met his niece—she would say he was busy with work, satisfied that she wasn't telling a lie. Massimo was *always* busy with work. Always. She'd lived with his grandfather as his private nurse for nine months and in that time Massimo hadn't made one trip home. She'd accepted the family line that Massimo was too busy to fly home from California regularly but had come to her own private conclusion during their marriage that it was nothing to do with his schedule preventing him from spending more time with his family. He simply didn't want to.

She would be glad when these evasions of the truth could be done with and they could tell his family they had separated. She hated lying, even if only by omission.

'Lindy mentioned it,' he admitted stiffly.

'Did you do anything about it?'

'I called him on the ship. He sounded fine.' His gaze dropped back to his laptop.

'He isn't fine.' Livia's heart had broken to see how

frail Jimmy had become. The elderly yet vital man who'd waged such a strong battle against his first diagnosis of cancer was fading, too weak to fly both legs of the mammoth journey to Fiji. It had been decided that a cruise was the safest way to get him to the other side of the world. Jimmy wanted to spend his ninetieth birthday with all his family around him, see corners of the world he'd never visited before and tread the soil he'd been raised on one last time.

Everything for him was now one last time.

'I know that.'

'Will you spend some proper time with him this weekend?' she asked. It was pointless adding that spending real time with Massimo was Jimmy's greatest wish. It was his parents' greatest wish too.

Massimo thought the gift of his money was enough. When he'd made his fortune, he'd bought his entire family new homes of their own and a car each. As his wealth had increased so had his generous gifts to them. It had been Massimo who'd paid for the private treatment during Jimmy's first diagnosis and all the associated costs including the agency fees for Livia's wages as his live-in nurse. It was Massimo who had bought the island his grandfather came from and spent a fortune building a complex for the entire family to stay on. It was Massimo footing the bill for the cruise the rest of the family were taking with Jimmy to reach the island. He'd chartered an ocean liner for their sole use.

Yet for all his generosity, he was spectacularly blind to the fact his family would much rather have his presence than his presents. He also seemed blind to the fact that time was running out for his grandfather.

'Yes.'

'You'll leave your laptop and phone switched off?'

'You know I can't do that.'

'I know you *won't* do that.'

His jaw clenched. 'We can talk about this later.'

She laughed mockingly. 'Later. Of course. Everything is always *later* with you, isn't it?'

Without any warning, Massimo slammed his fist against the panel beside his seat. 'And everything still has to be *now* with you. I said we could talk once I have completed my work but, as always, you don't listen. This is important and needs my attention. If you can't wait patiently for me to finish then I suggest you take yourself to the bedroom and give your mouth a rest.'

Massimo refused to feel guilt for his outburst, even when Livia's face paled before him.

True to form, she refused to let him get the last word, getting to her feet slowly and glowering at him. 'If anyone has a problem with listening it's you. If it doesn't involve your precious work then it's insignificant to you. It's been four months since you last saw me and you haven't even cared to ask how I've been. If I'd had any doubts that leaving you was the best thing I could do, an hour in your company has proven me right. You never cared for me. You've never cared for anyone.'

She walked away, not to the bedroom but to her original seat. There was dignity in the way she moved that, despite the acrimony that thickened the air between them, touched him. Livia was a strange mix of toughness and vulnerability, traits that had first moved him then infuriated him. Her toughness meant she did not know how to back down from an argument but the underlying vulnerability found her easily wounded. He'd never known the words to say to repair the wounds he'd unwittingly inflicted on her. Eventually he'd stopped trying.

Her partition rose and she disappeared from sight.

Massimo sighed his relief and rubbed his eyes. He hadn't slept in over twenty-four hours and was exhausted.

Ringing the bell, he ordered a fresh coffee when the stewardess appeared. Caffeine and sugar would keep him awake long enough to get his analysis done. Maybe then he'd be able to catch some sleep.

He tuned out Livia's husky voice when the stewardess turned her attention to his wife.

But he couldn't tune out her presence.

The data on the screen before him blurred. His head felt so heavy. All of him felt heavy, a weight compressing him from the top down and, even with the importance of the work that needed to be done, he found his thoughts drifting to the early days of their marriage, days when he'd believed nothing could come between them.

Nothing *had* come between them. Only themselves.

Livia tried to concentrate on the movie she'd selected from the thousands stored on the in-flight entertainment system—a system Massimo had had installed for her benefit—but the storyline passed her by in a haze. The first movie, a comedy, had passed her by too. This second one was a critically acclaimed thriller guaranteed to keep her tear ducts intact but, even with the sound on her headphones turned up high to drown out the incessant tapping of Massimo's fingers on his keyboard, he was all she could think about.

How had it come to this? How could a marriage

formed with such passion and joy disintegrate into such bitterness?

Movement caught her attention and she removed her headphones and straightened as the head stewardess approached to see if she would like anything.

'A blanket would be nice, thanks,' she replied. The air-conditioning on Massimo's jet was always set to freezing.

The blanket delivered, Livia was suddenly struck by the cabin's silence.

Lowering her partition, she looked across at Massimo. He'd fallen asleep.

His laptop was still open but the man himself was fast asleep, upright in his seat, his mouth slightly open as he breathed in and out heavily.

A tightness formed in her chest as she watched until, without thinking, she got to her feet and padded over to him.

For a long time, hardly daring to breathe, she drank in the features of the man she had once loved so much. His Fijian ancestry was stronger in him than in his sister. His skin was a deep olive, his thick hair the most beautiful shade of ebony. She'd liked it when he forgot to cut it, and had spent many happy hours snuggled on the sofa with him, Massimo talking, his head on her lap, Livia content to simply listen to his wonderful rich, deep voice and run her fingers through his hair. It was the closest to peace she had ever felt in her life.

She'd tried so hard to hold onto what they had but he had slipped away from her with the same ease her fingers had run through his hair.

Her throat closed, Livia carefully draped the blanket she'd been about to use for herself on his lap. She wanted to press the button that would tilt the chair back and turn it into a bed but was afraid the motion would wake him. Struck again by the dark circles around his eyes, she wondered when he'd last had a decent night's sleep. Or the last time he'd had a decent meal.

The compulsion to reach out her hand and stroke her fingers over his high cheekbones, to feel the texture of his skin on hers, to run her fingers through his hair… it all hit her so fast that her hand was inches from his face before she realised what she was about to do and stopped herself.

Her heart thumped wildly and for a moment she couldn't breathe.

Putting her hand to her chest, she backed away, afraid to be this close to him.

Afraid of what it did to her.

Massimo's eyes opened with a start.

He blinked rapidly, disorientated.

His laptop was still open but had put itself into sleep mode.

Had *he* fallen asleep?

Getting to his feet to stretch his legs, he felt a sudden chill on his thighs and gazed down in astonishment at the blanket that had fallen to the floor.

Where had that come from?

He stared over at Livia. Her partition was still up but, standing, he could see her clearly. She'd reclined her chair and was watching something on the television with her headphones in. A blanket covered her whole body up to her chin.

'Did you put a blanket on me?' He didn't mean to sound so accusatory but the thought of her doing that…

Her face turned towards him and she pulled the headphones off. 'Did you say something?'

Before he could answer one of the cabin crew entered. 'We will be landing in twenty minutes.'

The moment they were alone again, Massimo turned back to Livia. 'How long was I asleep?'

She shrugged.

He swore under his breath. He hadn't finished his analysis. Damn it, he'd promised the project manager that he would have it in his inbox before he reached the office that morning.

He bit back the demand he wanted to throw at her as to why she hadn't woken him and sat back down.

Livia had put the blanket on him. He knew that with a deep certainty and he didn't know if it was that simple gesture or that he was now behind on where he needed to be workwise that made his guts feel as if acid had been poured in them.

He felt close to snapping. Virulent emotions were coursing through him and his wife, the cause of all his angst, was reclined in her seat as nonchalant as could be.

But knowing her as well as he did, he knew her nonchalance was a sham. Livia did not do nonchalance.

Why had she put a blanket on him?

His eyes were better able to focus after his short sleep but, with their landing imminent, he put his laptop away and folded his desk up and secured it, all the while hating that he was fully aware of Livia sorting her own seating area out, avoiding looking at him as much as he avoided looking at her.

Los Angeles couldn't come soon enough.

Not another word was exchanged until the plane had landed safely.

Needing to escape the strange febrile atmosphere that seemed to have infected his flight crew as much as them, Massimo grabbed his laptop and got to his feet but the moment he left his seat, Livia was there facing him in the aisle, holding her bag tightly, clearly ready to make her own escape.

He stepped to one side to let her pass but she stepped to the same side too.

Their eyes met. Their gaze held, only momentarily, but long enough for him to see the pain she had become a master at hiding from him.

A sharp compression lanced his chest, as if his heart had become a rose in full bloom, its thorns spearing into him.

And then she blinked, cast her gaze to the floor, murmured, 'Excuse me,' and brushed past him.

Massimo swallowed away the lump in his throat and left his plane by the other exit.

CHAPTER THREE

Two hours after landing in Los Angeles, they were cleared to take off for the second leg of their mammoth journey to Fiji.

Livia had returned to the plane before Massimo. She guessed he'd gone to the private executive lounge in the airport to work. She'd taken herself for a walk, keeping her phone in her hand for the alert that the plane had refuelled and she could get back on, and tried to get hold of Gianluca, her youngest sibling. He hadn't answered and hadn't called her back either. She'd had no wish to go sightseeing or do any of the things most visitors with a short layover at LAX would do. Just breathing the air brought back the awful feelings that had lived in her the last dying months of their marriage.

She hated Los Angeles. She hated California. She'd loathed living there. For a place known as the Golden State, her life there had been devoid of sunshine.

At first, she'd enjoyed the novelty of it all. Compared to Naples and Rome it was huge. Everything was so much bigger. Even the sky and the sun that shone in it appeared greater and brighter. But then loneliness had seeped its way in. She had no friends there and no means to make them. Unlike Massimo, who spoke fluent English, her own English was barely passable. The glass home they'd shared was forty kilometres from downtown LA. An intensely private man, Massimo had deliberately chosen a home far from prying eyes. There were no neighbours. The household staff spoke only English and Spanish.

She'd become sick with longing for home.

Massimo hadn't understood. He hadn't even tried.

But there hadn't been any sunshine since she'd left him and returned to her home in Italy either.

It was strange to experience taking off in her second sunset of the day. She should have slept during the first leg of the journey but sleep had been the last thing on her mind, the last thing she'd been capable of. The sun putting itself to sleep now in LA would soon be awakening in Rome.

She yawned and cast her eyes in Massimo's direction. His partition was raised again but she could still hear the tapping of his fingers on the keypad. So much for talking. Silence for them truly had become golden.

A member of the cabin crew brought her pillows and a duvet and turned her seat into a bed while Livia used the bathroom to change into pyjamas, remove her make-up and brush her teeth.

She thought of the plane's bedroom and its comfortable king-sized bed. An ache formed in the pit of her stomach to remember the glorious hours they had spent sharing it. Massimo would never begrudge her sleeping in it now but she couldn't do it. She couldn't sleep in a bed they had shared knowing that when she woke the pillow beside her would be unused. That had been hard enough to deal with when they'd been together.

Massimo was on his feet stretching his aching back

when Livia returned to the cabin clutching her washbag. It was the same washbag she'd used when they'd been married and his heart tugged to see it.

She looked younger with her face free from make-up and plain cream pyjamas on. More vulnerable too.

The threads tugging at his heart tightened.

'I'm going to have a nightcap. Do you want one?'

Surprise lit her dark brown eyes before they fixed on his own freshly made-up bed. 'You're finished?'

He nodded. 'My apologies for it taking so long. I didn't factor in falling asleep.'

Her plump lips curved into the tiniest of smiles. 'I would have woken you but you looked exhausted.'

She looked exhausted. Her seat had been made up into a bed for her too but, however comfortable it was, it was not the same as sleeping in a proper bed. 'Why don't you sleep in our bed?'

Now the tiniest of winces flashed over her face. 'I'll be fine here, thank you. You should use it—you only napped for a couple of hours.'

The only time he'd been in the jet's bedroom since she'd left him was to use the en-suite shower. Sleeping in the bed he'd shared with her...the thought alone had been enough to make his guts twist tightly.

To see the same reluctance reflected in her eyes twisted them even harder.

He removed a bottle of his favourite bourbon and two glasses from the bar as the stewardess came into the cabin with a bucket of ice. Massimo took it from her and arched an eyebrow in question at Livia.

She hesitated for a moment before nodding.

As the stewardess dimmed the lights and left the

cabin, he poured them both a measure and handed a glass to Livia.

She took it with a murmured thanks, avoiding direct eye contact, carefully avoiding his touch. He could smell the mintiness of her toothpaste and caught a whiff of the delicately scented cream she used to remove her make-up and the moisturiser she finished her night-time routine with. The two combined into a scent that had always delighted his senses far more than her perfume, which in itself was beautiful. The perfume she sprayed herself with by day could be enjoyed by anyone who got close enough. Her night-time scent had always been for him alone.

Had any other man been lucky enough to smell it since they'd parted?

She sat on her bed and took a small sip of her bourbon. As she moved he couldn't help but notice the light sway of her naked breasts beneath the silk pyjama top.

Her nightwear was functional and obviously selected to cover every inch but the curves that had driven him to such madness were clearly delineated beneath the fabric and it took all his willpower to keep his gaze fixed on her face.

But her face had driven him to madness as much as the body had. With Livia it had always been the whole package. Everything about her. Madness.

After a few moments of stilted silence she said, 'Are you going to get some sleep too?'

Massimo knew what Livia was thinking: that having his own seat made into a bed was no indication that he actually intended to get any rest.

He shrugged and took a large sip of his bourbon, willing the smooth burn it made in his throat to flow through his veins and burn away the awareness searing his loins.

'If I can.' He raised his glass. 'This should help.' Enough of it would allow him a few precious hours of oblivion to the firecracker who would be sleeping at such close quarters to him.

'How long do we have until we reach Fiji?'

He checked his watch. 'Nine hours until we land at Nadi.'

'We get another flight from there?' Livia already knew the answer to this but the dimming of the lights seemed to have shrunk the generously proportioned cabin and given it an air of dangerous intimacy.

What was it about darkness that could change an atmosphere so acutely? Livia had grown up scared of the dark. The Secondigliano was a dangerous place in daylight. At night, all the monsters came out.

The dangers now were as different as night and day compared to her childhood and adolescence but she felt them as keenly. With Massimo's face in shadows his handsome features took on a devilish quality that set her stomach loose with butterflies and her skin vibrating with awareness.

'I've chartered a Cessna to fly us to Seibua Island.'

'You managed to get the name changed?' She couldn't remember the original name of the island Massimo's grandfather had been born and raised on.

'The paperwork's still being sorted but I've been reliably informed it's been accepted.' He finished his drink and poured himself another, raising the bottle at her in an unspoken question.

She shook her head. Marriage to Massimo had given her a real appreciation of bourbon but too much alcohol had a tendency to loosen her tongue, which she was the first to admit didn't need loosening. It also loosened her inhibitions. She'd never had any inhibitions around Massimo before but to get through the weekend in one piece she needed them as greatly as she needed to keep her guard up around him. All of this would be easier to cope with if her heart didn't ache so much just to share the same air as him again.

'Are you going to buy a Cessna of your own to keep there?'

He grimaced and finally perched himself on his bed. The overhead light shone down on him. 'The yacht's already moored there and can be used as transport. Whether I buy a plane too depends on how often the family use the island.' The resort created on the island would be available for the entire extended family to use as and when they wished, free of charge. The only stipulation would be that they treated it with respect.

'Knowing your sister it will be often.' It was doubtful Massimo would ever use it. His idea of a holiday was to take a Sunday off work.

She caught the whisper of a smile on his firm mouth but it disappeared behind his glass as he took another drink.

'When did your family get there?'

'They arrived three days ago.'

'Have you been to the island yet?'

'I haven't had the time.'

She chewed her bottom lip rather than give voice to her thoughts that this was typical Massimo, never having the time for anything that didn't revolve around work. He'd jumped through hoops and paid an astronomical sum for the island but those hoops had been jumped through by his lawyers and accountants. He'd spent a further fortune having the complex for the family built but, again, he'd had little involvement past hiring the architects and transferring the cash. Livia had signed off on the initial blueprint for the complex in the weeks before she'd left him. She had no idea if he'd even bothered to do more than cast an eye over it.

There was no point in her saying anything. It would only be a rehash of a conversation they'd had many times before, a conversation that would only lead to an argument. Or, as usually happened, it would lead to her getting increasingly het up at his refusal to engage in the conversation and losing her temper, and Massimo walking away in contempt leaving her shouting at the walls.

In any case, Massimo's sidelining of anything that wasn't work-related was none of her business. Not any more. If he wanted to blow his own money on projects and assets he had no intention of enjoying then that was up to him. If he wanted to keep his family on the fringes of his life for eternity then that was up to him too. He wasn't an adolescent like her youngest brother, Gianluca, who'd been born seven months after their father's death.

There was hope for Gianluca. Unlike their other siblings, who had succumbed to life in the Secondigliano, Gianluca's humanity was still there. The question was whether he had the courage to take Livia's hand and join her far from the violence and drugs that were such an intrinsic part of the Espositos' lives before it was too late and he was sucked into a life of crime from which his only escape would be in a coffin.

It was too late for Pasquale, who like their dead father had risen high in Don Fortunato's ranks, and too late for Denise who had married one of Pasquale's equally ambitious friends and was currently pregnant with their second child. Livia's siblings and her mother all knew Livia's door was always open for them. Gianluca was the only one she allowed herself to hope for. He could still leave without repercussions just as she had but time was running out. He'd recently turned eighteen. Should Don Fortunato decide Gianluca was worthy of joining his guard he would strike soon.

The man Livia had married, a man who abhorred violence and anything to do with illegal drugs, had made his choice when he was only a few years older than Gianluca. He'd chosen to leave Italy and leave his family, just as his own grandfather had done seventy years before him. The difference was his grandfather had left Fiji for the love of his life, an Englishwoman, and set up home with her in England. When their daughter Sera had married an Italian, Jimmy and Elizabeth had moved again, this time to Italy so they could stay close to their daughter. For them, family came first above all else. They were as close as close could be. All except for Massimo himself.

He didn't want to change. He saw nothing wrong with how he lived his life, nothing wrong with keeping a physical and emotional distance from the people who loved him. That was the choice he'd made and Livia had to respect that. She couldn't change it. She'd tried. When the realisation hit that his emotional distance from his family extended to her too, along with the recognition that this too would never change, she'd had no choice but to leave him.

She hadn't clawed her way out of the Secondigliano to spend her life as a trophy in a glass cabinet masquerading as a home.

While she had spent the past four months trying desperately to fix herself back together, for Massimo there had been nothing to fix. He'd got on with his life as if she'd never been a part of it.

Finishing her drink, she put the empty glass in the holder beside her bed and got under the covers. 'I'm going to get some sleep. Goodnight.' Then she turned her back on him and closed her eyes.

Massimo lay under his bed sheets, eyes wide open. He'd drunk enough bourbon to tranquillise an elephant but his mind was too busy. Except now it wasn't the project he'd spent over a year working on that stopped his mind switching off.

Turning his head, eyes adjusted to the dark, he watched the rhythmic rise and fall of Livia's duvet. He guessed she'd been asleep for around an hour now. He always knew when she was properly asleep and not just faking it. When she faked it, she lay rigid in absolute silence.

They'd slept together the first night they'd met—once they'd got talking at the hotel bar he hadn't let her out of his sight—and both of them had known it was no one-night stand. He'd been dozing in the aftermath, Livia wrapped in his arms, his body thrumming with the delights they'd just shared, when she'd mumbled something. That was his first experience of her sleep-talking. He'd quickly discovered that she talked a lot in her sleep. Sometimes the words were distinct. He remembered the feeling that had erupted through him the first time she'd mumbled his name. It had been ten times the magnitude of what he'd felt to be offered two hundred million dollars for the stupid game he'd developed during his boring university evenings.

But her dreams hadn't always been good. At least once a week he'd had to wake her from a bad one. The darkness of the life she'd lived until she'd left Naples at eighteen still haunted her.

Had another man woken her from the nightmares since she'd left him?

He pinched the bridge of his nose and willed the pain spearing him away.

Livia's sex life was no longer his business.

The thought of her with a lover was something that hadn't even occurred to him until she'd stepped onto his plane and now it was all he could think of.

In the four months since she'd left him, his own libido had gone into hibernation. From the feelings erupting through him now, he realised he'd shut down far more than his libido.

He'd shut down long before she'd left him.

Their marriage had begun with such high hopes and such certainty. They'd both been too foolish to realise that it was nothing but lust, a flaming passion that could only burn itself out.

He'd been intoxicated by her. He'd never met anyone like her: tough on the outside but marshmallow-soft inside. Straight talking. Capable of lancing with her tongue. But tender and compassionate. Someone who would drop everything if she were needed. Someone who would give everything they had if it were needed. Massimo had never been one for showing his emotions but being tactile with Livia had come naturally. She'd brought that side of him out right from the start.

And then the tide had turned. His assumptions that he

would be able to continue his life and work in the same way he always had but with his beautiful, vivacious wife to come home to had been quickly dispelled.

He should never have married her, that was the truth of it, but he'd been so swept up in the need to tie her to him and make her his in every way possible that he'd blinded himself to what marriage to a woman like Livia would actually entail. It entailed far more than he could give.

It was still dark when Livia woke. Groping for her phone, she looked at the time and was relieved to see they only had a couple of hours left until they landed.

Creeping out of her bed so as not to wake Massimo, she took her overnight bag from the compartment and made her way to the bedroom. She needed a shower. It was pure misfortune that the main bathroom was reached through the bedroom.

The moment she opened the bedroom door and stepped inside, she realised her mistake. The bathroom light was already switched on and the scent of Massimo's shower gel seeped through the gap in the door. Before she could beat a hasty retreat, the door opened and he stepped over the threshold as naked as the day he was born.

Startled caramel eyes met hers. All the air flew from her lungs.

Seconds passed that stretched like hours as they did nothing but stare at each other.

A compression formed in her chest and tightened her throat.

For a man who rarely worked out, Massimo had a physique to die for. Lean but muscular, his deep olive skin had only the lightest brush of fine dark hair over his defined pecs and the plane of his washboard stomach. The hair thickened considerably below his abdomen to the huge…

Her own abdomen contracted, heat rushing through her pelvis as she noticed—couldn't *help* but notice—his growing erection.

The heat in her pelvis spread. It suffused her cheeks with colour and she tightened her hold on her bag, crushing it against her chest.

Slowly, his features became taut, his nostrils flaring. His caramel eyes swirled with something she recognised, something that should have her spinning round immediately and leaving. But she couldn't. Her feet were rooted to the floor.

He'd had more work done on his tattoo, she noticed dimly, trying desperately hard not to let her gaze fall back below his waist, trying even harder to contain the rush of sultry warmth flooding her veins. His tattoo covered the entire bicep around his left shoulder, all in bold black lines. The large sun, the centrepiece that he had once told her symbolised his rebirth and represented the way he strove for perfection in all he did, was encircled by sharks' teeth, which represented power, leadership and protection, and they were now encircled by spearheads. She didn't know what the spearheads represented but knew they must mean something to him.

Instinct told her they represented something to do with her.

The sensation in her fingers that had almost had her touching his sleeping face earlier tingled again. An ache to touch his tattoo. To touch him. A yearning to feel the heat of his powerful body flush against hers, to be swept in his arms and to lose herself in the wonder she had always found in his lovemaking. It all hit her so quickly that if he had reached out for her she would have fallen into his arms in an instant.

More seconds stretched without a word exchanged but with that thick, sick chemistry shrouding them.

And then Massimo closed his eyes.

When he next looked at her, the swirling desire had gone.

He'd shut down again.

He turned and walked back into the bathroom, locking the door behind him.

CHAPTER FOUR

LIVIA GAZED OUT of the window of the Cessna they'd transferred to after landing at Fiji's Nadi airport and soaked in the oval-shaped patch of land that rose like a majestic tropical oasis from the South Pacific below. Ringed with golden sand and light turquoise shores that deepened to ultramarine, Seibua Island was far more beautiful and exotic than even its namesake had described.

Livia had only ever travelled from her Italian homeland to the US; the scents that exploded through her airways when she stepped onto the small airfield were ones she'd never had the pleasure of smelling before.

She stared up at the rising sun before closing her eyes and savouring the sensation of the most incredible warmth on her skin.

Then she cast a glance at Massimo to witness his reaction at his first steps on his grandfather's homeland.

Far from savouring anything, he'd immediately headed to the waiting golf buggy and was introducing himself to its elderly driver.

Like Livia, who'd changed into a knee-length red sundress, Massimo had donned summer clothing too, opting for a pair of black canvas shorts and a fitted navy T-shirt with the cover of a hellraising rock band's album on it. Ever the chameleon, he looked as divine in these casual items as he did in a full dinner jacket but it only made her think that he never looked better than when he wore nothing at all, and she had to push hard to rid her mind of the vivid image of him standing before her naked. It was a battle she'd been losing for the past four hours.

She forced a smile at the two young men who were removing their luggage from the small plane and loading it onto a second buggy, and walked over to Massimo, who introduced her to the man he employed to run the island for him, first in English then in Italian for her benefit.

She shook the extended hand from the friendly looking man and carefully said, 'It is nice to see you.'

She caught the dart of surprise that flashed in Massimo's eyes but he said nothing about her attempt at English, indicating only that she should get into the buggy.

She slid into the back and was relieved when Massimo climbed in the front beside the driver.

'How long until we get to the complex?' she asked. The island was bigger than she'd envisaged. Naively, she'd imagined something around the size of a small field with a solitary palm tree as a marker.

'Not long. Five or ten minutes.'

Soon the thick, scented flora they drove through separated and the golden sand she'd seen from the air lay before them, glimmering under the glorious sunshine.

Stunned, she craned her neck to take in the thatched chalets nestled—but not too closely together—along the length of a high rock formation that ended on the shore of the beach. A long wooden bridge led the eye to a further thatched chalet that appeared to rise out of the ocean itself. On the other side of the thatched cottages and lower down, separated from the beach by a wall, lay the chalet designated for Massimo's grandfather. Beside it lay a handful of smaller though no less beautiful chalets. To the right of all these dwellings was the centrepiece, the huge, multi-purpose lodge behind which, virtually camouflaged by the coconut palms and other tropical trees and foliage that thrived on the island, were the structures that housed the great kitchens and the island staff's living quarters. Further to the right, where the beach curved out of sight, were the mangrove saplings, recently planted in their thousands to protect the island from erosion and rising sea levels.

Everything Massimo had envisaged for the island of his grandfather's birth had come to life in spectacular fashion.

The driver stopped in front of the main lodge and said something to Massimo before jumping out.

Livia's heart almost dropped to her feet when Massimo followed suit and held his hand out to her.

Confused at this unexpected gesture, especially since they'd spent the past four hours after she'd inadvertently walked in on him naked ignoring each other's existence, she stared into the caramel eyes that were fixed on her with an intensity that belied the easy smile playing on his lips.

A child's cry rang out and in an instant she understood. Massimo's family were already there. He was holding his hand out because they must be watching.

She reached out and wrapped her fingers loosely round the waiting hand.

At the first touch of her skin to his, her heart flew from her feet to her throat and her fingers reflexively tightened.

For that one singular moment in time, the world paused on its axis as she stared into his soulful eyes and a rush of helpless longing swept through her, long-buried emotions rising up and clutching her throat.

And then the ground beneath her feet began to spin.

These were emotions she'd buried for a reason—because they had never been returned with the same depth with which she'd held them.

Turning her head and blinking the brief spell away from her vision, she was thankful to see Madeline on the steps that led to the main entrance of the lodge holding her infant daughter, Elizabeth. Dropping Massimo's hand, Livia hurried over to them and embraced her sister-in-law, careful not to squash baby Elizabeth, who immediately grabbed at her hair.

Massimo watched his wife and sister's embrace, watched them exchange enthusiastic kisses, watched his wife rub a finger against his niece's chubby cheek before lifting the child into her own arms, and had to fight to keep a lid on the emotions threatening to overwhelm him.

Livia had laughed at his suggestion that they have a child.

Slowly he made his way towards them, bracing himself for the rebuke that was certain to be coming.

Madeline didn't disappoint. After the obligatory kisses, she took Elizabeth back from Livia and hitched her to her hip. 'Massimo, meet your niece, Elizabeth. Elizabeth, this is the uncle you've heard about who's been too busy saving the world to meet you.'

Were it not for the large blue eyes of his six-month-old niece staring at him with fascination, he would have sworn at his sister. 'It's been a long journey here. Can you save the harassment until I've said hello to everyone else?'

His sister smiled beadily. 'Sure. The others are in the lodge waiting for you.'

The others were, in fact, his grandfather and his army of carers, and Massimo and Madeline's parents. Tomorrow night his grandfather's surviving siblings and their spouses, children, grandchildren and great-grandchildren would either fly or sail to the island for the birthday party. It would be the first time his grandfather had seen all but one of his siblings since he'd left the island paradise, one of the remotest and smallest of all the Fijian islands, for Europe. He'd been the first Seibua to leave. In the almost seventy years since his emigration the rest of the Seibuas had, one by one, left the island of their birth too in search of better opportunities to raise their families. Most had settled on Fiji's largest island, Viti Levu. The soon-to-be renamed Seibua Island had been uninhabited for over a decade before Massimo had purchased it.

The main lodge was everything the architect had promised. Massimo had wanted a space large enough to accommodate the entire extended family, whether it was for a sit-down meal or a party, and it had been created accordingly. Dining tables lined the walls to the left, plush sofas lined the walls to the right. A bar ran the length of the far wall. The space in between was large enough for a hundred people to dance or for an army of children to skid on and scuff the expensive flooring. He estimated that tomorrow evening there would be a minimum of fifteen children there to test it out.

For now, though, it was only immediate family there and the knotted weight of expectation that came with being them. Massimo hadn't seen any of them in over a year. But Livia had, and he watched her embrace his parents as if she were the child of their loins and not a mere daughter-in-law. She had never understood where his ambivalence to his family had come from. In his wife's eyes, he'd been raised with everything she'd wanted and been denied.

Livia's childhood had been torrid; filled with violence and menace, her father murdered before she reached double digits, her mother the manager of a wedding dress shop who sold drugs for extra cash along with the white lace creations. Her mother also received a monthly payment from Don Fortunato, the mafia boss Livia's father had protected. Blood money, Livia always disdainfully referred to it as. Money had never been an issue in the Esposito home. She'd told Massimo once of going into the back storeroom of her mother's shop and finding wads of cash wrapped in elastic bands in one of the boxes that was supposed to store garter belts. She'd estimated it at half a million euros. Money that belonged to Don Fortunato, stashed away until he came to reclaim it and launder it back into the world.

It had taken more guts than Massimo could comprehend for Livia to claw her way out of that violent, narcotic-infested world. She saw his childhood as idyllic, had no comprehension of what it was like to walk rain-lashed streets with holes in the soles of her shoes or to be the butt of school tormentors' jokes because the clothes you wore were two sizes too small and threadbare. He could have coped with being the butt of all the jokes if his parents had worked hard, as his one close friend's parents had, the father holding down two jobs, the mother working school hours, but they didn't. They hadn't. His father had worked in a shoe repair shop. By mutual agreement, his mother hadn't worked since Massimo's birth.

Life was for living! his father would proudly proclaim. Not for being a slave!

What did it matter if they could only afford to eat meat once a week? Their vegetable patch grew an abundance of nutritious food!

What did it matter if they couldn't afford to buy Massimo a new calculator when his was flushed down the toilet by his school tormentors? His brain was advanced enough to be its own calculator!

His brain was advanced enough to be its own calculator out of necessity, not design. And it had been advanced enough to know that if he wanted to make anything of his life it would have to come from him alone. From the age of thirteen, he'd worked for anyone who would employ him: running errands, stacking shelves, working on market stalls, cleaning offices. You name it, he'd done it. He'd bought his own computer and a phone, the rest of the money he'd stashed away for university, which was just as well as when it had come time for him to leave home for the wonder that was higher education, his parents had not had a single cent spare to help him.

It was during his university years that he'd created the platform game that had made him his initial fortune and also brought him closer to his grandparents. They'd moved to Rome when their daughter had married Massimo's Italian father and, their apartment being much closer to his university than his parents' home, had insisted he visit regularly for home-cooked food and a comfortable bed. It was in these years that he'd learned more about his grandfather's roots and heritage.

And now he was here in the place he'd visited only in his imagination, about to be closeted with his family for the first time in two years.

His parents' eyes were alight as he approached them.

What he intended to be a sedate, functional greeting was quickly turned into a greeting worthy of Hollywood. His father ignored his outstretched hand and pulled him into an embrace that would have squeezed the life out of a weaker man, then his mother did the same. Their exuberantly delivered words were lost amidst the planting of paternal and maternal kisses all over his face.

When he was finally able to disentangle himself, he turned to greet his grandfather and found himself faltering.

The wizened man sitting in a wheelchair with an oxygen tank attached…that was his grandfather? This was Jimmy Seibua?

Getting down to his haunches, Massimo stared into the filmy eyes that had once been the darkest chocolate then gently embraced him, his heart pounding with shock and pain.

It was like embracing a skeleton.

He hid his shock with the widest smile he could conjure. From the periphery of his vision he saw Livia speaking to one of his grandfather's medical team. He would talk to them too. Soon. When he was confident he could speak without ripping their heads off.

Soon the entire family was reclining together on sofas dragged together to form a square, his grandfather wheeled over to be with them, fresh coffee, pastries and fruit brought out for them to devour.

This should be a moment of great satisfaction for him but instead Massimo felt as if he'd been hit by an articulated lorry. His chest felt tight, as if all the air had been sucked out and his lungs and heart vacuum packed. He detested small talk at the best of times but right then he could hardly move his tongue to form simple words, responding to his brother-in-law's chat with grunts and monosyllables.

At his sister's instigation, he'd arranged for them to spend the day on the yacht he'd bought for the island, sailing out to a tiny atoll twenty kilometres away. This atoll was circled by a protected coral reef even more spectacular than the one surrounding Seibua Island and which cruise liners were forbidden from visiting.

Only another forty-eight hours to go until he could leave and return to his home and work in America.

He had a feeling these were going to be the longest forty-eight hours of his life. The distance between them had never felt greater. This was his family but he'd never felt a part of it. Part of *them*. Always he'd felt like the cuckoo in the nest. If he didn't have such a strong physical resemblance to his father and the colouring of his mother, he could easily believe he'd been adopted.

The only person he'd ever felt completely at ease with had been Livia but he now knew the ease had been a dopamine-induced illusion. She was sitting on the opposite sofa chatting to Madeline with baby Elizabeth on her lap, uncaring that her hair was being pulled by a tight, pudgy fist.

His estranged wife was more comfortable with his family than he was. The woman who'd laughed at having a child with him was laughing now, pretty white teeth gleaming where the sun's rays filtered through the high windows and bathed her in their light.

It was only when their eyes met that he saw the effort

it was costing her to maintain a carefree front. When he'd walked out of his bathroom naked and found her standing there...

He'd wanted to touch her with an ache that came from the very centre of his being.

The desire he'd thought had died with their marriage had come back to life as if it had never left. Livia still breathed in his blood. She pumped through his veins in a hot, relentless motion that seeped through his every pore, making his skin feverish.

There could be no going back. She was only there because of her love for his grandfather and her affection for the rest of his family.

Massimo waited until he'd drained his coffee before getting to his feet. 'I need to stretch my legs,' he announced. 'I'll see you all on the yacht in an hour.' Without waiting for a response, he strode out of the lodge and into the blazing sun.

His chalet was the one over the bridge and he headed towards it without breaking stride. His family didn't need him to entertain them. They were already settled in and relaxed in their surroundings, already tanned and glowing. All except his grandfather...

'Massimo, will you *wait*?'

Muttering a curse under his breath, he turned his head. Livia was hurrying in his direction, her hair flowing in a stream behind her.

'Problem?' he asked tightly when she reached him.

Livia snatched a breath of air. It had been years since she'd walked so quickly. 'I was going to ask you the same thing.'

His family had all turned their questioning eyes to her when he'd left the lodge. She'd shrugged apologeti-

cally and murmured that it had been a long flight before
following him out.

He grunted and set off again.

'Are you going to tell me what's on your mind?' she
asked when she caught up with him. Her short legs made
double his strides to keep pace.

'I'm going to call the owner of the agency.'

'What agency?'

'The one who supplied the nurses and carers who
were supposed to look after my grandfather. The agency
you used to work for.'

They both stepped onto the wooden bridge without
changing pace. It felt as substantial beneath her feet as
the earth itself. 'Why?'

'I chose that agency because my previous experience
with them was positive. I am disgusted that they've allowed him to get into this state. He's skin and bone.
When was the last time he had a shave? My grandfather
has shaved every day of his adult life and now he looks
like a homeless drug addict.'

They'd reached the door to their cabin but before he
could open it, Livia placed a hand on his wrist.

'I tried to warn you,' she said gently when he finally
met her gaze. A pulse throbbed in his jaw.

He closed his eyes then shook her hand away. 'I know
his cancer is incurable,' he bit out. 'That is no excuse for
allowing him to get in such a state.'

She sighed and followed him into the chalet. After
closing the door, she rested her back against it and tried
to think of the words to use that wouldn't add to his distress. For she was quite certain that his anger was nothing but a mask for his anguish at seeing first-hand how
close to death his grandfather really was.

'He's lost so much weight because he can't handle solid food any more,' she told him quietly. 'They can't shave him as often as he would like because his skin's become too sensitive. He can only cope with them doing it once a week.'

'You would make excuses for them,' he retorted scathingly. 'The medical profession always protects its own.'

'Even if I was still on the agency's books I wouldn't make excuses for medical negligence.'

The usually soulful eyes glittered menacingly. 'You accept they've neglected him?'

'No. They have given him exceptional care. The problem is it's been so long since you last saw Jimmy that the changes are more obvious to you.'

'I knew it wouldn't take long for you to get around to *my* supposed neglect of him.'

Livia sighed again in lieu of biting her tongue and in a vain effort to temper the anger rising in her. This was a weekend for celebration, not recriminations. Massimo was the one who had to live with his conscience, not her.

'Your grandfather is very ill, Massimo, but he's as comfortable and as pain-free as he can be. He's here on the island he loves with the family he loves. *You* made this happen, all of it. Don't spoil things for him by taking your anger at his condition out on those who have done their best for him.'

His jaw tightened as she spoke. For a long time he didn't respond, just stared at her until his nostrils flared and he gave a sharp nod. 'I need to call in with the office.'

This time her sigh was one of exasperation.

'I need to answer any questions the project manager has about the analysis and data before we set sail. Okay?'

She was glad he turned his back on her and strode through to the chalet's living room, his wretched phone already in his hand. It meant he didn't see the sheen of tears that suddenly filled her eyes.

CHAPTER FIVE

LIVIA TAMPED DOWN the gulf of feelings knotting her belly and boarded the white yacht. Although dwarfed in size by the cruise ship it was moored next to, it still dazzled with elegance. After their mammoth journey to the island she would have preferred to spend the day relaxing but this was the trip Madeline had forced Massimo to concede to. Livia knew what her sister-in-law was thinking: that forcing Massimo into close quarters would stop him hiding away.

Unfortunately, Madeline hadn't reckoned on Massimo boarding the yacht with his laptop case slung over his shoulder and his phone sticking out of his shorts pocket and Livia saw her lips pull in tightly. When they set sail, Livia was the only one secretly pleased when he made his excuses and disappeared inside.

Disappointment was writ large on his family's faces.

She met Madeline's gaze and shrugged apologetically.

Barely three hours with Massimo's family and she'd already made two silent apologies for him.

Sailing at a steady pace over the calm South Pacific, it took only an hour to reach the atoll. They whiled the time away in a lazy fashion, dipping in and out of the swimming pool and chatting. The captain anchored the yacht at a distance far enough away not to cause any damage to the precious reef but close enough for them all to see the clear turquoise water teeming with brightly coloured fish and all other manner of sea life. Madeline and Raul donned their snorkelling gear and jumped in, leaving baby Elizabeth in Sera's capable hands.

Livia looked out at Madeline and Raul having the time of their lives in the water, at Sera playing happily with her granddaughter, at her father-in-law Gianni, book in one hand, large cocktail in the other, at Jimmy napping in his wheelchair in a shaded part of the deck, at the chefs cooking up a storm on the barbecue and felt a sharp pang rip through her chest.

Massimo should be there with them.

She hurried down the stairs and slipped inside in search of him.

The interior of the yacht was vast and as sleek and as elegant as the exterior and refreshingly cool after the hazy heat on deck. It took a few minutes before she found him hidden in an isolated section of the saloon, tapping away on his laptop. So engrossed was he in his work that it took a few moments before he noticed her presence.

'Lunch is almost ready,' she said briskly.

'I'll be ten minutes.'

'And then you'll turn your laptop off and leave it off?'

'I can't.'

She inhaled deeply to smother her anger. 'Your family have been looking forward to spending time with you.'

'And they will.'

'When?' she challenged. 'Tomorrow, everything will be about the party and then you go back to LA. Today is the only day when it's just us and you're missing out.

You've travelled thousands of kilometres to be here. It's not going to kill you to turn your laptop off and spend some time with your family.'

His jaw clenched, his fingers now drumming on the table rather than tapping on his laptop.

Looking at the obstinate set of Livia's jawline, Massimo knew she wouldn't give him a moment's peace until he joined the rest of them on deck.

It wasn't that he disliked spending time with his family. Not really. It was that they were all so different from him. His approach to life was alien to them. They believed he worked too hard, never understanding that it was only when he was immersed in his work that he felt at peace with himself.

It would be easier to handle these few days with them if Livia weren't there. It was hard enough dealing with his family's suffocating love without adding his estranged wife and all the intense emotions she'd drawn back out of him into the mix.

How could he find ease in her company when his attention was consumed by her every movement? She stood a good five feet from him but awareness thrummed through him, a buzz on his skin, an itch in his fingers. Her black swimsuit was designed for functionality and not for flaunting her body but still he reacted as if she were wearing the skimpiest of bikinis. The itch in his fingers became unbearable when he noticed the smudge of mascara under her left eye from where she'd dried her face after her swim. He wanted to rub the smudge away.

He breathed in deeply through his nose and nodded. 'I'll turn my laptop off and join you in ten minutes.'

She inclined her head and backed away. Just when he

thought he was rid of her she fixed him with a hard stare counteracted by a quirking at the corner of her lips. 'If you get your phone out at all while we're on this yacht, I can't promise that it won't become fish food.'

Two hours later and Livia almost wished Massimo would return to the saloon and do more work.

After they'd eaten their long lunch; barbecued fish freshly caught that morning and an array of salads, she'd gone snorkelling with Madeline and climbed back on board to find Massimo had removed his T-shirt and draped it carelessly on the back of his chair.

Trying hard to blur his magnificent physique from her sight, she wrapped her beach towel around her waist while Madeline went straight to Raul, wrapped her arms around his neck and kissed the top of his balding head. In response, he twisted in his chair and squeezed her bottom.

Livia couldn't stop her eyes from seeking Massimo, her heart throbbing as she remembered a time when they'd been as tactile and affectionate together as his sister and brother-in-law were. Her insides heated to match the warmth on her skin when she found his gaze already on her. Was he remembering those heady, carefree days too...?

His eyes pulsed before he looked away and reached for the jug of fruit cocktail. He refilled his glass then filled another and pulled out the empty chair beside him. Livia sat, accepting the drink with a murmured thanks, and tried again to blur out his naked chest. Even with the parasol raised to shade them from the worst of the heat, the sun's rays were slow-roasting them. One of Jimmy's carers had taken him inside for a nap.

Madeline pulled a bottle of sunscreen from her bag. Once she and Raul had slathered themselves in it, she passed the bottle to Livia, who rubbed the lotion over her face, covered her arms, shoulders, the top part of her chest not covered by her swimsuit and her neck. But she couldn't reach all of her back.

'Here, let me.'

Of course Massimo would offer to help. They had a watching audience, just as they'd had when they'd arrived at the lodge and he'd offered his hand to help her out of the golf buggy. His offer was for their benefit. If not for them, he would probably let her burn.

Trying valiantly to keep her features nonchalant, Livia gave the bottle to Massimo and twisted in her seat so her back was to him.

The anticipation of his touch was almost unbearable. And when it came...

Her breath caught in her throat.

Darts of awareness spread through her, memories flooding her of the first time he'd applied sunscreen to her skin. They'd been on their honeymoon in St Barts. They'd sunbathed naked, secure in their privacy. Massimo had rubbed the lotion sensually over every inch of her skin. By the time he'd rolled her onto her back and driven deep inside her, she'd been wet and aching for him. It had been the quickest she had ever achieved orgasm.

Now, he applied the lotion to her back briskly. His indifference made her heart twist with sadness but she worked hard to keep her lips curved upwards.

His hands pulled away with an abruptness that made the twist in her heart turn to an ache.

'Turn around and I'll do your back,' she ordered,

proud that her voice was as bright as she intended for their watching audience.

As he was so tall and broad, there was a lot more skin to cover than the small area of exposed flesh on her own back.

Resisting the temptation to squirt it straight onto his back and have the fleeting enjoyment of watching him squirm at the quick shock of cold on his warm skin, she placed a healthy dollop into her palm, rubbed her hands together to spread it equally between them then placed them on his shoulder blades.

He still flinched.

She worked as briskly as he had to rub the lotion into his smooth skin.

When had she last touched his back? She couldn't remember. The coldness that had entered their marriage hadn't appeared overnight. It had accumulated over time until one day there was nothing but ice where once there had been love.

She had forgotten how much pleasure she got from simply touching him. Massimo carried so much on his shoulders. She'd loved to massage his knots away and feel him relax beneath her fingers. There were knots there now beneath the pads of her fingers, at the top of his spine and around his shoulder blades. Big ones.

Livia gritted her teeth and, dragging her hands from the knotted shoulders, swept down to the base of his back and covered the last bit that needed protection from the blazing sun.

The weight on his shoulders and the knots formed by it were none of her concern.

The moment she was done she pulled her hands away with the same abruptness that he'd done with her then breathed a quick sigh of relief when the captain appeared on deck, distracting everyone's attention. It was time to sail back.

His family's natural exuberance, which Massimo had never inherited, made sailing a noisy affair. The three women were in the pool swimming with his niece, laughing and splashing, leaving him at the table with his father, grandfather and brother-in-law, answering questions as best he could about the carbon filter he was days away from testing the prototype of. He could see the effort it was taking for them to concentrate.

He couldn't help his gaze drifting to the swimming pool, his attention as attuned as it had always been to Livia's every movement.

He was also intensely aware that she'd left her phone on the table and intensely ashamed that he wanted to snatch it up, take it somewhere private and trawl through all her communications over the past four months. He wondered how she would react if he were to throw it overboard and give it the same fate she'd threatened his own phone.

As if it were aware of his attention, her phone suddenly burst into life.

His father peered at it. 'Livia, Gianluca's calling,' he called to her.

'Coming!' She scrambled out of the pool, snatching her towel as she padded to the table, but her brother's call had gone to voicemail before she reached them.

Her brow furrowed. 'Excuse me a moment. I need to call him back.'

As she climbed the stairs to the top deck, Massimo's mother got out of the pool and joined them at the table.

'How is Gianluca doing?' she asked him in an undertone, concern writ large on her face. 'I know Livia has been very worried about him.'

But he never got the chance to ask what she was talking about for Madeline had sneaked up behind him and suddenly thrust a soaking Elizabeth into his arms. 'Here you go, Massimo. You can hold Elizabeth for me.'

'Where are you going?'

'Nowhere.' She stood at the balustrade with a cackle of laughter that produced laughs from his parents and a sound that could have been laughter too from his grandfather.

With a wriggling baby thrust upon him, Massimo filed away his mother's comment about Livia's youngest sibling as something to query later. Gianluca was the only member of Livia's family he'd met. He'd turned up at their wedding looking furtive, constantly looking over his shoulder. His behaviour, Livia had later explained, was a mirror of her own when she'd first left Naples, a habit it had taken her years to break.

He hoped Gianluca hadn't finally fallen into the life Livia had escaped from and which she'd so dearly hoped he would follow her out of.

Teenage boys were pack animals. That was Livia's theory for why he hadn't attempted to escape yet. He went around the Secondigliano with his gang of friends on their scooters, chasing girls, playing video games, employed by the brutal men who ran the territory to keep watch for enemies and the police. Livia was convinced that it was a life her brother didn't want but Massimo was equally convinced that Gianluca had been as seduced by it as the rest of her family had been and that sooner or later he would be seduced into committing a crime from which there would be no going back. Livia's strength of mind and moral code were rare.

He stood his niece on his lap and stared at her cherubic face and felt the tightness in his chest loosen. This little one would be raised with security and love. She would never be exposed to the danger and violence his wife and her siblings had lived.

Huge blue eyes stared back. Unable to resist, he sniffed the top of her head. She smelled of baby.

'When are you two going to have one of those?' Raul asked with a grin.

Ice laced like a snake up Massimo's spine in an instant.

All eyes focused on him...and the presence he sensed behind him. Livia had returned from her phone call.

She sat back down, phone clutched in her hand. 'It's not the right time for us to have a child,' she said and shrugged apologetically. 'You know the hours Massimo puts into his work.'

'You would work those hours if there was a child?' his mother said, looking at him with an air of bewilderment. It was a look he'd become used to during his childhood, a physical expression that the differences between Massimo and his family were felt as keenly by them as they were by him.

'My work is important,' he pointed out cordially. He didn't expect her to understand. To his parents, work was only important in as much as it paid the bills. That hadn't stopped his parents from accepting the luxury home he'd purchased for them and for which he footed all the bills *and* the monthly sum he transferred into their bank account for everything else they could possibly need. He did the same for his sister and his grandfather and for his father's siblings and their offspring. He would have done the same for his mother's siblings if she'd had any.

He had stopped them ever having to work again—work being something none of the extended Briatores had been enamoured with either—and still his work ethic bewildered them. He provided for them all and the source of their wealth came from the technology he was creating that would, hopefully, allow baby Elizabeth, along with future generations of Briatores, to live on a planet that wasn't a raging fireball. And still they stared at him with bewilderment, unable to comprehend why he worked as hard as he did.

'I know, but…' His mother must have sensed something from his expression for her voice trailed off.

Livia had no such sensibilities. Pouring herself a glass of fruit cocktail, she said, 'Your son is a workaholic, Sera. It makes for a lonely life for me. I could not bring a child into that.'

'You could get help,' his mother suggested hopefully.

Livia shook her head. 'In America, any help would be from English speakers. I've been trying to learn but it's very hard. I had a cut on my leg last year that needed stitching and it was very stressful trying to understand the staff at the hospital.'

Talk of that incident made Massimo's guts clench uncomfortably and his gaze automatically drift down to her leg. The scar, although expertly stitched and incredibly neat, was still vivid. Livia had gone for a swim in their outdoor pool in LA. One of the pebbled tiles around its perimeter had broken away leaving a sharp edge that she had sliced her calf on when hauling herself out of the pool. He'd been at his testing facility when she'd called to tell him about it, saying only that she'd cut her leg and needed help communicating with a medical practitioner about it. He'd sent Lindy, fluent in Italian, to deal with it and translate for her.

He'd been furious when he'd returned home that night and seen the extent of the damage. Seventeen stitches, internal and external. Her reply had been the coolest he'd ever received from her—up to that point anyway—Livia saying, 'I didn't want to make a drama out of it and worry you while you were driving.' He'd stared at her quizzically. Her lips had tightened. 'I assumed you would come.'

It wasn't his fault, he told himself stubbornly. He wasn't a mind reader. He couldn't have known how bad the damage had been.

The damage it had caused to their marriage in the longer term had been far more extensive.

'Look!' His sister's exclamation cut through his moody reminiscences.

Everyone followed Madeline's pointed finger. Holding Elizabeth securely in his arms, Massimo carried her to the balustrade. Swimming beside the yacht, almost racing them, was a pod of bottlenose dolphins.

Around thirty of the beautiful mammals sped sleekly through the water, creating huge white foams with their dives. It was as if they'd come to check them out and decided to stay for a while and play.

It was one of the most incredible sights he had ever seen and it filled him with something indefinable; indefinable because it was nothing he'd ever felt before.

He looked at Livia and the awed joy on her face and experienced a fleeting gratitude that she'd forced him from his work and enabled him to enjoy this priceless moment.

Elizabeth wriggled in his arms. He tightened his hold on her to stop her falling and, as he did, Livia's blame as to their childless state came back to him and the brief lightness that had filled his chest leached back out.

Livia tried her hardest to keep a happy front going but it only got harder as time passed. Gianluca hadn't answered her returned call and he hadn't called or left a message since.

And then there was Massimo.

The excitement of the dolphins racing so joyously alongside them had waned once they'd finally swum off and the lightness she'd witnessed in his eyes had quickly waned too. Was she the only one to notice his underlying tension? She would bet the knots on his shoulders had become even tighter.

Her assumption that he would keep the reasons for his anger to himself was dispelled when they returned to the island. His family retired to their chalets for a late siesta before dinner, leaving them together on the terrace of the lodge drinking a coconut and rum creation the head bar steward had made for them.

The moment they were alone, he fixed her with hard eyes. 'Why did you say all that rubbish about a baby?'

'What rubbish?'

'You let my family believe the issue of us not having children lies with me.'

'I'm prepared to pretend that our marriage is intact but I'm not prepared to tell an outright lie.'

'You're the one who didn't want a child. Not me.'

Confused, she blinked. 'When did I say I didn't want a child?'

His jaw clenched. 'You laughed when I suggested we have one.'

'Do you mean the time you suggested we have a child to cure me of my loneliness? Is that the time you're referring to?' Of course it was. It was the only time the subject of a baby had come up since their first heady days when they'd spoken of a future that involved children. 'I laughed at the suggestion, yes, because it *was* laughable. And even if you hadn't suggested a child as a sticking plaster for my loneliness I would still have laughed and for the reasons I shared with your mother—ours was no marriage to bring a child into.'

His hand tightened perceptibly around his glass. 'You made it sound like you're a neglected wife.'

'I *was* a neglected wife,' she bit back. 'Why do you think I left you? To pretend otherwise is demeaning—'

'You're here this weekend so my grandfather can spend what is likely to be his last birthday on this earth believing everything is fine between us,' he interrupted.

'We're not going to do that by pretending that you've suddenly turned into a model husband, are we? Your grandfather isn't stupid—none of your family are, and they're not going to believe a leopard can change its spots. I visited your family on my own and made excuses for you for over a year before I left and I've been doing the same for the last four months and they have been none the wiser about the state of our marriage. When we finally come clean that we've separated, the only surprise will be that it's taken me so long to see sense.'

Livia knew she was baiting him but she didn't care. She wanted him to argue with her. She'd always wanted him to argue back but he never did. It was a circle that had only grown more vicious as their marriage limped on; her shouting, him clamming up.

True to form, Massimo's mouth clamped into a straight line. He pushed his chair back roughly and got to his feet but before he could stride away as she fully expected him to do, he turned back around and glowered at her. 'Unless you want a fight over any divorce settlement, I suggest you stick to the plan and stop putting doubts about our marriage in my family's head. I don't care what my parents or sister think but I will not have my grandfather having doubts about us.'

'If you want a fight over the settlement then I'll give you a fight,' she said, outraged at his threat, 'but I *am* sticking to the plan! You've neglected your family for so long that they think it's normal that you neglect your wife too.'

'I'm not having this argument again.'

She laughed bitterly. Her hands were shaking. 'We never argued about it. Whenever I tried to tell you how unhappy I was, you walked away from me. You never wanted to hear it.'

'You were like a stuck record.' He made crablike pinching motions with his hands. 'I'm bored, Massimo,' he mimicked. 'I'm lonely, Massimo. Why do you work such long hours, Massimo?' He dropped his hands and expelled his own bitter laugh. 'See? I *did* listen. Maybe if you'd ever paused for breath between complaints I might have felt more incentivised to come home earlier each night.'

'I only complained *because* you work such stupid hours!'

His eyes were cold. 'I didn't force you to move to America. I didn't force you to marry me. You knew the kind of man I was before we married but you thought you could change me. Instead of solving your problems for yourself you sat around the house wallowing and complaining and expecting me to fix everything for you.'

'I never wallowed!' she said, outraged. Of all the things he'd just accused her of, for some reason that was the one that immediately bit the hardest. 'And as if I would have expected you to fix anything—you aren't capable of fixing anything to do with the human heart. You've spent so much time with your machines and gadgets that your heart has turned to metal.'

He took the three steps needed to smile cruelly down at her. 'You did nothing *but* wallow. And sulk. And complain. For the first few weeks after you left I thought I'd gone deaf.'

And then his smile turned into a grimace as he turned on his heel and, parting shot delivered, strode off leaving Livia standing there feeling as if he'd just ripped her heart out.

CHAPTER SIX

MASSIMO LOCKED THE bathroom door. He didn't trust Livia not to barge in.

He'd expected her to follow him to the chalet. Every step had been taken with an ear braced for a fresh verbal assault.

But the assault never came.

He turned the shower on and closed his eyes to the hot water spraying over his head.

Livia's defiant yet stricken face played in his retinas.

Guilt fisted his guts. He'd been cruel. The words had spilled out of him as if a snake had taken possession of his tongue.

Being here…with Livia, with his family, seeing how close to death his grandfather really was…it was all too much.

Hearing accusations of neglectful behaviour towards those he loved had driven like a knife in his heart.

He'd done his best for his family. They might not see him as much as they would like but he made up for his lack of presence in other ways.

And he'd done his best in his marriage. That his best did not live up to his wife's exacting standards was not his fault. Neglect seemed to suggest that she was a child who needed taking care of when they both knew Livia was more than capable of taking care of herself. This was the woman who'd survived the Secondigliano without being seduced by its violent glamour. This was the woman who'd discovered an affinity for nursing when the local doctor the neighbourhood gangsters visited to fix their gangland wounds recognised her coolness under pressure when one of her cousins got shot in the leg. From the age of fourteen Livia had been paid a flat fee of fifty euros a time to assist the doctor whenever required. Like Massimo, she'd stashed it away. Unlike Massimo, who'd saved his money in a box in his bedroom, never having to worry about his family stealing it from him, she'd kept her cash in a waterproof container under the vase in her father's grave. As she was the only mourner to place flowers on the grave, it was the only safe place she had for it.

She'd refused to be sucked into a life of crime. The only vice she'd picked up in her years where drugs were cheap and plentiful was cigarette smoking, which she'd quit when she'd achieved the grades needed to study nursing in Rome and taken all her cash and left the life behind her. She was as tough as nails. To suggest she needed caring for was laughable.

Finished showering, he rubbed his body with a towel then wrapped it around his waist. Bracing himself, he unlocked the door and stepped into the bedroom.

He'd been right to brace himself. Livia was sitting on the end of the bed waiting for him. But the fury he expected to be met with was nowhere to be seen. Her eyes, when he met them, were sad. The smudge of mascara was still visible.

After a moment's silence that felt strangely melancholic, she said, 'I don't want it to be like this.' It was the quietest he'd ever heard her speak.

He ran a hand through his damp hair and grimaced. 'I thought you wanted me to argue with you. Isn't that what you've always said?'

'Arguing's healthy, but this…?' Her shoulders and chest rose before slumping sharply, her gaze falling to the floor. 'I don't want us to be cruel to each other. I knew things would be difficult this weekend but…' Her voice trailed away before she slowly raised her head to meet his gaze. There was a sheen in her eyes that made his heart clench. 'This is much harder than I thought it would be.'

Massimo pressed his back against the bathroom door and closed his eyes. 'It's harder than I thought it would be too.'

'It is?'

He nodded and ground his teeth together. 'I shouldn't have said the things I said. I'm sorry.'

'I didn't know you felt like that.'

'I don't.' At her raised, disbelieving brow, he added, 'Not in the way I said it.'

'You made me sound like a fishwife.'

His lips curved involuntarily at the glimmer of humour in her tone. 'I was lashing out. Being with you…' The fleeting smile faded away. 'I can't explain how it makes me feel.'

'It just makes me feel sad,' she admitted with a whisper. Then she rubbed her eyes with the palms of her hands and took a deep breath. 'When the time is right for us to file the divorce papers, I won't be wanting a settlement.'

'I didn't mean it about fighting you. We can come to an—'

Her head shook. 'No. No settlement. You've given me enough money since we married. I've hardly spent any of it. I've enough to buy an apartment—'

'You were going to buy one when you went back to Rome,' he interrupted. 'You were supposed to let my lawyer know when you'd found somewhere.' He'd informed his lawyer and accountant that Livia would be purchasing a home in Italy in her sole name and that funds should be made available to her when she got in touch with them about it, no questions asked. He didn't care what she spent.

He'd specifically told them to go ahead without notifying him. He hadn't wanted to know when she'd made that last, permanent move out of his life for reasons he couldn't explain, not even to himself.

Massimo ran his eyes over his finances once a year when it was tax season and that was for scrutiny purposes. He would have noticed then, he supposed, that she hadn't bought herself a home.

'I've been renting my old place.' Actually buying herself a home of her own had felt too final, Livia realised. It would have been the ultimate confirmation that their marriage was over for good.

Had she been living in denial? And if so, what had she been holding out for? Miracles didn't exist. The cruel truth was that she and Massimo were wholly incompatible and she'd been a fool for believing differently. She'd known it when she'd left. It hadn't stopped her heart skipping every time her phone had buzzed only to plummet when his name didn't flash on the screen. It hadn't flashed once since their separation.

'Once everything's out in the open, I'm going to go

back to nursing,' she added, fighting back a well of tears. To cry in front of him would be the final indignity.

He rested his head back against the bathroom door with a sigh. 'You don't need to work, Liv.'

The simple shortening of her name…oh, but it made her heart *ache*. Massimo was the only person in the world who'd ever shortened her name. And then he'd stopped calling her Liv and started calling her Livia like everyone else. And then he'd stopped calling her anything.

Blinking away the tears that were still desperately trying to unleash, she sniffed delicately and gave a jerky nod. 'I need a sense of purpose. I like knowing the money in my pocket is earned by my own endeavours. I never wanted to be a kept woman.'

His throat moved before he gave his own nod. 'At least let me buy you a home like we agreed I would. The law entitles you to much more.'

And he would give it, everything the law said she was entitled to and more. If only he were as generous with his time as he was with his money…

But those were pointless thoughts to have. Massimo was who he was, just as Livia was who she was. They'd tried. They'd failed.

She just wished she could find a way to stop her heart from hurting so much.

'Thank you.' Swallowing hard to dislodge the lump in her throat, she got to her feet. 'I'll leave you to get changed. I'm going to make myself a coffee—would you like one?'

'That would be great, thank you.'

She smiled and left the bedroom and kept smiling as she made the coffee, smiling so hard that eventually the tears sucked themselves dry and her cheeks ached miserably in their place.

It didn't occur to her until she was standing under the shower an hour later that this was the first real conversation she and Massimo had had that hadn't descended to insults and recriminations in over a year.

The cloudless sky had turned deep blue, the sun a deep orange shimmering on the horizon when Livia ventured out of the chalet in search of Massimo. She found him on the wrap-around veranda drinking a bottle of beer and looking at his phone, wearing a pair of old battered jeans and a crisp white shirt, a booted foot hooked casually on his thigh.

It was the first time she'd been at the rear of their chalet and she tried hard not to let sadness fill her as she recalled poring over the architect's designs for it, imagining all the happy times she and Massimo would spend here. This chalet had been the only part of the complex Massimo had taken a real interest in. They'd chosen to build it high on the jutting mound of earth that, when the tide was low, could be walked to along a sandy pathway created by nature at its finest. This was supposed to be their own private hideaway in their private paradise. Their horseshoe swimming pool, garden and veranda were entirely hidden from prying eyes.

She hadn't been able to bring herself to think about the sleeping arrangements that night. Their chalet only had one bed. It was a huge bed but, still, it was only the one bed. She supposed she could sleep on the sofa. Massimo's long frame would never fit on it.

His eyes widened slightly when he looked up as she approached and he unhooked his foot and straightened.

The vain part of her bloomed to see his response. Although it was only a family meal they were going to have, she'd applied her make-up and done her hair with care. She'd been mortified to look in the mirror and see a huge smudge of mascara under her left eye.

But it wasn't vanity that had propelled her to make an effort. It was armoury. When she looked her best it had the effect of boosting her morale and for all the unspoken truce they'd forged, her emotions were all over the place. She needed every piece of armour she could find to hold herself together.

Massimo turned his phone off and tried hard to temper the emotions crashing through him. Livia had dressed casually in a pair of tight white three-quarter-length trousers and a shimmering red strappy top that stopped at her midriff. On her feet were high, white strappy sandals that elongated her frame but did nothing to diminish her natural curves.

A lifetime ago he would have beckoned her over, put his hands on her hips and pulled her to him.

The instant awakening of his loins proved, as if it needed proving, that nothing had changed. He still wanted her with an ache he felt deep in his marrow.

Inhaling deeply through his nose, he willed the thudding of his heart to steady.

'You're ready?' he asked.

She nodded.

He finished his beer and got to his feet.

In silence they walked the veranda to the front of the chalet and headed to the lodge. The tide had risen in the past two hours, the sandy path now mostly submerged beneath the powerful ocean and the colourful, tropical fish that swam in it. Its gentle rhythm was soothing.

His family had beaten them to the lodge and were all sitting around a set dining table chatting noisily. One of his grandfather's carers sat discreetly in a far corner of the lodge reading a book.

The meal passed quickly. His grandfather was tired and, fed by Massimo's mother, ate only his soup before retiring for the night. Madeline and Raul quickly followed, taking an increasingly fractious Elizabeth, who'd turned her nose up at all the offerings they'd tried to tempt her with. Considering it looked like mushed vomit, Massimo didn't blame her for smacking the plastic spoon out of her mother's hand. When his brother-in-law attempted to feed her, her little face turned bright red with fury. If Massimo had been offered that excuse for food, he'd have been tempted to screw his face up and bawl too.

He was about to rise and retire to the chalet to check in on work, when his father's suggestion of a game of Scopa, the traditional Italian game played with an Italian forty-card deck, gave him pause.

His mother's hopeful gaze made his ready refusal stick on his tongue before he could vocalise it.

He didn't need to look at Livia to know she was beseeching him with her eyes to accept too. Her earlier insistence that his family wanted only to spend time with him kept ringing in his ears.

He stretched his mouth into the semblance of a smile. 'Sure.'

The beaming grins made his chest tighten.

He signalled to the barman. Soon, a bottle of bourbon, a bucket of ice and four glasses had been taken to the outside table they now sat around. Massimo and his father formed a team and sat opposite each other, the ladies playing as the opposing team. Livia sat beside his father, his mother beside Massimo. He shuffled the cards, dealt them three each and four face up on the table. The first game of Scopa began.

What began as a sop to please his parents turned into a couple of hours' mindless fun under the warm starry sky. His parents were the most laid-back, easy-going people on the planet but when it came to card games, they became ultra-competitive.

And Livia's competitive streak came out too. His wife and mother were both determined to beat their spouses and were not above cheating to achieve this. When the women were two nil down, suddenly they both found it necessary to halt the game for frequent bathroom breaks.

Soon after this mysterious onset of bladder issues, he spotted his mother furtively pulling something out of her handbag, which, when she was challenged, turned out to be a king with a value of ten points. Rather than display any shame, his mother giggled. Livia though…her throaty cackle of laughter filled his ears and suddenly he was thrown back to his sister's wedding and the first time he'd heard it.

It was a sound that speared him.

Firmly dragging his mind away from that fateful first meeting, he confiscated the card but then found he couldn't stop his own burst of laughter when, barely a minute later, Livia stood to use the bathroom for the fourth time and two high-value cards slipped out of her top.

'Shameless,' he chided with a stern shake of his head.

'All's fair in love and war,' she replied, a gleam in her eye he hadn't seen for so long that suddenly he could fight the swelling emotions no more, body blows of longing and pain ravaging him.

He couldn't tear his gaze from her.

In the beat of a moment her amusement vanished and her dark brown eyes were swirling with more emotion than there were stars in the sky.

Hardly single-digit seconds passed as their stares remained fixed on each other but those seconds contained so much weight he felt its compression on his chest. He knew with a bone-deep certainty that she was thinking about their first meeting too and that the memory lanced her as deeply as it did him.

Then Livia turned her gaze from him.

'I really do need to use the bathroom,' she murmured, reaching down to pick up the illicit cards and placing them on the table.

In the plush ladies' room, Livia put her hands on the sink and dragged air into her lungs.

For a moment there her heart had felt so full of so many emotions that it had felt as if it could burst out of her chest.

Teaming up with Sera against their husbands had been so wickedly joyful that for a while she had forgotten that she and Massimo were estranged and preparing for a divorce.

For a short, glorious time, it had been like slipping on a pair of shoes that transported them to their early days when there had been as much fun in their marriage as there had been desire and love.

She had adored making Massimo laugh. He was such a serious person that to see his face light up had brought her more joy than anything. Laughter had been in short supply in her childhood so to discover this side of herself with him had been joyful in its own right.

Like the smiles she'd been unable to form in the four months since she'd left him, laughter had become a distant memory too. Until tonight.

Back outside in the warm evening air, she found the cards had been put away and the glasses empty. Sera and Gianni got to their feet as she approached the table and both apologised for having to call it a night. They were tired and needed to get some sleep.

Kissing them both goodnight, Livia poured herself another bourbon and watched them walk away.

The silence they left behind was stark. Apart from the white noise in her ears.

'I suppose we should go to our chalet too,' she said, avoiding Massimo's stare.

They'd spent a whole day travelling between time zones quickly followed by a day out at sea. All of this, when added to her frazzled nerves brought about by being with him again, was a recipe for exhaustion. Yet she felt anything but tired.

When he didn't answer, she stared up at the sky. The stars were in abundance that night, twinkling like gold diamonds in the vast blackness. She'd thought the sky in LA was big but here, on this island, it seemed to stretch for ever.

'I'll sleep on the sofa,' she added into the silence.

'No. You take the bed.' She felt his eyes on her. 'I've work I need to get on with.'

'The sofa's too small for you, and you can't work all night.' But he could. She knew that. He'd worked through the night on many occasions.

'I'll work for a few hours then sleep on the hammock.'

'We have a hammock?' That was the first she'd heard of it.

'I'm surprised you didn't notice it earlier. It's on the veranda by the outside table.'

'I probably didn't register it,' she murmured, taking a hasty sip of her bourbon.

She wouldn't have noticed any hammock because when she'd stepped out onto the veranda her eyes had been too consumed by Massimo to register anything else.

They finished their drinks and, as silently as they'd made the walk from their chalet to the lodge, walked the return journey together. The incoming tide now lapped the beach noisily, so deep beneath the bridge that if this had been her first sight of the island she would never have believed it could ebb back far enough for a sandy pathway to open up between the main island and their private peninsula.

But as much as she tried to distract herself with their surroundings she couldn't block out Massimo's lean frame striding beside her.

When they reached their chalet, he picked up the briefcase he'd left on their dining table.

Everything about this chalet was supposed to be theirs. Everything had been designed to their exact instructions; a love nest they'd imagined themselves escaping to whenever time allowed, designed and dreamed up before Livia had realised time would never allow it. For Massimo, time existed only for work.

He stared at her for a moment before his chest rose sharply. 'I'll work on the veranda. Sleep well.'

Her goodnight to him came out as a whisper.

He closed the door quietly behind him.

* * *

Massimo powered his laptop but, other than reply to a few urgent emails, found he didn't have the concentration to work.

Sighing heavily, he ran his fingers through his hair and closed his eyes.

It felt as if he'd slipped into a time loop, taken back to the days when he'd worked from the sprawling building that homed Briatore Technologies and found his concentration fighting a war with himself. Livia had taken back possession of his mind. She'd been all he could think of then. She was all he could think of now.

It didn't matter, he told himself grimly. One more full day and night and then that would be it for them. She would live her life in Italy and he would live his in LA.

Thinking he could do with another drink before attempting to sleep in the hammock he'd instructed be erected when he'd remembered the chalet he would share with his estranged wife had only one bed, he padded quietly back inside. Before he could switch the light on and head to the bar, he noticed a slant of light coming from beneath the closed bedroom door.

His heart fisted.

He'd left her over an hour ago, plenty of time for her to do her night-time beauty routine and fall asleep. Was she reading?

Was she wearing the cream pyjamas that managed to be both modest and yet revealing…?

He stepped closer to the bedroom door, his ears craning when he heard her voice. She was talking to someone.

A lover?

Hating himself yet unable to stop, he put his ear to the door. The wooden barrier muffled her words.

She laughed. It sounded pained. And then she said something distinguishable even through the muffling.

'Please. I love you.'

CHAPTER SEVEN

NIGHTMARES HAD PLAGUED Livia's life as far back as she could remember but it was rare for them to pepper her sleep over a whole night. After a night of exactly that and feeling distinctly unrefreshed, she showered and dressed quickly, choosing a black bikini, mid-thigh-length denim shorts and a loose white top.

Years of practice had allowed her to switch her mind off from her brother's problems—she would never have slept a wink if she hadn't—but last night his problems had been too great to stop her from worrying.

She had a feeling that even without Gianluca's issues overshadowing everything, she would still have had problems sleeping. She had never successfully learned to switch her mind off from her husband.

Their bed had been everything they'd been promised, like sleeping on a supportive cloud. Having never shared it with Massimo, she'd assumed she'd be all right sleeping in it alone but her twitchy body had betrayed her. This was a bed designed for lovers, chosen when divorce hadn't entered her head.

Before leaving the chalet she checked her phone, hoping Gianluca had messaged as he'd promised he would. Her chest loosened a fraction to see his simple message on the screen telling her he was fine and that nothing had happened.

The message did nothing to quell the sick dread curdling in her stomach.

Out on the veranda she wasn't surprised to find Massimo awake, dressed in the same clothes he'd worn the previous evening, and drinking a cup of coffee at the table. He must have made it while she'd been showering.

He would have heard the shower. He would have known she was awake. He hadn't thought to make her a coffee too.

It hurt that he hadn't thought of her, especially since she'd made him a coffee barely twelve hours ago. It had been an attempt at a peace offering she'd assumed—wrongly—that he'd accepted.

Her attention was caught by the hammock behind him swinging between the low roof of the chalet and one of the palm trees.

How had she not noticed it before?

Pushing petty thoughts of coffee aside, she inclined her head towards the hammock. 'How did you find sleeping on that?'

He shrugged in answer.

'I don't mind sleeping on it tonight.'

'No need,' he answered sardonically. 'It was fine.'

'But it doesn't seem fair...'

'I said no need,' he said through what sounded like gritted teeth before rising to his feet. 'I'm going to take a shower.'

Her eyes narrowed. Since when did Massimo wake up in such an obviously foul mood? She had a strong inkling his ire was directed at her, although she couldn't think what she'd done to cause it. 'Suit yourself. I'm going to make a coffee. I would offer you one but seeing as you've already taken care of yourself, I won't bother.'

His smile was as cutting as his tone had been. 'Good.'

Despite her much shorter legs, Livia made it to the chalet ahead of him.

Inside, he strode past her and into the bedroom, closing the door firmly behind him.

She scowled at the door and wished she had laser eyes that could cut through it and zap him.

She hoped he regretted suggesting the main bathroom be adjacent to where they slept.

In the small yet eye-wateringly expensive kitchen area, she opened a cupboard door, removed a glass mug then closed it with a slam. One small spoonful of sugar was thrown into the mug before she snatched an espresso pod and rammed it into the machine, then punched the button to get it working.

Alone in the bathroom, Massimo looked at the beauty paraphernalia left higgledy-piggledy all over the ledge and rammed his hands into his pockets to prevent them sweeping the entire lot onto the floor.

From the sounds of banging coming from the kitchen area, Livia was having more trouble controlling her own temper. But then, she always had.

His fury, he recognised in a dim, grim fashion, should be aimed at himself.

Until he'd heard her utter words of love to another, he'd never believed in his heart that she'd found someone else. The confirmation that she had a lover had come as a bigger blow than he'd ever imagined it could.

Seeing her in the flesh for the first time since hearing that confirmation had lanced him; a different pain from the constant ache he'd learned to live with since she'd left him. This pain went far deeper.

How could he go on pretending all was well in their marriage knowing another man had kissed those lips, knowing her pretty hands had touched another's body?

Was it for her lover that she'd cut her hair and added colour to it?

Nausea roiled deep in his stomach and he stripped his clothes off and threw them onto the floor, kicking his jeans for good measure.

Knowing that volatile emotions were usually his wife's domain only increased his temper.

Setting the temperature to cold, he stood under the frigid water for as long as he could bear it. It did little to temper the violent emotions churning in him.

After donning shorts and a T-shirt in his private dressing room—at least he was spared having to dress surrounded by Livia's clothing—he stepped back into the bedroom and this time was unable to stop his eyes falling to the neatly made bed.

It was a habit he'd never been able to break her out of. In LA she'd insisted on making it herself even though his housekeeping team would go into their bedroom later on and remake it to hotel standards.

The tightness in his lungs loosened a little.

He shouldn't take his unfathomable jealousy out on Livia. She had done nothing wrong. Their marriage was over.

But his calm rationale flew out of the window when he went back into the main living area and found her slumped on the sofa, her feet on the coffee table, ankles hooked together, fingers flying on the screen of her phone, concentration etched on her face. An empty glass mug lay on a coaster only inches from her bare feet.

More contact with her lover? he wondered bleakly.

She didn't look at him but a mutinous expression he recognised formed on her face. 'Are you going to tell me what I've done to upset you?'

'You haven't done anything,' he answered stiffly.

She made a pft sound he recognised. It had become a familiar sound in the months leading up to her leaving him.

'I didn't sleep well,' he confessed, attempting a less hostile tone.

'You said you'd been fine on the hammock.'

'It wasn't the hammock. I couldn't switch my mind off.' This much was the truth. How could he sleep when his mind tortured him with images of his wife with another man?

Now her eyes did rise to meet his. He saw suspicion in the dark brown depths. After long moments, she sighed and put her phone down on the coffee table. 'Okay,' she said with a shrug.

Massimo was an insomniac, Livia reminded herself. Switching his mind off enough to sleep was a battle he'd fought his entire life.

But never, not even when they'd been in the midst of their cold war, had he woken in such an obviously foul temper. She didn't believe for a minute that it was lack of sleep causing his current mood but experience had taught her the futility of trying to get him to open up.

Her phone vibrated and bounced on the table. Snatching it up, she read the message that had pinged in and sighed again.

'Problem?' Massimo asked.

Even though she could feel the animosity in his politely delivered question and even though his bad mood had perversely put her in a bad mood too, the growing panic in her belly needed an outlet.

She rubbed her eyes with the palms of her hands and looked back at him. 'Gianluca.'

A furrow grooved in his brow. 'What's happened?'

'Don Fortunato's requested a meeting with him.' She didn't need to tell him what that meant. She had spared him nothing about the world she'd grown up in. The meeting could only mean one thing—that Gianluca would be invited to 'prove' himself. If he proved himself successfully then he would become one of Don Fortunato's trusted foot soldiers, a marked step up from his current role as a watcher.

The groove deepened. 'Requested? So he hasn't met with him yet?'

'Not yet, no. He's been summoned to his home this evening.' If Gianluca wanted the life Don Fortunato was offering, this would be a summons he'd been hoping for. Their father's loyalty and death had marked all the Esposito children as foot soldiers of the future. Now it was Gianluca's turn to prove himself a man.

'What's he going to do?'

'I don't know.' She pinched the bridge of her nose and tried to calm her rabid thoughts. Pasquale had been summoned for this same meeting within days of his sixteenth birthday. Livia had lost him that night. Gianluca's immaturity must have been noted for he'd been given an extra two years before his summons. It felt as if she'd spent these two years doing nothing but beg him to take the lifeline she was offering and escape.

If he went ahead and met Don Fortunato tonight,

there would be no escape. Whatever he was tasked to do would be much more than dipping a toe in their criminal world.

'I've offered him money and I've already got a room set up for him at my apartment. He wants to leave but he's scared.' And she was scared too; far more frightened for her baby brother than she had ever been for herself.

'When did he tell you this?'

'Last night. He called when I was in bed.'

'Last night?' he clarified. There was an expression on his face, a flickering she couldn't interpret.

She nodded heavily. 'He's always known this day would come but inside he always thought it would be tomorrow. He's been happy roving around with his friends on their stupid scooters and chasing girls… How cruel is fate that the day it comes I'm on the other side of the world and unable to help him?'

All the plans she'd made to help him flee were worthless. She was too far away. Gianluca was technically an adult but emotionally he was still a child. She didn't know if he had the strength to break away without her own strength to encourage and sustain him.

She watched Massimo stride to the kitchen area and pull two glass mugs out of the cupboard.

'How did you escape, Livia?' he asked thoughtfully, placing both mugs in the coffee machine.

'You know how. I took my money and jumped on a train and never looked back.'

He put a large pod in the machine and pressed the button. 'You did that without help?'

'You know I did but I wasn't in his position.'

'Has Gianluca saved any money?'

'No.' Saving was an alien concept to her brother.

'I've offered to transfer him the money for his ticket out but he's scared to take it. He knows they're watching him.'

Frustration burned deeply enough for her to want to scream. Gianluca looked up to her. If she were in Italy she would be right there, her hand extended, a source of strength and a physical reminder that it was possible to leave and possible to build a good life outside the Secondigliano.

'Are you sure he wants to leave?'

'*Yes.* The summons has frightened him.' She managed a twisted smile then twisted her fingers together to stop herself biting the horrible gel stuff off her nails. 'I think my baby brother has grown up overnight.'

He stirred their coffees and carried them over, handing one to her.

Strangely, the hostility that had been shooting off him had gone.

He sat opposite her. 'Let me speak to him.'

'You? What for?'

'I can help.'

'How? You're as far away from him as I am.'

'But I have resources at my disposal that you don't. Have you heard of Felipe Lorenzi?'

She shook her head.

'He's ex-Spanish Special Forces and now runs his own security business protecting high-profile people. He only employs other ex-special forces. They're the best at what they do and used to dangerous situations. They can get him out safely.'

She stared at him dumbly. She'd confided in Massimo only because her fears for her brother had grown so large she'd felt as if she would explode if she kept them contained a minute longer. She hadn't expected him to offer help. It hadn't crossed her mind.

'You would do that?' she whispered. She hardly dared allow hope to fight through the fear. If they could get Gianluca out before his meeting with Don Fortunato, before he was tasked with something that would cross the line for ever and before he was made privy to the secrets that would put a mark on his head, then there was a good chance he would be left in peace.

He reached into his pocket and pulled out his phone. 'Leave it with me. By the time of my grandfather's party tonight, your brother will be out of the Secondigliano and free.'

Having Livia's brother to concentrate on and the preparations for the party that evening to oversee helped the day pass quickly. It kept Massimo's mind occupied. It stopped him having to think of the relief that had almost doubled him over to learn his wife hadn't been exchanging endearments with a lover.

She'd been talking to her brother.

But this only caused a shadow to form on his relief because he knew he had no right feeling relief. He had no business feeling what he'd felt.

Knowing how he should feel and behave did nothing to stop the twisting ache that had burrowed in his guts and set up home in his short time on the island. He had to get a grip on it. One day in the future Livia would find a new lover who could give her the happiness she deserved, a man who could give her the attention and time she needed.

He couldn't imagine meeting anyone for himself. A casual lover, possibly, if his body ever became receptive to a woman who wasn't his wife. He would certainly never marry again. Or have children. Before he'd met Livia he'd never even thought of having children. The subject had completely passed by his radar.

Her pointed remark that theirs had been no marriage to bring a child into had hit a nerve with its truth. He would be as lousy a father as he'd been a husband.

Before he could switch his mind away from his latest bout of acidic ruminations and call his PA for a business update, he spotted two figures approaching in the distance. Livia was returning from her walk with his grandfather. They'd gone for an exploration of the island that had been his grandfather's home together. She was the only member of the family Massimo felt comfortable for his grandfather to spend time alone with. If there was an emergency she would know exactly what to do.

Whatever his conflicting feelings towards his estranged wife, he would never deny that she was an exceptional nurse who'd cared for his grandfather with a devotion that had allowed the entire family to sleep at night. Her return to nursing would be other cancer sufferers' gain.

He failed to stop his heart blooming as she neared him. His blood stirred too, thickening the closer she came. She'd removed her T-shirt and tied it around her waist, exposing her bikini-clad breasts, which swayed gently as she walked towards him pushing the wheelchair. Her hair, normally worn loose, had been pulled into a high ponytail, no doubt to counter the heat coming from the blazing sun. Her golden skin had darkened in their short time on the island and it suited her beautifully.

His grandfather had fallen asleep. She adjusted the

parasol above him then gave Massimo a cautious smile.
'Any news?'

He looked at his watch. 'One hour.'

Felipe's wife, Francesca, was about to go into labour
with their second child so his right-hand man, Seb, was
coordinating events. Seb had been confident they could
get Gianluca out without anyone noticing their presence.
But this depended on Gianluca following the plan and
being in the right place at the right time without changing his mind.

If Gianluca had half the strength of mind his sister
had, then everything would go well.

If was a big word and Massimo had his doubts. He
hoped for Livia's sake that Gianluca went through with
it. He didn't like to think of her devastation if the opposite happened.

She would cope though. That was one thing he didn't
doubt. Livia was a tough cookie. The life she'd lived, the
life they were now trying to remove her brother from,
had made her that way.

This was the first time since he'd met her, though,
that the reality of her childhood had seeped into their
life together. Her childhood had always been stories nar-
rated from the safety and comfort of their bed, fables
completely removed from his own existence. He'd appreciated intellectually what an awful life it had been
for her but this was the first time he'd really *felt* it. It
was as if her fear had transplanted like ice in his heart.

'As soon as I have word, I will let you know,' he promised. Gianluca had been instructed to turn his phone off
in case it had a tracker in it. Massimo had already or-
ganised a replacement one for him.

'Thank you.' Her lips pulled together before her chest and shoulders rose then fell sharply. 'Whatever happens... thank you.'

His own chest inflated at this simple, sincere gratitude. He hadn't offered assistance out of any form of altruism. Livia had needed help and he'd been in a position to provide it...

He'd never seen fear on her face before. He defied any man in his position not to offer their help too.

It struck him then that in the whole of their marriage she had never asked for or needed his help for anything of importance. Not once. All she'd ever wanted from him was the one thing he'd been unable to give. His time.

Her shoulders rose again. 'I'm going to find one of Jimmy's carers and get them to put him to bed, then I'll be back out to help...if you want it?'

As she spoke, a golf buggy delivering the first batch of workers for the evening's party emerged from the thick forest. There was much to oversee to ensure the event went perfectly. His family had offered help earlier but he'd refused, told them to enjoy their last full day on the island. This was something he'd wanted to do himself. His last gift to his grandfather.

About to give the same refusal to Livia, he found his tongue forming words of its own accord. 'If you haven't anything better to do.'

Her smile this time was wide. 'Only sunbathing, which bores me.'

She wheeled his grandfather away.

He closed his eyes and breathed deeply, telling himself he'd accepted her offer so as to give her something to distract herself with while they waited for news on her brother.

The acid burning in his guts exposed that for the lie it was.

Livia, her head upside down, dried her hair on a low setting and tried to pretend she wasn't keeping an ear out for Massimo. He'd sent her back to their chalet over an hour ago saying he'd join her shortly. The party was due to start in thirty minutes and he still needed to shower and dress. This was cutting it fine even for the man who could get himself ready in ten minutes flat.

Together, they'd supervised the arrival of the vast volume of staff employed for the evening, the exquisite finger buffet the army of chefs had spent the day preparing, the decoration of the interior and exterior of the lodge, the quantities and varieties of drink, made sure the extra chalets some of the guests were staying in for the night were ready, and fielded a constant flow of calls.

During all this, Massimo had kept her updated on Gianluca. As of three hours ago her brother was in a hotel two hundred miles from Naples. Tomorrow he'd be moved from the hotel to her rented apartment.

Knowing her brother was safe and had turned his back on the life she too had fought so hard to escape from had left her dizzy with relief. Every part of her felt the relief, her lungs looser, her limbs stronger, her shoulders lighter. She could hardly wait to get back to Rome and smother him.

Massimo's help in extracting Gianluca...

She'd learned at much too young an age that to get through life she could only rely on herself. Self-reliance had been so inured in her that it had never occurred to her to ask for help. She'd always managed alone.

It was the first time anyone had ever removed a burden from her shoulders and her heart swelled in gratitude for it.

Maybe Gianluca would have found the nerve to leave on his own that day with nothing but a transfer of money from her and the promise of her apartment but there was no doubt that Massimo taking control of the situation had given Gianluca the final injection of courage he needed. *He'd* been the one to talk Gianluca round.

When Gianluca had called her from the hotel, he'd been relieved to be out but torn at all he was leaving behind. She understood those feelings. They were the same emotions she'd lived through. As dangerous an environment as the Secondigliano was, it was where their family and friends were. It was their home. Starting over was never easy.

Leaving Massimo had been harder than leaving her family. She'd never felt an atom of relief at leaving him, only overwhelming pain. The future without him had never appeared bright, only bleak.

There had been times that day when she'd found herself staring at him with a heart so full she'd felt the individual heavy beats vibrating through her body.

There had been times, too, when she'd had to turn her face away from him and blink back hot tears at all they had lost. Today, working together harmoniously, supporting each other, teasing each other, laughing… it was like being thrown back to the early days of their marriage.

Why had they thrown it away?

When she'd finished drying her hair, she heard yet another small plane flying low over the cabin. More guests arriving. Unfortunately—or fortunately, depending on your perspective of paradise being spoilt by a mile-long runway—the island only had the capacity to admit small aircraft, so half the guests were being flown in as the staff had been: tag-team-style. The remaining guests were sailing to the island on Massimo's yacht.

She'd just finished applying her lipstick when the bedroom door opened and Massimo's reflection appeared in the mirror.

She stared at him, her chest filling so hard and so quickly that it pushed the air from her lungs.

She cleared her throat and turned around to face him properly, trying desperately hard to mask the turbulence raging beneath her skin. 'I was about to send a search party out for you.'

Caramel eyes glittered. His throat moved a number of times before he responded with a gruff, 'I had a work call I needed to take care of. Give me ten minutes?'

She nodded.

He strode to the bathroom door and turned the handle.

As he pushed it open, he suddenly stopped and turned back to face her. His throat moved again. 'You look beautiful.'

CHAPTER EIGHT

THE SETTING SUN bathed the lodge in a warm golden glow. The glow bounced off the delicate lights that adorned the exterior of the lodge and the high trees nestled around it, creating a sight that made Livia sigh with pleasure. The abundance of flowering shrubs filled the air with exotic scents that seemed more pronounced than usual to her sensitised state.

The lodge's huge double doors were open. Music and chattering voices echoed out of it like a friendly greeting.

She walked in step with Massimo, heartbreakingly gorgeous in a black tuxedo and a black tie she doubted would stay around his neck for any length of time. In thirteen minutes flat he'd showered, dressed and trimmed his beard. He'd even tamed his thick black hair.

From the moment they'd closed their chalet door behind them, the urge to take his hand had been all-consuming. It swung by his hip as he made his graceful long strides. All she had to do was stretch her fingers...

Temptation was taken away when they entered the lodge. They were welcomed by a sea of happy faces all dressed in their finest clothes, embraces and smacking kisses flowing free and fast.

Madeline pounced at the earliest opportunity. 'Come

with me and introduce yourself to anyone you've never met before,' she hissed in Livia's ear. 'Everyone seems to know my name but I have no idea who lots of them are and I don't want to embarrass myself or them by saying so.'

Laughing, Livia happily stepped into the throng and introduced herself to the strangers, making sure to repeat their names for Madeline's benefit. A handful were Jimmy's old childhood friends, people who had once called this island home, others soldiers he'd befriended during his voluntary deployment in the Second World War. In all, there were ninety guests celebrating Jimmy's birthday with him. The language barrier between herself and the native English speakers was easy to overcome, she found, by simply placing her hand to her chest and reciting her name. After that, Madeline would take over and translate.

Getting everyone to the island for the party had been a logistical nightmare but the look on Jimmy's face proved all the effort Massimo had made and the vast expense had been worth it. Currently talking to an old schoolfriend who was in his own wheelchair and had his own carer in attendance, Jimmy was smiling from ear to ear.

Livia's heart swelled with love for the elderly man whose home she had entered as his nurse and left as his granddaughter-in-law. He had an inherent kindness and a decency about him that had shone through from their first meeting, qualities inherent in his daughter and granddaughter too. This was the kind of family Livia had longed for as a child. A family where you felt safe and cocooned in love. There had been love of a sort in the Esposito home but it was a hard love, the kind that came with conditions.

Her gaze drifted to Jimmy's grandson and some-how her heart swelled even more. Massimo was on his haunches chatting to a frail great-aunt. Massimo was different from the rest of his family in more ways than she could count but he had their decency. He had an un-limited quota of generosity running through his veins. All this, the purchase of the island, the building of the entire complex...all of that had been achieved by Mas-simo so Jimmy could spend his final birthday in the place of his birth.

The island would also be Jimmy's legacy. The staff employed to work full-time on the resort doubled as war-dens for the nature reserve. Jimmy's offspring and his siblings' offspring would enjoy this paradise for genera-tions to come. All of it courtesy of Massimo.

Massimo tried to concentrate on what his great-aunt, a woman he'd never met before, was saying to him. Her heavily accented English flew like a burr from her mouth. Her gratitude towards Massimo for arranging the party and ensuring she got to see her youngest brother for the first time in almost seventy years touched him. He imagined her as a young girl playing with his grand-father and their other siblings, the last generation of Seibuas to live, work and play here before their way of life had become unsustainable.

But it wasn't her accent that made it hard for him to concentrate. His lack of concentration was down to his wife.

She always looked beautiful but tonight... Beauty did not do her justice. He had to fight his eyes' desire to keep seeking her out but somehow he was always fully aware of exactly where she was. Right then, she was at the buffet table with his father.

The mid-thigh-length strappy black sequined dress she wore with its plunging neckline, the gold locket she wore around her neck, the gold hooped earrings that gleamed through the locks of her hair...

Everything about her glittered.

The Livia he'd first met had come back to life. The confident, gregarious woman with the throaty, dirty laugh, the woman who'd never found language to be a barrier for communication, she was here, radiating with the joy of life.

And why shouldn't she radiate in it? Life for Livia had been a hard-fought battle.

Where had this woman gone in those awful cold months before she'd left him?

He knew her brother's escape had something to do with her carefree mood but there had to be a greater explanation than that.

Suddenly her stance shifted and her eyes fell on him.

That feeling of being punch-drunk hit him again.

He had no idea how long they stared at each other. He barely recalled his last few minutes of conversation with his great-aunt either.

In need of a drink, he was manoeuvring his way around small children dancing vigorously, when his grandfather caught his eye and beckoned him over.

Massimo squatted to the same level as his wheelchair and took his frail hands into his own. It was like touching tissue paper. 'Are you enjoying the party, *Nonno*?'

'You have made an old man very happy. Thank you.'

Massimo would never get used to the raspiness of his

grandfather's voice. He squeezed the frail hands gently. 'My pleasure.'

The filmy eyes that had once been the same colour as Massimo's held his and the old gleam in them returned. 'What does an old man have to do to get a bourbon here?'

'I thought you'd been advised against drinking alcohol?'

'What does advice matter when you're dying?'

Massimo winced.

His grandfather twisted his hands so he was the one holding Massimo's. He leaned closer to him. 'I'm not afraid of death, Massimo. I've had a good life. All the people here remind me how good it's been. I've *lived*, and the short time I have left, I want to live that too.'

There was no guile in his grandfather's stare but Massimo had the strong impression the elderly man was trying to tell him something.

He kissed the bald head and wished he knew the words to tell his grandfather how much he meant to him.

By the time he returned with his grandfather's drink, a crowd had gathered around him. Not wanting to be snared in a large group and forced to make more small talk, he decided an upgrade from the beer he'd been drinking was in order and went back to the bar to order himself a large bourbon.

He was on his second when Livia sidled up to him.

'Hiding away?' she asked.

'Taking a breather.'

Dark brown eyes studied him, a combination of sympathy and amusement in them. Livia knew well how social situations made him feel.

She caught the barman's attention and ordered herself a bourbon too. 'This is a great party.'

'People are enjoying it?'

'Very much.' She nudged him with her elbow and pointed at one of the sofas. Two of the small children he'd almost tripped over earlier were fast asleep on it. A third, who'd gone a pale green colour, was eating a large scoop of ice cream, utter determination etched on her face. 'Someone needs to get that girl a sick bag.'

He laughed and was immediately thrown back to his sister's wedding again.

He'd approached Livia at the bar. She'd said something inane that had made him laugh. He wished he could remember what it was but it had slipped away the moment she'd said it, his attention too transfixed on her for words to stick.

She'd blown him away.

Those same feelings…

Had they ever really left him?

The music had slowed in tempo. The dance floor had filled, the children making way for the adults.

'We should dance,' he murmured.

Her chest rose, head tilted, teeth grazing over her bottom lip. 'I suppose we should…for appearances' sake.'

He breathed deeply and slowly held his hand out.

Equally slowly, she stretched hers out to meet his. The pads of her fingers pressed into his palm. Tingles shot through his skin. His fingers closed over them.

On the crowded dance floor, he placed his hands loosely on her hips. Her hands rested lightly on his shoulders. A delicate waft of her perfume filtered through his airwaves.

He clenched his jaw and purposely kept his gaze focused above her head.

They moved slowly in tempo with the music, their bodies a whisper away from touching...

'When did you take your tie off?' Livia murmured when she couldn't take the tension that had sprung between them any longer.

She'd been trying very hard not to breathe. Every inhalation sent Massimo's familiar musky heat and the citrus undertones of his cologne darting into her airwaves. Her skin vibrated with awareness, her senses uncoiling, tiny springs straining towards the man whose hands hardly touched her hips. She could feel the weight in them though, piercing through her skin.

Caramel eyes slowly drifted down to meet her gaze.

The music beating around them reduced to a burr.

The breath of space between them closed. The tips of her breasts brushed against the top of his flat stomach. The weight of his hands increased in pressure.

Heat pulsed deep in her pelvis.

Her hands crept without conscious thought over his shoulder blades. Heart beating hard, her fingers found his neck...her palms pressed against it.

His right hand caressed slowly up her back. She shivered at the darts of sensation rippling through her.

Distantly, she was aware the song they were dancing to had finished.

His left hand drew across her lower back and gradually pulled her so close their bodies became flush.

Her cheek pressed into his shoulder. She could feel the heavy thuds of his heart. They matched the beats of hers.

His mouth pressed into the top of her head. The warmth of his ragged breath whispered in the strands of her hair. Her lungs had stopped functioning. Not a hitch of air went into them.

A finger brushed a lock of her hair.

She closed her eyes.

The lock was caught and wound in his fingers.

She turned her cheek and pressed her mouth to his throat...

A body slammed into them. Words, foreign to her drumming ears but unmistakably words of apology, were gabbled.

They pulled apart.

There was a flash of bewilderment in Massimo's eyes she knew must be mirrored in hers before he blinked it away.

A song famous at parties all around the world was now playing. The floor was packed with bodies all joining in with the accompanying dance. Even the passed-out children had woken up to join in with it.

And she'd been oblivious. They both had.

The rest of the party passed in a blur, as if she'd been sucked into a time warp that had her in Massimo's arms on the crowded dance floor one minute, the next following him into their chalet. Had they even spoken since they'd left the dance floor?

Vague images flashed in Livia's mind. Jimmy, ably assisted by all the children under the age of ten blowing out the ninety candles on his cake. The exchange of goodbye kisses.

After the noise of the party, the silence in their chalet was deafening.

She stared at Massimo with a thundering heart and tried to think of something, anything to say to cut through this tension-filled silence but her brain seemed to have been infected with a fever.

His chest rose before he nodded his head in a decisive manner. 'I'll brush my teeth and leave you to sleep.'

Every inch of her body screamed in protest.

She managed to incline her head.

He turned and disappeared into the bedroom.

Massimo brushed his teeth vigorously, as if the bristles could brush away the longing raging through him.

One dance with Livia had smashed through his defences.

One touch of her hand had set his pulses racing.

One look in her eyes had set his heart pounding.

One press of her body against his had set the arousal he'd been suppressing by a thread off in an unstoppable flow that denial had no longer been able to contain.

He could still feel her lips against his throat. That one brush had marked him. His body still buzzed from the thrills that had been unleashed in that one short dance.

He wanted her with an ache that burned. He'd never *stopped* wanting her.

Done with his teeth, he slapped cold water over his face then stared hard at his reflection.

He was going to leave this bathroom, walk calmly through the bedroom, wish Livia a good night then go outside and sleep on the hammock.

He would not linger. He would not engage in conversation. He would not touch her.

To do any of these things would prise open the lid of the box they had both hammered shut. Their marriage was over for damn good reasons. In the morning they would say goodbye and fly to separate continents. The ripping of his heart at this thought meant nothing but an acknowledgement of his own failure. For a man who had succeeded on his own merits at everything he'd attempted in life, failure was a hard thing to tolerate. Their marriage had been a failure and much of that had been down to him. It was bound to sit uncomfortably.

He patted his damp face dry, shoved the towel back on the rail and moved purposefully out of the bathroom, through the bedroom that had been designed to be theirs, and through to the main living area...

Livia was in the kitchen area, her back to the counter, glass of water clasped tightly in her hand.

Their eyes met.

His heart squeezed unbearably but his steps did not falter.

'Sleep well,' he muttered as he continued to the door.

Only when he'd closed the door behind him did he pause for breath.

He closed his eyes and filled his lungs with resolve...

But he could still feel her eyes on him.

He fisted a hand and punched it into the palm of the other.

He tried to set off again. His legs and feet refused to cooperate.

Livia stared at the closed door for so long her eyes became fuzzy.

There was a cramping in her chest that made every breath she took an effort.

She wanted to run out after him and beg him to come back inside. She wanted to wrap her arms around him and kiss him; his mouth, his face, his neck, his chest, every inch of him.

She wanted his arms around her. She wanted to feel

the intense pleasure that had cemented the love they had once found together.

Deep in her soul she knew she would never find what they'd had with anyone else. It wasn't possible for a heart to love as deeply as hers had loved Massimo and move on without leaving a part of it with him.

And he had loved her too. He *had*. Self-preservation had had her denying his love but being with him again had unleashed the memories she'd suppressed about all the good times they'd had.

Those good times had been the best of her life.

She'd *had* to focus on the bad times that had destroyed them because to remember the good times would have been to remind herself in multicolour detail of all they had thrown away.

Resolve suddenly took her in its grip, pulling her out of the paralysis that had kept her immobile in her desperate thoughts.

Shoving her undrunk glass of water on the counter, she kicked her shoes off and put one bare foot in front of the other...

Without any warning the door flew open.

Massimo filled the doorway, breathing heavily through his nose, his hair dishevelled, caramel eyes pulsing.

There was a moment of stillness. Only a moment but it stretched and pulled like an invisible band looping around them, pulling tighter and tighter until the binds became too great and, feet moving in sync, they closed the distance between them.

Livia drank in the face she had never stopped dreaming about. Everything inside her had cramped. Except for her heart. That felt as if a hummingbird had nestled in it.

The throat she had unthinkingly kissed moved. The top three buttons of his shirt were undone. The dinner jacket he'd worn to the party had long been discarded with the tie that had adorned his neck.

This was Massimo; heartbreakingly handsome yet unkempt, lacking in vanity and dismissive of his own beauty. Yet he had made her feel feminine and beautiful. He had made her feel as if she were the only woman on this earth.

The look reflecting back at her now...

It made all those old feelings come roaring back to life.

The electrified air between them swirled as his hand inched to hers. Fingers locked together. Slowly, he lifted their hands to his chest as, equally slowly, his other hand touched her hair. Using the backs of his fingers, he stroked the strands.

How could hair feel alive? she wondered dimly, shivering as sensation tingled from the top of her head and spread through her heated veins.

Their entwined fingers tightened.

The hand in her hair dived through the locks and gently traced the rim of her ear.

Her legs weakened.

The hand at her ear slowly skimmed down the side of her neck. The hummingbird in her heart was trying to beat its way out. It almost succeeded when the eyes her gaze was locked on drew closer and closer, the lids closing, and the wide, firm mouth she had once believed she would kiss for ever brushed against her aching lips.

CHAPTER NINE

MASSIMO, EYES CLOSED, rested his mouth against the softest lips in creation and breathed Livia in.

He felt her quiver. The nails of the fingers entwined in his dug into his hand.

Emotions were erupting through him, so many it was impossible to pinpoint one and say *this* was what he was feeling.

The only certainty he could find was that this was where he needed to be.

He needed Livia's touch like a fish needed water.

And he needed to touch her like a drowning man needed air.

A tempest raged inside him, a storm crashing onto the drowning man.

Livia was the air he needed. She was on his mind with every breath he took.

The thunder of his heart vibrated through his bones. When she placed her small hand on the top of his chest he knew she must be able to feel it too.

He could feel her heartbeat through their tightly wound hands.

The fingers splayed on her soft neck drifted back up to spear her hair. He hadn't realised that he'd been afraid the changes she'd made to her hair would have changed its texture until relief had coursed through him on the dance floor to find it had the same silky feel.

He'd been as helpless not to touch her then as he was not to touch her now.

Livia was more than air. She was the fire in his heart, the water in his veins, the earth that kept him grounded.

Their lips moved slowly together, fused mouths parting, the kiss deepening.

Her sweet breath curled into his senses.

Their entwined hands released. Arms wrapped tightly around each other, bodies crushed together, tongues danced as the desire he had fought since she had stepped into the cabin of his private jet was finally set free.

A million tastes and scents and sensations filled Livia's starved senses. Being wrapped so tightly in Massimo's arms and being kissed so deeply and passionately was awakening the last parts of her she had kept locked away.

He'd torn the last of her barriers down but the feelings erupting in her were too heady, too familiar and too wondrous to be frightening.

If she were to be cast away on a desert island and allowed to choose only one person to join her on it, there was no question of who she would choose. Massimo. He was scarred on her heart and etched in her soul.

She didn't want to think of what she was doing—what they were doing. She needed this too much. Needed him too much.

Only now, as she drowned in the heady delights of his touch, did she understand how starved she'd been since she'd left him and how slowly time had crawled in those awful dark days.

To feel the crash of their hearts pounding so violently together through their embracing bodies…

Everything inside her bloomed wide open and light poured in.

Her stomach swooped as he lifted her into his arms.

He'd carried her like this on their wedding night, she remembered dreamily, pressing her mouth against his neck and inhaling the Massimo scent that had always made her stomach swoop all on its own.

There was such tenderness in the way he laid her down on the bed that the light that had poured inside her sparkled and glimmered through her skin and veins.

His hooded eyes glimmered too.

She could feel his hunger as keenly as she felt her own.

Gently he brushed away the locks of hair that had fallen across her face.

No words were spoken between them. No words were necessary.

She raised her hand and palmed his cheek. The bristles of his beard grazed against her skin.

Their mouths locked together.

The hand palming his cheek slipped around his neck, her other hand sliding around his waist, pulling him down so she could feel his solid weight on her. She needed to feel that brief crush of her lungs before he shifted to release the weight, needed the assurance that she hadn't fallen into a dream.

She couldn't bear it if this was nothing but a dream. She'd suffered too many dreams in those dark days where they would be making love only for her to wake to the cold reality of a lonely bed.

There had been nightmares too, ones where he'd found someone else. One in particular had stayed with her for days. She'd been walking down the street when she'd spotted Massimo walking arm in arm with a faceless woman. She'd run after them but couldn't catch them, screaming his name as loudly as she could but no sound coming out. She'd awoken from it with a start, tears soaking into her pillow and her heart cold with a fear a hundred times worse than she'd felt in the nightmares from her childhood.

Being with him like this, here, now, evoked only warmth in her soaring heart.

She was flying.

For now, tomorrow didn't exist.

There was only now.

His hands stroked down the sides of her breasts and down to her hips where he gathered the skirt of her dress and hitched it to her waist, his mouth raining kisses over her face, her hands scratching into his scalp. They only broke away so her dress could be pulled over her head and discarded.

She saw the pulse in his eyes as he dragged his stare over her body, naked save for the skimpy black knickers she wore.

Heat flooded her with an intensity that stole her breath when he dipped his head and kissed her breasts in turn, and now it was his shirt she was scratching at, grasping to untuck it.

Every part of Livia's body had been etched in Massimo's memory but he stared at her feeling as if he were seeing it all for the first time.

His memory had played tricks on him. He'd forgotten how damned sexy she was, how perfect she was.

He'd forgotten the way her legs writhed when she was hungry for him and to see them doing that now...

He kissed her breasts again, with more savagery than the first tender kisses he'd placed on them. He'd forgotten, too, how much she loved him lavishing attention on them. She was as receptive to his touch as he was to hers, the perfect fusion that had so blown his mind the first time they'd made love and every time after.

He moved down to her belly, divesting himself of his shirt as he went, then gripped her knickers in his fingers and pulled them down her legs to land in the pile their other clothing had formed. Working quickly, he removed the last of his own clothing too.

He could smell the musky heat of her excitement...

There was not a single thing about Livia that didn't set his blood aflame.

He kissed her thighs, digging his fingers into the pliant flesh, then ran his tongue between the soft mound of dark hair between her parted legs.

There was a clenching in his heart. Fresh memories assailed him of the first time he'd shaved her bikini line for her and trimmed the hair. She'd been about to make an appointment at a salon when he'd suggested with a wolfish gleam that he do it for her. Her eyes had pulsed with agreement.

It had been sexy. It had been fun. The trust she had bestowed in him had blown his mind as much as everything else they had shared. After that first time they'd adopted their own language for it. It had always ended with wild lovemaking.

Her bikini line now was smooth but the rest was as nature intended. It looked to him that she hadn't bothered with it since she'd left him. For a woman who always liked to feel her best as well as look her best, right down to always wearing matching underwear that no one other than him would see, this told him everything he needed to know.

Livia hadn't been with anyone since they'd parted.

No other man had buried his face between her legs and experienced her uninhibited wild responses, the soft moans and pleas...

No other man had teased her to orgasm with his tongue alone.

He *knew* he had no right to feel such relief at this. But he did.

Livia was *his*. Just as he was hers.

Gripping her hips, he snaked his tongue back up her petite, curvy body, inhaling her skin, tasting it, nipping it, the primal eruption that had so consumed him the first time they'd made love stronger than it had ever been.

She belonged to *him*. And he belonged to her. He would always belong to her.

Elbows resting either side of her face, he gazed down in wonder. The same ragged-breath wonder reflected right back at him.

Why had he let her go? How could he have let this beautiful, sassy woman walk away without a fight?

With a groan, he plundered her plump, delectable mouth. Her arms looped around his neck and she arched her back so her breasts crushed against his chest as they devoured each other with a hungry desperation. Her legs hooked around his thighs, encouraging him, and he drove inside her in one long thrust.

The relief at being in Livia's tight, slick heat was such

that he had to screw his eyes shut and drag in a breath lest he lose control immediately.

But, damn, a man could happily die like this.

Livia's head had gone. She'd lost control of her sanity when Massimo had brought her to orgasm using nothing but his tongue and now, with him sheathed so tightly inside her, the sensations were too incredible to do anything but cling tightly to him and soar in the heavenliness they were creating together.

The hummingbird that had nestled in her heart had broken free and she was flying high in the sky, reaching for the stars.

They made love with abandon, Massimo driving into her with fury tempered by tenderness, wet kisses, bites on necks, nails digging into skin, nothing existing but this moment, them, together, the fire that had always blazed so brightly between them reignited but now burning with the blue flame of desperation.

For the first time ever she found herself fighting release. She didn't want this to end. She wanted these wonderful feelings to last for ever.

From the concentration carved on Massimo's face and the pained desire she caught every time she looked in his eyes, he was fighting the same battle.

Squeezing her eyes shut tight, she pressed her mouth into his neck and fought the growing sensations pulsating deep inside her pelvis. But it was like fighting against the tide. The pleasure was just too much…

She forgot all about fighting when the pulsations turned into an eruption that spread through her like a rippling wave. All she could do was tighten her hold on him and submit to the waves carrying her as high as the soaring hummingbird of her heart.

* * *

Livia opened her eyes with a start and immediately rolled over to check Massimo was still there. She'd fallen asleep in his arms but at some point after drifting off she must have disentangled herself.

The night was still dark but hazy light filtered in from the moon and stars. She swallowed back her relief to find his solid form lying peacefully beside her, facing her on his side. His chest rose and fell steadily.

She inched closer and covered his hand, then gently brought it up over the mattress to her lips. She razed the lightest of kisses against his knuckles and soaked in every detail of his sleeping face.

Something sharp and painful filled her chest. The hummingbird had nestled back into her heart. If Massimo opened his eyes he would see its thrumming wings beating through her skin.

She swallowed again and tried to regain control of her suddenly erratic breathing.

She pressed her mouth back against his knuckles. His fingers twitched.

Feeling herself in desperate need of air, she released his hand and slipped out of the bed. She wrapped her robe around her naked body and padded out of the bedroom.

At the back of their chalet, down the steps of their veranda, was their private garden and swimming pool. Livia sank onto a sunlounger by the pool and stared at the sun peeking over the horizon.

The cusp of a new day was showing its face but for Livia this cusp was the beginning of the end. This was the day she would say goodbye to Massimo for good...

The realisation hit her like a cold slap.

She didn't want to say goodbye.

Her feelings for Massimo were as strong as they'd ever been and the feelings he'd had for her were still there too. He'd shown it with every look, every touch and every kiss.

Why had they let that love go? Why hadn't they fought for it? The love they had once shared had been *everything*.

Massimo had slipped away from her. That was the truth. It had been so gradual that to begin with she'd only sensed it. That was what had brought her fears and insecurities out and deepened her loneliness and homesickness. Everything had escalated from that.

She talked too much but he didn't talk enough. Not about the things that were important.

That needed to change.

She looked up at the brightening sky and breathed in the warm, fragrant air. The chirrup of awakening birds sounded all around her, a joyful sound that sparked hope in her heart.

Where there was life there was hope.

What they had was worth fighting for. All she had to do was make Massimo see that too.

Filling her lungs with resolve, Livia walked back into the chalet.

If she had any chance of saving their marriage, she needed her phone, which was in the bedroom.

She pushed the door open quietly.

Massimo lifted his head. He'd woken to an empty bed. He'd registered this little fact before his eyes had opened, an emptiness where warmth should be.

He breathed a little easier to see Livia's silhouette in the doorway.

'Are you okay?' he asked, his voice croaky from sleep. He had no idea what time it was other than it was early.

It was the deepest sleep he'd had in...since she'd left him.

She stared at him for the longest time before a smile curved over her beautiful face and she released the robe wrapped around her.

'I needed some air,' she said as she padded to the bed.

He pulled the sheets back and held his arms out for her, his body responding automatically to her unashamed nudity.

His desire for her was the one thing he'd never been able to turn off.

She nestled into his embrace.

He closed his eyes and breathed into her hair, his chest swelling. For long silent moments they did nothing but lie entwined together.

This would be the last time he held her like this.

'Why did you get spearheads added to your tattoo?' she murmured, tracing it gently with her finger before kissing it. 'I thought it was finished.'

'I thought it was finished too.'

His tattoo hadn't been finished but their marriage was.

He tightened the embrace. Regrets swirled in the air around them but it was too late for regrets. However good it felt to spend one last night with Livia, they were better off apart. They both knew that. You couldn't play on broken strings. The strings that had bound them together hadn't merely broken; they'd been irrevocably severed.

Whatever desire-driven thoughts had consumed him when they'd been making love didn't change the fact that he was better on his own. He worked better and functioned better.

Their lips found each other and the hunger that had always left him feeling starving when he was without her reared back to life.

They could have this, he thought dimly as she sank onto his length, her hair falling onto his face.

One last moment of bliss together before they said goodbye for good.

CHAPTER TEN

AFTER A LATE breakfast in the lodge, it was time to say goodbye. The guests who'd stayed the night left first until it was only Massimo, his immediate family and his grandfather's care team left.

Heart heavy, Massimo walked with them to the jetty where the cruise liner awaited. This return journey would be much shorter than the outward one. They were sailing to Viti Levu and flying to Rome from there on a private jet he'd chartered for them. After two months away from their homes, his family was looking forward to their return to Italy.

Unspoken between them all was his grandfather's health. It was the reason they were flying back. Jimmy had reserved all his energy for this stay on his birth land and his party. A two-month sail might be too late for him to have his last request of dying in his home met.

Madeline wrapped her arms around him and looked up at him with an unusually serious expression. 'Come home soon, Massimo. Please?'

Instead of the usual vague response he gave to these kinds of requests, Massimo found himself kissing his sister's cheek. 'I'll try.'

She tightened her hold. 'Try harder. We miss you.'

For the first time he found himself thinking that he *would* try.

Something had shifted in him. For all his dread at being cooped up on an island with his family, the weekend had gone much better than he'd anticipated. The more time he'd spent with them, the easier he'd found it. There had been an acceptance he'd never felt before. Or was it that he now looked at his family with fresh eyes?

Gazing over his sister's head, he saw his mother fussing with his grandfather's wheelchair. His mother loved to fuss. She was never happier than when doing things for those she loved, whether it was ironing shirts to within an inch of their lives or slaving over steaming bowls of simple home-cooked food to fill their bellies with. His father was the same too.

An old memory surfaced: sleeping on his sister's bedroom floor while his father had made a bed and wardrobe for Massimo's room. All the materials were old, reclaimed stuff but his father had made the entire lot himself right down to painting them in a colour of Massimo's choosing.

That had been his first practical exposure to the idea that something could start out as one thing and then be turned into something completely different.

Just as he was thinking that he'd finally found the root of his love of engineering and science, another memory surfaced, of the time his father found an old bicycle at a central rubbish-collection point. He'd brought it home, serviced it and painted it. By the time he presented it to Massimo—a gift for him to run his errands on—the bike looked brand new.

A wave of affection washed through him and he embraced his parents tighter than he usually did. For all the resentment he'd once felt at growing up poor, he'd never had to sleep with one ear alert to danger. He'd never had to worry about his sister being seduced into a life of crime.

After a cuddle with his niece, it was time to say goodbye to his grandfather. He sent a silent prayer that this would not be for the last time.

He watched them sail away with a weighted heart and a lump in his throat.

Beside him stood Livia, waving vigorously at his departing family.

However hard he tried to blur her from his vision she remained solid. Beautiful.

The lump that felt like granite in his throat grew. He felt all disjointed.

Abruptly, he turned on his heel and strode back down the jetty, scanning the sky for signs of the Cessna, which had taken the last of the party guests to Viti Levu and should be back by now to take Massimo and Livia to Nadi International Airport where his flight crew were waiting for them.

'Massimo?'

He closed his eyes and drew in a breath, slowing his pace enough for Livia to catch up with him.

The last thing he wanted was a long, protracted goodbye with his wife. He had enough tumultuous feelings ripping through him.

'Are you okay?'

'Yes.'

'You've hardly spoken to me since we got out of bed. Do you regret last night?'

That was Livia. Straight to the point, as always.

'I don't regret it. I just don't see any point in talking about it.'

'We spent the night making love. I would say that gives us lots to talk about.'

That was Livia too, always so keen to discuss *feelings*, as if feelings mattered a damn.

'Last night…' He closed his eyes again and sucked in another breath, fighting the heat that spread through his veins to remember how incredible it had been. 'I'm not saying it was a mistake but, with hindsight, it shouldn't have happened.'

'Why not?'

'We're getting divorced, Liv. I know we're going to wait for my grandfather to…' He couldn't vocalise the words. They were waiting for his grandfather to die before they went ahead with the legalities. 'It won't be long,' he finished. He didn't know if it was his grandfather's imminent death or the final severance of their marriage that caused his heart to constrict.

Dark brown eyes held his. 'Don't you have doubts?'

'Doubts?'

'About whether we're doing the right thing.'

'None.'

She flinched but didn't drop her stare. 'I do.'

'How can you have doubts?' he asked incredulously. 'This was your idea. You left *me*.'

Her slim shoulders rose. Her lips drew together before she said, 'I want to try again.'

His heart made a giant lurch. He took a step back and stared hard at her. 'One night of sex doesn't mend a broken marriage and our marriage *was* broken.'

'But we never tried to fix it. We were always too busy arguing…' She held her hands in the air. '*I* was always too busy arguing. You refused to argue. It doesn't matter who did what, the truth is we never sat down and talked and tried to find a way to fix things. We just gave up.'

'Some things can't be fixed. Our marriage is one of them and you were right to leave me. I'm sorry if last night has caused you to have doubts but—'

'Last night made me see the truth. We gave up too easily.'

'It changed nothing for me.'

Her burst of laughter sounded hollow. 'You *liar*.'

'I can't be the husband you want me to be.'

'You don't know what I want.'

'You screamed it in my face every day.'

'Then maybe you should have listened.'

'I'm not going to rehash old wounds.' He put his hand out, palm facing her; a visual sign to back up his words that he wanted this conversation to end. 'You wanted a divorce and I accepted it. It is the right thing for us to do. I'm going back to America and you're going back to Italy. That's it. Over.'

He started walking again.

'I *knew* you'd run away as soon as I brought the subject up.'

Ignoring her, he continued, craning his head to the sky again for sign of the plane. It should have been here thirty minutes ago.

'It's not coming.'

He stopped in his tracks.

'The plane. You keep looking out for it. It's not coming back today.'

Livia folded her arms across her chest and braced herself.

When he turned to look at her, his face was dark. 'What have you done?'

'I've cancelled the Cessna until tomorrow. We need to talk.'

'No, we need to go home. I have work and you have your brother waiting for you. I thought you were keen to see him and convince him that he's done the right thing in leaving.'

'He's safe,' she countered, 'and as long as he's got a gaming thing to play on and a mountain of food to eat, which he has, he won't be going anywhere. To save you time making wasted phone calls, I might as well confess that I've sent your flight crew on a sailing trip on your yacht. Even if you manage to get another Cessna to take you from the island to the mainland, you'll find it hard to leave Fiji itself.'

'What the...?' He swore loudly.

Bad language didn't faze her. She'd grown up in a home where every other word was punctuated with a curse.

His jaw clenching hard enough to snap, he pulled his phone out of his back pocket. 'I don't know what game you think you're playing but it won't work. My crew take orders from me, not from you.'

'When we married you told all your staff, flight crew included, that they were to take my orders as seriously as they took yours. Have you changed those orders?'

If looks could kill she would be dead on the ground beneath her.

'Call them if you want but you'll find they're already on the yacht drinking the champagne I ordered for them. They won't be fit to fly.' Massimo might be the undisputed brains in their marriage but when it came to planning, Livia could beat anyone. If she had any chance of getting him to stay on the island a little longer, she had to cut off all his options to leave.

Glaring at her, he punched his fingers against the screen of his phone. 'I shall charter another plane to take me home. You can stay here and rot.'

'You think you'll be able to charter a plane today? You'll be lucky to get one for tomorrow.'

'I'll take my chances.' He put his phone to his ear. A moment later he swiped it with another curse.

'If you were calling Lindy then I've already spoken to her. It's Saturday in Los Angeles…' The time difference had taken a while for Livia to get her head around but thankfully she'd found it worked in her favour. 'She's taking her daughter out for the day and keeping her phone switched off.'

'Lindy was never given instructions to obey you.'

'I asked her a favour and she agreed. It's her own private time so she's not in breach of her contract with you.'

There was a long pause of venom-filled silence.

Livia held her breath.

Then he smiled. His eyes remained blocks of ice. 'I don't need Lindy to charter a plane for me and I don't need her to book me into a hotel for the night if you're right that it's too short notice for me to charter a plane. You lose.'

'No, *we* lose,' she called to his retreating back. 'One extra day, Massimo, that's all I'm asking for. Call the flight company and have another Cessna flown in to take you off the island and check into a hotel while you wait for your flight crew to get back from their trip, or stay here with me and see if we can try and fix this marriage.'

'I am not willing to waste my energy fixing something that's beyond repair.'

'How can you say that when you've dedicated your working life on solutions for the greatest problems facing this earth that people said were beyond repair?'

'Those are problems that can be fixed by science and engineering. Our problems are fundamental.'

'I thought that about us too but now—'

Suddenly he stopped and spun round. If she hadn't stopped walking too she would have careered into him.

'But now, *nothing*. What you have done is deplorable. I need to be back at the facility first thing Monday. We have the prototype to test...'

'Why does it have to be you?' She strove to keep her voice steady but could feel the all too familiar anger rising. 'You employ four thousand people. Are you telling me not one of them can test the prototype for you? Why can't the project manager do it?' It was an argument she'd made countless times about all the different aspects of his business.

'It's a controlled environment that I need to oversee.' It was a variation of an answer he'd given countless times too.

'The only controlled environment is your heart,' she finally snapped.

His face contorted. 'I don't have to listen to this.'

'Oh, yes, you do. If you hadn't noticed, you're stuck on an island with me. There's nowhere for you to escape unless you pay someone to get you out.' Seeing he was about to walk away again, she grabbed hold of his wrist and took a deep breath to calm her rising temper and tremulous heart. The heavy thud of his pulse against her fingers gave her the courage to continue. 'Please, Massimo, give me this one day. The Cessna's scheduled to pick us up in the morning. When it gets here, if you still want us to go our separate ways then I'll accept it but if I ever meant anything to you, and if our marriage ever meant anything to you, please, give us this chance.'

Her tight chest loosened a fraction to see a softening in the icy gaze boring into her.

He dropped his gaze to her hand and gently prised her fingers from his wrist.

'Seeing as the options you've left me mean I'm going to be a day late getting home, I need to make some calls.'

'You'll stay?' She hardly dared to hope.

He met her stare again, his expression now inscrutable. 'I'll stay but only because of the situation you've engineered. I'm not staying for us. I have no wish to be cruel but I'm not cut out for marriage. It took our marriage for me to see that.'

Massimo, sitting on the veranda at the back of the chalet, ended his final call and rubbed his fingers over his head. The testing on the prototype he'd spent the last year working on had been put back twenty-four hours, the first time he'd ever deferred anything to do with work. Livia had smashed his carefully planned schedule on its head.

Why was she doing this? Revenge for all the late nights he'd spent in his facility? This devious streak was a side of her he'd never seen before.

Surely she wasn't serious about them trying again? After everything they'd been through and everything they'd put each other through, she wanted to patch their marriage back up? The idea was ludicrous.

They *had* tried, for two long years. He couldn't make her happy then so why did she think he could make her happy now?

He pushed away the thought that the first year of their marriage had been the best of his life. That was easily explained by the high levels of dopamine and other hormones induced by great sex.

He should never have made love to her last night. That was what had brought all this stupid, devious behaviour from her on. The hormones released by their lovemaking had messed with his head too but in the bright light of day the fog his brain had succumbed to had cleared and he could see with clarity again.

He hoped his blunt parting words had given her some much-needed clarity too.

A burst of frustration shot through him and, without thinking, he threw his phone onto the veranda's terracotta tiles. If not for the protective case around it, it would have shattered.

Scowling at the phone as if it were its own fault that it was on the ground, he got off his chair and reached down to pick it back up. As his fingers closed around it a pair of bare feet with pretty painted toenails appeared before him. Attached to the feet was a pair of smooth, bare legs, a scar running along the calf of one, attached to a curvy body wrapped in a sheer pale blue sarong beneath which Livia was very obviously naked. Her newly cut and highlighted chestnut hair was piled high on top of her head, locks spilling over a large pair of aviator shades.

He straightened, his foul mood deepening at the spark of response that flashed through his loins and darkening to see the bucket she carried under her arm, which had a bottle of champagne in it, and the two champagne flutes she held by the stems.

Seemingly oblivious to her presence being unwelcome, she placed everything carefully on the table without speaking and poured the champagne into the flutes. Then she had a large drink from one and removed her shades. Her eyes didn't even flicker at him.

Still not speaking, she then turned around and walked to the steps that led down to their private garden and pool. Before going down the steps, she paused.

He held his breath.

The sarong dropped to the ground.

He clamped his lips tightly together to smother the groan that formed in his throat.

What was she playing at now?

Whatever it was, he would not play along.

But he could not tear his eyes from the nymph-like form.

Her naked bottom swayed gently as she made her way slowly…seductively…down the steps to the thick, green lawn. When she reached the pool she dipped a toe in the water, then entered the pool, wading into it from the wide, gently sloping steps in the arch of the shallow end until she was waist deep. And then she began to swim, a slow breaststroke.

There was no suppressing the groan from his throat at the first frog kick of her legs.

Livia swam to the end of the pool and stopped. The water being only chest deep here, she pressed her hands together on the pool's ledge, rested her chin on them and stared out at the softly rippling waves of the ocean lapping only metres from the edge of the private garden and enjoyed the feel of the sun baking her skin.

Massimo's reaction to her entrapping him on the island hadn't surprised her but it had still hurt. But, whatever he'd said about not being cut out for marriage, she wasn't about to raise a white flag and admit defeat. She knew he still had feelings for her. She just had to break down his barriers for him to see that, with a little compromise and a lot of effort, they could have the life together they'd once dreamed of.

The barriers she'd erected to protect herself had been demolished in one blissful night. What did she have to lose?

Being here this weekend, with the man she loved and with the family she wished she could have had for her own… It had brought back everything she'd wanted for them, everything they'd had at the beginning of their marriage. Gentle teasing. Mutual support. Fun. Laughter. Love.

If she failed, at least she could look herself in the eye and say she'd tried. At least she'd be able to move on rather than being stuck in the awful limbo she'd spent the past four months existing in.

She sensed movement behind her before she heard it. Her heart began to thud but she didn't move, not even when the water rippled around her.

CHAPTER ELEVEN

MASSIMO FELT AS if he'd been drugged.

He'd kept his gaze fixed on Livia, telling himself again and again that he wouldn't play her game.

He'd still been telling himself that when he'd stripped his clothes off.

He'd still been telling himself that when he'd stepped into the water and swum to her.

She made no effort to acknowledge him, not even when he stood behind her.

His hands working of their own volition, he reached into her hair and pulled the pin holding it together out.

Her right shoulder made the smallest of movements but she still didn't acknowledge him.

Her hair tumbled down.

He smoothed it with his hands then pressed his nose into the fragrant silk while dragging his fingers down her back and then sliding them around her waist. 'Why did you cut it?' he murmured.

She leaned back into him with a soft sigh and moved her hands to slide them over his arms. Her nails scratched through the fine hairs of his forearms as her bottom wriggled provocatively against his arousal.

He slid his hand over her ribcage and cupped a

weighty breast. His blood had thickened so much that even his heart felt sluggish within the heavy beats.

The small hands pulled away from his arms and reached up behind her shoulders, her fingers groping for him. And then she twisted around to face him.

Her breasts brushed against his chest, her abdomen pressed against his arousal, her hands cupped his neck.

Colour heightened her face, the dark eyes black with desire, the plump lips parted...

Those lips...

Mouths fused together in a kiss of hard, passionate savagery as the desire between them unleashed like a coil springing free from its tight box.

This was how it had always been between them, he thought, in the hazy recess of his mind. One touch had always been enough to ignite the torch that blazed so brightly between them.

Gripping her hips, he lifted her from the water to place her bottom onto the pool's ledge, parted her legs with his thighs, and thrust straight inside her welcoming heat.

She gasped into his mouth then kissed him even harder.

His fingers digging into her hips, her fingers digging into his neck and scalp, mouths clashing together, he drove in and out of her, fast, furious, thrusting as deep as he could go, pain and pleasure driving them on and on to a climax that had her crying his name and Massimo finding himself separating from his body in a wash of brilliant colour.

It took a long time to come back to himself.

He barely remembered climbing out of the pool and collapsing into an entwined heap of naked limbs on the soft lawn. The afternoon sun above blazed down on them, its heat tempered by the breeze coming from the ocean.

'We should get some sunscreen on you,' he muttered.

Her lips pressed into his neck before she clambered upright and got to her feet. 'Don't go anywhere. I'll be back in a minute.'

When she'd disappeared from view, he rolled onto his back and stretched his limbs with a long sigh.

Slinging an arm across his forehead, he closed his eyes. There was a lethargy within him. His heart still thumped heavily.

He should get up and put his clothes back on before Livia came back with the sunscreen.

He knew what he *should* do. The trouble was his lethargic limbs refused to cooperate, just as his limbs had refused his mind's instructions not to play her sensual game in the pool.

His body had been Livia's slave from the moment they'd met.

He wanted to be angry with her for using her sexuality as a weapon against him but he couldn't. He understood what she was doing. His anger was directed at himself.

When she returned wearing her sarong and carrying two full flutes of champagne whilst also balancing the sunscreen and a couple of beach towels under her arm, he rolled onto his side and propped himself on his elbow.

'Livia, I'm sorry...'

'But this doesn't change anything?' she finished for him with a raised brow. She put the champagne and towels on the poolside table and removed her sarong.

'It's okay, Massimo,' she said as she spread the sarong out like a blanket on the lawn. 'Sometimes great sex is just that—great sex. Could you do my back for me, please?'

Livia sat with her legs stretched out on the sarong and waited for him to join her on it.

Massimo, she had discovered early on in their relationship, opened up more easily after sex, when his defences were down in the wave of euphoria that followed it.

She knew stripping naked and seducing him visually could be considered as fighting dirty but there was no shame in seducing her own husband. They both took great pleasure from making love. If she could go back in time and do one thing differently it would be to stop herself turning her back on him in the last months of their marriage. Without sex to keep the intimacy between them alive, the glue that had held them together had disintegrated. There had been nothing left.

But sex wasn't all a marriage could or should be and intimacy came in many forms.

She leaned forward, hugging her knees when he put his hands filled with sunscreen on her back.

Unlike when he'd worked the screen into her skin briskly on the yacht, he took his time. His touch was soothing. She closed her eyes to savour the sensation.

'What did I do to turn you away from me?' she asked quietly.

His hands paused in their work. 'I don't know what you mean.'

'Yes, you do. You turned away from me, Massimo. You stopped caring. Even if tomorrow you decide everything's still over for us, I need to know because the not knowing's killing me.'

Massimo clenched his jaw and breathed in deeply.

What was the point in discussing something that wouldn't make the slightest difference to anything? But she'd steered it so he had no choice. If she'd shouted her demands as she'd always done, he would happily walk away, as he always used to. But she was using temperance. Using the closeness of sex.

He rubbed the sunscreen into her lower back and forced his mind to disassociate from the soft skin beneath his fingers. 'You didn't do anything. We're just not suited. My work is my life. There isn't the space for anything more.'

'You didn't think that when we got together.'

'My feelings for you took me by surprise.' They'd floored him. 'I let those feelings guide me instead of sitting down and thinking them through rationally. You and I have a rare chemistry but, when you boil it down, it's nothing but adrenaline, dopamine, oxytocin, serotonin…'

'Do not reduce my feelings to a chemistry lesson.' An edge crept into her voice.

Good. The dopamine currently flowing through her needed to be extinguished.

'All the effects of desire and what we think of as love can be reduced to a chemical level,' he explained levelly. 'The overwhelming feelings we experience at the start of a relationship are a surge of chemical reactions but those chemicals are raised to unsustainable levels. Eventually they lessen, which is what happened to us.'

'Nice try at deflection but what happened to us is that you turned away from me.' She leaned forward and traced her finger along the scar on her leg. 'This cut was when I really felt it. You didn't care that I was injured.'

'I did care but you told me it wasn't anything serious.' But his first instinct had been to grab his keys and
speed straight to her. That had been the day after he'd
realised how far behind they were on the carbon filter
project because of basic errors *he'd* made. The first errors he'd made in his entire career. The day after he'd
woken Livia from a nightmare and held her trembling
body tightly to him and found himself developing his
own cold sweat at how badly he'd wanted to dive into
her head and rip out the terrors that plagued her.

That had been the moment he'd understood what a
dreadful mistake he'd made.

The fun, sexy marriage he'd envisaged for them had
become an all-consuming sickness in his blood. Livia
had taken full possession of his mind as well as his body.

He'd *had* to back away. Before he lost everything.

If she had given him the space he needed things
might have been very different but she hadn't and a
gulf had opened between them that had only solidified
how wrong they were for each other.

'I didn't want to worry you because I thought you
would drive to me,' she said wistfully. 'When we first
married, I slipped and bumped my head one evening.
Do you remember that? It wasn't anything serious but
you stayed home the next day to keep an eye on me.
You were worried about concussion even though I'm a
nurse and told you there was nothing to worry about.
Less than a year later you sent your PA to drive me to
hospital with a gashed leg.'

He'd sent his PA after first having to prise his car
keys from his own hands to drop them in Lindy's palm.

He shifted away from Livia's smooth, golden back
and got to his feet. 'Do you have any idea how much

work I missed in the first year of our marriage and how behind we got because of it?' He snatched up one of the beach towels she'd left on the poolside table. 'This carbon filter we're about to test should have been ready months ago.'

'That's because you have to micromanage everything.'

He secured the towel around his waist. 'It's my company.'

Her eyes found his. If she felt at a disadvantage remaining naked while he'd covered himself, she didn't show it. 'You employ some of the world's biggest brains. If you can't trust their skills and judgement then what does that say? It says you're either a control freak or you need to employ people who you do trust.'

'No, it says I take my responsibilities seriously.'

'You're in the position where you can allow others who are equally responsible and qualified to share the burden. You choose not to. You use the excuse of your work to cut yourself off from everyone who loves you and you still haven't explained why you cut yourself away from me. We were *happy*, Massimo. We were. And then we had nothing and I need to understand why and, please, for the love of God, don't explain it to me as a scientific formula. I get that we're nothing but atoms and dust but we're also conscious beings who feel and love and dream.'

Feeling in better control of himself, he took a seat at the poolside table and drank his champagne in one deep swallow. Bourbon would have numbed the agitation growing in his stomach much better but this would do.

He had to make her understand. Whatever delusions Livia had allowed herself to believe, he needed to dispel them. Since she'd left him, his world had reverted to its prior orderly calm. His time was where it needed to be—with his business. His mind was clutter-free. The stupid errors that had crept into his work were relegated to history. His wife would soon be relegated to history too. Everything would be as it should be.

'It's just the way I am. I was always different from the rest of my family.' Damn but he really could do with a bourbon. 'They didn't care if the clothes they wore were fraying at the seams or if there wasn't the money available to fix things that broke but I did. They think love alone can fix everything when in reality only hard work achieves anything. I love them in my own way but I never felt as if I belonged and I never wanted to settle for making do. I didn't set out to be rich but I did set out to be well off enough that I would never want for anything.'

Livia pounced on his choice of words. 'You love them in your own way? That implies you're aware of feeling love on something other than a chemical level.'

His eyes narrowed. 'You're twisting my words against me.'

'No, I'm pointing out your hypocrisy. You know perfectly well that love, however it is formed, is real but you're using science as an excuse to deny that what you and I had was real. I never had shoes with holes or clothes that didn't fit but, given the choice, I would have suffered that than live through my childhood. My father was always generous with his money and gave me everything I asked for but I was terrified of him.'

There was the barest flicker in the shuttered caramel eyes but it was enough for the faint hope in her heart to continue beating. 'Whenever he hugged me, all I felt was his gun digging into my chest from his pocket. When he was killed, I was upset because he was my father but I never grieved him like the rest of my family did because the bogeyman of my early childhood *was* my father. My mother was hardly ever there and when she was she would be high or drunk. I practically raised Gianluca—I was the one who took him to school every day and helped him with his homework and made sure he had a hot meal at night.

'Your parents are decent, law-abiding, loving people.' If she was going to fight, she might as well fight on his family's behalf too. But it wasn't just a fight for herself or for the Briatores. She was fighting for Massimo, for him to wake up and see all the joy of love and family that he was denying himself. She got to her feet and gathered the sarong as she continued, 'They could have worked longer hours or taken additional jobs to give you everything you wanted but they made the choice to be there for you whenever you needed them and I wish I could make you see how priceless that was.'

'From your perspective, anyone else's childhood would be priceless.'

'Maybe,' she conceded, wrapping the sarong around her. 'But we're talking about our own, not anyone else's. You are very different from your family but there are similarities. You have their generosity but yours is given in material ways where theirs is given in time.'

His fingers curved on the table but his eyes remained fixed on her. 'I cannot un-live my childhood just because yours was, on a sliding scale, much worse. It made me who I am. It taught me that anything I wanted or needed, I had to get by myself. My parents loved me, yes, but their love didn't change the reality of us being poor. It didn't solve anything. You could be right. I could be a control freak. But everything I have has been achieved by my own endeavours. Science is logical and it's real. It's where I feel most comfortable. It's where I belong but to do my best work, I need my mind to be free from clutter.'

It took her a moment to process the implication of what he'd just said. 'Are you calling me *clutter*?'

His response was unapologetic. 'You became a distraction. You demanded my attention when I needed to be focused.'

'All I ever *demanded* was your time.' Try as she might, she couldn't hide the rising anger. 'Since when is it a crime to want to spend time with your own husband?'

'That is my point perfectly encapsulated. I cannot produce my best work when I'm constantly worrying about you. I need to be free to focus without limits, not clock-watching, not worrying about you being lonely at home, not thinking I need to drive home because you're waiting for me with your dinner going cold.'

'My food wouldn't have gone cold if you'd bothered to let me know you were going to be late,' she retorted.

'That was never intentional.'

'And now you're contradicting yourself again. If it wasn't intentional you wouldn't have worried about it.'

Over the still air, Massimo's ringtone suddenly played out. He looked from Livia to the table on the veranda and back to her.

She gritted her teeth. 'Please. Leave it.'

But of course he wouldn't leave it. It might be *important*. Far more important than her and their marriage.

He strode away without a backwards glance.

She suspected bitterly that he would have cut their conversation short to answer it even if it were a cold caller.

Massimo had set himself up in a shaded part of the veranda, laptop open before him and his phone wedged to his ear. Furious with his retreat from their conversation and his deliberate immersion back into his work, Livia knew she needed to create a little distance between them before she snatched his phone off him and chucked it into the ocean. Doing that would only make things worse. If they could get any worse.

Of the many stories Jimmy had told her about his childhood on this island, the one that had fed Livia's imagination the most had been tales of the Seibua children playing in the naturally formed freshwater pool hidden in the thick forest. When she'd taken Jimmy for an exploration of the island, he'd pointed in the direction of its location and it was with that in mind, and conscious that the sun would soon begin its descent, that she set off.

By the time she passed the lodge, her fury had dimmed a little, enough for her to pass a message to Massimo through one of the staff members of where she was going. Just in case he missed her. Which he wouldn't, a knowledge that curdled her belly with bitter misery.

Her head streamed their conversation continually as she reached the red mangrove saplings planted at the edge of the shore; it echoed as she made her way inland past the black mangroves, which Massimo had explained were protection against the shallow flooding that occurred at high tide, still burred in her ears as she strode upwards to the white mangroves and onwards to the butterwoods until she reached the island's natural forest.

The pathway the Seibua children had taken had disappeared long ago but she'd walked in as straight a direction as she could and she was sure she would find it. If not, she'd go back.

Here, under the natural canopy of trees, the vegetation was dense with colourful wildlife and rich with sound. The heat was stifling but she didn't care. Large red-chested sociable parrots chattered noisily in squeaks and whistles, other less visible birds adding to the wonderful cacophony. None of them seemed bothered by her presence.

Soon, just as Jimmy had described, the canopy began to thin until she was standing in a small, sandy clearing centred around a startlingly clear pool of water no bigger than their private swimming pool. It was like stepping into a magical fairy tale.

She stood still for a moment to inhale the fresher air and enjoy the feel of the light wind on her face. At the water's edge two coconut palms stood tall and proud, their fronds dancing to the breeze's rhythm.

The last of her anger left her as she noticed the distinctive red heads and bright green bodies of Fiji Parrotfinches bathing happily in the pool. She wouldn't be surprised if a couple of deer and rabbits appeared and began communicating with her.

Livia removed her sandals and sat carefully on the stony wall encasing the pool. The Fiji Parrotfinches were not prepared to tolerate this and flew off back into the surrounding forest, leaving her in silence.

Her thoughts weren't silent though. They were screaming their rising desperation and panic in her ears.

Foolishly, she'd hoped Massimo would at least consider giving their marriage another try. The happiness they'd once shared...that had been *real*.

Why hadn't she fought sooner? There had been so much to fight for but they had both let it descend into cold acrimony. She bore as much responsibility for this as Massimo. Livia knew how to fight. Fighting was one thing she excelled at. She could shout and scream and stamp her feet but she hadn't done the most important thing, which was to listen. When he'd asked for space and peace she'd taken it personally. She'd allowed her insecurities and fears to take root. Instead of giving him what he'd asked for she'd pushed even harder.

Exhaustion washed through her. What did all this even matter? How could she fight for a marriage when her husband didn't see anything worth saving? He'd had a taste of life without her and found it preferable.

Oh, God, the *pain* that ripped through her. And then the panic. It was all there in her battered, frightened heart as the depth of her love finally screamed unfiltered to the surface.

Massimo was the love of her life. How could she ever sleep again if he slipped away for good? How could she ever breathe properly?

The tears that had threatened to unleash since she'd woken in his arms filled her eyes. She no longer had the strength to hold them back.

Hugging her knees to her chest, Livia bowed her head and wept.

CHAPTER TWELVE

THE SKY HAD turned golden when Massimo disappeared under the canopy of trees.

He hadn't planned to go in search of Livia. He'd fixed the business problem that had cropped up and had intended to keep working but the silence Livia had left when she'd slipped away without a word had been louder than the ocean. It had deafened him. Every time he'd looked at his laptop, nothing had penetrated his brain.

The disjointed feelings had returned with a vengeance.

He'd decided a brisk walk on the fine white sandy beach was in order but he'd barely taken ten paces when one of his workers had rushed up to tell him Livia had gone off in search of the freshwater pool in the forest.

He'd shrugged the message off and walked another ten paces when an image of Livia lost and alone in the forest had formed in his head. He'd performed an abrupt about-turn.

Mercifully, the worker knew exactly where the pool was located.

The forest canopy cast everything in shadow and he increased his pace, praying he was heading in the right direction and not meandering from the route.

How long had she been here? She'd walked away from their chalet a couple of hours ago. Had she even found the pool? The island was small but the forest was dense and large enough to lose yourself in.

Perspiration clung to his skin when he finally found the clearing but he didn't know if it was from the heat or the fear that had gripped his heart. The sky had turned a deeper orange in his time in the forest. There was little daylight left.

He exhaled a long breath of relief to see her there. She was sitting with her feet in the pool gazing down into the water.

On legs that felt strangely unsteady, he stepped over and crouched beside her.

Other than a long, defeated sigh, she made no reaction to his presence.

He followed her gaze to peer into the still, clear water. He couldn't see what had captivated her attention so greatly.

Long moments passed before she turned her face to him.

He sucked in a shocked breath.

Even under the fading light he could see the puffiness of her red eyes. Her cheeks and neck were blotchy.

'Have you been crying?' he asked in a hoarse voice.

Eyes dark with misery met his. Her pretty nose wriggled, her chin wobbled and her shoulders shook before her face crumpled and tears fell like a waterfall down her face.

Massimo froze.

Not once in the entirety of their marriage had he seen his wife cry.

A tiny fissure cracked in his heart.

Working on autopilot, he twisted round to take her into his arms and held her tightly. She clung to him, sobbing into his chest, her hot tears soaking his T-shirt.

Something hot and sharp stabbed the back of his eyes and he blinked violently to clear it.

'Tell me what the matter is,' he urged, kissing the top of her head and strengthening his hold around her. Livia's vulnerability was something he'd always sensed rather than seen, something she'd always striven to mask. To witness her like this, with all her barriers and defences stripped away...

The fissure in his heart splintered into a thousand crevices all filling with an emotion so painful it felt as if his insides were splitting into pieces.

Her shoulders shook and she slowly raised her face to look at him. There was a despairing quality when she whispered his name before the ghost of a smile flittered on her tear-drenched lips. 'For such a clever man you can be incredibly stupid.'

He never got the chance to ask what she meant for her lips found his and he was pulled into a kiss of such hungry desperation that his senses responded before his brain could stop it.

Desperation had formed in his own skin too, an agonising ache of need for the woman whose tears hurt him in a place he'd never known existed.

In a crush of arms they tumbled to the sandy ground. There was no attempt or need for seduction or foreplay, that hungry ache to be as one all-consuming. Deep inside him breathed a wish to crawl into Livia's skin and rip out every demon that had filled his beautiful, strong wife with such desolation.

Together, their hands tugged frantically at his shorts

and her bikini bottoms, anguished passion there in every touch and every kiss.

They clung to each other as he drove deep inside her, their mouths crushed together, bodies fused tightly. There was a hopeless urgency in their lovemaking he had never experienced before and it flowed through them both, every soft moan of pleasure from her mouth a cry, every gasp a sob, a feeling in his soul that his world was on the verge of collapse, all of it combining to heighten the pleasure and shadow it with despair.

Only the despair racked him when it was over and the heady sensations had seeped away from him.

But his heart still thumped painfully when he pulled away from her and covered his face.

This had to stop.

They were over. *Over.*

Why prolong the pain? Hadn't they hurt each other enough?

Long moments passed in heavy silence before he rolled onto his side and got to his feet. Pulling his shorts on, he muttered, 'It's getting dark. We should get back.'

She didn't answer, simply rearranged her clothing and ran her fingers through her hair. As she did so, he noticed something that made him pause, perplexed. One of her nails was missing…

He snatched at the diversion from all the weight crushing him. 'What happened to your nail?'

She shrugged. 'It fell off.'

'They're false?'

She nodded.

He had no idea why this disturbed him so much. 'Since when do you wear false nails?'

More to the point, since when did she *bite* her nails?

Livia had always taken pride in her nails. Even when she'd worked as a nurse and been forced to keep them short for practical reasons they'd been buffed and polished. This nail was so short and ragged the nail bed was exposed.

She shrugged again. 'They needed doing.'

Shrugging the subject away with the same indifference she'd dismissed it with, Massimo reached into his pocket for his phone and turned the torch app on. It was bright enough to lead them back through the forest in relative safety but, all the same, he made sure to keep Livia close to him as they headed back along the route he'd taken to reach her, resisting the urge to take her hand.

No more touching her. He would dine alone and sleep in a cabin far from her. Far from the temptation he'd proven himself incapable of resisting.

But those tears...

Where had they come from? Surely she hadn't been crying about them?

It disturbed him to recall how close he'd come to tears too. He hadn't cried since he was a small child.

When they emerged from the forest and into the young mangroves, the first stars had emerged in the night sky.

Livia looked up at them and wished their shining brilliance could penetrate Massimo's heart and make him see that what they had could shine with that same brilliance too.

The incoming tide had covered most of the beach and she sat on the stone wall that acted as a barrier and looked up again at the vast night sky.

She had no idea what the time was.

Time was slipping away from her as fast as Massimo was.

Her fight to save them was a fight she was losing. She could feel it in her soul.

She could still taste their lovemaking on her lips but here he was now, sitting beside her at a distance that meant she would have to stretch her arm out to touch him.

'Did you know I fell in love with your family before I fell in love with you?' she said into the still air. 'Before I met them, I was stone inside. I'd had to fight and work for everything I had, escaping the Secondigliano, getting into nursing, supporting myself through my degree...even getting my placement in oncology so I could be a cancer nurse was a battle. Keeping myself detached while not losing my compassion for my patients and their families was a constant fight.'

She'd worked hard and fought her entire life. But her marriage? She'd thrown that away with hardly a whimper and now she feared she'd left it too late to repair it.

He shifted, stretching his legs out. The lapping tide drew in inches from his toes.

'Your grandfather was the first patient I ever became attached to. His home was so *warm*. All those photos of you all everywhere...' She sighed to remember the feelings being in that home had brought about in her. Jimmy had been her third private placement after she'd been head-hunted by the agency to work as a private oncology nurse. 'I was used to family members dropping in for regular short visits with the other placements, but your family were always there. They fed him, watched television with him, read to him. They lifted his spirits better than any medicine. The love they all had for each other opened my eyes to what a family should be like: built on love and support and just being there for each other. I wanted that so badly I could taste it. And then I met you...'

She clasped her hands together, remembering how it had felt to lie naked and cocooned in Massimo's arms that first night, the beat of his strong heart thudding against her... Nothing had ever felt more right in her life.

It made her soul weep to think she might never feel that rightness again.

'I fell so *hard* for you,' she whispered. 'When you proposed, I imagined a family life like the one your family had. I imagined babies and lots of visits to and from your parents. I assumed your detachment from them was a result of you being a single man living on the other side of the ocean and that once we were married you would want to spend more time with them. It took me a long time to realise that my assumptions had been delusional.' She filled her lungs with the fresh salty air. 'I could have coped with all that if you hadn't started detaching yourself from *me*. It scared me, Massimo. I could feel you slipping away and I didn't know how to bring you back and I made everything worse with my reaction to it all. I knew you didn't respond well to confrontation but I still kept on confronting you because that's the only way I knew to deal with things. Growing up was a survival of the fittest. If someone upset you, you confronted them. You learned to never show weakness. To back down made you weak and made you a target. I try so hard not to be that woman any more.'

Those confrontational traits had become her default position, a cycle she hadn't known how to break out of.

'You have two ears and one mouth for a reason,' Massimo had once said to her on one of the rare times she'd been able to spark a reaction out of him.

Those were words she'd carried every day since she'd left him.

She'd stopped supporting him in his work. She'd become *resentful* of his work. All the wonderful qualities she'd fallen in love with…she'd forgotten them because he'd hidden them away. He'd turned into a recluse from her and she in turn had become a shrill person she despised.

Fresh tears welled behind her eyes.

She let them fall.

There was nothing to hide any more. This was her, stripped bare of the things she always kept locked away from him, the vulnerabilities she'd hidden as she'd always hidden them since she was too young to even know what vulnerability meant.

'I remember us going to that technology awards ceremony you were guest of honour at. I got talking to one of the other trophy wives…'

'You were *never* a trophy wife,' he interrupted tightly.

'Not to begin with but that's how I felt in the second year. The wife I was talking to asked me how many lovers you'd had since we'd married. You should have seen her face when I said none. She thought I was delusional. All rich men have lovers. But not you. I never doubted you. Even when you spent nights in your office rather than come home to me, I never once had suspicions you were seeing other women. It would have been easier to compete with a flesh and blood woman but your mistress was always your business and I grew resentful towards it. I hate myself for walking away and not fighting harder for us. I hate that I became so needy and resentful. We could have the marriage we once dreamed about but we both have to want it and work at it.'

Massimo had never felt the thuds of his heart as clearly as he did right then. The crash they made in his ears reverberated with the distant crash of waves and sluiced through his entire being.

'But that's the problem,' he said harshly. 'I don't want it. We did try, Liv, but it wasn't enough then and it wouldn't be enough now. You might not want to hear about our marriage being reduced to a scientific formula but everything that drove us to marry in the first place was because of the heightened chemicals overpowering our rationality. What you're feeling now is a reignition of those chemicals brought about by—'

'Don't you *dare*,' she interrupted with a tearful edge. 'Don't tell me what I feel. I *know* what I feel. I love you. I'm well aware that the early days of a relationship are driven by heightened emotions and hormones—that's what normal people call the honeymoon period—but for you to keep reducing the love we shared to science is an insult to every memory we created together. If you simply stopped loving me, at least have the guts to say so.'

Nausea swirled violently inside him. 'I don't know if what I felt for you was love or not. I don't know if it was real. The feelings I had for you were the strongest I have ever felt but you must see that even if it was love, it doesn't solve anything. The problems we had would still be there eating away at us.'

'I don't see that. Not if we're both prepared to work at it.' The hitch in her voice made his heart contract but he made himself stay focused and strong.

This was for the best. One day, when the intensity of

everything they'd shared these last few days had subsided, she would see that too.

'I'm afraid that I do see it like that,' he said in as even a voice as he could manage. 'I'm not prepared to return to a marriage that's a proven failure. I'm not prepared to put myself through that again. It isn't worth it.'

There was a moment of silence until, without any warning, she jumped off the wall and waded out into the ocean until she was standing thigh high in the water. The moon had risen, bathing her in a silvery glow.

'Do you know what I don't understand?' Her voice carried through the breeze and the waves. 'How you can work so hard to save the world we live in when you've no intention of enjoying anything it has to offer. And I don't see or understand how you can put your mind to *anything* and make it succeed when you won't put a fraction of that energy into saving our marriage.'

'A marriage is not a business.'

'You're right. A marriage involves feelings. A business won't care for you when you're sick or lonely.' She rolled her neck and turned. Treading slowly through the water, she seemed to become magnified as she neared him.

The expression on her face sent coldness snaking up his spine and through his veins.

'You might not think our love *worth* it or know if it was real or not but I do. My love was real. I left you and I fell to pieces. I don't know what was worse—living with the ghost you'd become or living without you. Being apart from you felt like I'd had my heart ripped out. Every day was a battle just to get out of bed. I have no idea how I kept the charade going when I visited your family or Gianluca.' As she spoke, her voice grew steadily colder to match the expression on her face. 'I don't care what you think about your feelings for me but don't you ever lie to yourself that my love for you was anything but pure. You were my whole world. I gave up everything to be with you but I wasn't even worth fighting for, was I? You just breathed a great sigh of relief to be rid of me and got on with your life. My God, I've been *pathetic*.'

She took a step back and brought the hand with the missing nail to her face and stared at it as if she were seeing it for the first time before looking back at him. 'I'm no better than my mother. She would sit at the kitchen table late at night biting her nails while she waited for my father to come home.'

Massimo had seen many emotions from Livia in their time together but this was the first time she'd ever looked at him with contempt.

'And you're no better than my father.'

As insults went, that was the worst she could have thrown at him. A hot cauldron of anger rose in him. 'Do not compare me to that man.'

'His work, if you can call it that, came first in his life, just as yours does.'

Rising to his feet, Massimo flexed his hands and leaned forward to speak right into her face. 'Your father was killed in a gangland shooting. That was his work. You dare compare it to mine? My work has the potential to save the world from catastrophe!'

'And that's all that matters to you,' she spat back but still in the same controlled voice. 'Your work. At least my father loved his family.'

'Love?' He burst into a roar of incredulous laughter. 'You were terrified of him!'

'I was terrified because he was a monster but even monsters can love their family. He loved us and he wasn't afraid to show it but you... You shut out everyone who loves you. You want to know why I cut my hair?' She turned and parted her hair at the back of her scalp.

His heart throbbing madly, his guts cramped, confounded and disjointed that his temper was fraying at the seams while Livia had hers under such tight control, he blinked rapidly and leaned forward to see what she was showing him. Even with only the moon and the stars to illuminate them, he could see the exposed section she'd parted contained a small bald patch.

'Stress-induced alopecia,' she explained tightly, releasing her hair as she looked back at him. 'I had it cut and layered to cover it when I had my nails done last week because my pride couldn't bear for you to look at me and think I'd suffered in any way without you. I was trying to prove to myself, too, that I was over you and now I know I am because all the love I had for you... you've just killed it.'

His nausea had returned with a vengeance. 'Livia...'

'I don't want to hear any more of your excuses.' Her eyes blazed with a hardness he'd never seen before, a look he instinctively knew she hadn't given since leaving Naples. 'I'm not *prepared*...' she dragged the word out with a sneer '...to waste another atom of energy on a man who refuses to give me an inch of what he devotes to his business. Enjoy the rest of your life—I hope you and your business are very happy together.'

The footprints she made in the sand as she walked away with her head held high were covered by foaming ocean within moments of being created.

CHAPTER THIRTEEN

THE RETURN JOURNEY was harder than the outbound journey had been. Livia had debated the idea of making her own way back to Italy but reluctantly decided against it. It would take twice as long as it would to fly with Massimo and she wanted to be at home with her brother.

She had walked away from him with her head held high and kept her own company since, her emotions veering from humiliation to anger and back again. The only emotion she wouldn't allow herself was despair.

Her anger was directed only at herself.

She *had* been pathetic. Not only in her marriage but in the aftermath, after she'd walked away. When she should have reclaimed her life and moved on, she'd become stuck in purgatory, unable to sever the emotional ties that had kept her bound to Massimo.

They were severed now.

Their only communication since her disastrous attempt at reconciliation had been a text message from him that morning informing her they would be leaving the island in ten minutes.

She'd spent the night in Madeline's chalet. She neither knew nor cared where Massimo had slept.

During the short flight on the Cessna to Nadi airport, she'd refused to look at him and rebuffed his few attempts at conversation. When they'd boarded his jet, she'd taken her original seat, stuck her earphones in and selected the most mindless movie she could find.

The moment they were in the air, she'd put the physical barrier around her seat up. It went perfectly with the metaphorical barrier she'd erected.

The one good thing about this return journey was that Massimo would only be travelling as far as LA with her. She had no doubt he would go straight to his precious facility.

When one of the cabin crew asked if she would like something to eat she readily accepted and forced the warm baguette filled with smoked cheese and prosciutto into her cramped stomach.

She would never allow her feelings to prevent her from eating ever again.

She had no idea if Massimo ate. She refused to look.

She still refused to look at him when they landed in LA, even when he hovered by her seat as if trying to get her attention.

'Take care of yourself,' he muttered after she'd ignored him for as long as he could tolerate.

And then he was gone.

She didn't expel a breath until he'd left the cabin.

The baguette she'd eaten felt as if it wanted to expel itself out of her system. She held it down and left the plane too, escorted by a hefty security guard to a private lounge. She didn't have to worry about bumping into Massimo. He would already be in his car.

But he wasn't in his car.

Livia's heart came to a shuddering halt when the lounge door opened a few minutes later and Massimo stood at the threshold looking paler than she'd ever seen him.

She knew what was wrong before he spoke, her heart already aching for him before the words came out.

'My grandfather had a bad turn on the flight home. They don't think he's going to make it.'

The only illumination in the room Massimo sat in came from the machines hooked to his grandfather's weakening body. The incessant beeping from them grated in his head like nails on a chalkboard.

He'd shifted the armchair as close to the bed as he could get it. His parents were sleeping in a spare room down the corridor. The medical team were resting in the adjoining room. His sister had gone home for the night, making Massimo promise to call her if anything changed.

Nothing had changed in the two days his grandfather had been home. Nothing apart from his steadily weakening heart.

Jimmy Seibua was dying. But he was dying in the home he loved. His bedroom had been turned into its own hospital room with everything needed to keep him comfortable and pain-free until nature finally took its course.

The door opened.

He didn't need to look to know it was Livia. He would know her movements blindfolded.

'Hot chocolate,' she said softly.

He took one of the steaming cups from her with a muted thanks.

She placed her own cup on a ledge before pulling a thermometer from the dedicated medical cupboard and running it gently over his grandfather's forehead. After logging the reading and checking the equipment he was hooked to, she pulled the other armchair closer and sat beside Massimo. 'He's comfortable. That's the most important thing.'

Massimo nodded.

In the two days they'd been holed up in his grandfather's home, Livia had left only once, a short trip to her apartment on the other side of the city to check in on her brother.

He could never put into words how grateful he was to have her there. Her calm, compassionate presence soothed his family's nerves.

It soothed his nerves too. She could easily save her compassion for the rest of his family and pretend he didn't exist but she didn't.

'How are you doing?' she asked quietly.

He shrugged. He didn't know how he was doing. He felt battered from the inside.

'Have you eaten?'

'I'm not hungry.'

Her small hand rested on his and gave a gentle squeeze. It lasted only seconds but it spread a little warmth into his cold veins.

He had to stop himself from reaching over to snatch her hand back and keep it tucked in his.

She stayed with him for the next hour. They didn't speak but it was a companionable silence. When she whispered that she was going to try and get a few hours' sleep, the warmth she'd brought into the room left with her.

Time dragged on. The clock on the wall ticked slowly. The first hint of daylight seeped through the curtains.

Needing to stretch his legs, Massimo got to his feet and walked to his grandfather's dressing table. His mother had placed a dozen framed photos on it for him, his grandparents' wedding photo taking pride of place. Massimo picked it up and smiled sadly at the two beaming faces. How young they had been. How happy. And how in love. They'd met during his grandfather's deployment in the Second World War. His grandmother, who'd come from a wealthy English family, had worked for a secret government agency during that period. She'd kept those secrets for all her life. The only concrete facts Massimo knew were that they had met and fallen in love. His grandfather had left his home on the other side of the world permanently to marry her. Her parents, dismayed that she'd fallen for a man with skin they considered too dark, had disowned her. Massimo's grandparents had never allowed their subsequent poverty to get them down. They'd got on with life as best they could, raising a daughter, Sera, who was their pride and joy. When Sera married the Italian Gianni Briatore, they hadn't hesitated to follow her to Italy and make it their home.

He tried to imagine the challenges they'd faced. A mixed race couple in a time when mixed race marriages were frowned upon and in a time when most of the world was reeling from unimaginable horrors. Yet they had remained strong. Their love had endured. He didn't think it a coincidence that his grandfather was first diagnosed with cancer within a year of his grandmother's death.

His hand trembled as he placed the frame back on the dresser. His knuckles brushed the picture next to it, the one photo he'd spent two days blurring from his vision. This time, he picked it up.

It was his own wedding photo. He and Livia were in the centre, his parents to his left, his sister and grandfather to Livia's right.

If smiles could be converted into energy, Livia's could have powered a small country.

Massimo's own joy was there too on his beaming face. The camera didn't show that Livia's hand had been squeezing his bottom when the photo was taken.

Their wedding day had been the happiest of his life.

His grandfather coughed.

Abandoning the photo, Massimo hurried to his side and took his hand.

His grandfather's eyes were open. He coughed again. And then he smiled.

The love behind that smile could have fuelled the same country as Livia's and it filled Massimo's chest and spread through his veins.

He returned the smile.

He didn't notice the tear that had leaked from his eye until it rolled down his chin and landed on their joined hands.

The filmy eyes closed and his grandfather drifted back to sleep.

He never woke up again.

Three hours later, with the family he loved at his side, Jimmy Seibua took his last breath.

Livia switched the dishwasher on and dried her hands absently on the front of her black trousers, wishing there were something else she could do but there wasn't a single mark left to wipe down. She'd scrubbed the kitchen so hard it gleamed.

She felt heartsick to her core.

She'd sat with her brother during the full Requiem mass for Jimmy. Gianluca had held her hand and kept her supplied with tissues. She was so proud of him and grateful for his support but she couldn't stop her heart from wishing it were Massimo's hand she'd been holding.

Stupid heart. One day it would catch up with her brain and let him go for good. All the resolutions she'd made had been destroyed before she'd had a chance to put them into practice.

But what else could she have done? Massimo's family had wanted her there while they'd nursed Jimmy in his final days. She'd wanted to be there too, with the old man who'd given her the most precious gift she could have received. A family.

The wake was being held in a marquee in the garden of Sera and Gianni's home. Caterers had been brought in for the refreshments, allowing family and friends to drink and reminisce his memory unhindered.

After an hour of it, Livia had needed to escape and slipped into the house to hide in the kitchen. Massimo's immediate family knew now they were getting divorced. He'd told them shortly after Jimmy's death. All had privately told her that their marriage was their own business but, divorce or not, she would always be family to them.

She wished that could be true and wished that when she said goodbye to them all later it wouldn't be for the last time.

She needed a clean break. There was no way she could move forward with her life if Massimo's family remained a central part of it. She would be permanently reminded of all she had lost.

She hoped they understood. She hoped they could forgive her.

'What are you doing?'

She turned her head to find Massimo at the kitchen door, his brow creased. His suit looked slightly baggy. Unsurprisingly, Massimo had lost weight. Livia doubted he'd eaten a full meal since they'd left the island.

She supposed he would go back to LA tonight. She was surprised he hadn't gone back after Jimmy's death and returned for the funeral. He'd stayed with his parents. She didn't think she was imagining the growing closeness between them. She could only hope it was a closeness that lasted.

'Cleaning up.'

'You didn't have to do that.'

She shrugged and stared at the floor. It hurt too much to look at him. 'I wanted to.'

Massimo closed the door and stood with his back to it. 'I want to thank you.'

'For what?'

'Everything you did for my grandfather and for all the support you've given my family.'

She raised her shoulders. It wasn't a shrug but he knew what she was trying to convey. That she didn't want or expect thanks. It was something she'd done because it was the right thing to do and because she couldn't not do it.

He wondered if she had any idea what a difference she'd made this last week.

Their last conversation before his grandfather had been taken ill…he'd hurt her so badly. She'd put her heart and her pride on the line for them to have a future together and he'd thrown it back at her and denounced the love they'd shared as anything worth fighting for.

And yet here she was, still there, still giving the support he'd once taken for granted. Because he had taken it for granted. He'd become so damned frightened of his own feelings that he'd forgotten how good it had felt to go home and unload what was on his mind to her receptive ears and to lie in her arms and feel her massage the tension from his head and his shoulders. The errors he'd made... They hadn't been Livia's fault. They'd been his alone. But he'd punished her for them.

He'd pushed her away and shut her out one cold retreat at a time when he should have wrapped his arms around her and told her he loved her every single day.

After the funeral service, she'd joined the line of mourners waiting their turn to give their personal embrace to Massimo, his sister and their parents. She should have been by his side.

If she'd been at his side and he'd had her strength to lean on he would have found it easier to endure. He'd found everything easier to endure with Livia by his side. He'd forgotten that too.

'When are you going home?' she asked, breaking the silence.

'Tonight.'

'What's happened with the prototype?'

'Nothing. I've deferred the testing again until I get back.'

The raise of her shoulder seemed to indicate something different from her first raise but this was a shrug he couldn't interpret.

'Come back with me.' The words left his mouth before he could stop them.

Her eyes shot up to meet his. 'What?'

He rested the back of his head against the door as everything suddenly became clear. 'Come back with me. To Los Angeles.'

She just stared at him, lips parted but no sound coming out.

'Those things I said on the island. I didn't mean them...'

'They sounded convincing to me.'

'I love you.' And as he said the words aloud he felt a physical shift inside him.

'No!' Her voice ricocheted through the kitchen like a bullet.

'Livia—'

'I don't want to hear it.' She pressed her hands to her ears then finally met his eye. The pain reflecting back at him almost tore him in two. 'And I don't want to be the salve for your grief.'

'It's not about my grief.' How had he been so *blind*? 'I've been...'

'I don't want to hear another word of your lies.' Her shoulders rose in shudders and her throat moved before she turned away to take her bag from the counter. 'It's too late. I don't believe you. And even if I did, the answer would still be no. I could never trust my heart with you again.' She slung the strap of her bag over her shoulder and stood before him. When her eyes met his this time, they were devoid of emotion. 'I need to go.'

Something cold scratched deep in his throat.

He'd never fully recognised the love that had always reflected back at him until now that it was gone.

He moved to one side to let her pass.

She walked out of the kitchen without looking back. When he could no longer hear her footsteps and all that remained was the lightest linger of her fragrance, his knees finally gave way and he sank to the floor.

Head clasped in his hands, he breathed in deeply, calling himself every name under the sun until he could hold it back no longer and punched the nearest cabinet.

The crack it made echoed through the walls closing in around him.

He brought his hand to his face. Blood poured from his knuckles but he felt no pain.

The only pain came from the bleeding in his heart.

His grandfather's words at his party about having lived... Finally he understood them.

For the first time since he'd been a small child, Massimo wept.

He understood *everything*.

He understood that the blood in his veins never pumped as hard as it did when he was with Livia. She brought him to life. She had brought him back to his family. She had brought joy and love to his cold heart. She had lit the way and pulled him out of the darkness he hadn't realised he'd become lost in.

He understood, finally, that he could live in the warmth of her love or die in the cold of that darkness.

Livia hauled the shopping bags into the ground-floor apartment and closed the door with her bottom, craning her ears for the sound of the gaming console. Since she'd returned to her apartment after Jimmy's funeral two weeks ago, the sound of fast cars racing had become the background music of her life. She never complained about it. She needed the noise to drown the sound of her tortured thoughts.

Today, though, the apartment was quiet.

'Gianluca?' she called.

Her brother appeared as she was putting the bags on the side.

'Guess what?' he said, grinning and waving his phone in that goofy way of his.

'What?'

He looked as proud as a strutting peacock. 'Massimo's giving me a job.'

The name landed like a cold sharp shock against her face, just as it did every time Gianluca uttered it. She took a moment to compose herself. 'A job? Working for him? You're moving to America?'

His grin widened. 'You're not getting rid of me that easily. He's opening his European headquarters in Rome and has offered me a job on the security team.'

'He's opening headquarters *here*?'

Gianluca had the grace to look sheepish. 'He told me his plans the night of Jimmy's funeral after you'd gone but said not to say anything until everything was confirmed.'

So desperate had Livia been to get away from Massimo that she'd left the wake without her brother. Gianluca hadn't cared that she'd forgotten him. He'd had a great time getting drunk on bourbon with Massimo.

'You were told not to tell me?'

The sheepish expression morphed into the same confusion as she knew she must be showing. 'He didn't say not to tell you specifically. Just said it was best to keep it quiet until he'd bought the premises and knew for certain it would go ahead.' The confusion turned into beaming pride. 'And I kept my mouth shut exactly as he asked.'

'You certainly did. A job in security?' That was quite a step for an eighteen-year-old who'd never held down a job and had left school with only minimal qualifications. She had to practically crack her skin to get a smile to form. 'This is wonderful news. Congratulations. I didn't realise the two of you had kept in touch,' she added casually.

She should have guessed though. Since Massimo had brought in the team to help Gianluca escape the Secondigliano without reprisals, her brother had developed a serious case of hero worship.

Hearing him go on and on about how marvellous her estranged husband was... It was frustrating, to put it mildly. But she had the sense to reason with herself that if her brother was going to hero-worship anyone and use them as a base to model himself on, better it be Massimo than one of the men who had terrorised their lives.

'He's going to pay for me to take some courses too, so I can build on my qualifications. He said if I work hard, I could one day run his security for him.'

'This is wonderful,' she repeated. And it was. Truly. Livia had tried very hard not to be concerned that her brother hadn't been actively looking for work, telling herself he needed time to get used to this new life in a new city without the safety net of their family and his friends. She'd planned to give him a month to settle in before broaching the subject, when all along Massimo had already decided to give him a chance.

That was a big thing for him to do, she acknowledged. He knew full well what a handful Gianluca could be.

Handful or not, she'd been glad to have him around, and not only because it meant he was safe. His playful puppy-like ways were a welcome distraction from the painful ache in her frozen heart.

She dug into one of the shopping bags, pulled out the fresh tagliatelle she'd purchased and threw it at him.

He caught it easily.

'Put the water on and get this cooked. There's ricotta and spinach in the other bag. I'm going back to the shop to buy a bottle of prosecco. We need to celebrate!'

She hurried out of the apartment, Gianluca's protests that he didn't know how to cook pasta a distant ringing in her ears.

As soon as the door shut behind her, her smile dropped.

She walked down the street, her mind in a whirl.

Massimo was opening a headquarters here? In the city she lived in? The city he'd actively avoided throughout their marriage?

He'd once mooted the idea of opening a headquarters in London but that had been over a year ago, a throwaway musing of an idea. He hadn't mentioned it when they'd been in Fiji...

She firmly pushed the thought of Fiji from her mind. Every time a memory from it flashed through her, the nausea that seemed to have become a constant presence in her stomach swirled harder. It swirled now, strong enough to make her giddy.

As she passed a steakhouse, a customer opened its doors, unleashing the aromas being cooked within. Smells she would normally find tempting swirled through Livia's airways, increasing the nausea.

Suddenly fearing she really was going to be sick, she rested one hand against a wall, the other to her roiling stomach and forced as much air as she could into her lungs.

It seemed to take an age to pass.

When she finally felt capable of continuing, she looked up, but instead of her gaze fixing on the shop she was heading for, it landed on the neon-green cross on the other side of the street.

She didn't even realise she was staring at it until a small child walked into her. The mother, who was pushing a pram with a tiny baby in it, apologised but her words sounded like an echo in Livia's ears.

Thoughts of prosecco all but forgotten, she crossed the busy road and entered the pharmacy.

She'd stopped taking her pill when she'd left Massimo. They hadn't used protection when they were in Fiji. The thought hadn't even occurred to her, not even when she'd cuddled baby Elizabeth or when they'd had that angry conversation about babies.

Why had that been? She'd taken her pill religiously throughout their marriage. She'd wanted a baby with Massimo but it had been something they'd both agreed was for the future. And then their marriage had become so cold that it would have been cruel to bring a baby into it.

Two minutes later she walked out, a pregnancy test tucked in her bag.

Twenty minutes after that she was back in her apartment and in the bathroom, having given Gianluca the cash to go out and buy them food—he'd burnt the tagliatelle—and prosecco.

But he would have to drink the prosecco himself.

The test was unambiguous. She was pregnant.

Her head swimming, she did the only thing that made sense. She reached into her bag for her phone and called Massimo.

He answered on the third ring. 'Liv?'

Just hearing his voice made her heart clench and tears fill her eyes.

She squeezed them shut.

'Livia? Are you there? Is something wrong?'

She could hardly hear her own dull voice over the roar in her ears. 'I'm pregnant.'

CHAPTER FOURTEEN

THE SUDDEN PEAL of the doorbell only added to the pounding in Livia's head.

'If it's for me, I'm not in,' she shouted to her brother, who was playing on his games console in the living room.

Mercifully, Gianluca was a selfish teenager and had been oblivious to there being anything wrong with her when he'd returned with their takeaway. He'd also been oblivious when she'd eaten only half of her portion, using her lack of appetite as an opportunity to consume more food for himself, and oblivious to there being anything out of the ordinary when she'd announced immediately after eating that she was going to get an early night.

The bell rang again.

Grabbing her pillow, she pulled it over her head and burrowed deeper under the covers.

She would wallow for one night, she'd decided. Discovering she was pregnant was an exceptional circumstance that merited wallowing.

But...

For all the fear an unexpected pregnancy had brought there had also been the first flutterings of excitement.

Deciding that suffocating herself was probably bad for the baby, she removed the pillow and put it back under her head and stared at the ceiling.

She put a tentative hand up her nightshirt and pressed it against her belly. It didn't feel any different but a tiny life form was growing in there. A life created by her and Massimo.

Massimo...

She closed her eyes.

She couldn't decide if fate was being cruel or kind. When she'd finally found the strength to move forward with her life it played this most magical of tricks on her. She would never be free of him now.

She'd struggled to move on as it was. She'd kept a smile on her face, used iron willpower to stop herself biting her nails and gone through the motions of re-claiming her life but the wrench in her heart hadn't even started to heal yet.

She lived in hope rather than expectation.

She lived with an ache that left her always feeling cold. The sun could shine as hard as it wanted but she never felt it any more.

A knock on her bedroom door interrupted her wallowing.

She sat up, expecting Gianluca's face to appear and the request of money to be given.

But it wasn't her skinny brother who walked into her bedroom.

She blinked a number of times, certain she must be imagining the towering figure standing there, dressed in snug black jeans, a black T-shirt and a tan leather jacket. Her immediate impression was that he hadn't shaved since his grandfather's funeral.

She had to clear her throat to get any words out. 'What are you doing here?'

Massimo closed the door and gazed at the woman he loved sitting like a princess in her bed. He soaked in every detail of the face he'd missed so much.

'You didn't think I would take the news of you being pregnant and not come straight to you?'

Her brow creased in confusion. 'Do you have a time portal? I only told you two hours ago?'

'I would have been here sooner but I couldn't find my car keys and I'd already sent my driver home for the night. I walked.'

'You were already in Rome?'

'I never left.'

Now her whole face creased.

He grinned and removed his jacket, draping it over her dressing-table chair without taking his eyes from her. God, it felt so good seeing her. Knowing he was in the same city as Livia but unable to reach out to her had almost killed him. He took a step towards her. 'I've bought a house here.'

She shrank back as if afraid he was going to touch her. 'Since when?'

'The sale went through yesterday. I was going to wait a little longer for a few of the other pieces to fall into place before I came to you.'

The wariness in her eyes almost killed him too. 'Came to me for what?'

'To see what else it would take for you to believe that I do love you and that you can trust your heart with me.'

Since his epiphany at his grandfather's funeral, he'd done a lot of thinking.

Everything Livia had said about him was true. He

did shut people out. Livia was the only person he'd ever let in but the moment he'd felt her get too close, the moment his heart had truly opened for her, he'd slammed it back shut and pushed her away.

He'd got so used to doing everything for himself, to relying only on himself that he'd convinced himself that it was the only way to be. He'd got so used to everything he touched turning into gold that when he'd made the first basic errors of his career he'd automatically blamed Livia for them, forgetting that he was only human.

She'd brought such joy into his life and, fool that he was, he'd turned his back on that joy and turned his back on her.

He'd pushed his parents away too. He'd been a condescending, arrogant bastard about the choices they'd made. They'd chosen family over money and he'd been too blind to appreciate the sacrifices they'd made so he could have that security. He'd taken their love for granted. He'd never had to walk his sister to school or cook her meals as Livia had done for Gianluca. He'd never slept with a weapon under his pillow out of fear. The threadbare clothes he'd been so ashamed to wear had always been lovingly repaired, the holes in his shoes fixed until the shoes could be replaced. He'd been so focused on creating his own future that he'd never taken the time to appreciate all the things he'd had right there. Love. Security. An abundance of affection. All the things that when added together made life worth living.

He'd been blind about everything.

But Livia had seen everything clearly.

He didn't blame her for dismissing his half-formed declaration of love.

Along with all his thinking he'd done a lot of doing.

The path to bringing her back into his life had been clear. He'd needed to rebuild her trust with actions rather than words.

Her shoulders rose before she brought her knees up and wrapped her arms around them. 'Not this again,' she whispered. 'I told you, it's too late. I've moved on.'

'Nature doesn't think so or you wouldn't be pregnant.'

'Nature is a joke.'

'A wonderful joke.'

She rested her chin on her knees. 'You're happy?'

'That we're having a baby together? Liv, there is only one thing that could make me happier than I feel at this moment but I will get to that shortly. Why didn't you tell me you'd come off the pill?'

Colour flamed her cheeks. 'I didn't think.'

'And I didn't think to ask if you were still on it.' He pulled his T-shirt over his head.

'What are you doing?' she asked, alarm in her voice but something different in her eyes.

'Showing you something.' Dropping the T-shirt on the floor, he kicked his boots off and climbed onto the bed. Then he leaned forward to take her rigid hand and placed it on his left bicep. Eyes holding hers, he said, 'The spearheads on this tattoo... One of the meanings for it is willpower. I had it done to remind myself to remain strong. I needed that reminder when you left me otherwise I would have chased after you and begged you to come back to me.'

He moved her hand so it rested on his chest above his beating heart. 'I married you because the madness of my attraction to you compelled me to. I knew my feelings for you ran deep and I assumed what I felt for you was love but I didn't know it could grow deeper. I didn't know my feelings for you would take root in my soul and that you would become my reason for breathing. You challenged me on so many levels I didn't know where I ended and you began. When you left me I felt as if I'd been freed from madness itself. I threw myself back into my work a liberated man and I would have worked myself into an early grave rather than stop for a minute and open myself to the pain beating right here in this cold, shrivelled heart that losing you caused.'

He reached for her hair with his free hand and ran his fingers down the silky locks he loved so much. 'I'm sorry for pushing you away. I'm sorry for shutting you out. I'm sorry for throwing your love back at you and demeaning everything we meant to each other. I'm sorry for every minute of hurt I caused you.'

She opened her mouth but he put a finger to her lips.

'I'm sorry for doing nothing when I knew how miserable you were in LA.'

'Don't,' she whispered, turning her cheek. 'My loneliness was my fault too. I should have gone out and had English lessons and taken art classes or something.'

'Art classes?'

She shrugged. 'Something that got me out of the house. Something that stopped me being dependent on you for my happiness.'

That reminded him of something he'd meant to ask her on the island. 'Have you had English lessons since we separated?'

'I started an online course. I didn't get very far. My head wasn't in the right place for new information to sink into it.'

He rubbed his thumb along her cheekbone, his heart swelling. 'There was a lot I could have done to make your life easier and if you come back to me, I swear things will be different. I'm moving back to Italy.'

Her eyes found his again. There was a glimmer of something in them that gave him hope.

'Everything you said before we left the island was right, including what you said about my relationship with my family,' he said quietly. 'How can I build a proper relationship with them if I'm living on the other side of the ocean?'

'Is that why you're opening a base here in Rome?'

He nodded and slid his hands down her cheeks to cup her face. 'Partly. But mostly for you. Your life is here and my life is with you…if you'll let me back in it. That's all I want. To be with you. It took losing you for me to see how much I need you.'

A tear spilled out and rolled down her cheek and over his hand. 'You said that about our marriage. That you hadn't realised how unsuited you were to marriage until you married me.'

'I said a lot of things. I believed a lot of things.'

'So why should I believe you now?' Livia wanted to believe him more desperately than she had ever wanted to believe anything but she was frightened. Her heart had been wrung too many times to bloom properly any more.

'Because now my head is clear. I want to make our marriage work more than I have ever wanted anything and I'm willing to do whatever it takes for it. You're my priority, now and for ever…you and our baby.' He could hardly believe he was going to be a father. 'I was waiting for confirmation of the sale of my house in LA before I came to you…' He gave a rueful smile. 'Your news about the pregnancy brought me to you a few days earlier than I anticipated. I wanted to be able to look you in the eye

and give you categorical proof that you're more important to me than anything else. The house I've bought here
in Rome is in your name.' Another rueful smile. 'I'm
hoping you will let me share it with you. If not, it's yours
to keep. I'll still need a base in LA but I'm hoping you'll
come with me and choose a house for us to share there.
A house you're comfortable in, in a neighbourhood you
can feel at home in. There's a lot that I'm hoping for but
whatever happens from this point forward is up to you.'

'And what if I say no?'

He closed his eyes and inhaled deeply through his
nose. 'Then I will have only myself to blame and I will
have to be content with having a child with you even if I
can't be your husband. All I would ask is that you allow
me to be a proper father to it.'

Livia blinked back the fresh tears blurring her vision
so she could look at him properly.

Ringing from the soulful caramel eyes was nothing
but sincerity.

Her heart thumped and expanded.

'Let me get a few things straight,' she said slowly. 'In
the last two weeks you've bought me a house, bought
new business premises here in Rome, offered my de-
linquent brother a job and put your house up for sale in
LA. Have I missed anything?'

'I think that's everything.'

'And you've done all this for me?'

He shifted forward and pressed the tip of his nose to
hers. 'You're my life, Livia. Everything I have is yours.'

Her heart expanding a little more, she nudged her face
a little closer to place the softest of kisses to his lips. 'I
need you to promise me something.'

'Anything.'

Her hands crept onto his shoulders. 'Don't ever push me away again.'

'Never.' Now he placed the softest of kisses to her lips. 'Does this mean…?'

She hooked her hands around his neck. The blooming in her heart was growing with every breath she took. Staring deep into his eyes, she smiled. 'It means yes. To everything.'

The eyes staring back at her were searching. 'Do you think you can ever love me again?'

She kissed him once more and kept her mouth there, breathing him in, filling her lungs and her senses with the taste and scent she'd believed she would never enjoy again. She moved her lips away long enough to say, 'Massimo, you are etched in my heart. I've loved you since the day I met you and I will love you until the day I die.'

'You're etched on my heart too. And my soul. There is only you.'

And with those words her blooming heart swelled and reached out to join with his for ever.

A long while later, naked and replete in each other's arms, Massimo suddenly pulled himself out of the light sleep he'd fallen into.

With everything that had happened that evening, the full, wonderful magnitude of their situation finally hit him. 'We're having a baby.'

Livia giggled softly and kissed his chest. 'Yes, we are!'

'Have I told you recently how much I love you?'

'Not recently enough.'

He told her. And then he showed her.

EPILOGUE

LIVIA STOOD AT the front of the chalet's veranda, her hands on the wooden balustrade, and watched in awe at the rain lashing down. From her vantage point, she could see the main part of Seibua Island and all the surrounding ocean.

In the distance, she spotted one of the staff running through the rain in exaggerated leaps and grinned. If baby Sera weren't sleeping in her crib, Livia would be out there running a dance through it too. Massimo thought her a little bit mad for loving the rainy season so much but for her it was perfect. It unleashed Seibua Island's scents so that even the dullest of them filled the air with their potency and made the landscape a glimmering sheen of verdant brilliance. The rainbows that came when the sun blazed through the rain were the most glorious sight. She hoped one appeared soon.

The buzzing of her phone distracted her from her rainbow watch and she pulled it out of her shorts pocket, rolling her eyes at yet another of her brother's joke messages. She quickly fired a message back telling him he should be working and got an indignant reply that it was early morning in Rome and even the birds weren't awake yet. Smiling widely, she put her phone back in her pocket and resumed her position on the veranda.

While she scanned in all directions, she saw her mother-in-law poke her head out of her chalet door and laughed when she immediately whipped it back in.

In truth, it wasn't only Massimo who thought her a little mad for her love of the rain. His entire family thought the same. None of them understood how magical she found it, how without it there would be no rainbows and none of the glorious colour that now filled her life.

She remembered reading something once, how without the dark we wouldn't see the stars. That was how she felt about the rain.

She laughed again when she saw Jimmy make his escape from the lodge to go dancing in it as he'd watched her do numerous times. He saw her looking and waved wildly.

She waved back, waving harder when Massimo, who'd been caught in the lodge when the downpour started, came out to join their three-year-old son, his bemusement obvious even from the distance that separated them.

Her heart swelled to see him scoop their son into his arms and swing him around. She didn't need to be close to hear Jimmy's squeal of laughter. It was a sound locked in her memory bank.

And then her heart swelled enough to burst when, right above their dancing heads, the clouds parted and the multicoloured arc appeared in all its glory.

It appeared to be shining just for them.

* * * * *

DEALING HER FINAL CARD

JENNIE LUCAS

CHAPTER ONE

"BREE, wake up!"

A hand roughly shook Bree Dalton awake. Startled, she sat up with a gasp, blinking in the darkness.

Her younger sister was sitting on the edge of the bed. Tears sparkled on Josie's pale cheeks in the moonlight.

"What's happened?" Bree dropped her bare feet to the tile floor, ready to run, ready to fight anyone who had made her baby sister cry. "What's wrong?"

Josie took a deep breath.

"I really messed up this time." She wiped her eyes. "But before you freak out, I want you to know it's going to be fine. I know how to fix it."

Rather than be comforted by this statement, Bree felt deepening fear. Her twenty-two-year-old sister, six years younger than Bree, had a knack for getting into trouble. And she was wearing the short, sexy dress of a Hale Ka'nani cocktail waitress instead of their gray housekeeping smock.

"Were you working at the bar?" Bree demanded.

"Still worried about some man hitting on me?" Josie barked a bitter laugh. "I *wish* that was the problem."

"What is it, then?"

Josie ran a hand over her eyes. "I'm tired, Bree," she whispered. "You gave up everything to take care of me. When I was twelve, I needed that, but now I am so tired of being your burden—"

"I've never thought of you that way," Bree said, stung.

Josie looked at her clasped hands. "I thought this was my chance to pay off those debts, so we could go back to the Mainland. I've been practicing in secret. I thought I knew how to play. How to win."

A chill went down Bree's spine.

"You gambled?" she said numbly.

"It fell into my lap." Josie exhaled, visibly shivering in the warm Hawaiian night. "I'd finished cleaning the wedding reception in the ballroom when I ran into Mr. Hudson. He offered to pay me overtime if I'd serve drinks at his private poker game at midnight. I knew you'd say no, but I thought, just this once..."

"I told you not to trust him!"

"I'm sorry," Josie cried. "When he invited me to join them at the table, I couldn't say no!"

Bree clawed back her long blond hair. "What happened?"

"I won," Josie said defiantly. Then she swallowed. "At least I did for a while. Then I started losing. First I lost the chips I'd won, then I lost our grocery money, and then..."

Cold understanding went through Bree. She finished dully, "Then Mr. Hudson kindly offered to loan you whatever you needed."

Josie's mouth fell open. "How did you know?"

Because Bree knew bullies like Greg Hudson and how they tried to gain the upper hand. She'd met his type before, long ago, in the life she'd given up ten years ago—before she'd fallen in love, and her life had fallen apart. Before the man she loved had betrayed her, leaving her to the sheriff and the wolves—orphaned and penniless at eighteen, with a heartbroken twelve-year-old sister.

But oh, yes. Bree knew Greg Hudson's type. She closed her eyes, feeling sick as she thought of the hotel manager's hard eyes above his jovial smile, of his cheerful Hawaiian shirt that barely covered his fat belly. The resort manager had slept with many of his female employees, particularly amongst the lower-paid housekeeping staff. In the two months since the Dalton sisters had arrived in Hawaii, Bree had wondered more than once why he'd gone to such trouble to hire them from Seattle. He claimed the girls had been recommended by their employment agency, but that didn't ring true. Surely there were many people looking for jobs here in Honolulu.

Josie had laughed at her, teasing her for being "gloomy and doomy," but as Bree had scrubbed the bathrooms and floors of the lavish resort, she'd tried to solve the puzzle in her mind, and her bad feeling only grew. Especially when their boss made it clear over the past few weeks that he was interested in Josie. And made it equally clear the one he really wanted was Bree.

But of course Josie, with her innocent, trusting spirit, never noticed evil around her. She didn't fully understand why Bree had given up gambling, and insisted they work only low-wage jobs for the ten years since their father died, keeping them under the radar of unscrupulous, dangerous men. Josie didn't know how wicked the world could be.

Bree did.

"Gambling doesn't pay." She kept her voice calm. "You should know that by now."

"You're wrong. It does!" Josie said angrily. "We had plenty of money ten years ago." She turned and looked wistfully at the window, toward the moonlit Hawaiian night. "And I thought if I could just be more like you and Dad…"

"You were using *us* as role models? Have you lost your mind?" Bree exploded. "I've spent the last decade trying to give you a different life!"

"Don't you think I know that?" Josie cried. "What you've sacrificed for me?"

Bree took a deep breath. "It wasn't just for you." Her throat ached as she rose to her feet. "How much money did you lose tonight?"

For a moment, her sister didn't answer. Outside, Bree heard

the distant plaintive call of seabirds as Josie stared mutinously at the floor, arms folded. When she finally spoke, her voice was barely audible.

"A hundred."

Bree felt relief so fierce she almost cried. She'd been so afraid it would be worse. Reaching out, she gave her sister's shoulder a squeeze. "It'll be all right." She exhaled in relief. "Our budget will be tight, but we'll just eat a little more rice and beans this month." Wiping her eyes, she tried to smile. "Let this be a good lesson…"

But Josie hadn't moved from the end of the bed. She looked up, her face pale.

"A hundred *thousand,* Bree," she whispered. "I owe Mr. Hudson a hundred thousand dollars."

For a second, Bree couldn't understand the words. Lingering tears of relief burned her eyes like acid as she stared at her sister.

A hundred thousand dollars.

Turning away, Bree started to pace, compulsively twisting a long tendril of blond hair into a tight ringlet around her finger as she struggled to make sense of all her worst fears coming true. She tried to control her shaking hands. Tried desperately to think of a way out.

"But I told you, you don't have to worry!" Josie blurted out. "I have a plan."

Bree stopped abruptly. "What is it?"

"I'm going to sell the land."

Her eyes went wide as she stared at her sister.

"There's no choice now. Even you must see that," Josie argued, blinking fast as she clasped her hands tightly in her lap. "We'll sell it, pay off the debt, and then pay off those men who are after us. You'll finally be free—"

"That land is in trust." Bree's voice was hard. "You don't get possession until you're twenty-five or married. So put it out of your mind."

Josie shook her head desperately. "But I know how I could—"

"You can't," she said coldly. "And even if you could, I wouldn't let you. Dad put that land into an unbreakable trust for a reason."

"Because he thought I was helpless to take care of myself."

"Because from the day you were born, you've had a knack for trusting people and believing the best of them."

"You mean I'm stupid and naive."

Controlling herself, Bree clenched her hands at her sides.

"It's a good quality, Josie," she said quietly. "I wish I had more of it."

And it was true. Josie had always put concern for others over her own safety and well-being. As a chubby girl of five, she'd once wandered out of their Alaskan cabin into the snow, hoping to find their neighbor's cat, which had disappeared the day before. Eleven-year-old Bree had searched their rural street with their panicked father and half a dozen neighbors for hours, until they'd finally found her, lost in the forest, dazed and half-frozen.

Josie had nearly died that day, for the sake of a cat that was found later, snug and warm in a nearby barn.

Bree took a deep breath. Her little sister's heart was as big as the world. It was why she needed someone not nearly so kind or innocent to protect her. "Are they still playing?"

"Yes," Josie said in a small voice.

"Who's at the table?"

"Mr. Hudson and a few owners. Texas Big-Hat, Silicon Valley, Belgian Bob," she said, using the housekeeping staff's nicknames for the villa owners. Her eyes narrowed. "And one more man I didn't recognize. Handsome. Arrogant. He kicked me out of the game." She scowled. "The others would've let me stay longer—"

"You would have just lost more," Bree said coldly. Turning away, she went behind her closet door and yanked off her oversized sleep shirt, pulling on a bra and then a snug black T-shirt. "We'd owe a million dollars now, instead of just a hundred thousand."

"It might as well be a million, for all our chance of paying," Josie grumbled. "For all the good it will do them if I don't sell that land. They can't get blood out of a stone!"

Bree pulled on her skinny dark jeans over her slim legs. "And what do you think will happen when you don't pay?"

"Mr. Hudson will make me scrub his floors for free?" she replied weakly.

Coming around the closet door, Bree stared at her in disbelief. "Scrub his *floors?*"

"What else can he do?"

Bree turned away, muttering to herself. Josie didn't understand the situation she was dealing with. How could she? Bree had made it her mission in life to protect her from knowing.

She'd hoped they would find peace in Hawaii, three thousand miles away from the ice and snow of Alaska. She'd prayed she would find her own peace, and finally stop dreaming of the blue-eyed, dark-haired man she'd once loved. But it hadn't worked. Every night, she still felt Vladimir's arms around her, still heard his low, sensual voice. *I love you, Breanna.* She still saw the brightness of his eyes as he held up a sparkling diamond beneath the Christmas tree. *Will you marry me?*

Ugh. Furiously, Bree pushed the memory away. No wonder she still hated Christmas. Let other women go home to their turkeys and children and brightly lit trees. To Bree, yesterday had been just another workday. She never let herself remember that one magical Christmas night when she was eighteen, when she'd wanted to change her life to be worthy of Vladimir's love. The night she'd promised herself that she would never—for any reason—gamble or cheat or lie again. Even though he'd left her, she'd kept that promise.

Until now. She reached into the back of her closet, pulling out her black boots with the sharp stiletto heels.

"Bree?" Josie said anxiously.

Not answering, Bree sat down heavily on the bed. Putting her feet into her boots, she zipped up the backs. It was the first time she'd worn these stiletto boots since she was a rebellious teenager with a flexible conscience and a greedy heart. It took Bree back to the woman she'd never thought she would be again. The woman she'd have to be tonight to save her sister. She glanced at the illuminated red letters of the clock. Three in the morning. A perfect time to start.

"Please, you don't have to do this," her sister whimpered. Her voice choked as she whispered helplessly, "I have a plan."

Ignoring the guilt and anguish in her sister's voice, Bree rose to her feet. "Stay here." Squaring her shoulders, she severed the connection between her brain and her pounding heart. Emotion would only be a liability from here on out. "I'll take care of it."

"No! It's my fault, Bree, and I can fix it. Listen. On Christmas Eve, I met a man who told me how..."

But Bree didn't wait to hear whatever cockamamy sob story someone might have fed her softhearted sister this time. She grabbed her black leather motorcycle jacket and headed for the door.

"Bree, wait!"

She didn't look back. She walked out of the tiny apartment and went down the open-air hallway to the moss-covered, crumbling concrete steps of the aging building where all the Hale Ka'nani Resort's staff lived.

It's just like riding a bike, Bree told herself fiercely as she raced down the steps. Even after ten years away from the game, she could win at poker. She *could*.

Warm trade winds blew against her cold skin. Pulling on her black leather jacket, she went down the illuminated paths of the five-star resort toward the beautiful, brand-new buildings used by wealthy tourists and the even wealthier villa owners, clustered around the edge of a private, white-sand beach.

My heart is cold, she repeated to herself. *I feel nothing.*

The moon was full over the Pacific, leaving a ghostly trail across the black water. Palm trees swayed in the warmth of the Hawaiian breeze. She heard the distant call of night birds, smelled the exotic scent of fruit and spice mingling with the salt of the sea.

Above her, dark silhouettes of tall, slender palm trees swayed in a violet sky twinkling with stars. Even with the bright full moon, the night seemed black to her, wide and endless as the sea. She followed the illuminated path around the deserted pool between the beach and the main lobby. As she grew closer to the beach, she heard the sound of the surf build to a roar.

The open-air bar was nearly empty beneath its long thatched roof. Hanging lights swayed in the breeze over a few drunk tourists and cuddling honeymooners. Bree nodded at the tired-eyed bartender, then went past the bar into a connecting hall that led to the private rooms reserved for the villa owners and their guests. Where rich men brought their cheap mistresses and played private, illegal games.

Opening the door, Bree stumbled in her stiletto boots.

Clenching her hands at her sides, she took a deep breath and told her heart to be a lump of ice. Cold. Cold. Cold. She had no feelings of any kind. Poker was easy. By the time she was fourteen, she'd been fleecing tourists in Alaskan ports. And she'd learned the best way not to show emotion was not to feel it in the first place.

Never play with your heart, kiddo. Only a sucker plays with his heart. Even if you win, you lose.

Her father had said those words to her a million times growing up, but she'd still had to learn the hard way. Once, she'd played with all her heart. And lost—everything.

Don't think about it. But in spite of her best efforts, the memory brought a chill of fear. She'd been so determined to leave that life behind. What if she'd forgotten how to play? What if she'd lost her gift? What if she couldn't lure the men in, convince them to let her ante up without money, and get the cards she needed—or bluff them into believing she had?

If she failed at this, then... Bree felt a flash of sweat on her forehead. Running for the Mainland might be their only option. Or, since they had no money or credit cards and it was doubtful they'd even make it to the airport before they were caught, *swimming* for the Mainland.

She exhaled, forcing her body to calm down and her heart to slow. *It's just poker,* she told herself firmly. *Your heart is cold. You feel nothing.*

Bree went all the way down the long, air-conditioned hall. A large man weighing perhaps three hundred pounds sat at a polished oak door.

She forced a crooked smile in his direction. "Hey, Kai."

The enormous security guard nodded with a single jerk of his chins. "What you doing here, Bree? Saw your sister take off. She sick or something?"

"Something like that."

"You working in her place?" Kai frowned, looking over her dark, tight jeans, her black leather jacket and black stiletto boots. "Where's the uniform?"

"This is my outfit." Her voice was cool as she stared him down. "For poker."

"Oh." His round, friendly face looked confused. "Well. Okay. Go in, then."

"Thanks." Forcing the ice in her voice to fully infuse her heart, she pushed open the door.

The private room for the villa residents had a cavernous ceiling and no windows. The walls were soundproofed with thick red fabric that swooped from a center point on the ceiling. The effect made the room glamorous and cozy and claustrophobic all at once. To Bree, it felt like entering the tent of a sheikh's harem. But as she approached the wealthy men who were playing at the single large table, if there was a stab of fear down her spine, she didn't feel it.

She'd succeeded. She'd turned off her heart.

There were no women players. The only females in the room stood in a circle behind the men, smiling with hawkish red lips, wearing low-cut, tight silk gowns. At the table, she saw the dealer, Chris—what was his last name?—whose eyes widened with surprise when he saw her.

The four players at the table were Greg Hudson and three owners she recognized: a Belgian land developer, a long-mustached oil man from Texas and a short, bald tycoon from Silicon Valley. But where was the arrogant stranger Josie had mentioned? Had he already quit the game?

Whatever. It was time to play.

In her black leather jacket and jeans, Bree pushed through the venomous, overdressed women. Without a word, she sat down at one of the two empty seats at the table around the dealer, beside Greg Hudson.

"Deal me in," she said coolly.

The men blinked, staring at her in shock that was almost comical. One of the men snorted a laugh. Another frowned. "Another cocktail waitress?" one scoffed.

"Actually," Bree said with a grin, "I'm with the housekeeping staff, and so was my sister."

The men glanced at each other uncertainly.

"Well, well. Bree Dalton." Greg Hudson licked his lips, looking at her with beady eyes in his florid, sweaty face. "So. Did you bring the hundred thousand dollars your sister owes me?"

"You know we don't have that kind of money."

"Then I'll send my men to take it out of her hide."

Bree's knees shook beneath the table, but she did not feel fear. Her body might feel whatever it liked, but she'd disconnected it from her heart. Crossing her legs, she leaned back in her chair. "I will play for her debt."

"You!" He snorted. "What will you wager? This game has a five-thousand-dollar buy-in. You could scrub the bathrooms of the entire Hale Ka'nani Resort for years and not have that kind of money."

"I offer a trade."

"You have nothing of value."

"I have myself."

Her boss stared at her, then licked his lips. "You mean—"

"Yes. I mean you could have me in bed." She looked at him steadily, feeling nothing. Her skin felt cold, her heart as frozen as the blue iceberg that sank the *Titanic*. "You wanted me, Mr. Hudson. Here I am."

There was a low whistle, an intake of breath around the room.

Bree slowly gazed around the table. She had everyone's complete attention. Without flinching, she let her gaze taunt each man in turn, all of them larger, older and more powerful than she could ever be. "Who will take the gamble?"

"Well now." Looking her over, the Texas oil baron thoughtfully tilted back his cowboy hat. "This game just got a lot more interesting."

In the corner of her eye, she saw a dark, hulking shadow come around the table. A man sat down in the empty chair on the other side of the dealer, and Bree instantly turned to him with languid eyes. "Allow me to join your game, and I could be yours...."

Bree's voice choked off midsentence as she sucked in her breath.

She knew those cold blue eyes. The high cheekbones, sharp as a razor blade. The strong jaw that proclaimed ruthless, almost thuggish strength. So powerful, so darkly handsome, so sensual.

So impossible.

"No," she whispered. Not after ten years. Not here. "It can't be."

Vladimir Xendzov's eyes narrowed with recognition, and then she felt the rush of his sudden searing hatred like fire.

"Have you met Prince Vladimir?" Greg Hudson purred.

"Prince?" Bree choked out. She was unable to look away from Vladimir's face, the face of the man she'd dreamed about unwillingly for the past ten years.

His cruel, sensual lips curved as he leaned back in his chair.

"Miss Dalton," he drawled. "I didn't know you were in Hawaii. And gambling. What a pleasant surprise."

His low, husky voice, so close to her, so real, caused a shiver across her skin. She stared at him in shock.

Her one lost love. Not a ghost. Not a dream. But here, at the Hale Ka'nani Resort, not six feet away from her.

"So what's on offer? Your body, is it?" Vladimir's words were cold, even sardonic. "What a charming prize that would be, though hardly exclusive. Shared by thousands, I should imagine."

And just like that, the ice around her heart exploded into a million glass splinters. She sucked in her breath.

Vladimir Xendzov had made her love him with all the reckless passion of an innocent, untamed heart. He'd made her a better person—and then he'd destroyed her. Her lips parted. "Vladimir."

He stiffened. *"Your Highness* will do."

She didn't realize she'd spoken his name aloud. Glancing to the right and left, she matched his sardonic tone. "So you're using your title now."

His blue eyes burned through her. "It is mine by right."

She knew it was true. His great-grandfather had been one of the last great princes of Russia, before he'd died fighting the Red Army in Siberia, after sending his wife and baby son to safety in Alaskan exile. As a poverty-stricken child, Vladimir had been mocked with the title at school. When he was twenty-five, he'd told her that he never intended to use the title, that it still felt like a mockery, an honor he hadn't earned—and was worthless, anyway.

But apparently, now, he'd found a use for it.

"You didn't always think so," Bree said.

"I am no longer the boy you once knew," he said coldly.

She swallowed. Ten years ago, she'd thought Vladimir was the last honest man on earth. She'd loved him enough to give up the wicked skills that made her special. When he'd held her tight on a cold Alaskan night and begged her to be his bride, it had been the happiest night of her life. Then he'd ruthlessly deserted her the next morning, before she could tell him the truth. When she needed him most, he'd stabbed her in the back. Some *prince*. "What are you doing here?"

His lip curled. Without answering her, he turned away. "The table is full," he said to the other players. "We do not want her."

"Speak for yourself," one of them muttered, looking at Bree.

Looking around, she jolted in her chair. She'd forgotten the other men were there, looking at her like hungry wolves at a raw mutton chop. The beautiful, sexily dressed women standing in a circle behind them were glaring as if they would like to tear her limb from limb. Perhaps she'd taken her act a little too far.

Feel nothing, she ordered her shivering heart. *I have ice for a heart.* She looked away from the large, powerful men and sharp-taloned women. They couldn't hurt her. The only man who'd ever been able to really hurt her was Vladimir. And what more could he do, that he hadn't done already?

One thing, a cold voice whispered. Ten years ago, he'd taken her heart and soul.

But not her virginity.

And he never would, she told herself fiercely. Bree didn't know what Vladimir Xendzov was doing in Honolulu, but she didn't care. He was ancient history. All that mattered now was protecting Josie.

To save her little sister, Bree would play cards with the devil himself.

With an intake of breath, she lifted her chin, ignoring Vladimir as she looked around the table. "It is for this first game only that I offer my body. If I lose, the winner will get me, along with all the money in the pot. But if I win—" *when* I win, she amended silently "—I will only bet money. Until I possess the entire amount of my sister's debt."

As she spoke, her heart started to resume a normal beat. Bluffing, playing card games, was home to her. She'd learned poker when her father had pulled her up to their table in Anchorage and taught her at the tender age of four. By six, shortly after her mother had died two months after giving birth to Josie, Bree was a child prodigy accompanying her father to games—and, when he saw how much money she could make, his partner in crime.

Leaning forward, she looked at each man in turn, ignoring the death stares of the women behind them. "What is your answer?"

"We are here to play poker," another man complained. "Not for hookers."

Bree twirled her long blond hair slowly around one of her slender fingers and looked through her lashes at the Silicon Valley tycoon. "You don't recognize me, do you, Mr. McNamara?"

"Should I?"

She gave him a smile. "I guess not. But you knew my father, Black Jack Dalton." She paused. "Have you enjoyed the painting you paid him to steal from the archives of the Getty Museum in Los Angeles? When did you learn it was a fake?"

The Silicon Valley tycoon stiffened.

"And Mr. Vanderwald—" she turned to the gray-haired, overweight man sitting beside her boss "—twelve years ago you were nearly wiped out, weren't you? Investing in an Alaskan oil well that never existed."

The Belgian land developer scowled. "How the devil did you—"

"You thought my father conned you. But it was my idea. It was me," she whispered, lowering her eyelashes as she ran her hand down the softly worn leather of her black motorcycle jacket. "It was all me."

"You," the fat man breathed, staring at her.

She was doing well. Then, from the corner of her eye, she felt Vladimir's sardonic gaze. It hit her cheek and the side of her neck like a blast of ice. Her heart skidded with the effort it took to ignore him. He was the one man who'd ever really known her. The mark she'd stupidly let see behind her mask. She felt his hatred. Felt his scorn.

Fine. She felt the same about him. Let him hate her. His hatred bounced off the thickening ice of her scorn for *him*. She'd thought he was so perfect and noble. She'd killed herself trying to be worthy. But when he'd learned the truth about her past, he'd deserted her, without giving her a chance to explain.

So much for his honor. So much for his *love*.

Bree's lips twisted. Turning away, she gave the rest of the men a sensual smile. "Win this first hand, and you'll have me at your mercy. You'll get your revenge. Humiliate me completely. Take my body, and make your last memory of me one of your own pleasure." She gave a soft sigh, allowing her lips to part. "My skills at cards are nothing compared to what I can do to you in bed. I've learned the art of seduction. You have no idea," she whispered, "what I can do to you. A single hour with me will change your life."

Her act was one hundred percent fraud, of course. She, know the art of seduction? What a joke. She'd have no clue what she'd do with a man in bed. Since Vladimir, she'd been very careful never to let any man close to her. At twenty-eight, she was a virgin. But she did know how to bluff.

The men were riveted.

"I'm in," Greg Hudson croaked.

"And me."

"I accept."

"Yes."

As the men at the table agreed, Bree would have been frightened by all the looks of lust and desire and rage, if she hadn't frozen her heart against emotion.

But the last set of ice-blue eyes held no lust. No desire for domination. Just pure, cold understanding. As if Vladimir alone could see through all her tricks to the scared woman beneath.

"As you wish," he said softly. He gave a cold smile. "Let's play."

His low, sensual voice slid through her body. When she looked into Vladimir's eyes, fear pierced her armor. *Pierced her heart.* She wanted to leap up and run from his knowing gaze, to keep running and never stop. It took every ounce of her willpower to remain in the chair.

Clutching her jacket around her for warmth, she wrenched her gaze away, gripping the black leather so no one could see that her hands were shaking. "Then let's begin."

At Greg Hudson's nod, Chris the dealer dealt the cards. Ignoring the spiteful whispers and daggered glances of the trophy girls, Bree stared at her cards, facedown on the table.

She couldn't let herself think what would happen if she lost. Couldn't even imagine what it would be like to let any of these angry, fat, ugly men take their revenge on her virginal body through rough sex.

But even more awful would be having Vladimir win. Giving her virginity to the man who'd once broken her completely? She couldn't survive it. Not from him.

Just win, she ordered herself. All she had to do was take this first hand, and her virginity would no longer be on offer. It would be a long night of poker trying to win a hundred thousand dollars. But this was the most important hand.

Closing her eyes, she silently prayed. Then she picked up the cards. Careful not to let any of the players see them, she looked at them.

It took every ounce of her skill not to gasp.

Three kings. She had three kings, along with a four and a

queen. Three kings. She nearly wept with relief. It was as if fate had decided she was gambling for the right reasons and deserved to win.

Unless it was more than fate…

She looked up through her lashes toward the young dealer. Could he be helping her? Chris was about Josie's age, and he'd come twice to their apartment for dinner. He wasn't exactly a close friend, but he'd spoken many times with irritation about Greg Hudson's poor management skills. "You would do a better job of running this resort, Bree," he'd grumbled, and she'd agreed with a smile. "But who wouldn't?"

Now, catching her eye, the young dealer gave her a wink and a smile.

Sucking in her breath, Bree looked away before anyone noticed. Her eyes accidentally fell on Vladimir's. His eyebrows lowered, and she gulped, looking back down at her cards, hastily making her expression blank. Had he seen? Could he guess?

The dealer turned to his left. "Your Highness?"

Because of his placement at the table, Vladimir was the first one required to add a bet to the pile of chips already in the middle of the table from the ante. "Raise."

Raise? Bree looked up in surprise. He was looking straight at her as he said, "Five thousand."

Texas Big-Hat cursed and threw his cards on the table. "Fold."

"Call," Silicon Valley said, matching Vladimir's bet.

"Call," Mr. Vanderwald puffed, a bead of sweat dripping down his forehead.

"Call," Greg Hudson said.

All eyes turned to Bree.

"She's already all in," Greg Hudson said dismissively. "There's nothing more she can wager."

He was right, she thought with a pang. She couldn't match Vladimir's raise, and that meant even if she won the hand, she couldn't win anything beyond the twenty-five thousand dollars' worth of chips currently in the center. What a waste of three kings…

Bree suddenly smiled. "I call."

"Call?" Greg Hudson hooted. "You have an extra five thousand dollars hidden in the back pocket of those jeans?"

She stretched back her shoulders and felt the eyes of the men linger on the shape of her breasts beneath her black T-shirt. "I can match the bet in other ways. Instead of just an hour in bed, I'll offer an entire night." She tilted back her head, allowing her long blond hair to tumble provocatively down her shoulders. "Many chances. Multiple positions. As fast or slow or hard as you like it, all night long, and each time better than the last. Against the wall. Bent over the bed. In my mouth."

She felt like a total fool. She hoped she sounded like a woman who knew what she was talking about, not a scared virgin whose idea of lovemaking was vague at best, based only on movies and novels. But as she looked at each man at the table they seemed captivated. She exhaled. Her mask was holding. She was convincing them. Even Chris the dealer looked entranced.

Vladimir alone seemed completely unaffected. Bored, even. His lips twisted with scorn. And his eyes—

His blue eyes saw straight through her. A hot blush burned her cheeks as she said to him, "Do you agree my bet is commensurate with your five thousand dollar raise?"

"No," Vladimir said coldly. "That is not a call."

Her heart sank. "You…"

He gave her a calm smile. "That is an additional raise."

"A…a raise?" she echoed uncertainly.

"Obviously. Let us say…your added services are equivalent to an additional five thousand dollars? Yes. A full night with you would surely be worth that." He lifted a dark eyebrow. "Would you not agree?"

"Five thousand more?" Greg Hudson's voice hit a false note.

Catching himself, he shifted uncomfortably in his chair and snickered, "Fine with me. I'm half *raised* already."

"Good," Vladimir said softly, never looking away from Bree. "So we are in agreement."

Bree's brow furrowed as she tried to read his expression. What on earth was he doing?

Trying to help her? Or giving her more rope to hang herself with?

Repressing her inner tumult, she stared him down. *In for a penny...* She lifted her chin. "If it's worth five more, then why not ten more?"

The corners of Vladimir's mouth lifted. "Yes, indeed. Why not?" He looked around the table. "Miss Dalton has raised the wager by ten thousand dollars."

To her shock, one by one the men agreed to her supposed "raise," except for the Belgian, who folded with an unintelligible curse.

And just like that—oh, merciful heavens—there was suddenly a pile of chips at the center of the table worth *seventy-five thousand dollars.*

She looked at each man as they discarded cards and got new ones from the dealer.

Don't play the hand, her father had always said. *Play the man.*

She forced herself to look across the table at Vladimir. His face was inscrutable as he discarded a card and got a new one. When she'd played him ten years ago, he'd had a tight style of play. He did not bluff, he did not overbet—the exact opposite of Bree's strategy.

He lifted his eyes to hers, and against her will, her heart turned over in her chest. His handsome face revealed nothing. The poverty of his homesteading Alaskan childhood, so different from hers, had pushed him to create a billion-dollar business across the world, primarily in metals and diamonds. He was so ruthless he had cut his own younger brother out of their partnership right before a multimillion-dollar deal. It was said Vladimir Xendzov had molten gold in his veins and a flinty diamond instead of a heart. That he wasn't flesh and blood.

But if Bree closed her eyes, she could still remember their last night together, when they'd almost made love on a bearskin rug beneath the Christmas tree. She could remember the heat and searing pleasure of his lips against her skin in the deep hush of that cold winter's night.

I love you, Breanna. As I've never loved anyone.

No one else had ever called Bree by her full name. Not like that. Now, as they looked at each other across the poker table, they were two enemies with battle lines drawn. Everything she'd ever thought him to be was a dream. All that was left was a savagely handsome man with hard blue eyes and an emotionless face.

She turned away. Greg Hudson and the Silicon Valley tycoon were far easier to read. She watched her boss get three new cards, saw the sweat on his face and the way he licked his thick, rubbery lips as he stared down at his hand. Hudson had nothing. A pair of twos, maybe.

She looked at Silicon Valley. His lips were tight, his eyes irritated as he stared down moodily at his cards. He was probably already thinking about the twenty thousand dollars he'd wagered in the pot. She hid a smile.

"Miss Dalton?" Chris the dealer said. Stone-faced, she handed in the four of spades. Waited. And got back...

A queen.

She forced herself not to react, not even to breathe. Three kings and two queens. *A full house.*

It was an almost unbeatable hand. Careful not to meet Vladimir's eyes, she placed her cards facedown on the table. How she wished she could raise again! If only she had more to offer, she could have finished off her sister's debt right now—with a single hand!

Don't be greedy, she ordered herself. Seventy-five thousand dollars was plenty. Once she had it safely in her possession, the offer of her body—and unbeknownst to the men, her virginity—would be off the table.

But still. A full house. Her heart filled with regret.

"Raise," Vladimir said.

She looked up with a frown. Why would he raise now?

His eyes met hers. "Fifteen thousand."

"Fold." With a growl, Silicon Valley tossed his cards on the table. "Damn you."

Greg Hudson nervously wiped his forehead. For several seconds, he stared at his cards. Then he said in a small voice, "Call."

They all looked at her. Bree hesitated. She wanted to match Vladimir's raise. *Yearned* to. She had an amazing hand, and the amount now in the pot was even more than her sister's debt. But without anything more to offer, she was already all in. Even if she won, she wouldn't get the additional amount.

If only she had something more to offer!

"Well?" Vladimir's eyes met hers. "Will you call? Perhaps," he said in a sardonic voice, "you wish to raise your offer to an entire *weekend* of your charms?"

Bree stared at him in shock. A weekend?

She didn't know why he was helping her—or if he thought he could hurt her. But with this hand, it didn't matter. She was going to win.

"Great idea," she said coolly. "I'll match your raise with a full weekend of my—how did you put it? My charms?"

Vladimir's lips turned up slightly at the edges, though his eyes revealed nothing.

Heart pounding, she waited for Greg Hudson to object. But he didn't even look up. He just kept staring at his own cards, chewing on his lower lip.

It was time to reveal cards. Vladimir, based on his position at the table, went first. Slowly, he turned over his cards. He had two pairs—sevens and nines.

Relief flooded through Bree, making her body almost limp. She hadn't realized until that moment how scared she'd been that even with her completely unbeatable hand, Vladimir might find a way to beat her.

Greg Hudson's cards, on the other hand, were a foregone conclusion. He muttered a curse as he revealed a pair of threes.

Blinking back tears, Bree turned over her cards to reveal her full house, the three kings and two queens. There was a smattering of applause, exclamations and cursing across the room. She nearly wept as she reached for the pile of chips at the center of the table.

She'd saved Josie.

She'd won.

Bree's legs trembled beneath her as she rose unsteadily to her feet, swaying in her high-heeled stiletto boots. She pushed the bulk of the chips toward Greg Hudson, keeping only a handful for herself. "This pays my sister's debt completely, yes? We are free of you now?"

"Free?" Greg Hudson glared at her, then his piggy eyes narrowed. "Yes, you're free. In fact, I want you and your sister off this property tonight."

"You're firing us?" Her jaw dropped. "For what cause?"

"I don't need one," he said coldly.

She stiffened. She hadn't seen that coming. She should have. A small-minded man like her boss would never stand being beaten in a card game by a female employee. He'd already resented her for weeks, for the respect she'd quickly gained from the staff, and all the notes she'd left in the suggestion box, listing possible ways to improve his management of the resort.

"Fine." She grabbed her handful of chips and glared at him. "Then I'll tell you what I should have written up in the suggestion box weeks ago. This resort is a mess. You're being overcharged by your vendors, half your employees are stealing from you and the other half are ready to quit. You couldn't manage your way out of a paper bag!"

Mr. Hudson's face went apoplectic. "You—"

She barely heard him as he cursed at her. These extra chips, worth thousands of dollars, would give both Dalton girls a new start—buy them a plane trip back to the Mainland, first and last months' rent on a new apartment, and a little something extra to save for emergencies. And she would go someplace where she'd be sure she never, ever saw Vladimir Xendzov again. "I'll just cash in these chips, collect our last paychecks, and we'll be on our way."

"Wait, Miss Dalton," Vladimir said from behind her in a low, husky voice.

Her body obeyed, without asking her brain. Slowly, she turned. She couldn't help herself.

He was sitting calmly at the table, looking up at her with heavily lidded eyes. "I wish to play one more game with you."

Nervousness rose in her belly, but she tossed her head. "So desperate to win your money back? Are times so tough for billionaires these days?"

He smiled, and it did not meet his eyes. "A game for just the two of us. Winner take all."

"Why would I do that?"

Vladimir indicated his own entire pile of chips. "For this."

The blood rushed from her head, making her dizzy. "*All* of that?" she gasped.

He gave her a single nod.

Greg Hudson made a noise like a squeak. Sweat was showing through his tropical cotton shirt as he, along with everyone in the room, stared at the pile of chips. "But Prince Vladimir—Your Highness—that's a million dollars," he stammered.

"So it is," he replied mildly, as if the amount were nothing at all—and to Vladimir, it probably wasn't.

A single bead of sweat broke out between Bree's breasts. "And what would you want from me?"

His blue eyes seared right through her. "If I win," he said quietly, "you would be mine. For as long as I want you."

As long as he wanted her? "That would make me your...
your slave."

Vladimir gave her a cold smile. "It is a wager I offer. You.
For a million dollars."

"But that's—"

"Make your choice. Play me or go."

She swallowed, hearing a roar of blood in her ears.

"You can't just buy her!" her ex-boss brayed.

"That's up to Miss Dalton," Vladimir said. He turned his
laserlike gaze on Bree. "So?"

Though there were ten other people in the room, it was so
quiet she could have heard a pin drop. All eyes were on her.

A million dollars. The choice she made in this moment
would determine the rest of her life—and Josie's. They could
pay off their father's old debts to unsavory men, the ones that
had kept them in virtual hiding for the past ten years. Josie
would be free to go to college—any college she wanted. And
Bree could start her own little B and B by the sea.

They'd no longer have to hide or be afraid.

They'd be free.

"What is the game?" she said weakly. "Poker?"

"Let's keep it easy. Leave it to fate. One card."

Her eyes widened. "One..."

His gorgeous face and chilly blue eyes revealed nothing as
his sensual lips curved. "Are you feeling lucky, Miss Dalton?"

Was she feeling lucky?

Taking a million dollars from Vladimir would be more than
sweet revenge. It would be justice for how he'd coldly abandoned her when she'd needed him most. He'd destroyed ten
years of her life. She could take this one thing from him. A
new life for her and Josie.

But risk being Vladimir's slave—forever? The thought made
her body turn to ice. It was too much to risk on a random card
from the deck.

Unless...it wasn't so random.

She looked sideways beneath her lashes at Chris, the dealer. He lowered his head, his expression serious. Was that a nod? Did she have a sympathetic ally? She closed her eyes.

How much was she willing to risk on a single card?

Are you feeling lucky, Miss Dalton?

Bree exhaled. She'd just won a hundred thousand dollars in a single game. She slowly opened her eyes. So, yes, she felt lucky. She sat back down at the table.

"I accept your terms," she stated emphatically.

Vladimir's smile widened. "So to be clear. If my card is higher, you'll belong to me, obeying my every whim, for as long as I desire."

"Yes," she said, glancing again at Chris. "And if mine is higher, you will give me every chip on that table."

"Agreed." Vladimir lifted a dark eyebrow. "Ace card high?"

"Yes."

They stared at each other, and Bree again forgot there was anyone else in the room. Until someone coughed behind her, and she jumped, realizing she'd been holding her breath.

Vladimir turned to the dealer. "Shuffle the deck."

Bree put the chips she'd won in the last game into a little pile and pushed them aside. "I will select my own card."

Her opponent looked amused. "I would expect no less."

They both turned to Chris, who visibly gulped. Shuffling carefully, with all eyes upon him, he fanned out the facedown cards. He turned them toward Bree, who made her selection, then toward Vladimir, who did the same.

Holding her breath, Bree slowly turned her card over.

The king of hearts.

She'd drawn the king of hearts! She'd won!

She gasped aloud, no longer able to control her emotions. Flipping her card onto the table to reveal the suit, she covered her face with her palms and sobbed with joy. After ten years, fate had brought the untouchable Vladimir Xendzov into her hands, to give her justice at last. Parting her hands, she lifted her gaze, waiting for the sweetness of the moment when he turned over his own losing card, and his face fell as he realized he'd lost and she'd won.

Vladimir looked down at his card. For an instant, his hard expression didn't change.

Then he looked up at her and smiled. A real smile that reached his eyes.

It was an ice pick through her heart.

"Sorry, Bree," he said casually, and tossed his card onto the table.

She stared down at the ace of diamonds.

Her mind went blank. Then a tremble went through her, starting at her toes and moving up her body as she looked at Vladimir, her eyes wide and uncomprehending. She dimly heard Greg Hudson's annoyed curse and the other men's cheers, heard the women's snide laughter—except for the woman directly behind Vladimir, who seemed to be crying.

"You—you've…" Bree couldn't speak the words.

"I've won." Vladimir looked at her, his blue eyes electric with dislike. He rose from his chair, all six feet four inches of him, and said coldly, "You have ten minutes to pack. I will collect my winnings in the lobby." As she gaped at him, he walked around the table to stand over her, so close she could feel the warmth of his body. He leaned nearer, his face inches from hers.

"I've waited a long time for this," he said softly. "But now, at last, Bree Dalton—" his lips slid into a hard, sensual smile "—you are mine."

CHAPTER TWO

BREE'S heart stopped in her chest.

As Vladimir turned away, she struggled to wake up from this bad dream. She looked down at her overturned card on the table. The king of hearts looked back at her. Bree should have won. She was supposed to win. Her brain whirled in confusion.

"Wake up," she whispered to herself. But it wasn't a dream. She'd just sold herself. Forever. To the only man she hated.

Blinking, she looked up tearfully at the young dealer, who she'd thought was her ally. Chris just shook his head. "Wow," he said in awe. "That was a really stupid bet."

Bree gripped the edge of the table with trembling hands. Staggering to her feet, she turned on Vladimir savagely. "You cheated!"

From the doorway, he whirled back to face her. *"Cheated?"*

He went straight toward her, and the crowds parted for him, falling back from his powerful presence and his expression of fury. He looked as cold as a marble statue, like an ancient tsar of perfect masculine beauty, of despotic strength and ruthless cruelty. He reached for her, and she backed away, terrified of the look in his eyes.

Vladimir dropped his hands. His posture relaxed and his voice became a sardonic drawl. "You are the one who cheats, my dear. And you'd best hurry." He glanced at his platinum watch. "You now only have—nine minutes to pack before I collect my prize."

She gasped aloud. His *prize?*

Her body—her soul!

Turning without another word, Vladimir stalked out the door with a warrior's easy, deadly grace. Everyone in the room, Bree included, remained silent until the door closed behind him. Then the crowd around her burst into noise, and Bree's knees went weak. She leaned her trembling hands against the table. Her ex-boss was yelling something in her ear: "Nine minutes is too long. I want you out of the Hale Ka'nani in five!"

Greg Hudson looked as if he were dying to slap her across the face. But she knew he couldn't touch her. Not now. Not ever.

She was Vladimir Xendzov's property now.

How could she have been so stupid? How?

Bree had never hated herself so much as she did in that moment. She rubbed her eyes, hard. She'd thought she could save her hapless baby sister from the perils of gambling. Instead, she'd proved herself more stupidly naive than Josie had ever been.

The warm, close air in the red-curtained, windowless room suddenly choked her. Pushing past the annoyed blonde who'd stood behind Vladimir's chair, Bree ran for the exit, past a startled Kai who was guarding the door. She rushed down the hall, past the deserted outdoor bar, into the dark night.

She ran up the hill, trying to focus on the feel of the path beneath her feet, on the hard rhythm of her breathing. But she was counting down her freedom in minutes. Eight. Seven and a half. Seven.

Her right foot stumbled and she slowed to a walk, her breath a rasp in her throat. The moon glowed above her as she reached the apartment building she shared with her sister.

Bree shivered as a warm breeze blew against her clammy skin. Rushing up the open-air stairs of the aged, moss-covered structure, she shook with fear. He would take everything from her. Everything.

She'd been stupid. So stupid. He'd set his trap and she'd

walked right into it. And now Josie would be left alone, with no one to watch out for her.

Bree started to reach for the doorknob, then stopped. Her body shook as she remembered the poker chips she'd been so proud to win—all of which she'd left behind. With a choked sob, she covered her face with her hands. How would she ever explain this disaster to Josie?

The door abruptly opened.

"There you are," Josie said. "I saw you come up the path. Did you manage to…?" But her sister's hopeful voice choked off when she saw Bree's face. "Oh," she whispered. "You… you lost?"

Josie spoke the words as if they were impossible. As if she'd never once thought such a thing could happen. Bree had never lost big like this before—ever. Even tonight, she would have won, if she hadn't allowed Vladimir to tempt her into one last game. Her hands clenched at her sides. She didn't know who she hated more at this moment—him or herself.

Him. Definitely him.

"What happened?" Josie breathed.

"The stranger was Vladimir," Bree said through dry lips. "The man who kicked you out of the game was Vladimir Xendzov."

Josie stared at her blankly. But of course—she'd been only twelve when their father had died, and Bree had set her sights on the twenty-five-year-old businessman with a small mining company, who'd returned to Alaska to try to buy back his family's land. She'd hoped to con him out of enough cash to pay off the dangerous men who'd tracked them down and were demanding repayment of the money Black Jack and Bree had once stolen.

She'd fallen for Vladimir instead. And Christmas night, when he'd proposed to her, she'd decided to tell him everything. But his brother told him first—and by then, it was in the newspapers. Without a word, he'd abruptly left Alaska, leaving eighteen-year-old Bree and her sister threatened by dangerous men—as well as the sheriff, who'd wanted to toss Bree into jail and Josie into foster care. So they'd thrown everything into their beat-up old car in the middle of the night, and headed south. For the past ten years, they'd never stopped running.

"You lost? At poker?" Josie repeated, dazed. Her eyes suddenly welled up with tears. "This is all my fault."

"It's not your fault," Bree said tightly.

"Of course it is!"

Josie was clearly miserable. Looking at her little sister's tearful face, Bree came to a sudden decision. She grabbed her duffel bag.

"Pack," she said tersely.

Josie didn't move. Her expression was bewildered. "Where are we going?"

Bree stuffed her passport into her bag, and any clean clothes she could reach. "Airport. You have two minutes."

"Oh, my God," Josie breathed, staring at her. "You want to run. What on earth did you lose?"

"Move!" Bree barked.

Jumping, her sister turned and grabbed her knapsack. A scant hundred seconds later, Bree was pulling on her hand and yanking her toward the door.

"Hurry." She flung open the door. "We'll get our last paychecks and—"

Vladimir stood across the open-air hallway. His broad-shouldered, powerful body leaned casually against the wall in the shadows.

"Going somewhere?" he murmured silkily.

Bree stopped short, staring up in shock. Behind her, Josie ran into her back with a surprised yelp.

He lifted a dark eyebrow and gave Bree a cold smile. "I had a feeling you would attempt to cheat me. But I admit I'm disappointed. Some part of me had hoped you might have changed over the last ten years."

Other hulking shadows appeared on the stairs. He hadn't come alone.

Desperately, Bree tossed her head and glared at him defiantly. "How do you know I wasn't just hurrying to be on time to meet you in the lobby?"

Vladimir's smile became caustic. "Hurrying to meet me? No. Ten years ago you could barely be on time for anything. You'd have been late to my funeral."

"Oh, I'd be early for your funeral, believe me! Holding flowers and red balloons!"

His blue eyes gleamed as he came toward her in the shadows. She felt Josie quivering behind her, so as he reached for her, Bree forced herself not to flinch or back away.

"People don't change," he said softly. He pulled the duffel bag from her shoulder. Unzipping it, he turned away from her, and she exhaled. Then, as he went through the bag, she glared at him.

"What do you think I have in there—a rifle or something? Didn't anyone ever tell you it's rude to go through other people's stuff?"

"A woman like you doesn't need a rifle. You have all the feminine weapons you need. Beauty. Seduction. Deceit." Vladimir gazed at her with eyes dark as a midnight sea. His handsome, chiseled face seemed made of granite. "A pity your charms don't work on me."

As she looked at him, her throat tightened. She whispered, "If you despise me so much, just let me go. Easier for you. Easier for everyone."

His lips curved. "Is that the final item on your checklist?"

"What are you talking about?"

"You've tried running, insulting me, accusing me of cheating, and now you're *reasoning* with me." Zipping up the bag, he pushed it back into her arms and looked at her coldly. "What's next—begging for mercy?"

She held the bag over her heart like a shield. "Would it

work?" she breathed. "If I begged you—on my knees—would you let me go?"

Reaching out, Vladimir cupped her cheek. He looked down at her almost tenderly. "No."

She jerked her chin away. "I hate you!"

Vladimir gave a low, bitter laugh. "So you did have a checklist. It's fascinating, really, how little you've changed."

If only that were true, Bree thought. She didn't have a plan. She was going on pure instinct. Ten years of living a scrupulously honest life, of scraping to get by on minimum-wage jobs, and taking care of her sister, had left Bree's old skills of sleight of hand and deception laughably out-of-date. She was rusty. She was clumsy and awkward.

And Vladimir made it worse. He brought out her weakness. She couldn't hide her feelings, even though she knew it would be to her advantage to cloak her hatred. But he'd long ago learned the secret ways past the guarded walls of her heart.

"You can't be serious about making me your slave forever!" she snapped.

"What?" Josie gasped, clinging to her arm.

Vladimir's eyes were hard in the moonlight. "You made the bet. Now you will honor it."

"You tricked me!"

He gave her a lazy smile. "You thought that dealer was going to stick his neck out for you, didn't you? But men don't sacrifice themselves for women anymore. Not even for pretty ones." He moved closer to her, leaning his head down to her ear. "I know all your tells, Bree," he whispered. "And soon... I will know every last secret of your body."

Bree felt the warmth of his breath on her neck, felt the brush of his lips against the tender flesh of her earlobe. Prickles raced through her, making her hair stand on end as he towered over her. She felt tiny and feminine compared to his powerful masculine strength, and against her will, she licked her lips as a shiver went down her body.

Vladimir straightened, and his eyes glittered like an arctic sea. "This time, you will fulfill your promises."

He made a small movement with his hand, and the three shadows on the stairs came forward, toward the bare light outside their apartment. Vladimir strode down the steps without looking back, leaving his three bodyguards to corral the two Dalton sisters and escort them down the concrete staircase.

Two luxury vehicles waited in the dimly lit parking lot. The first was a black SUV with tinted windows. The second... Bree's feet slowed.

"Bree!"

Hearing her sister's panicked voice behind her, she turned around and saw the bodyguards pushing Josie into the backseat of the SUV.

Bree clenched her hands as she went forward. "Let her go!"

Vladimir grabbed her arm. "You're coming with me."

"I won't be separated from her!"

He looked at her, his face hard and oh, so handsome in the moonlight. "My Lamborghini only has two seats." When she didn't move, he said with exaggerated patience, "They will be right behind us."

Glancing at the SUV parked behind the Lamborghini, Bree saw her sister settled in the backseat as the bodyguards climbed in beside her. Bree ground her teeth. "Why should I trust you?"

"You have no choice."

He reached for her hand, but she ripped it away. "Don't touch me!"

Vladimir narrowed his eyes. "I was merely trying to be courteous. Clearly a waste." He thrust his thumb toward the door of the bright red Lamborghini. "Get in."

Opening the door, Bree climbed inside the car and took a deep breath of the soft leather seats' scent. Fast cars had once been her father's favorite indulgence, back when they'd been conning rich criminals across the West, and Black Jack had been spending money even faster than they made it. By the time her father died of lung cancer, only debts were left. But the smell of the car reminded her of the time when her father had been her hero and their mattresses had been stuffed with money—literally. Unwillingly, Bree ran her hand over the smooth leather.

"Nice car," she said grudgingly.

With a sudden low laugh, Vladimir started the engine. "It gets me where I need to go."

At the sound of that laugh, she sucked in her breath.

His laugh...

She'd first heard it at a party in Anchorage, when Vladimir Xendzov was just a mark, half owner of a fledgling mining company, who had come to Alaska looking to buy the land her father had left in an ironclad trust for Josie, then just twelve years old. Bree had been hoping she could distract Vladimir from the legal facts long enough to disappear with his money. Instead, when their eyes met across the room, she'd been electrified. He'd grabbed an extra flute of champagne and come toward her.

"I know who you are," he'd said.

She'd hid the nervous flutter in her belly. "You do?"

He gave her a wicked smile. "The woman who's coming home with me tonight."

For an instant, she'd caught her breath. Then she'd laughed in his face. "Does that line usually work?"

He'd looked surprised, then he'd joined her laughter with his own low baritone. "Yes," he'd said almost sheepishly. "In fact, it always does." He'd held out his hand with a grin. "Let's try this again. I'm Vladimir."

Now, as his eyes met hers, his expression was like stone. He yanked hard on the wheel of the Lamborghini, pulling the car away from the curb with a squeal of tires. Bree glanced behind them, and saw her sister's SUV was indeed following them. She exhaled.

She had to think of a way to get out of this prison sentence.

She looked at the passing lights of Honolulu. The city sparkled, even in the dead of night.

Deals can always be made. Her father's words came back to her. *Just figure out what a man wants most. And find a way to give it to him—or make him think you will.*

But what could a man like Vladimir possibly want, that he didn't already have?

He was frequently in the business news—and nearly as often in the tabloids. He was the sole owner of Xendzov Mining OAO, with operations on six continents. His company was one of the leading producers of gold, platinum and diamonds around the world. He was famous for his workaholic ways, for his lavish lifestyle, and most of all for the ruthless way he crushed his competition—most spectacularly his own brother, who'd once been part-owner of the company before Vladimir had forced him out, the same day he'd abandoned Bree in Alaska. For ten years, the two brothers' brutal, internecine battles had caused them both to lose millions of dollars, tarnishing both their reputations.

Ala Moana Boulevard was deserted as they drove away from Waikiki, heading toward downtown. Along the wide dark beach across the street, palm trees stretched up into the violet sky. They passed Ala Moana Center, which was filled with shops such as Prada, Fendi and Louis Vuitton—brands that Bree had once worn as a teenage poker player, but which as a hotel housekeeper she couldn't remotely afford. Vladimir could probably buy out the entire mall without flinching, she thought. Just as he'd bought her.

Bree rolled down her window to breathe the warm night air. "So tell me," she said casually. "What brings you to Honolulu?"

He glanced at her out of the corner of his eye. "Don't."

"What?"

"Play whatever angle you're hoping to use against me."

"I wasn't…"

"I can hear the purr in your voice." His voice was sardonic.

"It's the same one you used at the poker table, whipping the male players into a frenzy by offering your body as the prize."

Anger rushed through her, but she took a deep breath. He was right—that wasn't exactly her proudest moment. She looked down at her hands, clenched in her lap. "I was desperate. I had nothing else to offer."

"You weren't desperate when you played that last card against me. Your sister's debt was already paid. You could have walked away."

Tears burned the backs of her eyes. "You don't understand. We are in debt—"

"Fascinating." His voice dripped sarcasm.

Didn't he have even the slightest bit of humanity, even a sliver of a flesh-and-blood heart? Her throat ached as she looked away. "I can't believe I ever loved you."

"Loved?" Changing gears as they sped down the boulevard, he gave a hard laugh. "It's tacky to bring that up. Even for you."

Ahead of them, she saw the towering cruise ships parked like floating hotels at the pier. She blinked fast, her heart aching. She wished both she and Josie were on one of those ships, headed to Japan—or anywhere away from Vladimir Xendzov. She swallowed against the razor blade in her throat. "You can't be serious about taking me to bed."

"The deal was made."

"What kind of man accepts a woman's body as a prize in a card game?"

"What kind of woman offers herself?"

She gritted her teeth and blinked fast, staring at the Aloha Tower and the cruise ships. Without warning, Vladimir suddenly veered the Lamborghini to the right.

Glancing behind them, Bree saw the SUV with her sister continuing straight down the Nimitz Highway, a different direction from the Lamborghini. She turned to him with a gasp.

"Where are you taking my sister?"

Vladimir pressed down more firmly on the gas, zooming

at illegal speeds through the eerily empty streets of downtown Honolulu in the hours before dawn. "You should be more concerned about where I am taking you."

"You can't separate me from Josie!"

"And yet I have," he drawled.

"Take me back!"

"Your sister has nothing to do with this," he said coldly. "*She* did not wager her body."

Bree cursed at him with the eloquence of Black Jack Dalton himself, but Vladimir only glanced at her with narrowed eyes. "You have no power over me, Bree. Not anymore."

"No!" Desperate, she looked around for a handy police car—anything! But the road was empty, desolate in the darkest part of night before dawn. "I won't let you do this!"

"You'll soon learn to obey me."

She gasped in desperate fury. Then she did the only thing she could think of to make him stop the car. Reaching between the seats, she grabbed the hand brake and yanked upwards with all her might.

Bree's neck jerked back and tires squealed as the fast-moving car spun out of control.

As if in slow motion, she looked at Vladimir. She heard his low gasp, saw him fight the steering wheel, gripping until his knuckles were white. As the car spun in a hard circle, the colored lights of the city swirled around them, then shook in chaos when they bumped up over a curb. Bree screamed, throwing her hands in front of her face as the car plummeted toward a skyscraper of glass and steel.

The red Lamborghini abruptly pulled to a stop.

With a gulp, Bree slowly opened her eyes. When she saw how close they had come to hitting the office building, she sucked in her breath. Dazed, she reached her hand through the car's open window toward the plate glass window, just inches away, literally close enough for her to touch. If Vladimir weren't such a capable driver... If the car had gone a little more to the right...

They'd have crashed through the lobby of the skyscraper in an explosion of glass.

Her reckless desperation to save her sister had very nearly killed them both. Bree was afraid to look at him. She coughed, eyes watering from the cloud of dust that rose from the car's tires. She slowly turned.

Vladimir's silhouette was framed by a Gothic cathedral of stone and stained glass on the other side of the street. A fitting background for the dark avenging angel now glaring at her in deathly fury.

"The airport." His breathing was still heavy, his blue eyes shooting daggers of rage. "My men are taking your sister to the *airport,* damn you. Do you think I would hurt her?"

Heart in her throat, Bree looked back at him. "How would I know?"

He stared at her for a long moment. "You," he said coldly, "are the only one who's put her at risk. You, Bree."

As he restarted the car and drove down the curb, back onto the deserted road, a chill went down her spine.

Was he right?

She put her hand against her hot forehead. She'd spent ten years protecting her sister with all her heart, but from the moment she'd seen Vladimir, her every instinct was wrong. Every choice she made seemed to end in disaster. Maybe Josie *was* better off without her. "Your men will take her straight to the airport? Do you promise?"

"I promise nothing. Believe me or don't."

Bree's body still shook as they drove out of downtown, eventually leaving the city behind, heading north into the green-shadowed mountains at the center of the island. As they drove through the darkly green hills of Oahu, moonlight illuminated the low-slung clouds kissing the earth. She finally looked at him.

"Josie doesn't have any money for a plane ticket," she said in a small voice.

"My men will escort her onto one of my private jets, and she'll be taken back to the Mainland. A bodyguard already procured her last paycheck from the hotel. And yours, since you no longer need money."

Bree's mouth fell open. "I don't need money? Are you crazy?"

"You are my possession now. I will provide you with everything I feel you require."

"Oh," she said in a small voice. She bit her lip. "So you mean you'll feed me and house me? Like…like your pet?"

His hands tightened on the steering wheel. "A pet would imply affection. You are more like…a serf."

"A serf?" she gasped.

"Just as my ancestors once had in Russia." He looked at her. "For the rest of your life, you will work for me, Bree. For free. You will never be paid, or allowed to leave. Your only reason for living will be to serve me and give me pleasure."

Bree swallowed.

"Oh," she whispered. Good to know where she stood. Setting her jaw, she looked out at the spectacular vista of sharp hills on either side of the Pali Highway, then closed her eyes. At least Josie was free, Bree thought. At least she'd done one thing right before she disappeared forever.…

Her eyes flew open. *No.* She sat up straight in her seat. She wasn't going to give up so easily. She'd find a way to escape her fate. She *would!*

She folded her arms, glaring at him. "Where do you intend to hide me, Vladimir? Because I hardly think your shareholders would approve of slavery. Or *kidnapping.*"

"Kidnapping!" Vladimir spoke a low, guttural word in Russian that was almost certainly a curse. "After so many years of lies, do you even know how to tell the truth?"

"What else would you call it when you—"

"You had the money to pay your sister's debt. You were free to leave. But you chose to gamble out of pure greed. And now you're too much of a coward to admit you lost." He turned to her, his blue eyes like ice in the moonlight. "I let your sister go because you're the one I want to punish, Bree. Only you." He gave a slow, cold smile. "And I will."

CHAPTER THREE

VLADIMIR watched a tumult of emotions cross Bree's beautiful face. Rage. Fury. Grief. And most of all helplessness.

It was like Christmas and his birthday all at once.

Still smiling, he turned back to the deserted, moonlit road and pushed down on the gas of the Lamborghini, causing it to give a low purr as it sped through the lush mountains of Oahu's interior.

When he'd first seen young Josie Dalton at the poker game, getting lured in over her head by the hotel manager, he hadn't recognized her. How could he? He'd never met the kid before. He'd just thought some idiot girl was letting herself get played.

He hadn't liked it, so he'd tried to get her out of the game. An unusually charitable deed for a man who now prided himself on having a cold, flinty diamond instead of a heart.

Once, he'd tried to protect his younger brother. Once, he'd believed in the woman he loved. Now he despised weakness, especially in himself. But three months ago, after nearly dying in a fiery crash on the Honolulu International Raceway, he'd taken his doctor's advice and bought a beach house on a secluded stretch of the Windward Coast, to recuperate.

He'd had no clue Bree was in Hawaii. If he'd known, he'd have gotten up from his hospital bed and walked to the airport, broken bones and all. What man in his right mind would seek out Bree Dalton? That would be like yearning for a plague or other infectious disease.

She was poison, pure and simple. A poison that tasted sweet as sugar and spicy as cinnamon, but once ingested, would destroy a man's body from within, like acid. And that's just what she'd done ten years ago. Her scheming, callous heart had burned Vladimir so badly that she'd sucked all the mercy from his soul.

She'd done him a favor, really. He was better off without a working heart. Being free of sympathy or emotion had helped him build a worldwide business. Helped him get rid of a business partner he no longer wanted.

Bree had betrayed him. But so had his younger brother, in revealing that deception to a newspaper reporter while their first major deal was on the line. Burned, Vladimir had ruthlessly cut his brother out of their company, buying him out for pennies. Then he'd announced his acquisition of mining rights in a newly discovered gold field in northern Siberia. A year later, at twenty-six, Vladimir was worth five hundred million dollars, while his twenty-four-year-old brother was still broke and living in the Moroccan desert.

Though Kasimir hadn't remained penniless for long. Even living like a nomad in the Sahara, thousands of miles from the ice and snow, he'd found a way to start his own mining company, one that now rivaled Xendzov Mining OAO. Vladimir's eyes narrowed. He'd allowed Kasimir to peck away at his business for long enough. It was time for him to destroy his brother once and for all.

But first…

Vladimir's lips curled as he drove the Lamborghini through the hills toward the Windward Coast. He glanced at Bree out of the corner of his eye.

He'd told himself for years that his memory of her was wrong. No woman could possibly be that lovely, that enticing.

And it was true. She wasn't. At eighteen, she'd still been a girl.

Now, at twenty-eight, she was the most beautiful woman

he'd ever seen. Her fragility and mystery, mixed with her outward toughness, made her more seductive than ever.

And soon, he'd know her every secret. As they drove down the hills into a lush, green valley, a cold smile lifted Vladimir's lips. He would satisfy his hot memory of her—the thirst that, no matter how many cool blondes he took to his bed, still haunted him in dreams at night. He would satiate himself with her body.

He'd be disappointed by the experience, of course. His memory had amplified her into a goddess of desire. No woman could be that extraordinary. No woman could kiss that well. No woman could set such a fire in his blood. He'd built her up.

He would enjoy cutting her down.

From the moment Vladimir had heard her sultry voice at the poker table, and seen her slender, willowy body in the tight dark jeans and black leather jacket, her hazel eyes like a deep, mysterious forest and her full pink lips like the luring temptation into heaven—or hell—his every nerve ending had become electrified in a way he hadn't felt in a long, long time.

At first he'd thought it was fate. When she'd taken him up on his final bet, he'd realized the two Dalton sisters must have been working some kind of con. It was the only explanation. He could think of no other reason for Bree Dalton, the smartest, sexiest, most ruthless con artist he'd ever met, to be working as an underpaid housekeeper in a five-star Hawaiian resort.

But now he'd teach proud, wicked Bree a lesson she'd never forget. He'd have her as his slave. Scrubbing his floors. And most of all, pleasuring him in bed. He looked at her, at the way her long blond hair glowed in the moonlight, at the fullness of her breasts trembling with each angry breath. Oh, yes.

"Your girlfriend is going to hate you for this," she muttered.

In the distance, Vladimir could see the violet sky growing light pink over the vast dark Pacific. "I don't have a girlfriend."

She glared at him. "Yes, you do."

"Wouldn't I know?"

"What about the woman whose breasts were pressed against your back throughout the poker game?"

"Oh." He tilted his head. "You mean Heather."

"Right. Heather. Won't she object to this little master-slave thing with me?"

He shrugged. "I met her at the pool a few days ago. She was perhaps amusing for a moment, but..."

"But now you're done with her, so you're heartlessly casting her aside." Bree's jaw set as she turned away. "Typical."

"Do not worry. I have no intention of casting *you* aside," he assured her.

"A famous playboy like you? You'll tire of me in bed after the first night."

He found the hope in her voice insulting. Women did not wish to be cast out of his bed. They begged to get in. Hiding his irritation, he gave her a sensual smile. "Do not fear. If that happens, I'll find some other way for you to serve me. Scrubbing my floors. Cleaning my house..."

Her cheeks turned a girlish shade of pink, but her voice was steady as she said, "I'd rather clean your bathroom with my *toothbrush* than have you touch me."

"Perhaps I'll have you clean my house naked," he mused.

"Sounds like heaven," she muttered, tossing her head.

Driving along the edge of the coast, he stroked his chin with one hand. "Perhaps I'll allow my men to enjoy the show."

That finally got her. Bree's eyes went wide as her lips parted. "You..." She swallowed, looking pale. "You wouldn't."

Of course he wouldn't. Vladimir had no intention of sharing his hard-won prize—or even the image of her—with anyone. He wasn't much of a sharer, in any case. A man was stronger alone. With no gaps in his armor. With no one close enough to slow him down, or stab him in the back.

Looking away from Bree's pale, panicked face—somehow he didn't enjoy seeing that expression there as much as he'd thought he would—he turned the Lamborghini into the road to his ultraprivate, palatial Hawaii mansion. The guard nodded at him from the guardhouse and opened the ten-foot-tall electric gate.

"Relax, Bree." Vladimir ground out the words, keeping his eyes on the road. "I don't intend to share you. You're my prize and mine alone."

In the corner of his eye, he saw her tight shoulders relax infinitesimally. *This is supposed to be her punishment,* he mocked himself. *Why reassure her?*

But frightening her wasn't what he wanted, he decided. He had no interest in seeing her pitiful and terrified. He wanted to conquer the real Bree—proud and sly and gloriously beautiful. He didn't want to be tempted, even once, to feel sympathy for her.

Vladimir stopped the red car in the paved courtyard in front of his enormous beachside mansion, built on the edge of a cliff, with one story on the courtyard side, and three stories facing the ocean.

"This is yours?" she breathed.

"Yes."

"I didn't know you had a place on Oahu." She bit her lip, looking up at the house. "If I'd known you were here…"

"You wouldn't have come to Honolulu to try your con?"

"Con?" She looked genuinely shocked. "What are you talking about?"

"What do you call that poker game?"

Her big hazel eyes were wide and luminous in the moonlight.

"The worst mistake of my life," she whispered.

Her heart-shaped face was pale, her pink lips full, her expression agonized. In spite of her tough-girl clothes, the black leather jacket and stiletto boots, she looked like a young, lost princess, trapped by an ogre with no hope of escape.

A trick, he told himself angrily. *Don't fall for it.* He turned

off the ignition. Grabbing her duffel bag, he got out of the car.
"Come on."

Closing the door behind him, he stalked toward the front
door without looking back. He'd bought this twenty-million-
dollar house three months ago, sight unseen, an hour before he
was released from the hospital in Honolulu. The lavish estate
on the windward side of the Oahu shore was set on the best
private beach near Kailua.

He went into the sprawling beach house, and heard the sound
of her stiletto boots on the patterned ohia wood floor. They
passed through the large, expansive rooms. Floor-to-ceiling
windows on both sides of the house revealed the Ka'iwa Mountain Ridge in one direction, and in the other, the distant pink-
and-lavender dawn breaking over the Pacific and the distant
Mokulua Islands.

But Vladimir was used to the view. Sick of it, in fact. He'd
spent weeks cooped up like a prisoner here, as he recuperated from the car race that had nearly killed him, gritting his
teeth through physical therapy. No wonder, within a month of
being here, he'd started seeking amusement in Honolulu, half
an hour away, at a private poker game. The fact that it was illegal to gamble at any resort in Hawaii just added to the spice.

At the end of the hall, Vladimir opened double doors into
the enormous master bedroom, revealing high ceilings, an elegant marble fireplace and a huge four-poster bed. Veranda
doors opened to a balcony that overlooked the infinity pool
and the ocean beyond it. He dropped Bree's duffel bag on the
bed and abruptly turned to face her.

She ran straight into him.

Vladimir heard her intake of breath as, for one instant,
he felt the softness of her body against his own. Electricity
coursed through his veins and his heart twisted as all his blood
coursed toward his groin. He looked down at her beautiful,
shocked face, at her wide hazel eyes, at the way her pink lips
parted, full and ripe for plunder.

Mouth parted, she jumped back as if he'd burned her.

"Give a girl some notice, will you," she snapped, "if you're just going to whip around like that!"

Her tone was scornful. But it was too late.

He knew.

For years, Vladimir had told himself that their passionate, innocent affair had all been one-sided—that she'd tricked him, creating a hunger and longing in him while she herself remained stone cold, focused only on the money she intended to steal from him. But just now, when he'd felt her body against his, he'd seen her face. Felt the way her body reacted. And he'd suddenly known the truth.

She felt it, too.

"You...you should..." Her voice faltered as their eyes locked. As they stood beside the four-poster bed, the brilliant sun burst over the horizon, coming through the tall east-facing windows, bathing them both in warm golden light. Everything he'd ever hungered for, everything he feared and despised, was personified in this one woman. *Breanna.*

Her long blond hair shimmered like diamonds and gold. Her eyes shone a vivid green, like emeralds. Her skin was pale and untouched, like plains of virgin white snow. Hardly aware of what he was doing, Vladimir reached out and stroked a gleaming tendril of her hair. It was impossibly soft.

He heard her soft intake of breath. "Please. Don't."

"Don't?" He looked into her eyes. "You want me," he said in a low voice. "Just as I want you."

Her luscious lips fell open. Then with a scowl, she shook her head fiercely. "You're out of your mind!"

"Don't you recognize the truth when you see it? Or have you forgotten how?"

"The only *truth* is I want you to leave me alone!"

Twining his fingers through her long blond hair, he pulled back, tilting her head to expose her throat.

"Whatever your words say," he whispered, "your lips won't lie."

And he ruthlessly lowered his mouth to hers.

His kiss was an overpowering force, savage enough to bruise. His grip was unyielding, like steel. Bree felt herself being crushed against his hard body.

Kiss? More like plunder. His lips were hard and rough. She felt his powerful hands on her back, felt their warmth through her leather jacket. The muscles of his hard chest crushed her breasts as he wrapped his arms tighter around her. He pushed her lips wider apart with his own, taking full possession of her mouth.

The tip of his tongue touched hers, and it was like two currents of electricity joining in a burst of light. Against her will, repressed desire exploded inside her, and need sizzled down her body like fire.

Her hands somehow stopped pushing against his chest, and lifted to wrap around his neck. It had been so long since she'd been touched by anyone, and he was the only man who'd ever kissed her. The only one she'd ever wanted. The man she'd loved with all her heart, the man who'd brought her to life and made her new.

Vladimir. As he kissed her, she sighed softly against his mouth. For ten long years, she'd dreamed of him every aching night. And now, at last, her dream was real. She was in his arms, he was kissing her....

But he'd never kissed her like this before. There was nothing loving about this embrace. It was scornful. Angry.

One of his legs pushed her thighs apart. His hands moved up to entwine his fingers in her hair, yanking her head back.

"No," she whimpered, feeling dizzy as she wrenched away. She put an unsteady hand to her forehead. "No."

Vladimir stared down at her. His gaze seemed almost bewildered. She heard the hard rasp of his breath, and realized that he, too, had been surprised. Then his face hardened.

"Why should I not kiss you?" He walked slowly around her, running one hand up her arm and the side of her neck. "You belong to me now, *kroshka.*"

Kroshka? She didn't know what it meant, but it didn't sound very nice.

Stopping in front of her, he cupped her chin. He handled her carelessly, possessively, as a man might handle any valuable possession—a rifle, a jewel, a horse. Insolently, he traced his hand down her bare neck. "I intend to take full possession of my prize." His hand slid over her black T-shirt to the hollow between her breasts. "Soon you will be spread across my bed. Aching for me." His hand continued to slide down her waist. Gripping her hip, he suddenly pulled her hard against his body. "Your only reason to exist now is to serve me."

Shaking, she tried to toss her head. Tried to defy him. Instead, her voice trembled as she asked, "What are you going to do to me?"

"Whatever I please." He moved his hand up her body, cupping her breast over the T-shirt, tweaking her aching nipple with his thumb. As she gasped, he smiled. "But you will please me, Bree. Have no doubt about that."

She wanted to beg him to let her go. But she knew it would do no good. Vladimir's handsome, chiseled face was hard as granite. There was no mercy in it. But she couldn't stop herself from choking out, "Please don't do this."

"My touch wasn't always so distasteful to you," he said softly. He ran his hands down her shoulders, pulling off her black leather jacket and dropping it to the marble bedroom floor. "Once, you shuddered beneath me. You wanted me so badly you wept."

Bree swallowed. She'd once been sure of only two things on earth: that Vladimir Xendzov was the last honorable man in this selfish, cynical world. And that he loved her.

"Ya tebya lyublyu," he'd whispered. *I love you, Breanna. Be my wife. Be mine forever.*

He'd been a different man then, a man who laughed easily, who held her tenderly, a fellow orphan who looked at her with worship in his eyes. Now, his handsome face was a lifetime harder. He was a different man, hard and rough as an unpolished diamond, his blue gaze as cold as the place that had been his frequent home for the past ten years—Siberia.

His grip on her tightened as he said huskily, "Do you not remember?"

Blinking fast, she whispered, "That was when I loved you."

His hands grew still.

"You must think I'm a fool." Dropping his arms, he said coldly, "I know you never loved me. You loved my money, nothing more."

"It might have started as a con," she said tearfully, "but it changed to something more. I'm telling you the truth. I loved—"

"Say those words again," he exclaimed, cutting her off in a low, dangerous voice, "and you'll regret it."

She straightened her spine and looked at him defiantly.

"I loved you," she cried. "With all my heart!"

"Be quiet!" With a low growl, he pushed her back violently against the bedpost. "Not another word!"

Bree's heart pounded as she saw the fury in his eyes. She could feel the hard wood against her back, feel his chest against hers with the quick rise and fall of her every breath.

Abruptly, he released her.

"Why did you really come to Hawaii?" he said in a low voice.

She blinked fast, able to exhale. "We got offered jobs here, and we needed them."

He shook his head, his jaw tight. "Why would you take a job as a housekeeper? With your skills?" His eyes narrowed.

"You were surprised to see me at the poker table. If you're not here to con me, who was your mark?"

"No one! I told you—I don't do that anymore!"

"Right," he said sarcastically. "Because you're honest and pure."

His nasty tone cut her to the heart, but she raised her chin. "What are *you* doing here? Because the last time I checked, there weren't many gold mines on Oahu!"

He stared at her for a long moment. "Do you truly not know?" His forehead furrowed. "It was in the news…."

"I've spent the last decade *avoiding* news about you, chief. Not looking for it!"

"Three months ago, I was in an accident," he said tightly. "Racing on the Honolulu International Speedway."

An accident? As in—hurt?

She looked him over anxiously, but saw no sign of injury. Catching his eye, she scowled. "Too bad it didn't kill you."

"Yes. Too bad." His voice was cold. "I am fine now. I was planning to return to St. Petersburg tomorrow."

Her heart leaped with sudden hope. "So you're leaving—"

"I'm not in any hurry." He gripped her wrists again. "Nice try changing the subject. Tell me why you came here. Who is your mark? If not me, then who?"

"No one!"

"You expect me to believe we met by coincidence?"

She bared her teeth. "More like bad luck!"

"Bad luck," he muttered. He moved closer to her, and his grip tightened. She felt tingles down her body, felt his closeness as he pressed her against the carved wooden post of the bed. His gaze fell to her lips.

"No," she whispered. "Please." She swallowed, then lifted her gaze. "You said…I could just clean the house…."

He stared at her. His blue eyes were wide as the infinite blue sea. Then he abruptly let her go.

"As you wish," he said coldly. "On your back in my bed, or

breaking it scrubbing my floor—it makes little difference to me. Be downstairs in five minutes."

Turning on his heel, he left the bedroom. Bree's knees nearly collapsed, and she fell back against the bed.

Vladimir didn't believe she'd ever loved him. When he'd abandoned her to the sheriff that cold December night in Alaska, he'd truly believed that her love for him had just been an act. And now he was determined to exact revenge.

His punishing, soul-destroying kiss had been just the start. An appetizer. He intended to enjoy her humiliation like a lengthy gourmet meal, taking each exquisite course at his own leisure. He would feast on her pride, her body, her soul, her memories, her youth, her heart—until nothing was left but an empty shell.

With a silent sob, Bree dropped her face in her hands.

She was in real trouble.

CHAPTER FOUR

SEVEN hours later, Bree had never felt so sweaty and filthy in her life.

And she was glad.

With a sigh, she squeezed her sponge over the bucket of soapy water. There was still almost no dirt—she guessed Vladimir's team of servants had cleaned the place top to bottom the day before. But he'd still made her scrub every inch of the enormous house's marble floor. She narrowed her eyes. Tyrannical man. Her back ached, as did her arms and legs. But—and this was the part she was happy about—she'd done it all with her clothes on. He'd thought a little cleaning could humiliate her?

Leaning back on her haunches, Bree rubbed her cheek with her shoulder and smiled at the newly shining kitchen floor.

This house was a beautiful place, she'd give him that. Glancing through the windows as she'd worked all day, surreptitiously plotting her escape, she'd seen an Olympic-sized infinity pool clinging to the edge of the ocean cliff. On the other side of the house, across the tennis courts, she'd seen a cluster of small cottages on the edge of the compound, where she guessed Vladimir's invisible army of servants lived. Yes. She'd never seen such an amazing villa estate before.

But for all its luxury, it was still a prison. Just as, for all of Vladimir's dark, brooding good looks, he was her jailer.

She scowled, recalling how he'd enjoyed watching her on all fours, scrubbing his home office that morning. Her stomach had growled with hunger as Vladimir ate a lavish breakfast, served on a tray at his desk. The delicious smells of coffee and bacon had been torture to Bree, following a night where she'd had no food and barely two hours' sleep. His housekeeper, after watching with dismay, had disappeared. But Bree was proud of herself that she hadn't given Vladimir the satisfaction of seeing her whimper.

No more whimpering, she vowed.

Bree jumped as Vladimir suddenly stalked into the kitchen, his posture angry. He stomped into the room and opened one of the doors of the big refrigerator.

Biting her lip, she looked away, scrubbing the floor harder with her sponge. But he was making so much noise, she glanced at him out of the corner of her eye.

He grabbed homemade bread from the cupboard and ripped off a hunk. Tossing it onto a plate, he chopped through it with a big knife, like a grim executioner with an ax. She gulped, watching in bewilderment as he added cheese, chicken, even mustard and tomato. He opened the fridge and added a bottle of water and then a linen napkin to the tray. His Italian leather shoes were heavy against the marble floor as he came over to her, holding out the tray with a glower.

"Your lunch," he said coldly.

Her belly rumbled in response. She'd had nothing to eat since a cheerless Christmas dinner yesterday, a bologna sandwich eaten alone at the end of her housekeeping shift. Sitting back on her haunches, Bree wiped her sweaty forehead and looked up at him.

Unlike her, Vladimir had taken a shower, and looked sleek, urbane and civilized in a freshly pressed black button-down shirt and black trousers. His tanned skin glowed with health, smelling faintly of soap and sandalwood.

While she...

She wasn't feeling so pretty. She'd peeled off her boots to work barefoot on the wet floor. Her long blond hair was twisted into a messy knot at the back of her head, to lift it off her hot neck. Her T-shirt was sweaty all the way through, and in the humidity of Hawaii, even with air-conditioning she knew she looked like a swamp creature from a 1950s horror movie.

She narrowed her eyes. If he thought she was going to lick his boots with gratitude for the simple courtesy of lunch, he had another think coming. His *serf!*

She looked at the tray. He waited.

"I don't like tomatoes," she said pleasantly.

Vladimir dropped the tray with a noisy clatter on the floor beside her. "Tough. I have no desire to cater to you, and Mrs. Kalani decided to take the rest of the day off."

Bree looked up at him, and a slow grin lifted her cheeks. "She gave you a hard time about me, didn't she?"

"Enjoy your lunch." He pointed to an immaculate section of the floor. "You missed a spot."

Vladimir had thrown the tray down as if she were the family golden retriever. Rising to her feet after he left, she washed her hands, then took the tray to the dining table like a civilized person, ready for a fight if he came back to give her one. Somewhat to her disappointment, he didn't.

Once she'd removed the tomatoes, the freshly baked bread made the rest of the sandwich delicious. Honey mustard was a nice touch, too. And the cold, sparkling water was just what she'd wanted. She wiped her mouth.

He was still a brute. Her eyes narrowed as she remembered his cold words.

For the rest of your life, you will work for me, Bree. For free. You will never be paid, or allowed to leave. Your only goal, until you die, is to serve me and give me pleasure.

He didn't know who he was dealing with. She finished off the cold water and tidied up the tray. He thought a little house-cleaning would kill her? She'd been training for this for the past ten years.

She was going to escape this captivity. As soon as she could formulate a plan.

As the afternoon wore on, Bree scrubbed her way fiercely up the stairs and then cleaned five guest bedrooms, which had already been as sparkling clean as the rest of the house. But as she reached the master bedroom, the sun was starting to lower in the western sky, and her whole body ached. She couldn't stop yawning. Looking at the four-poster bed, she was tempted to take a short power nap. Vladimir would never know, she told herself. Climbing onto the large, soft bed, she closed her eyes—just for a few minutes.

With a gasp, Bree sat up suddenly in bed. The room was now dark. She looked over at the clock. It was almost seven o'clock. Dinnertime.

She'd slept for hours.

Feeling sweaty and gross, her body aching, Bree rose stiffly from the still-made bed, stretching her arms over her head. She rubbed her eyes with her knuckles. So where was her slave driver? Why hadn't he discovered her napping? Tsar Vladimir the Terrible must be hard at work, she decided, planning a new way to humiliate her, or dreaming up some nefarious new attack on his brother. When she'd been cleaning his home office, he'd been talking rather intensely in Russian on the phone. But even then, his smoldering gaze had slowly wandered over her backside as she scrubbed the floors on all fours.

Fine. Let him look.

With a deep breath, Bree closed her eyes. As long as he didn't touch. As long as she didn't have to feel his lips, hot and hard against her own, as he held her so tightly against his body...

"You're awake."

At the sound of Vladimir's husky voice from the doorway, she jumped, whirling around. "You—you knew I was sleeping?" she stammered.

His gaze was intense as he came toward her. "Yes."

She felt suddenly very small as his tall body loomed over hers. She licked her lips. "So why didn't you wake me up and start bossing me around?"

Reaching out, he brushed a tendril of hair out of her eyes. "Because you looked like an angel."

His voice was low. Sensual. Bree's eyes widened as she looked up—no, not at his lips! His *eyes!* Trembling with awareness at how they were once again alone in his bedroom, she tightened her hands at her sides. "Um. Thanks. For letting me borrow your bed." She edged away from it. "I should probably be getting back to work…."

His eyes glimmered. "*Our* bed."

"What?"

Vladimir's large hand wrapped around the post's polished wood. "You called it my bed. It is ours."

Her lips parted. Then she folded her arms protectively against her chest. "Look. Whatever our wager was, you can't actually expect me to…"

"Expect you to what?"

"Sleep with you."

"You were serious when you offered it as a prize." He looked down at her. "'My skills at cards are nothing compared to what I can do to you in bed,' you said." His tone was mocking. "'A single hour with me will change your whole life,' you said!"

Shivering, she looked away. "I was bluffing," she said in a small voice. "I don't know how to do those things." Her cheeks colored, and shame burned through her as she looked at the marble floor. "I've never been with a man before. I've never even kissed a man—since…" She bit her lip and muttered, "Not since you."

He stared at her. "You're a *virgin?*"

His voice dripped disbelief. A lump rose to her throat, and she nodded.

"Right," he said scornfully. "You're a virgin."

She lifted her head in outrage. "You think I'm a liar?"

"I know you are." His cool blue eyes met hers. "You lie about everything. You can't help it. Lying is in your blood."

Lying is in your blood. Before Bree's mother died, her parents had been regular law-abiding citizens, childhood sweethearts married at eighteen, high school teachers who mowed the lawn in Alaska's short, bright summers and shoveled snow through eight-month winters. Her mother had taught English, her father science. Then, at thirty, Lois Dalton had contracted cancer. Newly pregnant with her second child, she'd put off chemo treatments that might risk her baby. Two months after Josie's birth, Lois had died. Jack Dalton lost his wife, his best friend and, some said, his mind....

He'd quit his job as a teacher. He left the new baby with a sitter. And every day, after he picked up Bree from first grade, he took her to backroom poker games. First in Anchorage, and then to ports where Alaskan cruises deposited new tourists each day. With each success, his plans had grown more daring. And they'd worked. At first.

Pushing the memory aside, Bree shook her head. "I'm not lying. I'm a virgin!"

"Stop it. You made the bet. You made your bed." Vladimir lightly trailed his hand above her head, along the carved wooden post. "Now you will sleep in it."

She glared at him, setting her jaw. "I only made that bet because I was desperate—because I had nothing else remotely valuable to offer! For Josie—"

"Josie was safe. You had more than enough."

A sudden thought struck Bree, and she caught her breath. "Did you...let me win?" she whispered. "Is that why you kept raising the stakes—why you egged me on during the game? So that I could cover Josie's debt?"

His jaw tightened. "I thought she was some innocent kid that Hudson had lured into the game. Not like you." His eyes flashed as he looked down at Bree. "You could have walked away. But when I offered you the one-card gamble, you accepted. There was no desperation. It was pure greed. And it told me what I needed to know."

She swallowed. "What?"

"That you hadn't changed. You were still using your body as bait."

She took a deep breath and whispered, "I never thought in a million years that I would lose that game." Exhaustion suddenly swamped her like a wave. Tears rose to her eyes. "And if you were any kind of decent man, you would never expect me to actually…"

"To what? Follow through on your promise?" He gave a hard laugh. "No, what kind of monster would expect that?"

Bree exhaled. "How stupid can I be, appealing to your better nature?"

"I won. You lost." He folded his arms, staring at her with his eyes narrowed. "You have many, many faults, Bree Dalton. Almost too many to count. In fact, your faults are like grains of sand on a beach that stretches across the whole wide world…"

"All right, I get it," she muttered. "You don't exactly admire me."

"…but I never thought," he continued, his eyes glinting, "that you'd be a sore loser."

Bree stared up at him mutinously. Then, setting her jaw, she turned away and stomped over to the bucket of cold water. She snatched up the scraggly sponge and held it up like a sword.

"Fine," she snapped. "What do you want me to scrub? The bottom of your Lamborghini? The concrete around the pool? A patch of mud by the garden? I don't even care. But we both know your house is already *clean!*"

His sensual mouth curved at the edges. Gently, he took the sponge out of her hand and dropped it with a soft splash into the bucket. "You can stop cleaning anytime you want."

She searched his eyes. "I can?"

He put his hands on her shoulders, looking down at her.

"Come to bed with me," he said quietly.

Flashes of heat went up and down her body. His hands on her shoulders were heavy, sensual, like points of light. With an intake of breath, she ripped herself away from him.

"Dream on," she said, tossing her head with every ounce of bravado she possessed.

He shrugged. "Then I'll have to find some other way to make you useful."

Bree started to reach for the bucket and sponge, but he stopped her. "No. You are right. Enough cleaning." He gave a sudden wicked grin. "You will cook for me."

Her jaw dropped. He must have forgotten the last time she'd cooked for him, taking a romantic date idea from a magazine. It had been romantic, all right—she'd nearly burned the cabin down, and then the firemen had been called. "You can't be serious."

Vladimir lifted a dark eyebrow. "Because you're still a terrible cook?"

She glared at him. "Because you know I would poison you!"

"I know you won't, because we will share the meal." He leaned forward and said softly, "Tonight I am craving…something delicious." She saw the edge of his tongue flick the corner of his sensual lips. "Something sinful."

Even though he was talking about food, his low voice caused a shiver of awareness down her spine. She swallowed.

"Well, were you thinking chicken noodle soup from a can?" she suggested weakly. "Because I know how to make that."

"Tempting. But no." He tilted his head. "A goat cheese soufflé with Provençal herbs."

Her mouth dropped. "Are you kidding?"

"Try it." His lips turned up at the corners. "You might like it."

"I might like to eat it, but I can't cook it!"

"If you cook it, I will allow you to have some."

"Generous of you."

"Of course." Innocently, he spread his arms wide. "What am I, some kind of heartless brute?"

"You really want me to answer that?"

He gave a low, wicked laugh. "It's a beautiful night. You will come out onto the lanai and cook for me."

"Fine." She looked at him dubiously. "It's your funeral."

And so half an hour later, Bree found herself on the patio beside the pool, in the sheltered outdoor kitchen, struggling to sauté garlic and flour in garlic oil.

"This recipe is ridiculous!" She sneezed violently as minced thyme sprinkled the air like snowflakes, instead of coating the melted butter in the soufflé pan. "It's meant for four cooks and a sous-chef, not one person!"

Vladimir, who sat at the large granite table with an amazing view of the sunset-swept Pacific beyond the infinity pool, sipped an extremely expensive wine as he read a Russian newspaper. "You're exaggerating. For a clever woman like you, surely arranging a few herbs and whipping up a few eggs is not so difficult. How hard can it be to chop and sauté?"

She waved her knife at him furiously. "Come a little closer and I'll show you!"

"Stop complaining," he said coldly, taking another sip of merlot.

"Oh," Bree gasped, realizing she was supposed to be whisking flour and garlic in the hot olive oil. She tried to focus, not wanting to let Vladimir break her, but cooking had never been her skill. Supervising a kitchen staff? No problem. Cracking the eggs herself? A huge mess. She suddenly smelled burning oil, and remembered she was supposed to keep stirring the milk and white wine in the pan until it boiled. As she rushed across the outdoor kitchen, her bare feet slid on an egg white she'd spilled earlier. She skidded, then slipped, and as her tailbone slammed against the tile floor, the whisked egg yolks in her bowl flew up in the air before landing, wet and sticky, in her hair.

Suddenly, Vladimir was kneeling beside her. "Are you hurt, Breanna?"

She stared at him. She felt his powerful arms around her, protective and strong, as he lifted her to her feet.

Trembling, Bree stared up at him, wide-eyed. "You called me Breanna."

He stiffened. Abruptly, he released her.

"It is your name," he said coldly.

Without his arms encircling her, she felt suddenly cold and shivery and—alone. For a moment she'd seen an emotion flicker in his eyes that had made her wonder if he...

No. She'd been wrong. He didn't care about her. Whatever feelings he'd once had for her had disappeared at the first sign of trouble.

Right?

Bree had certainly never intended to love him. The night they'd met, she'd known him only as the young CEO of a start-up mining company, whose family had once owned the land her father had bought in trust for Josie a few years before. "Promise me," Black Jack had wheezed from the hospital bed, before he died. "Promise me you'll always take care of your sister."

In her desperation to be free and keep Josie safe, Bree had known she'd do anything to get the money she needed. And the best way to make Vladimir Xendzov careless about his money was to make him care about her. To dazzle him.

But from the moment they'd met, Bree had been the one who was dazzled. She'd never met a man like Vladimir: so honest, so open, so protective. For the first time in her life, she'd seen the possibilities of a future beyond the next poker game. She'd seen she could be something more than a cheap con artist with a rusted heart. He'd called her by her full name, Breanna, and made her feel brand-new. *I love you, Breanna. Be my wife. Be mine forever.*

Now she blinked, staring up at him in the deepening twilight. Vladimir was practically scowling at her, his arms folded, his blue eyes dark.

But the way he'd said her name when he'd held her... His voice had sounded the same as ten years ago. Exactly the same.

Vladimir growled a low Russian curse. "You're a mess. Go take a shower. Wash the food out of your hair. Get clean clothes." He snatched the empty saucepan from her hand. "Just go. I will finish this."

Now, that was truly astonishing. "You—you will cook?"

"You are even more helpless in the kitchen than I remembered," he said harshly. "Go. I left new clothes for you in the bedroom upstairs. Get cleaned up. Return in a more presentable state."

Bree's lips were parted as she stared at him. He was actually being nice to her. No matter how harsh his tone, or how he couched his kindness inside insults, there could be no doubt. He was allowing her to take a shower, to change into clean clothes, like a guest. Not a slave.

Why? What could he possibly gain by kindness, when he held all the power? "Thank you." She swallowed. "I really appreciate—"

"Save it." He cut her off. Setting down the pan on the granite island of the outdoor kitchen, he looked at her. "At least until you see the dress I've left on your bed. Take a shower and put it on. Afterwards, come back here." He gave her a hard, sensual smile. "And then...then you can thank me."

Vladimir should have known not to make her cook.

He'd thought that Bree, at age twenty-eight, might have improved her skills. No. If possible, she'd grown even more hopeless in the kitchen. The attempt had been a complete disaster, even before the raw yolks had been flung all over—perhaps a merciful end before they could be added to the burned, lumpy mess in the sauté pan.

Cleaning up, he dumped it all out and started fresh. Forty

minutes later, he sat at the table on the patio and tasted his finished soufflé, and gave a satisfied sigh.

He would not ask Bree to make food again.

Vladimir knew how to cook. He just preferred not to. When he was growing up, his family had had nothing. His father tried his best to keep up the six-hundred-acre homestead, but he'd had his head in the clouds—the kind of man who would be mulling over a book of Russian philosophy and not notice that their newborn calf had just wandered away from its mother to die in a snowdrift. Vladimir's mother, a former waitress from the Lower Forty-Eight, had been a little in awe of her intellectual husband, with his royal background. Her days were spent cleaning up the messes her absentminded spouse left behind, to make sure they had enough wood to get through the winter, and food for their two growing boys. It was because of their father's influence that Vladimir and Kasimir had both applied to one of the oldest mining schools in Europe, in St. Petersburg. It was because of their mother's influence they'd managed to pay for it, but in a way that had broken her husband's heart. And that was nothing compared to how Vladimir had found the money to start Xendzov Mining OAO twelve years ago. That had been the spark that started the brothers' war. That had caused Kasimir to turn on him so viciously.

Vladimir's eyes narrowed. His brother deserved what he'd gotten—being cut out of the company right before it would have made him insanely rich. He, Vladimir, had deserved to own the company free and clear.

Just as he owned Bree Dalton.

He had a sudden memory of her stricken hazel eyes, of her pale, beautiful face.

You called me Breanna.

Rising from his chair, Vladimir paced three steps across the patio. He stopped, staring at the moonlight sparkling across the pool and the ocean beyond.

She really must think he was a fool. She must have no respect whatsoever for his intelligence, to think that she could look at him with those beautiful luminous eyes and make him believe she'd actually loved him once. It would not work. They both knew it had always been about money for her. It still was.

I've never been with a man before. I've never even kissed a man since you.

Reaching for his wine glass, he took a long drink and then wiped his mouth. She was a fairly good liar, he'd give her that. But he was immune to her now. Absolutely immune.

Except for her body.

He'd enjoyed watching her scrub his floors, watching the sway of her slender hips, of her backside and breasts as she knelt in front of him. He'd wanted to take her, then and there.

And he would. Soon.

Their kiss had been electric. He still shuddered to remember the softness of her body as she'd clung to him. The scent of her, like orchids and honey. The sweet, erotic taste of her lips. He'd intended to punish her with that savage kiss. Instead, he'd been lost in it, in memory, in yearning, in hot ruthless need.

Gritting his teeth, he roughly tidied up the outdoor kitchen, slamming the dirty pans into the sink. No matter how he tried to deny it, Bree still had power over him. Too much. When he'd seen her slip and fall on this floor, her cry had sliced straight through his heart. And suddenly, without knowing how, he'd found himself beside her, helping her to her feet.

You called me Breanna.

Irritated, he exhaled, setting his jaw. He glanced up toward the house. It had been almost an hour. What was taking her so long?

He grabbed a plate and served her a portion of the soufflé, then took a crystal goblet from the cupboard on the lanai. He carried them both over to the tray on the granite table, beside the open bottle of merlot. He looked out at the shimmering pool, at the crashing waves of the dark ocean below the cliff. He tried to relax his shoulders, to take a deep breath.

After he'd nearly died in the car crash on the raceway, his doctor had arrived from St. Petersburg and told him he needed to find a less risky way to relax. "You're thirty-five years old, Your Highness," the doctor had said gravely. "But you have the blood pressure of a much older man. You're a heart attack waiting to happen." So Vladimir, wrapped up in bandages over his broken bones, had grimly promised to give up car racing forever, along with boxing and skydiving. He'd bought this house and started physical rehabilitation. He'd done yoga and tai chi.

Or at least he'd tried.

He hadn't made it through a single yoga class. The more he tried to calm down, the more he felt the vein in his neck throb until his forehead was covered with sweat. The pain of doing nothing, of just sitting alone with his thoughts, left him half-mad, like a tiger trapped in a cage.

He'd done extreme sports because they made him feel something. The adrenaline stirred up by thinking he might die was a reminder that he was still alive. The never ending sameness of his work, of one meaningless love affair after another, sometimes made him forget.

And *yoga* was supposed to relax him? Vladimir grumbled beneath his breath. Stupid doctors. What did they know?

He'd already had twelve weeks of twiddling his thumbs, "healing" as ordered, while knowing his brother was in Morocco, tying up various gold and diamond sources in underhanded ways. When his leg had healed enough for him to drive, Vladimir had bought the new Lamborghini to go to the weekly private poker game at the Hale Ka'nani Resort. Then he'd found Bree, who drove him absolutely insane. Even more than yoga.

But what the hell was taking her so long? The dinner he'd made was growing cold. Scowling, he looked up at the second-floor bedroom balcony. How long could it take for a woman to shower?

"Bree," he yelled. "Come down."

"No," he heard her yell back from the open French doors of the balcony.

He set his jaw. "Right now!"

"Forget it! I'm not wearing this thing!"

"Then you won't eat!"

"Fine by me!"

This dinner wasn't going at all as he'd envisioned. Growling to himself, Vladimir left the dinner tray on the table and raced inside. Taking the stairs two at a time, he went down the hall and shoved open the double doors to the master bedroom, knocking them back against the walls.

Bree whirled around with a gasp.

Vladimir took one look and his mouth went slack. His heart nearly stopped in his chest.

She stood half-naked, wearing the expensive lingerie, a pale pink teddy and silk robe he'd had a servant buy for her in Kailua. "Make it tacky," Vladimir had instructed. "The sort of thing a stripper might wear."

He'd meant to humiliate her. In spite of Bree's corrupt, hollow soul, she'd always dressed modestly. She never showed any skin—ever. Even when she'd done her best to entice the men at the poker game, she'd lured them with her words, with her electrifying voice, with her angelic face and slender body. But she'd been completely covered from head to toe, with jeans and a leather jacket.

Vladimir had never seen this much of her bare skin. Not even the night ten years ago when he'd proposed, when they would have made love if they hadn't been interrupted. The lingerie should have looked slutty. It didn't.

The pale pink color reflected the blush on her cheeks. She looked innocent and young. Like a bride on her wedding night.

Anger and frustration rushed through him. Each time he tried to humiliate Bree or teach her a lesson, she stymied him.

Furious, he crossed the bedroom. Reaching out his hand, he heard her intake of breath as he ripped off the short silken robe, dropping it to the floor. His eyes raked over the creamy skin of her bare shoulders. The slip of silk beneath barely reached the tops of her thighs, and the flimsy bodice revealed most of the curves of her breasts. He saw the thrust of her nipples through the silk, and was instantly hard.

Bree's cheeks burned red as she glared at him. "Are you happy?"

"No," he growled. He roughly pulled her into his arms. "But I will be."

Her eyes glittered. "So you won me in a poker game. Is this what you wanted, Vladimir? To make me look like your whore?"

He saw the shimmer in her eyes, the vulnerability on her beautiful face, heard the heart-stopping tremble of her voice, and felt that same strange twist in his chest. *It's nothing more than an act to manipulate me,* he told himself fiercely. Damn her!

"You sold yourself to me of your own free will," he growled. "What other word would you use to describe a woman who does such a thing?"

He heard the furious intake of her breath, saw the rapid rise and fall of her chest. But as she drew her hand back to slap him, he caught her wrist.

"Typical feminine reaction," he observed coldly. "I expected more of you."

"How about this," she hissed, ripping her arm away. Her damp blond hair slid against the bare skin of her shoulders. *"I hate you."*

His lips curled. "Good."

"I wish to God we'd never met. That any man but you had won me." Her eyes flashed fire. "I'd rather be right now in the bed of any man at the table—"

Her voice ended with a choke as he yanked her against his body. "So you admit, then, that you are exactly as I've said. A liar, a cheat and a whore."

Her beautiful hazel eyes widened beneath the dark fringe of lashes. Then she swallowed and looked down. "I was a liar, yes, and a cheat, too, but never—never the other," she said in a small voice. She shook her head. "I haven't tried to con anyone for ten years. You changed me." Her dark lashes rose. "You made me a better person," she whispered. The pain and bewilderment in her eyes made her seem suddenly young and fragile and sad. "And you left."

And he felt it again—the tight twist in the place where his heart should have been. As if he were an ogre standing over a poor peasant girl with a whip.

No! Damn it! He wouldn't feel sorry for her!

He'd show her that her overt display of a wobbly lower lip and big hazel eyes had no effect on him whatsoever!

Bree Dalton didn't have feelings, he told himself fiercely. Just masks. He glared at her. "Stop it."

"What?"

"Your ridiculous attempt to gain my sympathy. It—"

It won't work, he meant to say, but his throat closed as he was distracted by the rise and fall of her breasts in the tiny slip of blush-colored silk when she breathed. He could see the shape of her nipples and the way they trembled with every hard breath.

And he was rock hard. Their mutual dislike somehow only made him desire her more, to almost unsustainable need. What magnetic control did she have over his body? Why did he want her like this? She was a confessed liar, a con artist. She wished she'd lost her body to any man but him. How could he want her still? It was almost as if she wasn't his slave at all, but he was hers.

And that enraged him most of all.

A low growl came from the back of his throat. He was in control. Not her.

His hands tightened into fists, his jaw clenching. He wanted to push Bree against the bed, to kiss her hard, to plunge himself inside her and make her scream with pleasure. He wanted to make her explode with pure ecstasy, even while she hated him. A grim smile curved his lips. She would despise herself for that, which would be sweet indeed.

But when he took her, it would be in his own time. At his free choice. Not because she'd driven him to madness by her taunts and the seductive sway of her nubile body.

He wouldn't let her conquer him.

His shoulders ached with tension as he turned away, fighting for self-control. He looked around the master bedroom with a derisive curl on his lip. "I can see you did not finish scrubbing this floor before you took your long lazy nap. You will finish it now. While I watch."

Her expression changed. Snatching up the frayed sponge, she grabbed the bucket of cold wash water from the floor and, in a posture of clear fury, knelt down. He watched her slender, delectable body, wearing only the tiny slip of pink silk, moving back and forth on all fours as she scrubbed the floor. His mouth went dry.

Bree looked up.

"Enjoying the show?" she said coldly.

Without a word, Vladimir turned and left the bedroom. He returned a moment later with his own dinner tray and red wine. Still not speaking, he sat down in a cushioned chair near the marble fireplace. Calmly he unfolded his fine linen napkin across his lap.

"Now I am," he replied.

Sitting back comfortably in his chair, he took a sip of merlot. He had the satisfaction of seeing her eyes widen, of seeing her scowl. Then she turned back to her work, and he had the even greater satisfaction of watching Bree on all fours, her body frosted with silvery moonlight, scrubbing his floor with a sponge and a pail of water.

Outside the veranda window, the full moon lit up the shimmering dark Pacific. The large master bedroom was full of shadows, lit only by a single lamp near his massive four-poster bed. With the flick of a remote, Vladimir turned on the gas fireplace, adding soft flickering firelight to better see his dinner—and the floor show. His solid silver knife and fork slid noisily against the pure bone china, edged with 24 karat gold, as he cut the Provençal goat cheese and Gruyère soufflé. Watching her, he took a bite.

It was exquisite. He sighed in true, deep pleasure.

"Tasty?" Bree muttered, not looking at him.

"You have no idea." His homemade soufflé was indeed delicious, but he wasn't referring to the food.

"I hope you choke and die," she said sweetly.

"Don't forget the area by the bed." He watched Bree's nearly naked body shimmy as she scrubbed. His eyes ran along her slender, toned legs, the sweet curve of her backside, her plump breasts hanging down as they swayed, barely covered by the whisper-thin silk hanging from her shoulders.

Hmm. He didn't want to enjoy it *this* much. He shifted uncomfortably in his seat, moving his plate closer to his knees.

"Of course, *Your Highness.*" Giving him an *I-wish-you-were-dead* glare, Bree stomped—if a woman could be said to stomp while she was crawling—over to the foot of the bed, dragging the bucket behind her. It changed her body's position, giving Vladimir an entirely different view.

He was now sitting directly behind her. All he needed to do was get down on his knees, grab her hips in his hands and pull her sweet bottom back against his groin. It was suddenly all he could think about.

You're in control, he ordered himself. *Not her.*

But his body wasn't listening. A bead of sweat formed on his forehead. His hands clenched on the silver tray in his lap. Well, why not just take her? Bree was his property. His serf. His slave. She'd sold herself to him freely, taunting him with her sexual skill. *You have no idea what I can do to you.* An untouched virgin—Bree? Impossible. She was an experienced seductress. He'd wanted her. Waited for her. For ten years. So what was stopping him?

Vladimir watched the bounce of her breasts and slow up-and-down motion of her hips as she scrubbed the floor angrily.

Not a damned thing.

He heard a loud crash of breaking china. He'd risen to his feet without even knowing it. The tray had fallen from his lap, and his dinner was now a mess of broken crockery.

At the noise, Bree leaned back on her haunches, brushing a tendril of hair out of her face with her shoulder. Turning her luscious body in the tiny, clinging silk teddy, she glared at him. "I'm not cleaning that."

Then she saw the look in his eyes. Twisting away with an intake of breath, she started to scrub the floor again. This time with enough panicked force to dig right through the marble to the house's foundation and straight through the earth to Russia.

He stepped over the broken china. He stopped behind her. He fell to his knees.

"I'm not done," she choked out.

Wrapping his body around her back, he reached in front of her. He put his larger hand over hers, forcing the sponge to be still. His hand tightened as she tried, without success, to keep scrubbing. Caught between two opposing forces, the sponge ripped apart.

Bewildered, she leaned back with half a sponge in her hand. "Look what you did," she said, blinking fast. "You destroyed it. After everything it tried to do for you…"

"Bree," he said in a low voice.

Dropping the sponge, she closed her eyes, wrapping her arms around her shivering body. "Don't…"

But he was ruthless. Grabbing her hips with both hands, he pulled her body back against his own. He felt the rapid, panicked rise and fall of her ribs beneath the chain of his arms. Felt the sweet softness of her backside pressing into his hard, aching groin.

Slowly she opened her eyes and twisted her head to glance at him. Her skin was flushed, her cheeks pink. Her lips parted. He saw the nervous flicker of her tongue against the corner of her mouth.

And he could bear it no longer.

Roughly turning her in his arms, he pulled her to face him, body to body. Twining his hands in her tangled hair, he savagely lowered his mouth to hers.

For an instant, she stiffened. Then, with a little anguished cry, her lips melted against his own. She wrapped her arms around him, and in a rush, their grip tightened as they embraced in the devouring passion of a decade's hunger.

CHAPTER FIVE

BREE had to push him away. She should. She *must*.

She couldn't.

His kiss was hard, even angry—passionate, yes, but nothing like the tender way he'd once embraced her. His chin was rough with five-o'clock shadow, and his powerful arms held her tightly against him as they knelt facing each other, bodies pressed together. Even through his black trousers, she could feel how much he wanted her. And she wanted him.

You are my serf, he'd informed her coldly. *Your only reason for living, until you die, is to serve me and give me pleasure.* She'd been enraged. She was no man's slave.

But he wasn't taking her by force, as her lord and master. No—she couldn't kid herself about that. Because no matter how badly he treated her, she still wanted him. She'd never stopped wanting him....

Vladimir's body moved as he took full, hard possession of her lips, stretching her mouth wide with his own, teasing her with his tongue. His hands moved against her back, sliding the thin, blush-colored silk teddy like a whisper against her naked skin. Her breasts felt heavy and taut, her nipples sizzling with awareness.

As he slowly kissed down her neck, her head fell backward. Breathless with need, she closed her eyes. His tongue flicked her collarbone, his hands cupping her breasts through the silk.

"Breanna," he whispered. "You feel so good. Just like I dreamed you would…"

His breath was warm against her skin as he lowered his head to suckle her through the silk.

She gasped. The sensation of his hot wet mouth against her hard, aching nipple flooded her nerve endings with pleasure. Her fingertips dug into his shoulders as her toes curled beneath her. She pulled him closer.

He sucked gently through the silk, and she felt the fabric move softly, caressing her skin. With agonizing slowness, he pulled the bodice down, and cupped her naked breasts. She felt the roughness of his palm as he rubbed her, then pinched her taut nipples, presenting first one, then the other, to the wet, welcoming warmth of his mouth. Lost in sweet pleasure, she held her breath….

She almost wept in frustration when he suddenly pulled away from her, leaving her bereft. Rising to his feet, he picked her up off the floor as if she weighed nothing at all. He carried her three steps to the bed, then tossed her on the white bedspread.

Eyes wide, Bree leaned back against the pillows and watched as Vladimir stood beside the bed, unbuttoning his shirt. His gaze locked with hers as he undid the cuffs and tossed the shirt to the floor. She had a brief vision of his tanned, muscled chest laced with dark hair before he fell on top of her, pulling her to him for a hard, hungry kiss.

It wasn't gentle or kind. It was primal, filled with fury at his unwilling need. She felt the heavy weight of his muscular body as he pushed her against the mattress. And as he kissed her, the world seemed to spin in a blinding flash of light. She kissed him back fiercely, desperately, forgetting pride and past pain beneath the overwhelming demand of desire.

Without a word, he ripped the pale pink silk teddy off her unresisting body. He looked down at her, now dressed only in the silk G-string panties he'd given her.

"I wanted you to learn your place." His voice was low, almost choked. Reaching out, he stroked her bare breasts in wonder, even as his other hand stroked up and down the length of her nearly naked body. "Instead you teach me mine." His dark blue eyes lifted to hers. "Why do you not touch me? Why do you hold back?"

She remembered her bravado at the poker table, the way she'd bragged about her skills in bed. Her cheeks flooded with heat. "I want to," she whispered. "I don't know how."

"You—don't know how?" he said in disbelief.

"I…" She swallowed. "I might have implied more than my skills actually deserve. At the poker table…"

"I don't give a damn about the game." He gripped her hand. "Just touch me. If you want to please me, touch me. If you want to punish me," he groaned, guiding her palm to stroke slowly down his chest to his belly, "touch me."

Vladimir truly had no idea that she was a virgin. Her fingers shook as she let him guide her, stroking his hard muscles, his hot, bare skin. She'd told him, but he hadn't believed her.

Suddenly, she didn't want him to know. Because how would he react if he learned the pathetic truth—that even after he'd abandoned her, she'd never wanted another man to touch her? Would his eyes fill with scorn—or pity?

She shuddered. He must never realize how much of a fool she'd been, or how thoroughly he'd destroyed her ten years ago.

She had to fake it.

Pretend to be the experienced woman he believed her to be.

So how would a sexually adventurous woman behave?

Trembling, Bree reached for his shoulders. Tossing her head with bravado, she rolled him beneath her on the bed. He did not resist, just looked up at her with smoldering eyes dark with lust. Trying to seem as if she was comfortable straddling him, with her breasts naked for a man for the first time, and wearing nothing but the tiny silk G-string, she gazed down at him. He did have an incredible body…and as long as she didn't look directly into his deep blue eyes, those eyes that always saw straight through her...

With an intake of breath, she slowly stroked down his bare chest to the waistband of his black trousers. Shaking with nerves, trying to act confident, she lowered her head.

And she kissed him.

Her lips were tentative, scared. Until she felt his mouth, hot and hard against hers, sliding like liquid silk as he kissed her back. He deepened the embrace, entwining her tongue with his. He tasted like sweet wine and spice and everything forbidden, everything she'd ever denied herself. His lips were soft and hard at once, like satin with steel. He let her set the rhythm and pace, let her lead.

And she forgot her fear. Her hands explored the warm, smooth skin of his hard chest, the edges and curves of his muscles. She stroked his flat nipples and the rough, bristly hair that stretched down his taut torso like an arrow. She heard his ragged intake of breath, and when she glanced up and saw his mesmerized expression, her confidence leaped. It was working! Growing bolder, she ran her fingertips beneath the edge of his waistband, swaying her splayed body against the thick hardness between his legs.

She'd meant it as an exploration. He took it as a taunt. With a growl, he pushed her back against the bed. Pulling off his pants and boxers, he kicked them to the floor.

She gasped when she saw him naked for the first time. He was huge. She couldn't look away. But as he pulled her back into his arms, crushing her breasts against his chest as he took possession of her mouth with a hard, hungry kiss, she forgot that fear, too.

He kissed slowly down her body, moving from her neck to the valley between her breasts to the flat plain of her belly. His hot breath enflamed her skin. Pushing her legs apart with his hands, he nuzzled her tender, untouched thighs. He kissed the edges of her G-string panties, and she felt the brief flicker of his tongue through silk.

She gasped. Need pounded through her, making her body shake as she felt his mouth move between her legs, gently suckling secret places there. She felt the heat and dampness of his tongue, teasing her on the edge of the fabric, and her back arched against the mattress. With a little cry, she stretched out her arms to grip the sheets, feeling as if she might fly off the bed and into the sky.

His fingers stroked the smooth silk, and she heard the rasp of her own frantic breathing. With tantalizing slowness, he reached beneath the fabric, stroking her wet core with a feather-like touch. He pushed a single thick fingertip an inch inside her, bending his head to suckle the top of her mound through the silk panties, and her back arched higher, her body grew tighter, and her breathing quickened, so much she started to see stars.

She heard the ripping of fabric as he destroyed the wisp of silk and tossed it to the floor.

"Look at me."

Against her will, she opened her eyes. Holding her gaze, he lowered his head between her naked thighs and fully tasted her with his wide tongue.

She cried out as she felt him tantalize, then lick, then lap her wet core. Her body twisted with the intensity of the pleasure even as her soul was torn by the intimacy of his gaze. Her heart hammered in her throat. Closing her eyes, she turned away so he could not see her tears.

His tongue changed rhythm; now he was using just the tip on her taut, sensitive nub. It was perfect. It was torture. His tongue swirled in light circles, barely touching her. She ached deep inside, wanting to be filled, wanting to have him inside her. Pleasure was building so hard and fast that her body could barely contain it. She felt an agony of need. With a whimper, she tried to pull away, but he held her firmly, not allowing her to escape from his hot, wet tongue.

Pleasure built higher and higher. "Please," she panted, nearly crying with need. "Please."

Holding her down, Vladimir thrust two thick fingertips inside her, then three. Still lapping her, he stretched her wide, his free hand pushing her back against the bed, while his tongue tormented her wet, slick core. And suddenly, she fell off a cliff. Her body exploded. She cried out as waves of ecstasy crashed around her, and she flew.

Quickly sheathing himself in a condom from the bedstand, he positioned himself between her legs. With a single rough thrust, he shoved himself all the way inside her. Gripping his shoulders, Bree cried out as sudden pain tore through her pleasure.

When Vladimir felt the barrier he hadn't expected, he froze, looking down at her in shock.

"You were—a virgin?" he breathed.

Bree's eyes squeezed shut, her beautiful face full of anguish as she turned it away, as if she didn't want him to see. He didn't move, unable to fathom the evidence he'd felt with his own body. "Why didn't you tell me?"

Trembling beneath him, she slowly opened her eyes again—limpid hazel eyes that glimmered like an autumn lake dark with rain. "I did," she whispered. She took a ragged breath. "You didn't believe me."

Vladimir stared at her beautiful face. Around him, the whole world suddenly seemed to shake and rattle. But the earthquake was in his own heart. He felt something crack inside his soul.

Everything he'd thought about Bree was wrong.

Everything he'd believed her to be—*wrong*.

With a ragged intake of breath, he pulled away. Sitting back on the bed, he choked out, "I don't understand."

"Don't you?" She sat up against the headboard, and her eyes shimmered in the silver-gold moonlight dappling the high-ceilinged bedroom. She licked her lips. "When you didn't believe me, I started hoping I could keep my virginity a secret. So you wouldn't..."

She stopped.

"So I wouldn't what?"

Her lips trembled as she tried to smile. "Well, it's pathetic, isn't it?" She didn't try to cover her nakedness, as another woman might have done. She just looked straight into his eyes, without artifice, without defenses. "There was no other man for me. Not before you. And not after."

Staring at her, Vladimir felt as if he'd just been sucker punched.

She'd told him the truth. All these years he'd thought of Bree Dalton as a liar, or worse. But even when she'd looked him in the eyes and told him she was a virgin, he hadn't believed her.

Who was the one who didn't recognize the truth when he saw it?

Who was the one who'd forgotten how?

Setting his jaw, he looked at her grimly. "And Alaska?"

She looked down, her eyelashes a dark sweep against her pale skin. "Everything your brother tried to tell you, that Christmas night he burst in on us, was true," she said softly. "I never had the rights to sell Josie's land. I was trying to distract you, so you'd put down earnest money in cash before you realized it, and my sister and I could disappear into a new life."

"To con people somewhere else."

"It was all I knew how to do." Bree lifted her gaze. "It never occurred to me that I could change. Not until..."

Her voice trailed off.

Yes, Vladimir, I'll marry you. He could almost hear her joyful, choked voice that Christmas night, see the tears in her beautiful eyes as she'd thrown her arms around him and whispered, "I'm not good enough for you, not by half. But I'll spend the rest of my life trying to be."

Now, his hands tightened into fists. "You had plenty of chances to tell me the truth. Instead, you let me find out about your con from Kasimir. You let me shout at him and throw him out of your cabin as a damned liar. You let me leave that night, still not knowing the truth. Until I started getting phone calls the next morning, and discovered from reporters that everything he'd told me about you was true."

"I wanted to tell you. But I was afraid."

"Afraid," he sneered.

"Yes," she cried. "Afraid you wouldn't listen to my side. That you'd abandon me, and I'd be left with no money and no defenses against the wolves circling us. I was afraid," she whispered, "you'd stop loving me."

That was exactly what had happened.

"If that is true, and you were truly intending to change purely because of this *love* for me," he said, his voice dripping scorn, "why didn't you go back to your old life of cheating and lying the instant I left?"

Her eyes widened, then fell. "It wasn't just for you," she muttered. "It was for me, too." She looked up. "And Josie. I wanted to be a good example. I wanted us to live a safe, boring, respectable life." Hugging her knees to her chest, she blinked fast, her eyes suspiciously wet. "But we couldn't."

"You couldn't be respectable?"

"We never felt safe." She licked her lips. "Back in Alaska, some men had threatened to hurt us if I didn't replace money we'd stolen. But my father had already spent it all and more. It was a million dollars, impossible to repay. So for the last ten years, I made sure we stayed off the radar. No job promotions. No college for Josie. Never staying too long anywhere." Bree's lips twisted. "Not much of a life, but at least no legs got broken."

His hands clenched as he remembered the angry looks of the players at the poker game, when she'd told them how she'd cheated them. "Why didn't you tell me about this?"

"I did," she said, bewildered at his reaction. "A few times."

"You told me you had debts," he said tightly. "Everyone

has debts. You didn't tell me some men were threatening to break your legs."

She took a deep breath, her face filled with pain.

"Not mine," she whispered. "Josie's."

Vladimir rose to his feet. Still naked, he paced three steps, clenching his hands. His shoulders felt so tense they burned. He was having a physical reaction.

If he'd been wrong about Bree, what else had he been wrong about?

He stopped as he remembered his brother's face, contorted beneath the lights of the Christmas tree. *You're taking her word over mine? You just met this girl two months ago. I've looked up to you my whole life. Why can't you believe I might know more than you—just once?*

But Vladimir, two years older, had always been the leader, the protector. He could still remember six-year-old Kasimir panting as he struggled through the snowy two miles to school. *Wait for me, Volodya! Wait for me!*

But he'd never waited. *If you want to follow me, keep up, Kasimir. Stop being slow.*

Now, as Vladimir remembered that long-lost adoration in his brother's eyes, his heart gave a strange, sickening jump in his chest. Tightening his jaw, he pushed the memory away. He looked at Bree.

"No one will ever threaten you or yours again."

Her lips parted. "What will you do?"

He narrowed his eyes. "They threatened to break a child's legs," he said roughly. "So I'll break every bone in their bodies. First their legs. Then their arms. Then—"

"Who are you?" she cried.

He stopped, surprised at the horror on her face. "What?"

"You're so ruthless." She swallowed. "There is no mercy in you. It's true what they say."

"You expect me to, what—give them a cookie and tuck them into bed?"

"No, but—" she spread her arms helplessly "—break every single bone? You don't just want to win, you want to crush them. Torture them. You've become the kind of man who..." Her eyes seared his. "Who'd destroy his own brother."

For a moment, Vladimir was speechless. Then he glared at her. "Kasimir made his own choice. When I wouldn't listen to his words about you, he told the story to a reporter. He betrayed me, and when I suggested we split up our partnership, it was his choice to agree—"

"You deliberately cheated your own brother," she interrupted, "out of millions of dollars. And you've spent ten years trying to destroy him. You don't just get revenge, Vladimir. You deal a double dose of pain—breaking not just their legs, but their arms!"

Pacing two steps, he clawed back his dark hair angrily. "What would you have me do, Breanna? Let them threaten you? Pay them off? Let them win? Let my brother take over my company? Not defend myself?"

"But you don't just defend yourself," she said. "You're ruthless. And you revel in it." Her eyes lifted to his. "Has it made you happy, Vladimir? Has destroying other people's lives made yours better?"

He flashed hot, then cold. As they faced each other, naked without touching, in a bedroom deep with shadows and frosted with moonlight, a mixture of emotions raced through his bloodstream that he hadn't felt in a long, long time—emotions he could barely recognize.

Bree took a deep, ragged breath.

"I loved you. I loved the honest, openhearted man you were." Tears glistened like icicles against her pale skin. "The truth is, I love him still."

Vladimir sucked in his breath. *What was she saying?*

"But the man you are now..." She looked at him. "I hate the man you've become, Vladimir," she whispered. "I hate you now. With all my heart."

He took a single staggering step. He held out his hand and heard his own hoarse, shaking voice. "Bree…"

"No!" She nearly fell off the bed to avoid his touch. Snatching the crumpled, pink silk robe off the floor, she covered her naked body. "I should never have let you touch me. Ever!"

She fled from the bedroom, racing down the hall.

For an instant, Vladimir stood frozen, paralyzed with shock.

Then, narrowing his eyes, he yanked on a pair of jeans and followed her grimly. Downstairs, he heard the door that led to the pool bang. He followed the sound outside. From the corner of his eye, beneath dark silhouettes of palm trees against the sapphire sky, he saw a pale flash going down the cliff toward the beach.

He followed. Striding around the pool, he pushed through the gate and went down steps chiseled into the rock, leading to the private, white-sand beach. At the bottom, surrounded by the noisy roar of the surf lapping the sand at his feet, he looked right and left.

Where was she?

The large Hawaiian moon glowed like an opalescent pearl across the dark blue velvet ocean, its light sparkling like diamonds.

I loved the honest, openhearted man you were. Her poignant words echoed in his mind. *I hate the man you've become.*

Closing his eyes, he thought of how he'd spent the past ten years, constantly proving to himself how hard and heartless he could be. Betraying others before they could even *think* of turning on him.

Half the world called him ruthless; the other half called him corrupt. Vladimir had worn their hatred like a badge of honor. He'd told himself that it was the fate of every powerful man to be despised. It only proved he'd succeeded. He'd conquered the world. He'd just never thought it would be so…

Meaningless. Bleakly, he looked out toward the dark waves of the Pacific.

Has it made you happy? Has destroying other people's lives made yours better?

The warm breeze felt cool against his bare skin. He'd loved her so recklessly. The night he'd proposed to her, in front of the crackling fire that dark, cold Christmas, had been the happiest of his life.

Until Kasimir had burst into her cabin and called Vladimir a fool for falling into a con woman's trap. The fighting had woken up her kid sister upstairs, so after tossing his brother out, he'd gone back to his hotel alone. He'd been woken by the ringing of his cell phone—and questions from a *Wall Street Journal* reporter.

Vladimir put a hand to his forehead.

For the past ten years, this woman he'd called a liar and a whore had been quietly working minimum-wage jobs, in a desperate attempt to provide an honest life for her young sister. While he…

Vladimir exhaled. He'd done exactly what she said. He'd cut all mercy from his heart, to make damn sure no one ever made a fool of him again. He'd closed himself off completely from every human feeling, and he'd tried to eradicate the memory of the woman who'd once broken him.

The moon retreated behind a cloud, and he saw a shadow move. He stumbled down the beach, and as the moon burst out of the darkness, he saw her.

Silvery light frosted the dark silhouette of her body as she rose like Venus from the waves. His heart twisted in his chest.

Breanna.

CHAPTER SIX

BREE stood alone in the surf, staring bleakly out at the moon-lit ocean, wishing she was far, far away from Hawaii. She felt the waves against her bare thighs, felt the sand squish beneath her toes. She shivered in the warm night, wishing she was a million miles away.

How could she have given him her virginity?

How could she have let him kiss her, touch her, make her explode with pleasure? *How?*

Allowing Vladimir to make love to her had brought back all the memories of the way she'd once loved him. How could she have allowed herself to be so vulnerable? Why hadn't she been able to protect herself, to keep her heart cold?

Because he'd always known how to get past all her defenses. Always. He hadn't forced her. He hadn't needed to. All he'd done was kiss her, and she'd surrendered, melting into his arms. And she'd been able to hold nothing back. Her feelings had come pouring out of her lips. How she'd loved him.

How she hated him.

When Vladimir had said that no one would ever threaten her or Josie again, she'd been relieved. Grateful, even. Then he'd spoken with such relish about breaking all their bones.

Bree had no love for the men who'd made their lives a mis-ery over the past ten years. But she would have paid back every penny if she could. And seeing Vladimir, the prince she'd loved at eighteen, turned into this…this *monster*…was unbearable.

She'd thought the man she'd loved had betrayed her. But it was far worse than that.

The charming, tender-hearted man she'd loved was dead. Dead and gone forever. And left in his place was nothing but a selfish, coldhearted tycoon.

She missed the man she'd loved. She missed him as she hadn't allowed herself to do for a full ten years. The way he'd held her, respected her, the way he'd made her laugh. He'd still been strong, but he'd looked out for those weaker than himself.

But that man was gone—gone forever.

Tears streamed unchecked down her cheeks as she bowed her head and cried in the moonlight. Even the cool water of the ocean couldn't wash away her grief and regret.

For all these years, she'd pompously lectured Josie that she must be strong as a woman—must never give a man power over her. Bree wiped her eyes.

She was a fraud. She wasn't strong. She never had been.

"Breanna."

She heard his low, deep voice behind her. Whirling around with a gasp, she saw him walking at the edge of the surf, coming toward her.

"Vladimir," she whispered, taking an involuntary step back into the ocean. "You followed me?"

"I couldn't let you go." He walked straight into the waves, never looking away from her. Moonlight traced the strong muscles of his naked chest, and the dark hairline leading to the low-slung waistband of his jeans.

She folded her trembling arms over her wet, flimsy robe. "What more could you possibly do to hurt me?"

His eyes were dark and hot, his voice low. "I don't want to hurt you. Not anymore. Never again."

"Then what do you want?" Then suddenly, Bree knew, and her body shook all over. Backing away, she held up her hand. "Don't—don't come any closer!"

But he didn't stop. He waded nearer, until the water rose

higher than his thighs, to his lean, sexy hips, where the wet jeans clung.

Vladimir's gaze fell to her body. Looking down, she realized her robe was completely soaked and sticking to her skin. Even in the moonlight, the color of her nipples was visible through the translucent, diaphanous pink silk.

They stood inches apart, waist-deep in the ocean. Their eyes locked. A current of electricity flashed through her.

"I won't be your possession, Vladimir," she whispered. "I won't be your slave."

His lips curved. "How could a woman like you," he said, "ever be any man's slave?"

A large wave pushed her forward, and the palm she'd held out against him fell upon the hot, bare skin of his solid chest. Without moving her hand, Bree looked up at him. Her heart was beating wildly.

"But you're mine." His dark eyes gleamed as, grabbing her wrists, he pulled her tightly against his body. Twining his hands through her wet hair, he cupped her face and tilted her mouth upwards. "You've always been mine."

"I'm not—"

"Your own body proved it. You belong to me, Breanna. Admit it."

She shook her head wildly. "I despise you."

"Perhaps I deserve your hatred." His words were low, barely audible over the surf and the plaintive cry of faraway seagulls. "But you belong to me, just the same. And I'm going to take you."

As the surf thundered against the beach, Vladimir lowered his mouth to hers.

His kiss was searing, passionate. But she realized something had changed. As he held her against his body like a newly dis-covered treasure, his lips were exploratory, even tender. His kiss was full of yearning and heartbreak—of vulnerability.

It was the kiss she remembered. The exact way Vladimir had kissed her when Bree's world had been reborn.

A choked sob came from the back of her throat. Wrapping her arms around his shoulders, she kissed him back with all the aching passion of lost time. Standing on the edge of the moon-drenched ocean, they clung to each other as the waves tried, but failed, to pull them apart.

Without a word, he lifted her against his naked chest. Their wet bodies dripped water as he carried her out of the ocean, back to the white-sand beach. And as he carried her up the moonlit cliff path that led to the villa, she closed her eyes, clinging to him.

You're mine. You've always been mine. Your own body proved it.

It was true. Even though she hated him, it had always been true.

Bree was his. And whether she wished it or not, she always would be.

Vladimir left a trail of sand and water as he crossed the floor of their bedroom, then gently lowered Bree to her feet beside the bed.

Neither of them spoke. Almost holding his breath, he slowly stroked down her soft arms to her slender waist. He undid the silken tie of her robe. Never taking his eyes from hers, he peeled the wet, translucent silk off her shoulders and dropped it to the floor.

She now stood before him naked and beautiful, her eyes luminous in the moonlight. Looking at her, this sensual angel, Vladimir trembled, racked with desires both sacred and profane.

He'd taken her virginity. He couldn't undo that.

But he could change her memory of it.

Pulling her naked body into his arms, against his bare chest, he cupped the back of her head, tangling his hands in her long wet hair, and lowered his mouth to hers.

This time, without so much anger and prejudice in his heart, he finally felt her inexperience, the way she held her breath as she hesitated, her lips shy, then tried to follow his lead. He noticed everything he hadn't wanted to see.

This time, he did not plunder. He kissed her softly. Slowly. His lips suggested, rather than forced; they taught, rather than demanded. He let her set the pace. He felt her small body tremble in his arms, and then, with a deep sigh from the back of her throat, she relaxed. Her arms reached around his neck, and he felt her mouth part for him, offering freely what he'd earlier taken like a brute.

As Vladimir held her naked, soft form, still wet from the ocean, waves of desire pummeled his own body with need. But he controlled himself. He would not take her roughly. This time, he would give her the perfect pleasure she deserved. The night he'd wanted to give her long ago…

Standing beside the four-poster bed, he kissed her for a long time, holding her tight. The two of them swayed in the shadows of the bedroom. Her soft breasts felt like silk, brushing against his bare chest. His ran his hands over the smooth, warm skin of her back, beneath her wet hair.

Their kiss deepened. He did not force it, and neither did she. It just happened, like magic, as the hunger grew like fire between them. He felt the tip of her tongue brush his, and his whole body suddenly felt electric. He could almost see colors in bursts of light behind his closed eyes, like an illumination in the darkness. She was his guiding light and North Star. His one true point.

He held on to her as if, by kissing her, he could go back in time and be the openhearted young man he'd once been. The fearless one…

Bree's hands moved slowly down the sides of his body, pausing at the recent scars. She drew back to look at his skin. "The racing accident did this?"

He didn't trust himself to speak, so he gave a single unsteady nod.

Her fingers traced the other scars she saw. "And this?"

"Boxing."

"And this?"

"Skydiving."

"So reckless," she sighed. "Don't you know you could die?"

"We're all going to die," he said roughly. "I was trying to feel alive."

Her fingertips explored, accepted fully. As she touched his scars, he held his breath, feeling his soul laid bare.

"Still sorry the car accident didn't kill me?" he said in a low voice.

She stopped at the waistband of his jeans and looked up at him with troubled eyes. For a moment, she didn't answer. Then she shook her head, moving her hand over his heart.

"No," she whispered. "Because I think the man I loved is still inside you."

He grabbed her wrist. "He's dead and gone."

She raised her eyes.

"Are you sure?" she said softly.

The look in her hazel eyes made Vladimir's heart twist in his chest. It was as if she knew exactly who he was, scars and all. As if she saw right through him. Straight to his broken soul.

Turning away without a word, he unzipped the fly of his jeans. He wrestled the wet denim to the floor. Grabbing her wrists, he pulled her to the bed, with her naked body on top of his. The feeling of having her like this—Breanna, the woman he'd hated for ten years, the first and last woman he'd let himself love—left him dizzy.

"I'm not that man," he said aloud, to both of them.

Pulling her wrists from his grip, she put her hands on either side of his face.

"Let me see," she whispered. Lowering her head, she kissed him.

As her sweet mouth moved against his lips, the weight of her naked body pressed against him, and it felt like heaven. Her hands moved slowly across his skin, down his arms, to his hips. Lowering her head, she followed the same path, kissing down his chest to his flat belly.

When he felt the heat of her breath against his thighs, he squeezed his eyes shut, suddenly afraid to move. She paused. Then, tentatively, she reached out her hand and stroked him, exploring the length of his shaft. He gasped softly. Then he felt her weight move on the bed, and suddenly her lips and breath were on him. He felt her mouth against him, her tongue stroke his shaft to the tip.

He gasped again.

She moved slowly, and he suddenly realized this was new to her; she'd never explored any man so intimately before. The thought of this—that she'd waited all this time for him, only for him—was too much for him to endure. He felt her soft warm mouth enfold him, and he sucked in his breath. One more flicker of her tongue—

Sitting up, he grabbed her, rolling her over. Lying on top of her, he looked straight into her eyes and breathed hoarsely, "No, Breanna. No."

Putting his hand on her cheek, he lowered his head to hers. As he kissed her lips, his hands stroked her satin-soft skin, cupping her breasts. Moving down her body, he kissed first one breast, then the other, with hot need, suckling her until she gasped. His fingertips caressed down her belly. When he reached the mound between her legs, he stopped. His body was shaking, screaming for him to push inside her.

But he did not. He moved abruptly to the bottom of the bed. Taking one of her feet in his hands, he slowly kissed it, suckling her toes, tasting salt from the Pacific on her sweet, warm skin. He felt her tremble as he kissed the hollow of her foot, then moved up her leg to her calf, and the tender spot behind her knee. When he reached her thighs, he pressed them apart, spreading her.

He risked a glance upward. Her face was rapt, her eyes tightly closed. He heard the rasp of her breath and felt the tremble of her legs as she nervously tried to close them. Smiling to himself—he could hardly wait to give her this pleasure—he held her legs splayed and kissed slowly up the soft skin of her thighs. He moved higher and higher, teasing her with his breath, until he finally spread her wide. Lowering his head, he took a long, deep taste.

He had the satisfaction of hearing her cry out as her body shook with need. Slowly, deliberately, he moved his tongue, widening it to lap at her, then pointing the tip to penetrate a half inch inside her. He felt her body get tighter and tighter, saw her back start to arch off the mattress, as before. But this time, he wanted to give her more.

Flicking his tongue against her swollen nub, he pushed a thick knuckle of his folded finger just barely inside her. She felt wet, so wet for him. One of her hands rested on his head, clutching his hair, no longer trying to pull him away, embarrassment and fear forgotten beneath the waves of pleasure. Her other hand gripped the tousled white sheets of the bed. Her body grew tense and tenser beneath him, until she started to lift off the mattress, as if gravity itself were losing power over her. She held her breath, and then with a loud cry, she exploded. He felt her body contract hard around his knuckle.

Sheathing himself in another condom—except this time, his hands shook so badly he nearly dropped it—he positioned himself as she was still gasping in kittenish cries of pleasure. He wanted to plunge himself inside her.

But *he did not*.

Even now, he forced himself to stay in control. He entered her body inch by inch, stretching her wide to fully accept him, doing it slowly, so that she could feel him inside her, and he could feel every inch of her. Her eyes opened with wonder, locking with his own. They never looked away as he slowly filled her, so slowly that the exquisite pleasure almost felt like pain. He finally pushed himself inside her, all the way to the hilt.

And he forgot to breathe. She felt so good. This was ecstasy he'd never felt before. *Faster,* his body screamed. *Harder, faster, deeper, now!*

But with a will of iron, he gritted his teeth and ignored his body's demand. He forced himself to go slow for her, in a way he'd never done before for any woman. He wanted this to be what she would remember from her first night of making love. Not the ruthless, rough, crude way of before.

Gripping her hips to steady his pace, he started to slowly ride her. Her hands held his backside, pulling him more tightly inside her, deeper, and deeper still.

He felt her body tighten again, and as he lowered his head to suckle her breasts—first one, then the other—his hardened body moved in a circular motion against hers as he thrust inside her.

Closing her eyes, she clutched his shoulders, digging her nails into his flesh. Vladimir's heart was pounding in his throat with the need to explode inside her, but he forced himself to relax, to wait. He just needed to see her face light up, to hear her gasp. He just needed to feel her tighten around him one more time....

He pounded inside her, harder and deeper, and her hips lifted to meet the force of his thrust. Lowering his head once more, he kissed her. As their lips met, he heard her suck in her breath, felt her body tighten....

And then she screamed, even louder than she had before. In that same instant, he finally let himself go. It felt so good.... So good...

Stars exploded behind his eyes, and his own ecstatic shout

rang in his ears. Their joined cries of pleasure echoed in the quiet moonlit night, louder than the distant roar of the sea.

Afterwards, they collapsed into each other's arms. Exhausted, he held her close, kissing her temple, whispering her name like a prayer. "Breanna…"

Vladimir woke abruptly when he heard his cell phone ringing. Blinking in surprise, he saw gray dawn breaking over the clouds. He'd slept all night in Bree's arms.

He looked down. She was still sleeping, cradled naked against his chest.

He'd lowered his guard and slept with a woman in his arms—something he'd never been able to do with anyone but her. The tension in his shoulders was gone. His head didn't hurt. His heartbeat was soft and slow. It was the best sleep he'd had since the accident.

Was this what peace felt like?

His phone buzzed again. Getting up quietly from bed, he picked it up from the nightstand and left the bedroom. Closing the door silently behind him, not wanting to wake her, he put the phone to his ear. "Yes?"

"Your Highness." It was John Anderson, his chief of operations. "The Arctic Oil merger is now urgent. Your brother just had a huge oil find in Alaska. On the land he bought last spring from that Spaniard, Eduardo Cruz."

"Wait," Vladimir growled. His hands were shaking as he went down the hall to his office. So much for peace. He could feel his heartbeat thrumming in his neck, hear his own blood rushing in his ears. His brother had that effect on him. He closed the office door. "Go."

"Sir, if the find is as substantial as it seems, oil might soon flood the market, causing the price to drop…."

Vladimir paced as he listened, clawing back his hair. Usually business calmed him, because he relished a fight. But not when the news involved his brother.

Volodya, Volodya, please wait for me! Closing his eyes,

Vladimir could still see his baby brother's chubby face as he'd toddled after him through the snow those long-ago, hungry winters. Sometimes supplies at the homestead grew lean, and Vladimir had gone out with their father to hunt rabbits. *I want to hunt, too.* Once, Kasimir had idolized his big brother. Now, he enjoyed taunting and hurting Vladimir any chance he could get. Kasimir would probably be the death of him.

As his COO droned on, Vladimir barely listened. He felt weary. For ten years now, he'd fought this fight. There was no longer any joy in it. He'd taken up hobbies like car racing, risking death for the sake of cutting a few seconds off his time. He'd taken women, in endless, meaningless one-night stands. He'd been starving to feel something. Anything. But lately, even the thrill of cheating death had brought only a tiny blip.

There were no new worlds to conquer. He'd been going through the motions for a long time. He felt nothing.

Not until last night.

Not until Breanna returned to him.

He exhaled. *Breanna.*

She made him *feel,* after years of deadness. She'd brought pleasure. Yearning. Anger. Guilt. Desire. All wrapped up in a chaotic ball. He felt as if he'd just woken out of a coma, after years of dull gray sleep.

Perhaps he was incapable of love, with a soul twisted and gnarled like a tree split by lightning. He'd told her the truth: he'd never be the man he'd once been—naive and trusting enough to give away the shirt off his back. Not even for a woman like her.

Barely hearing his COO's voice, Vladimir looked through the window of his villa's home office. The bright Hawaiian dawn was burning through the low-swept morning clouds still kissing the green earth. The sky was turning blue, as blue as the sparkling ocean below.

He had the sudden memory of Breanna rising from the waves in the moonlight last night, her short silk robe stuck to her like a second skin as rivulets of water streamed down her breasts to her thighs. Vladimir shuddered, turning instantly hard. Instead of satiating him, making love to her had only increased his hunger.

"…So what should we do, Your Highness?" his COO finished anxiously.

Vladimir blinked, realizing he hadn't been listening to the man for the past ten minutes. But he suddenly felt bored by business matters—completely bored. Even though it involved his brother. "What is your opinion?"

"We'll have someone at our Alaska site infiltrate your brother's mining operation to see if the data is accurate. If it is, we can try to influence the political process to delay their building. We could even consider some kind of sabotage at the mine. Although of course it would in no way be traceable back to you, sir…."

You're ruthless. And you revel in it. The realization of how low he'd sunk caused Vladimir to flinch. "No."

"But, Your Highness…"

"I said no." Clawing back his hair, he paced across his office with his phone at his ear, prowling in circles around his desk.

"So what are your orders, Your Highness? How shall we make sure your brother does not succeed?"

Vladimir abruptly stopped. He'd been wrong about Breanna.

Could he have similarly been wrong about Kasimir, over-reacting to his brother's betrayal?

It was an accident. His brother's voice had been muffled, humble, on the phone the next day from St. Petersburg. *When you wouldn't believe me, I was angry and drunk at the airport bar. I didn't realize the man sitting next to me was a reporter for the* Anchorage Herald. *Forgive me, Volodya.*

Vladimir's hands tightened into fists. But he hadn't accepted the apology. He'd been angry, humiliated, haunted. And he feared his stupidity might jeopardize the Siberian mining rights that were about to come through, rights that could make or break the fledgling company. "If you can't trust my leadership, we should end this partnership."

"Leadership? I thought we were supposed to be equals," his brother had retorted. When Vladimir maintained a frosty silence, Kasimir had said harshly, "Fine. I'll keep the rights in Africa and South America. And you can go to hell."

Vladimir had been angry enough to let his brother go without telling him about the Siberian rights worth potentially half a billion dollars. He'd effectively cheated Kasimir out of his half.

Perhaps... He took a deep breath. Perhaps Kasimir had some cause to seek revenge against him.

"You will do nothing." Now, Vladimir stared out the window toward the palm trees and blue sky. "My brother's operation in Alaska does not affect us. Leave him alone. May the best company win."

"But, sir!"

"Xendzov Mining can win in a fair fight."

"Of course we can!" the man replied indignantly. He continued in a bewildered voice, "It's just that we've never tried."

"No more dirty tricks," Vladimir said harshly.

"It will be harder—"

"Deal with it."

The man cleared his throat. "You were expected in St. Petersburg today for the signing of the Arctic Oil merger. How long do you wish us to delay...?"

Vladimir gritted his teeth. "I will be at the office tomorrow."

"Good." He audibly exhaled. "With ten billion dollars on the line, we don't want anything to—"

"Tomorrow." Vladimir hung up. Tossing his phone on his desk, he left the study, with its computers and piles of paperwork. Walking outside to the courtyard, he stopped by the pool. Closing his eyes, he turned his face toward the bright morning sun. He felt the warmth of the golden light, and took a breath of the exotic, flower-scented air.

I think the man I love is still inside you.

He's dead and gone.

Are you sure?

Slowly, Vladimir opened his eyes. He looked up at the twenty-million-dollar mansion that he'd bought as a refuge, but which had felt like a prison.

Bree Dalton had brought it to life. As she'd done to him.

But what right did he have to keep her prisoner?

He'd told himself she deserved it. She was the one who'd betrayed him ten years ago, then foolishly wagered her body in a card game. Let her finally face the consequences of her actions.

He paced around the edge of the pool, then stopped, clawing back his hair. But she'd offered her body in desperation. He'd abandoned her without a penny in Alaska, with men threatening them for money. And yet, even under that pressure, Bree had managed to come through the fire with a soul as pure as steel.

He still wanted to find those men and break their legs, their arms. Every bone in their bodies. But there was something he wanted even more.

He wanted Breanna.

His long-dormant conscience stirred, telling him he had no right to keep her. If he truly believed that she'd never meant to betray him, that she'd wagered herself only to protect her little sister, then he should let her go. If he kept her as his slave, it would make him no better than the criminals who'd imprisoned her with debts. He was selfish, but not a monster.

Wasn't he?

Pushing the thought away, he pulled out his cell phone and made a few calls. One to an investigator. The other to his secretary, to arrange a Russian visa. Then he picked a wild orchid from the garden and went back inside the house. He'd given his household staff the day off, after Mrs. Kalani's reaction to his treatment of Bree yesterday. So the enormous kitchen was quiet as he made her a breakfast tray. Putting the orchid in a vase, he walked up the stairs to their bedroom.

Breanna was still drowsing in bed. But as he pushed open the door, she sat up, tucking the sheet modestly over her naked breasts.

"Good morning," she said shyly.

Vladimir went to the bed. She looked so innocent and fresh and pretty, the epitome of everything good. He put the breakfast tray into her lap. "I thought you might be hungry."

"I am." Her cheeks blushed a soft pink as she looked down at the tray, with its toast and fresh fruit and fragrant flower. "Thank you." Looking up, she gave him a sudden wicked smile. "Last night left me really, really hungry."

The bright, teasing look on her face took his breath away. He said abruptly, "I have to go to St. Petersburg today."

Her face fell. "Oh." Looking away, she said stiffly, "Well. Good. I'll be glad to be free of you."

"Too bad." Turning her face roughly, he cupped her cheek. "You're coming with me."

Her eyes lit up. Then she scowled, glaring at him. "Because I'm your property and slave, right? Because you get to boss me around and take me wherever you want, right?"

He kissed her bare shoulder. "You got it."

She shivered as his lips touched her. "You are such a jerk—"

Leaning over the tray, he kissed her lips, long and thoroughly, just to remind her who was in charge. Her lips parted so sweetly, it took all his strength to stop. He needed to order his private jet to leave within the hour. He had no time to make love to her.

But as he drew away, he saw that the white cotton sheet had fallen from her heedless hands, revealing the glory of her naked, trembling breasts. Against his will, he leaned forward to kiss her again, and they both jumped as they heard the breakfast tray crash to the floor.

Bree gave an impish laugh. "Maybe you should consider paper plates. I know you're rich and all, but honestly, I can't clean up all your broken china."

With a growl, Vladimir pushed her back against the bed.

"Don't worry. You'll never clean for me again," he whispered. "From now on…there's only one thing I want you to do for me."

Forcing his conscience to be silent, he lowered his mouth to hers. As he tasted the sweetness of her lips, he knew he wouldn't give her up. She was his. He'd won her—she belonged to him, for as long as he desired her. If that meant he was a monster, so be it.

I think the man I love is still inside you.

He's dead and gone.

Are you sure?

As Vladimir felt her naked body move like silk beneath him, she gave a trembling sigh. She wrapped her arms around his neck and pulled him down to heaven.

Yes. He was sure.

CHAPTER SEVEN

Russia.

As a child, Bree had traveled down the rocky, forest-covered Alaskan coast with her father, seeking gullible tourists off cruise ships for poker games. Her favorite village had been Sitka, once the capital of Russian America. At twelve, she'd looked across the gray, frozen Bering Sea and dreamed of the distant, ancient, mysterious land of the tsars.

When wooden Orthodox churches were being hacked out of the wilderness in Alaska, St. Petersburg was already a century old, built on the orders of a tsar. She'd dreamed of someday seeing the palatial Russian city, the onion domes of its cathedrals shining with silver and gold.

But Bree never dreamed she'd come here as the cosseted mistress of a prince. For two days now, she'd been living in his three-story palace outside the city, built like a fortress on a hill, overlooking the Gulf of Finland on the Baltic Sea. She'd spent her days shopping in the most exclusive boutiques of the city, accompanied by his bodyguards and his chauffeur.

She spent her nights in Vladimir's bed. He came to her in the middle of the night, waking her, making love to her in darkness, setting her body ablaze from the inside out. He burned her with the fire of their mutual need. Each night, she fell asleep in his arms, satiated with pleasure.

But each day, she woke up in the cold gray winter dawn, bereft and alone.

Vladimir was extremely busy, working on the Arctic Oil merger. Even if he was using her only for sex, she shouldn't take it personally. Right? That was what she'd expected. Wasn't it? She should be grateful for this life he'd given her, one of luxury, pleasure and comfort. Most women would envy her. She should make the best of things.

So she tried.

Left alone all day, she went shopping, as Vladimir had ordered. Four bodyguards took her out in a black limousine with bulletproof glass. Expensive designer shops closed their doors to all other customers so Bree could shop alone, quite alone, with only sycophantic store clerks for company.

Maybe it would have been fun if Vladimir had been with her. Or Josie. Bree missed her sister like a physical ache in her heart. She'd tried multiple times over the past few days to call her, but Josie never answered. Bree tried to squelch her worries. Surely Josie was fine. It was just her own loneliness, playing tricks on her mood, that made Bree anxious.

But after two exhausting days of shopping, shocked at the outrageous prices, she was desperate to find something, anything, else to do. "Buy a wardrobe of winter clothes," Vladimir had said, shoving his credit card into her hand. "And lingerie." Wanting to be done, she'd randomly grabbed two items the clerks were pushing on her—a long, puffy black coat and an expensive lingerie set with a white lace bustier, G-string and garter belt—and practically ran from the store. The bodyguards formed a tunnel to her waiting black limo, and she fled past the annoyed faces of Russian women waiting outside.

But now, on her third day in St. Petersburg, as she sat alone at a very long table in the empty palace, eating an elegant lunch prepared by the Russian-speaking housekeeper, Bree felt a rush of pure relief when her cell phone rang. She snatched it up. "Hello?"

"What are you wearing?"

At the sound of Vladimir's low, sensual voice, her shoulders relaxed. "I thought you might be Josie."

"Sorry to disappoint you."

"I'm glad to hear your voice." Her hand tightened on her phone. "I'm, um, wearing my old flannel pajamas and big bootie slippers from home."

"Sounds sexy. Want to come over?"

"Come where?"

"To my office."

She blinked. "Why?"

"I have a fifteen-minute break coming up. I thought I'd have you for lunch."

A shiver of sensual delight went through her at his words. Straightening in her antique chair, she retorted, "Forget it. I'm not going to rush over to your office like some kind of booty-call delivery service. I might be your sex slave, but I do have some standards."

"I think you'll change your mind when you hear what I want to do to you...."

She listened to his low growl of a voice describing his intentions in graphic detail, and her hand went limp until the phone fell from her grasp and clattered to the floor. She snatched it up.

"I'll be right there," she said breathlessly. Clicking off, she pulled her new lingerie from the designer bag and tugged it on. Covering herself with the black puffy coat, that trailed to her ankles, she replaced her slippers with black stiletto boots and went outside, where a bodyguard held open her limousine door.

Bree's heart pounded as the chauffeur drove into the heart of St. Petersburg. She barely saw the elegant buildings lining the snowy streets and icy Neva River. All she could think about was what waited for her. *Who* waited for her.

The limo arrived at a sprawling eighteenth-century building. A bodyguard opened her door and said in heavily accented English, "This is office, miss."

She looked up and down the block. The structure seemed to stretch endlessly along the avenue. "Which one?"

The bodyguard looked at her. "All. Is Xendzov building."

"All of it?" Bree looked at the classically columned building in shock. It was one thing to theoretically know that Vladimir was rich. It was another to see this enormous building, an entire city block, and know it represented a mere fragment of his worldwide empire.

Swallowing nervously, she went into the foyer and took an elevator to the top floor. Down the hall, through a wall of glass, she saw men in suits packed around a conference table, some of them pounding the tabletop as they argued, while secretaries refilled their coffee cups and took notes.

Vladimir looked devastatingly powerful and ruthless, in a shirt and tie. And clearly, she wasn't the only woman to think so. She noticed how the secretaries walked a little more slowly and swayed their hips a little more around him. The beauty of Russian women was justly famous. Their skirts were short, their hair long, their stiletto heels high. They clearly knew their feminine power and were willing to sacrifice comfort in order to hold a man's attention.

Bree's confidence tumbled. If Vladimir was surrounded by women like this, why on earth had he sent for her? The sexy playfulness of her errand disappeared. What a laugh. It was like dialing out for a hamburger, when he was surrounded by steak!

He would laugh in her face when he got a good look at her in this stupid lingerie. Her cheeks burned and she started to turn around.

Their eyes met through the glass.

Spinning on her heel, Bree practically ran down the hallway. If she could just reach the elevator...

His hand gripped her upper arm, whirling her to face him. "Where are you going?"

She licked her lips, looking up at this broad-shouldered, powerful man standing in his own building, surrounded by his paid employees. Vladimir had rolled up his shirtsleeves, revealing sleekly muscled forearms laced with dark hair. His tie had been loosened around his thick neck, as if he'd been fighting corporate war all day.

She tried to pull away, but his grip was like iron. "I never should have come here," she said. "Haven't you humiliated me enough?"

Vladimir frowned, drawing closer. "What are you...?" People passed them in the hall, two men in suits and three women in tiny skirts, all looking at them with intense interest. Narrowing his eyes, he growled, "Come with me."

He pulled her into the nearest private office, closing the door behind them. She wrenched her arm away, blinking fast. Her eyes were stinging with unshed tears as she tossed her head. "You're out of your mind if you think..."

She gasped as, without a word, he roughly yanked open her oversized coat. He saw the lingerie, the white lace bustier, G-string panties and garter belt, and drew in a breath. He looked at her darkly.

"And *you* are out of your mind," he said in a low voice, "if you think I'm going to let you leave."

He ripped off her long coat, dropping it to the floor. Pushing her against the wall of the private office, he kissed her hard. Bree's body stiffened as his mouth plundered hers. She felt the soft, demanding steel of his lips against her own. Against her will, a moan came from the back of her throat, and her arms lifted to wrap around his neck.

His hands roamed over her body. He cupped her breasts, then undid her bustier in a single motion, dropping the white lace from her skin. Still kissing her passionately, he pushed her toward the desk, which he cleared with a sweep of his arm, knocking papers and computer topsy-turvy to the floor.

She could not resist. As he pressed her back against the desk, she relished the feeling of his weight. He kissed down her neck to her bare breasts, ravishing her body, and she panted, suddenly breathless with need. Her hands reached beneath his shirt to stroke his taut, hard chest.

Then she heard a noise at the door.

Dazed, Bree looked over and saw a man staring at them from the doorway. He said something in Russian, before Vladimir turned his head. The man's mouth snapped shut, his face red with the apparent effort of choking back his words. Turning, he left instantly, closing the door behind him.

But the damage was done. The man had seen her draped nearly naked across Vladimir's desk. Horrified, Bree said angrily, "That man's got some nerve, bursting into your office without warning!"

"This is his office—" Vladimir leaned back on the desk, tilting his head "—not mine."

"What?" she squeaked, sitting up.

"My office is on the other side of the building. Would have taken too long."

He leaned forward to kiss her, but she jerked back, nearly falling off the desk. "Are you crazy? I'm not going to fool around with you in someone else's office!"

"Why not?" he said lazily. "What does it matter? This building is mine. This office is mine. Just as you..."

She folded her arms over her naked breasts, glaring at him. "Just as I am?"

"Yes." Standing up, he tucked a tendril of hair behind her ear and said huskily, "Just as you are."

A pain went through her chest. His words were playful, but he was speaking a truth she'd been trying to conveniently forget: that Vladimir owned her. She was his property.

Bree's cheeks flooded with shame as she remembered the expression on the man's face when he'd seen Vladimir lying on top of her on the desk. He'd looked at her as if she were a prostitute. And glancing down at herself in only a G-string and garter belt, a sex-time delivery service, Bree felt a lump rise in her throat. Leaning down, she picked up the discarded bustier off the floor.

The smug masculine smile dropped from Vladimir's face. "What are you doing?"

She put on the long black coat, stuffing the bustier into the pocket. "Returning to my prison."

"Prison?" he repeated. "I have given you a palace. I've given you everything a woman could possibly desire."

"Right." She zipped the puffy coat all the way to her throat. As she turned away, she felt like crying.

Vladimir stopped her at the door. "Why are you so sad?"

The ache in her throat made it impossible to talk. She shook her head, unable to meet his eyes.

"You were—embarrassed?"

"Yes," she choked out.

"But why?" he demanded. "He is nothing. No one. Why do you care?"

Bree lifted her eyes. "Because I, too, am nothing," she whispered. "And no one."

He shook his head in exasperation. "I don't understand what you're talking about."

To you. I am nothing and no one to you. She turned her head. "I don't expect you to understand."

"Fine," he said coldly. "If you don't want to be here, go home."

She lifted her gaze hopefully. "Home to my sister?"

"Our home! Together!"

Her shoulders slumped. She stared down at her feet.

"There is no *together* at the palace," she said in a small voice. "There's just me. Alone."

"You know I am dealing with a complex merger, Breanna," he said tightly. "I have no time to—"

"I know." Her lips twisted. "I should just be grateful you show up in my bed in the middle of the night, right? Grateful you're so very, very good to me."

He ground his teeth, his eyes dark.

"I gave you my credit card. You should have bought out half the city by now. You should be enjoying yourself. You can buy whatever you wish—clothes, furs, shoes. And a ball gown. It is supposed to be fun."

"Fun," she muttered.

He scowled. "Is it not?"

"Shopping all by myself in a foreign city, as your bodyguards keep other people out of the store, and six different salesgirls try to convince me that a puce-colored burlap sack with ostrich feathers looks good on me...?" Bree shuddered. "No. It's not fun." She indicated the long black coat. "This is the sum total of my purchases."

He blinked. "The coat?"

"And the lingerie."

"Damn it, Bree, you aren't in Hawaii anymore. I told you to buy warm clothes."

"Who cares if I feel warm?" She glared at him. "I'm just your possession. My feelings don't matter."

He stared at her, and the air around them suddenly became electrified. "Of course they matter." He took a single step toward her. "Breanna—"

A knock sounded at the door. An older man poked his head in, an American with wire-rimmed glasses and anxious eyes. "Your Highness. Excuse me."

"What is it, Anderson?" Vladimir demanded.

The man looked at Bree and then cleared his throat. "We've reached an impasse, sir. Svenssen is demanding we retain every member of his company's staff."

"So?"

"Arctic Oil has a thousand employees we don't need. Drillers. Cafeteria workers in Siberia. Accountants and secretaries. Dead weight."

Dead weight. Bree's spine snapped straight. He would no doubt consider her and Josie *dead weight,* too, with their ten years of backbreaking, low-paying cleaning jobs. Every month, they'd experienced the painful uncertainty of never knowing if their jobs would last, or if they'd be able to pay their bills. Biting her lip, she glanced up and saw Vladimir watching her. His eyes narrowed.

"Tell Svenssen," he said slowly, "we'll find places for all his current employees. At their current pay level or better."

His employee gaped, aghast. "But, sir! Why?"

"Yes, why?" Bree echoed. She took a deep breath and gave him a trembling smile. "Don't tell me you've actually got a heart."

His lips abruptly twisted. "To the contrary." He turned back to Anderson. "I merely want to ensure that we're well staffed for future expansion."

"Expansion?" The man visibly exhaled in relief.

Vladimir lifted a dark eyebrow. "That should simplify your negotiations." Turning to Bree, he took her hand. "I will be unavailable for the rest of the day," he said softly.

"You will?" she breathed.

"But Prince Vladimir—"

He ignored the man. Pulling Bree from the office, he led her down the hall to the elevator. As he pushed the button, she looked at him, her heart in her throat.

"Where are we going?"

He tilted his head, giving her a boyish grin that took her breath away. "I'm going to show you my beautiful city."

His voice was casual. So why did she feel as if something had just changed between them, changed forever? She tried not to feel his strong, protective hand over her own, tried not to feel her own heart beating wildly. "But your merger is important. You said—"

"My people will manage. Let them earn their overpriced salaries."

"But why are you doing this?"

"I've realized something." Vladimir's eyes were ten shades of blue. "You belong to me."

She exhaled. "I know," she said dully. "You already said—"

"You belong to me." He cupped her cheek. "That means it's my job."

"What is?"

He looked intently into her eyes, and then smiled. "To take care of you."

Vladimir's mouth fell open as he stared at the beautiful angel who stood on a pedestal before him. Literally.

"Do you like it?" the angel said anxiously. "Do you approve?"

Bree was trying on her fourth designer ball gown, a strapless concoction in pale blue that revealed her elegant bare shoulders, the curve of her breasts and her slender waist above wide skirts of shot silk. She looked like a princess. Ethereal. Magical.

Intoxicating.

"I can't possibly let you buy this," the enchanted beauty said fretfully. "You won't let them tell me how much it costs, but I'm sure it's very expensive."

Vladimir lifted his hand, signaling to the five saleswomen who were hovering around them in the luxury designer atelier. "We will take it."

With a happy gasp, the salesgirls descended on Bree with sewing pins and measuring tape, to shape the couture gown perfectly to her body. Bree looked at them in dismay. But it was nothing compared to the sick expression he'd seen on her face when his COO had wanted to fire all the workers he called "dead weight."

Vladimir had lied. He wasn't planning an expansion. He'd just been unable to bear the emotions he'd seen on Bree's face: the anger, the powerlessness, the desperation. It reminded him how she'd spent ten years wasting her talents in minimum-wage jobs, because the man she'd trusted to protect her had left her to face all her enemies alone.

Now, she bit her pink, full lower lip. "I shouldn't let you do this."

"It's already decided." Rising to his feet, he felt glad once more that he'd decided to take the day off and spend it with her, leaving even the bodyguards behind. He put his hand on her shoulder. "You need a dress. I'm taking you to a very elegant ball for New Year's Eve."

Bree's dark-fringed hazel eyes went wide. "You are?"

"You will be," he said huskily, "the most beautiful woman there."

"I—I will?"

Her cheeks blushed in girlish confusion. Her charming innocence, at such odds with the wickedly seductive vixen she'd been when she'd shown up at his office building in lingerie hours before, made Vladimir want to kiss her.

So leaning forward, he did.

Her lips felt hot and velvety-soft. Her mouth parted for him, and he deepened the kiss. With a gasp, Bree started to wrap her arms around him.

Then she winced, pulling away. Rubbing her arm, she looked down at her skin. She'd been pricked by the needle of the salesgirl attempting to pin the waist of Bree's bodice.

Vladimir saw a small red dot of blood on Bree's skin, and was blinded by instant, brutal rage. He turned on the hapless girl and spoke harsh words in Russian.

The salesgirl choked back a sob and answered him with a flurry of begging and excuses. He stared at her, implacable as stone.

The salesgirl fell to her knees in front of Bree, holding the hem of the blue silk ball gown as she gazed up with imploring eyes.

Bree looked up at him uneasily. "What's she saying?"

"She's begging for mercy," Vladimir said coldly. "She's

saying she's the sole support of an aging mother and two-year-old son, and she's begging you to intervene with me, so I don't have her fired."

"You wouldn't do that!"

"I have just told her I will."

"What?" Bree gasped, staring at him. "No!"

"She hurt you," he said tightly.

"It wasn't her fault!" Bree tugged on the young woman's arms, forcing her to rise. "I'm the one who moved. And you're the one who kissed me! She never meant to stick me with her needle!"

"What does her intention matter? The pain for you was the same."

Bree was staring at him as if he were crazy. "Of course it matters! Why would I punish her for something that she didn't even mean to do? It was an accident!"

It was an accident. The memory of his brother's miserable, humbled voice on the phone ten years ago floated unbidden through Vladimir's mind. *Forgive me, Volodya. I'm sorry.*

"Don't have her fired. Don't!"

Bree's beautiful face came into focus. "Josie and I have been fired like this before." Her eyes were pleading as she clutched his arm. "You don't know what it's like, to always know that your boss or a single customer can just snap his fingers and take away your livelihood and your pride and your ability to feed your family." She swallowed, her heart-shaped face stricken. "Please don't do this."

Vladimir's lips parted. He didn't even realize he'd agreed to her request until he saw Bree's beautiful face light up with happiness. He dimly heard the grateful sobs of the Russian girl, but as Bree threw her arms around him, he felt only her. Saw only her.

"Thank you," she whispered. She drew back, tears sparkling in her eyes. "And thank you for that huge tip you gave her as an apology. I never expected that." A smile lifted Bree's trembling lips. "I'm starting to think you might have a heart, after all."

Huge tip? Looking down, Vladimir saw that his wallet was indeed open in his hand, and was now considerably lighter. The salesgirl was holding a wad of rubles, weeping with joy as she shared the unexpected largesse with the others.

"It was kind of you, to care for her."

His cheeks burned as he turned back to Bree. "I don't give a damn about her."

"But—"

He cut in. "I did it for you."

She took a deep breath.

"That's why I know you have a heart," she whispered.

And Vladimir knew she was right. Because in this moment, his heart was beating erratically, misfiring, racing.

Taking her hand in his own, he pulled her down from the pedestal. "I just want you to be happy," he said roughly. He didn't know how to manage this reckless, restless yearning he felt every time he looked into her beautiful face, every time he touched her. He looked down at her hand, nestled so trustingly in his. "I want to give you a gift."

"You already did."

"Tipping a salesgirl doesn't count."

She looked down at the exquisite blue ball gown. "You're buying me this dress."

"I want to do something for you," he growled. "Something you actually care about. Anything."

Her eyes went wide with dawning, desperate hope.

"Set me free," she choked out.

Let Bree go? He couldn't. *Wouldn't.* After ten years, he'd found her again. What were the chances of them walking into the same poker game in Hawaii? Surely fate had placed her there for a reason?

She'd brought sunlight and warmth into his life. But if he

let her go, she might leave. He couldn't take that risk. Not now. She meant too much.

Folding his arms, he scowled. "You lost fair and square."

"But this is what I want, more than anything—"

"*No,* Breanna." He set his jaw. "Something else."

Crushing disappointment filled her eyes. She looked down. "My birthday is in a few days. Let me fly back to the States and spend it with my sister. I'm worried about her...."

"Josie is fine. My men left her in Seattle, as she requested. She has money. She is fine."

"So why haven't I been able to reach her phone?" She swallowed. "I've always taken care of her...."

"She's a grown woman," he said, irritated. "And you coddle her like a child."

Her eyes flashed. "Coddle!"

"Yes, *coddle.* She will never grow up until you allow her to make her own choices, and live with the consequences!"

Bree stiffened. "Like you did, you mean—cheating your brother out of the company?"

He glared at her. "He chose to leave, rather than accept my leadership. It made him strong. Strong enough to be my rival!"

"Your enemy, you mean!"

Controlling himself, Vladimir exhaled. "Breanna, I don't want to fight."

She licked her lips, then shook her head. "I don't, either. But I have a reason to protect Josie. I told you, there are men who want to hurt us...."

With a harsh word and a clap of his hands, Vladimir scattered the salesgirls, leaving him alone with Bree in the dressing room. Coming closer, he put his hands on her shoulders and said in a low voice, "Those men won't be bothering you."

She blinked. "They won't?"

"My people tracked them down. One of the men was already dead, unfortunately." Vladimir gave a grim smile. "But the other two will never bother you or Josie again."

Her eyes were huge. "What did you do?" she whispered. "Tell me you didn't...break anything."

Vladimir narrowed his eyes. "I wanted to. But I respected your request. I paid them off. Also, my investigator gathered enough evidence to have them both thrown in prison for the rest of their lives. If they ever cross your path again, even accidentally, that information will go to the local police. And they will die in jail." He looked at her blank face, suddenly uncertain. "Is that satisfactory?"

"Satisfactory?" She took a deep breath, then with a sob, threw her arms around him. "Thank you," she whispered. "We're free!"

He looked down at her, wiping the tears off her cheek gently with his thumb. "I'll never let anyone hurt you or your sister, Breanna. Ever again."

Her lower lip wobbled. "Thank you."

Seeing her reaction, he wanted to do more. He heard himself say, "And I'll have my men look around Seattle. See if they can track Josie down."

"Okay," she sniffled.

"Do you have any idea where she might be?"

She shook her head. "We used to say that when we got back to the Mainland, if we had money, we'd start our own bed-and-breakfast, or a small hotel." Her cheeks flushed. "But the truth is, that's my dream, not hers. She wants to go to college."

"Don't worry. I'll find her." Pulling his phone out of his pocket, he turned away. He was stopped by Bree's small voice.

"People call you ruthless. But it's not true."

Slowly, he turned to face her.

Bree's hazel eyes were luminous, piercing his soul. "When we met, I thought you'd changed completely from the man I loved. But you're still the same, aren't you?" she whispered. "The other man—he's just the mask you wear."

Vladimir's forehead broke out in a cold sweat. He felt bare

beneath the spotlight. "You're wrong," he said roughly. "I *am* ruthless. Selfish, even cruel. Don't believe otherwise."

She shook her head. "You're afraid people will take advantage, so you hide your good heart—"

"Good heart?" He grabbed her shoulders, looking down at her fiercely. "I am selfish to the bone. I will never put someone else's interests ahead of my own. I cannot *love,* Bree. That ability is no longer in me. It died a long time ago."

"But—"

"Would a good man keep you prisoner against your will?"

She lifted her gaze. Her hazel eyes were suddenly troubled, opaque, full of shadows.

"No," she whispered.

No. That one word caused an unexpected wrench inside him. As the two of them stood in the huge private dressing room of the designer atelier, her expression became impassive—her poker face. He wondered what she was thinking. In this moment, when he felt so strangely vulnerable, his insight into her soul suddenly disappeared.

"I'm not a good man, Bree," he said in a low voice. To prove it further—to both of them—he lowered his mouth to hers, kissed her hard enough to bruise. She kissed him back with fierce passion, but he felt her withholding something he wanted. Something he needed.

Unzipping her blue ball gown, Vladimir kissed the bare skin of her neck. Her hair smelled like sunlight and passion fruit, like vanilla and the ocean, like endless summer.

Her strapless silk bodice fell, revealing her white bustier. They were surrounded by mirrors on three sides, and as he saw endless reflections of him touching her, he felt so hard he wanted to take her roughly, against the wall. So he did. As the dress fell to the hardwood floors, he unzipped his pants and lifted her, shoving her roughly against the mirrored wall. Barely pausing to sheath himself in a condom, he thrust inside her. Wrapping her legs around his hips tightly, she clutched his shoulders as he filled her, slamming her against the wall. Five thrusts and she was moaning. Ten thrusts and she clutched her fingertips into his shoulders as her body tightened, her back arching. Fifteen thrusts and she screamed with pleasure in cries that matched his own.

Afterwards, for an instant, panting and sweaty, he just held her, his eyes closed. Then slowly he released her legs, letting her body slide down his. The passion had been hotter than ever.

But he knew something had changed between them. An unbridgeable gap.

"Get dressed," he said. "We have dinner reservations."

"Fine," she said dully, not meeting his eyes.

He zipped up his pants, and she put on her new clothes, the slim-fitting black pants, sheer black top over a black camisole, and black leather motorcycle jacket he'd bought for her earlier at a department store on Nevsky Prospekt. All afternoon, he'd insisted on buying everything he saw in her size, anything she could possibly want to wear for the rest of her life, for any season and any event.

Compensating, he thought. Though he knew she couldn't be bought.

Even if he'd bought her.

"Before dinner," he said brightly, despising the false cheer in his voice, "I wish to buy you something truly special. A fur coat. White mink, perhaps, or Barguzin sable—"

Bree shook her head. "No, thanks."

"Russian furs are the best in the world."

Her eyes were cold. "I don't want a fur."

He set his jaw. "You're pouting."

"No." She looked away. "I just used to have a dog when I was a kid," she mumbled. "I loved that dog. We used to explore the forest all summer long. He had a soul. He was my friend."

She was talking about her dog? Vladimir exhaled. He'd been bracing for her anger, since the only thing she really wanted was the one thing he wouldn't, couldn't, give her. Relieved, he lifted his hand and lightly traced the bare skin of her collarbone. "I still don't understand the connection."

"I'll put it in simple terms." Pulling away from him, she folded her arms. "No fur."

"As you wish," he whispered, taking her hand in his own. He felt her shiver. He looked at her. Her expression was completely unreadable. He sighed. "Come."

Leaving the dressing room, he went out to meet with the salesgirl and finish the details of the order, arranging for the hand-stitched ball gown to be delivered the next day. Vladimir took Bree outside, where his bodyguard awaited them beside his bulletproof limo.

"Where are we going?"

"You'll see."

"I'm tired of shopping."

"You'll like this."

Twenty minutes later the limo pulled to a stop. Helping her out himself, Vladimir led her past two security guards into a tiny, high-ceilinged shop in the belle epoque style, with gilded walls and colors like a cloisonné Easter egg. Everything about the jewelry store bespoke elegance, taste and most of all money.

"What are we doing here?" Bree scowled. "I thought we had dinner reservations!"

He gave her a teasing smile. "This won't take long."

A short, plump man with wire-rimmed glasses and a short white beard, wearing an old-fashioned pin-striped suit with a vest, came eagerly from behind one of the glass cases. "Welcome, welcome, Your Highness," he said in Russian.

"Speak in English so she'll understand."

"Of course, Prince Vladimir." Tenting his hands, the jeweler turned to Bree and switched to accented English. "My lady. You are here for a necklace, yes? For the New Year's Eve ball at the ancient palace of the Romanov tsarina?"

Bree glanced up at Vladimir. "Um. Yes?"

He smiled back at her, feeling a warm glow at the thought

of spoiling her. "I wish to buy you a little something to wear with the ball gown."

"I don't need it."

"*Need* has nothing to do with it." He lifted a dark eyebrow. "Surely you won't deny me the small pleasure?"

Her scowl deepened. "No. How could I?"

He ignored her insinuation. "Surely," he said teasingly, "you will not tell me that diamonds remind you of a former pet? That they possibly have a *soul?*"

She looked down at the floor.

"No," she whispered. "A diamond is just a cold, heartless stone." Vladimir frowned. She suddenly seemed to recall she was speaking to the CEO of Xendzov Mining, one of the largest diamond producers in the world. Flashing him a wry smile, she amended, "But they are pretty. I'll give you that."

"So you'll let me buy you something."

"Don't you have a closetful of diamonds back home? I'm surprised you don't use them like rocks to decorate your garden."

"My company produces raw diamonds. We sell them wholesale. The fine art of polishing them into exquisite jewelry is not our specialty." He lifted his hands to indicate the little jewel box of a shop. "This is the best jewelry store in the world."

"Really? In the world?"

He gave her a sly smile. "Well, the best in St. Petersburg. Which means it is the best in Russia. Which means, naturally, that it is the best in the world."

Staring at him for a moment, she shook her head with a sigh. "All right." Her tone was resigned. "Since it seems I have no choice."

Vladimir had truly expected this to be a quick stop en route to dinner at the best restaurant in the city. He'd assumed Bree would quickly select one of the most expensive necklaces in the store: the looped rope of diamonds, the diadem of sapphires, the emerald choker that cost the equivalent of nine hundred thousand dollars. But an hour later, she still hadn't found a necklace she wanted.

"Six million rubles?" she said now, staring down incredulously at the ropes of diamonds patiently displayed by the portly jeweler. "How much is that in dollars?"

He told her, and her jaw dropped. Then she burst into laughter. "What a waste!" She glanced at Vladimir. "I won't let you spend your money that way. Might as well set it on fire."

He didn't have nearly the same patience as the jeweler. "Money isn't a problem," he said tightly. "I have more than I could spend in a lifetime."

"Lucky you."

"I mean it. After you make a certain amount, money is just a way to keep score."

"You could always donate the money to a charity, you know. If you hate it so much," she said tartly.

He gave a low laugh. "I didn't say I hate it. If nothing else, it gives me the opportunity to drape you in diamonds."

"Against my will."

"I know you will love them. All women do."

"*All* women?"

That hadn't come out right. "It's a gift, Bree. From me to you."

"It's a chain." She reached out a hand and touched the glittering diamond rope resting on the glass case, then said bitterly, "Diamond shackles for an honored slave." She looked up at the jeweler. "No offense."

"None taken, my lady."

She looked at Vladimir. "Thanks for wanting to buy me a gift. But I don't need a chain to remind me of my position."

Vladimir felt irritated. He'd wanted to buy something that would please her, to distract her from the one thing he would not give: her freedom. "I am trying to make you happy."

"I can't be bought!"

"You already were," he said coldly.

Bree gave an intake of breath, and her eyes dropped. "Fine. Buy it for me, then. Because you're right. You can do whatever you want."

Her voice dripped with icy, repressed fury.

This was turning into a disaster. Vladimir's intention in bringing her here had been to make her cry out in delight, clapping her hands as she threw her arms around him in joy. But it seemed no cries of joy would be forthcoming.

He forced his clenched hands to relax. "I think we're done." Turning away from the jewelry case empty-handed, leaving the disappointed jeweler behind them, Vladimir put his hand on her back. It was an olive branch, an attempt to salvage the evening. "Fine. No diamonds. But you will enjoy dinner."

"Yes," she said. "Since you are telling me to enjoy it, I must."

They were very late for their reservation. But when they finally arrived at the restaurant, adjacent to an exclusive hotel on the Nevsky Prospekt, he had the satisfaction of seeing Bree's mouth fall open.

Art-nouveau-style stained glass gleamed in a wall of windows. Shadowy balconies and discreet curtained booths overlooked the center parquet floor, filled with tables covered with crisp white linen. White lights edged the second-floor balustrade, and tapering candles graced the tables with flickering light as uniformed waiters glided among the planted palm trees, serving rich, powerful guests.

The maître d' immediately recognized Vladimir. "Your Highness!" Clapping his hands, he bowed with a flourish and escorted them to the best table.

"Everyone is looking at us," Bree muttered as they walked across the gleaming parquet.

Relieved she was finally talking to him again, Vladimir reached over to take her hand in his. "They're looking at you."

As they were seated, Bree's cheeks were pink, her eyes glowing in the flickering light of the candles and warmth of the high-ceilinged restaurant. Soaring above them on the ceiling were nineteenth-century frescoes, country scenes of the aristocracy at play.

When the waiter came, Vladimir ordered a short glass of vodka, then turned to Bree. "What would you like to drink?"

She tilted her head. "The same."

"It's vodka."

"I'm not scared."

"Are you sure?" He lifted a dark eyebrow. "You don't strike me as much of a drinker."

She shrugged. "I can handle myself."

Her bravado was provocative. He looked at her beautiful, impassive face, at the way her dark eyelashes brushed her pale skin, at the way her stubborn chin lifted from her long, graceful neck. He wondered what she would say if she knew what he was thinking.

"Your Highness?" the waiter said in Russian.

Vladimir turned back to him and gave the order. After the man left, Bree said abruptly, "Where did you learn Russian? It wasn't at school."

"How do you know?"

"I don't," she admitted. "But I know you and your brother grew up on the same land that now belongs to Josie—or will, in three years." She tilted her head. "It's funny we never met. Both of us growing up in the same state."

"That land was in our family for four generations. A thousand miles from anything. You know." He drummed his fingertips on the table, looking for the waiter with the vodka. "So we kept to ourselves. My father spoke Russian with us. He was proud of our history. He homeschooled us. In the long winters, we read Pushkin, Tolstoy." Vladimir's lips twisted. "It was my mother who made sure our home had food and wood. The land is our legacy. In our blood."

"Why did your mother sell it to my father?"

His body tightened. "I was desperate for money to start

our business. Kasimir absolutely refused to sell. He'd made some deathbed promise to our father. But I knew this was the only way."

"You had nothing else to sell? You couldn't take a loan?"

"Mining equipment is expensive. There is no guarantee of success. Banks offered to loan us a pitiful amount—not nearly enough to have the outfit I wanted. We'd already sold the last item of value our family possessed—a necklace that belonged to my great-grandmother—to help fund college in St. Petersburg. *Spasiba*," he said to the waiter, who'd just placed their drinks on the table. Reaching for his vodka, he continued, "So I talked to my mother. Alone. And convinced her to sell."

"Behind your brother's back?" Bree's eyes widened. "No wonder he hates you."

Knocking back his head, Vladimir took a deep drink and felt the welcoming burn down his throat. "I knew what I was doing."

"Really." Bree's cheeks were pink, but her troubled gaze danced in the flickering candlelight. "Do you know what you're doing now?"

"Now?" He set his glass back on the table with a clunk. "I am trying to make you happy."

Her eyes were impassive. "Without letting me go."

Reaching across the table, he took her hand in his larger one. "I have no intention of letting you go. Ever."

"Why?" She swallowed, then glanced right and left at all the well-dressed people around them. "You could have any woman you want. Even the gorgeous secretaries at your office…"

"But I want only the best." His hand tightened over hers. "And the best is you."

She stared at him, then shook her head. "I can see how you twist women's hearts around your little finger."

"There's only one woman I want." He looked at her beautiful, stricken face over the flickering candle. "I've never forgotten you, Breanna. Or stopped wanting you."

He felt her hand tremble before she wrenched it from his grasp. She reached wildly for her untouched glass of vodka and, tilting back her head, drank the whole thing down in a single gulp.

That gulp ended with a coughing fit. Reaching around her, he patted her on the back. Her face was red when she finally managed a deep breath, wheezing as she quipped, "See? I know how to handle vodka. No problem."

Somewhat relieved by her deliberate change of subject, Vladimir laughed, his eyes lingering on her beautiful face. He'd said too much. And yet it was oddly exhilarating. The adrenaline rush of emotional honesty put skydiving to shame, he thought. About time he tried it.

The waiter returned to take their order, and Vladimir requested a dinner that included Astrakhan beluga caviar and oysters, vodka-marinated salmon and black risotto, steak in a cream sauce and a selection of salads, breads and cheeses. Bree shook her head in disbelief when the exotic food started arriving at the table, but ninety minutes later, as she gracefully dropped the linen napkin across her mostly empty plate, she was sighing with satisfied pleasure.

"You," she proclaimed, "are a genius."

He gave her a crooked grin, ridiculously pleased by her praise. "I've come here a few times, so I knew what to order."

"That was perfect." She rose to her feet. "If you'll excuse me."

"Of course." Vladimir watched her disappear down the hall toward the ladies' room, and realized he was sitting alone at the best table in the most famous restaurant in St. Petersburg, grinning to himself like a fool. Feeling sheepish, he looked around him.

His gaze fell on a face he recognized, of a man sitting alone in a booth on the other side of the restaurant. This particular man in this particular place was so unexpected that it took him thirty seconds to even place him, though they'd spent many hours across the same poker table over the past two months. The Hale Ka'nani hotel manager, Greg Hudson. What was he doing in St. Petersburg?

Perhaps the man was on vacation. In Russia. In winter. Telling himself he didn't care, Vladimir turned his chair away, so the man was out of his sight.

Today was the best day Vladimir had had in a long time. Even though leaving subordinates to handle the merger so he could spend time with his mistress was reckless, irresponsible, foolish. Even though he'd likely lose a fortune retaining all the employees of Arctic Oil. Even so.

Instead of feeling guilty, he kept smiling to himself as he recalled how Bree's eyes sparkled when she was angry at him. The way her body had felt, pressed against his in the mirrored dressing room of the boutique. She was fire and ice. She was life itself.

"Hawaii has changed you completely." His doctor had been shocked by the test results that morning, when Vladimir stopped on the way to the office. "You've recuperated from your injury better than I ever dreamed. Even your blood pressure is improved. What have you been doing? Yoga? Eating bean sprouts? Whatever it is, clean living is making you healthy. Keep it up!"

With a laugh, Vladimir glanced down at his empty vodka glass and half-eaten plate of beef rib eye drenched in sauce. Clean living? No. *Good* living. It wasn't yoga and bean sprouts. It was laughter, good company and lots of sex.

It was Breanna.

Vladimir shifted impatiently in his chair, craning his head to look past the waiters and candlelit tables toward the wood-paneled hallway. His lips rose in unconscious pleasure when he saw Bree coming back down the hall.

Then a dark figure came out of the shadows to accost her. Seeing Greg Hudson, Vladimir rose to his feet. Bree looked surprised, then angry, as the man spoke to her. Vladimir clenched his jaw as he strode rapidly toward them. Hudson's eyes went wide when he saw him coming. Turning, he ran out of the restaurant.

"What did he say to you?" Vladimir demanded.

Bree turned with a carefully blank look on her face. Her poker face, he thought, but he could see her lips trembling. Her gaze dropped. "Nothing."

"Tell me."

"He…" She licked her lips. "He told me he's in St. Petersburg to collect a debt, and happened to see me." Her eyes carefully remained on the gleaming parquet floor. "He said he's going to be very rich in a few days, and he would pay a lot of money to be my next lover. He wondered if there was some kind of waiting list."

Anger made Vladimir's vision red. He started to turn, his hands clenched. "I will kill him."

"No. Please," Bree whispered. She put her hand on his arm. "Just take me home."

People in the restaurant were staring at them, whispering behind their hands. "But we already ordered dessert," he said tightly. "Chocolate cake. Your favorite."

"I just want to go." Her cheeks were red. "And forget this day ever happened."

Forget this day ever happened? The wonderful day he'd spent with her—the hours he'd spent watching her laugh, telling her the truth, buying her things, trying so hard to please her—as he'd never tried to please any woman? "I don't want to forget."

She looked away. "I do."

Shoulders stiff, Vladimir went across the restaurant and tossed thirty thousand rubles on their table. Getting her leather coat, he wrapped it around her shivering shoulders and led her out into the cold, dark night. As his chauffeur drove their limousine home, Vladimir looked out at the snowy streets of

St. Petersburg. It had been the best day of his life, but it had ended with Bree in tears.

He wanted to blame the fat little hotel manager. But he knew there was one person at fault for the way she'd been so crudely insulted as a woman who could be bought and sold at any man's will.

Vladimir himself.

CHAPTER EIGHT

THE next night, Bree paused as she got ready for the New Year's Eve ball. She looked wanly out the tall curved window of their bedroom.

The wintry Gulf of Finland on the Baltic Sea looked nothing like Hawaii's warm turquoise waters. It was even worse than Alaska's frigid sea. Even in the weak, short hours of daylight, the Russian waves were choppy and gray. But the sun had set long ago, and the world was dark. The black, icy water here could suck the life out of you within seconds if you were dumb enough to fall into it.

Kind of like falling in love with a man who would neither love you back nor set you free.

Bree closed her eyes. Yesterday, the workaholic tyrant had been neither workaholic nor a tyrant, playing hooky from work to entertain her. Letting people keep their jobs in his merger. Tipping that saleswoman at the boutique. Getting rid of the men who'd threatened Bree and her little sister. And more.

I've never forgotten you, Breanna. She would never forget the stark vulnerability in his blue eyes. *Or stopped wanting you.*

Bree trembled with emotion, remembering. Thank heaven she'd been able to cover her reaction by gulping that nasty-tasting vodka. She should probably be grateful for Greg Hudson, too. His words had brought her back to reality with a snap.

Bleakly, she opened her eyes. She was alone in their bedroom, with one leg propped up on the bed, pulling on sheer black stockings as she got ready for the New Year's Eve ball. Her beautiful haute-couture princess gown was on the bed, waiting to go over her new black lace bra, panties and garter belt. Vladimir had bought out every expensive store in the city. "I am trying to make you happy," he'd said. But she couldn't be bought that way. Only two things could make her happy, and they were the very things he would not or could not give her. Freedom. Love.

I am selfish to the bone. I will never put someone else's interests ahead of my own.

She couldn't let herself fall for him. She'd loved him once, and it had nearly killed her. She'd lost everything.

Never again. Unless they were equals, loving him was only a different kind of bondage. Especially since, in the eyes of the world, Bree was nothing more than his whore.

Hadn't meeting with her ex-boss proved that?

"Well, well, what a pleasant surprise," Greg Hudson had drawled, stepping into her path in the hallway last night. "If it isn't the poker-playing maid herself."

She'd been shocked to see her former boss's beady eyes and sweaty face. Instead of a tropical shirt, he was dressed in the required jacket and tie, probably borrowed from the restaurant, since they didn't fit his lumpy body.

"Mr. H-Hudson," she'd stammered. "What are you doing in St. Petersburg?"

"Call me Greg." He came closer, crowding her space in the darkened hallway. "I'm here to collect a big debt. Thought I'd celebrate at the best restaurant in town."

"You left the Hale Ka'nani?"

His expression darkened. "I got fired. The hotel's owner found out I took a bribe." He tilted his head, his eyes sly. "Didn't you ever wonder why I hired you and that sister of yours?"

Bree sucked in her breath as all her old worries came back. "Someone bribed you to hire us? Who?"

Leaning forward, he wheezed, "Even he didn't think I'd be as successful as I was. In a few days, I'll be paid, and given a huge bonus. I'll be rich enough to pay you directly, for services rendered. I want to be on your waiting list. Name your price." He'd stroked her upper arm, and she'd caught the scent of whiskey, heavy and sour, on his breath before he saw Vladimir and turned away. "Come to me when Xendzov is done with you."

Bree's face burned as she remembered the humiliation of that moment. She'd been completely unprepared for it. And even more unprepared for the suspicion that had slithered into her soul ever since.

Who would have paid Greg Hudson to hire the Dalton sisters at the Honolulu resort?

All night Bree had stared up at the bedroom ceiling in the dark gray light, going through countless scenarios in her mind. It could have been one of her father's old enemies. Or...it could have been Vladimir himself. To make her his prisoner forever, to enjoy at his will.

I've never forgotten you, Breanna. Or stopped wanting you.

She sighed. But that didn't make sense, either. He'd been surprised to see her. She'd seen it in his face, in his body. He'd had no idea she was in Hawaii.

So who?

Vladimir had been an extraordinarily tender lover last night, but even as he'd made her body shake and gasp with pleasure, her soul had been haunted by the question. Finally, at breakfast that morning, before he'd left for work, he'd stated, "I'm sorry you were insulted last night. It will never happen again."

"Thank you," she'd murmured, though they both knew it was a lie. There was no way he could prevent that. If she wasn't insulted to her face, she'd still be able to see it in people's eyes.

She was his possession. Nothing more, nothing less.

Now, staring out at the dark, wintry night, Bree felt an ache in her throat. She finished pulling on her stockings, attaching them to her garter belt. If only she had someone to talk to about this. If only she could talk to Josie...

Vladimir's voice was husky behind her. "Are you ready?"

With an intake of breath, Bree turned to face him. He stood in the doorway, half in silhouette. He looked broad-shouldered and impossibly handsome in a dark, exquisitely cut tuxedo. She tried not to notice. "Have you found Josie?"

"Josie?" he repeated absently. He came toward her, his blue eyes gleaming as they traced slowly down her nearly naked body in the black lace. "Forget the ball. Let's stay home for New Year's Eve."

She felt his gaze against her skin the same as if he'd stroked her with his fingers. Her breath caught in her throat, and she trembled with desire and something more—something that went straight to her heart. She wrapped her arms around herself. "My sister. Have you found her yet?"

He blinked, then his eyes lifted to hers. "Not yet. My investigator did trace her back to Hawaii."

"Hawaii!" Something was wrong. Bree could feel it. "Why would she go back?"

He shrugged. "Perhaps she forgot something at your old apartment."

"Spending every penny she owns, just to go back for some old sweater or something?"

Vladimir pressed his lips together. Bree saw him hesitate, then reluctantly say, "Apparently she was trying to get the police to take an interest in your case. But they laughed at her, both in Seattle and Honolulu." He looked at Bree sideways. "They thought our wager sounded like a lovers' game between consenting adults."

"Right." She had a sick feeling in the pit of her stomach. "So where is she now?"

He shook his head. "The trail went cold."

Josie was missing? Bree opened her mouth, then stopped.

Telling him her fears would do no good. She feared it wou
only set off another tirade from him about how Josie was
grown woman and that Bree should allow her sister to face her
own consequences.

And for all she knew, he was right. For ten years, her fears
had been on overdrive where Josie was concerned. How was
Bree supposed to know when it was rational to worry and
when it was not?

"We'll find her." Vladimir was watching her. "Don't worry."

"I'm not," she lied.

"Good." Reaching into his pocket, he held out a flat, black
velvet box. "This is for you."

She flinched when she saw the jewelry box. He'd known
she hated the diamond necklace, but *he'd bought it anyway*.
The chain of her captivity.

"You went back and bought it," she said dully.

He glanced at the blue silk ball gown draped across their
bed. "It goes with your dress."

Ice filled her heart, rushing through her like a frozen sea.
In spite of all appearances to the contrary yesterday, he didn't
care about her feelings. He wanted to dress her to appear well.
Like a show dog on display. "You are too kind."

A smile curved his sensual mouth, as if he knew exactly
what she was thinking. "Open it."

"You."

"Don't you want to see it?"

"No." Closing her eyes, she lifted her hair. "Just do it," she
choked out.

Bree heard the box snap open. She felt the warmth of his
body as he moved to stand behind her. She felt a heavy weight
against the bare skin beneath her collarbone. It was surpris-
ingly heavy. Frowning, she opened her eyes.

A simple gold chain hung around her neck, with an enormous green pendant wrapped in gold wire. Shocked, she

...ched the olive-green jewel, the size of a robin's egg. "What's ...is?"

"It's a peridot," he said quietly. "Carved from a meteorite that fell to Siberia in 1749. It once belonged to my great-grandmother."

Bree's mouth fell open. "Your—"

"The pendant was a wedding gift from my great-grandfather, before he sent her and their baby son into exile. To Alaska."

Bree felt the roughness of the peridot beneath her fingertips. The sharp crystalline edges had been worn smooth by time.

"We sold this necklace to a collector, to help pay for college." He ran a finger along the chain. "It took me years, and a large fortune, to get it back." He put his hand over the stone, near her heart, and lifted his gaze. "And now it is yours."

Bree gasped. Feeling the weight of the necklace and the warmth of his hand, she looked down at the stone. In the shadowy bedroom, the facets flashed fire, green like the heart's blood of a dragon. "I...I can't possibly keep this."

"Too late." Vladimir's handsome face was expressionless.

"But it's too valuable." She swallowed as her fingers stroked the gold chain against her skin. Their hands touched, and she breathed, "Not just the worth of the stone, but the value to your family..."

Drawing back, he said harshly, "It is yours." He turned away. "Finish getting ready. I will wait for you downstairs."

She suddenly felt like crying. "Wait!"

He stopped, his back stiff, his hands clenched into fists.

"This should belong to someone you care about," she whispered. "Someone...someone special."

He didn't turn around.

"You are special to me, Breanna," he said in a low voice. "You always have been."

She couldn't just let him leave. Not when he'd proven to her, once and for all, that she was more than a paid concubine. As he headed for the door, she rushed across the room, catching him from behind. Wrapping her arms around his body, she pressed her cheek against his back. "Thank you."

Slowly he turned around in her arms.

"I need you to know. You are more than just my possession." His darkly handsome face was stark. Vulnerable. "You are..."

"What?" Her throat ached.

"My lover."

Unable to speak, she nodded.

Wiping her cheek with his thumb, he said in a low voice, "Come. Get dressed. We don't want to be late." He gave her a crooked smile. "I don't want to miss kissing you at midnight."

Seeing that boyish, vulnerable smile, her heart twisted. "No. We don't want to miss that."

He picked up her silk ball gown from the bed, and she stepped into it. As he pulled it up around her, she felt his fingers brush against her spine. She looked back at him with an intake of breath. His gaze was hungry, his eyes dark as the midnight sea. She should expect more than just a kiss to celebrate the New Year.

She wasn't his girlfriend. She wasn't his wife. But perhaps...

Her fingertips ran softly over the necklace that had once belonged to a Russian princess, and a green stone that two hundred and fifty years ago had landed in Siberia from the farthest reaches of space. Perhaps he did care for her, after all.

Could that caring ever turn to something more? To love?

I cannot love. She heard the echo of his hard voice. *That ability is no longer in me. It died a long time ago.*

As Vladimir finished zipping up the ball gown, he turned her to face him. Brushing tendrils of hair from her face, he looked down at her with electric blue eyes. "Are you ready?"

Looking up at his handsome face, Bree tried not to feel anything. But her heart slammed against her ribs.

His forehead furrowed. "Bree?"

She turned away with a lump in her throat. "I, um, need some lipstick." Going to the mirror, she made her lips bright

Chanel red. Lifting the silk hem of her gown, she stepped into her expensive shoes with sparkling crystals decorating the four-inch heels, and took a deep breath. "Ready."

Downstairs in the foyer, Vladimir took a sharply tailored black coat from the closet, wearing it over his tuxedo. Then he removed a black hanging bag from the closet. He unzipped it. In dismay, Bree saw white fur.

He noted her expression. "Don't worry. It's fake."

Dubiously, she reached out and stroked the soft white fur. "It seems real."

"Well." His lips curved in amusement. "It's *very* expensive. Twice the price of the real thing." Lifting the white fur coat from the bag, he wrapped it around her bare shoulders. "I can't have you getting cold, *angel moy,*" he said softly.

"What does that mean?"

"My angel."

She bit her lip, faltering. "I'm nobody's angel."

He smiled. Pulling her close by the lapels of the white faux fur, he looked down at her. His blue eyes crinkled. "Wrong."

Bree's heart squeezed so hard and tight she couldn't breathe. Still smiling, he held out his arm and led her outside into the cold, frosty night.

The limousine whisked them to a small town on the edge of St. Petersburg, to a palace that had once belonged to a Romanov tsarina three hundred years before. Bree's eyes widened as the road curved and she got her first view of it. With a gasp, she rolled down the window for a better look.

Beneath the frosted winter moon, she saw the palace that had once been a summer getaway for the Russian royal family. The elegant structure, wide and sprawling, looked like a wedding cake, decked with snow. The limo drove up the avenue, past a wide white lawn lit up by flickering torches.

The limo stopped, and a valet in breeches and an eighteenth-century wig opened Bree's door and helped her out. Feeling the shock of cold, bracing air on her face, she looked around in awe. She touched the green peridot against her skin, beneath her white fur. Standing in this courtyard, she could almost imagine herself as the princess of an ancient, magical land of eternal winter.

She could almost imagine she was a Russian prince's bride. *His bride.* As Vladimir took her hand in his own, smiling at her with so much warmth she barely even needed a coat, she could not stop herself from wondering, just for an instant, what it would be like to be his wife. To be the woman he loved, the mother of his children.

"Are you still cold?" he murmured as they passed the bowing doormen.

She shook her head.

"But you're shivering."

"I'm just happy," she whispered.

Stopping inside the palace doors, he pulled her into his arms. Kissing the top of her hair, he looked down at her with a smile.

"At last," he said softly. "I have what I wanted."

Searching his gaze, Bree sucked in her breath. That smile. She couldn't look away. It was so open. So…young. He looked exactly like the young man she'd first fallen in love with, so long ago.

The man she'd never stopped loving.

As he took her hand to lead her down the elegant hallway, Bree nearly stumbled in her sparkling high-heeled shoes.

She was in love with him.

She could no longer deny it, even to herself.

Vladimir took her into the ballroom, and Bree barely noticed the exquisite, lavishly decorated space, the gilded walls or the crystal chandeliers high above. She barely spoke when he introduced her to acquaintances. As he led her out onto the dance floor, she didn't see all the gorgeous people all around them.

She saw only him. She felt only his arms around her, and the rapid thrum of her own heart.

She loved him. It was foolish. It was wrong. But she could no more stop herself than she could stop breathing. She loved him.

For hours, they danced together. They drank champagne. They ate. They danced some more. For Bree, it all flashed by in a moment. In his arms, she lived a lifetime in every precious minute. The regular laws of time were suspended. Hours sped by in seconds.

Suddenly, as they were dancing, the music stopped. Lifting her cheek from his chest in surprise, Bree saw it was nearly midnight.

Vladimir looked down at her as they stood unmoving on the dance floor, and as the last seconds of the year counted down, for Bree it was as if time not only became suspended, but was reversed. His gaze locked with hers, and ten years disappeared.

She was eighteen and he was twenty-five. They were in each other's arms. The world was new. Brand-new.

He cupped her face. "Breanna…"

Cheers went up around them in the ballroom as she heard the last seconds of the year counted down in a jumble of languages, German, French, Chinese, Spanish, English, and Russian loudest of all.

"Pyat…"

"Cheteeri…"

"Tree…"

Lowering his head, Vladimir said huskily, "Let's start the New Year right…"

"Dva…"

"Ahdeen…"

His lips pressed against hers, smooth and rough, hard and sweet. He kissed her, and fire flashed not just through her body, but her soul.

"S'novem godem!" Raucous cheers and the sound of horns and singing revels exploded across the ballroom. "Happy New Year!"

When Vladimir finally pulled away from their embrace,

Bree stared up at him, her heart in her throat. She swayed, nearly falling over without his arms around her.

"*S'novem godem,*" he murmured, cupping her cheek tenderly. "Happy New Year, *angel moy.*"

She looked up at him.

"I love you," she choked out.

He stared at her, his eyes wide.

All around them, people were dancing to the music of the orchestra, laughing, drinking champagne, kissing each other. But Vladimir was completely still.

Tears filled Bree's eyes as she gave him a trembling smile. "Even when I hated you, I loved you," she whispered. "When I made the wager in Hawaii to be yours forever, part of me must have been willing to lose that bet, or I never would have made it." She licked her lips. "You have always been the only man for me. Always."

He did not answer. His face was pale, his blue eyes as frozen as a glacier.

A chill of fear sneaked into her soul.

"And what I need to know is…" She bit her lip, then lifted her gaze to his. "Can you ever love me?"

Vladimir's eyes suddenly narrowed. He cleared his throat.

"Excuse me," he said shortly. He walked past her, leaving her alone on the dance floor.

Mouth agape, Bree turned and stared after him in amazement. Her cheeks went hot as she noticed exquisitely dressed Russians and other wealthy, beautiful people staring at her with open curiosity. Embarrassed, she walked off the dance floor.

She'd never felt so alone. Or so stupid.

She lifted her hand to the necklace, to the heavy weight of the peridot against her bare skin.

He cares for me, she repeated to herself silently. *He cares.*

But even that beautiful jewel seemed small consolation, considering that she'd just confessed her love for him, and he'd left her without a word.

Maybe he was called away on urgent business. At midnight. On New Year's Eve. She clawed back tendrils of her long blond hair. Why had she told him she loved him, and worse, asked if he could ever love her back? She knew he couldn't! He'd told her that straight-out, from the start!

Oh, God. She covered her face with her hands. She was an idiot.

Maybe when he came back, she could give a hearty laugh, as if it had all been a joke. She could tell him she'd been pretending to have Stockholm syndrome or something. She could be persuasive with her lies, as she'd been long ago. She could turn off her soul and disconnect from her heart. She knew how.

But...

She pulled her hand away. *She didn't want to.* She was tired of bluffing. She didn't want to be that con artist anymore. Ever again.

And sometimes telling the truth, showing her cards, would mean she lost the game.

She gave a ragged laugh. She'd never expected the cost to be this high. Snatching a flute of champagne from a passing waiter, she tried to sip it nonchalantly, as if it was quite enjoyable to be standing on the edge of the dance floor in a blue Cinderella gown, alone in a crowd of strangers. But as minutes passed, she suddenly wondered if Vladimir was even coming back. For all she knew, he'd already jumped into the limo and was heading for the airport.

Why not? He'd abandoned her before. Without a single word.

She squeezed her eyes shut. *Please don't leave.*

A prickle went up her spine as she felt someone come up behind her. Vladimir, at last! In a rush of relief, she turned.

But it wasn't Vladimir. A different man stood before her, slightly younger, slightly thinner, but with the same hard blue eyes—only filled with cold, malevolent ruthlessness.

"Kasimir?" Bree whispered. "Kasimir Xendzov?"

"Having a good time?" he replied coldly. Before she could

answer, he grabbed her arm and pulled her away from the crowd, into a private alcove. She stared at him. She'd met him only once before, in Alaska, the Christmas night he'd burst in upon them, desperate to tell his brother the truth about Bree's con. He'd been twenty-three then, barely more than a boy. Now…

Bree shivered. Now he was a man—the type of man you would never want to meet in a dark alley. She yanked her arm away from his grasp. "What do you want? If you've come to find your brother—"

"I haven't come to see my brother." Kasimir gave her a cold smile. "I came for you."

"Me?" she breathed.

"It's about…your sister."

"Josie?" An icy chill went down her spine. "What about her?"

He came closer, invading her personal space. She instinctively backed away. He straightened, and his eyes glittered. "I've married her."

"What?" Bree gasped.

He gave her a cold, ruthless smile. "Your little sister has become my dear, dear wife."

"I don't believe you!"

For answer, he pulled something from his pocket and held it out to her on his palm. Josie's cell phone. Bree snatched it up. There could be no doubt. She saw the colorful rhinestones that her sister had glued to the back in the shape of a rainbow.

"I asked her to marry me some time ago," Kasimir said, "and she refused. Until you disappeared. Then she came back. She offered to do anything, *anything,* if I would only save you from my evil brother. Marriage was my price."

"But why would you want to marry her?" Then suddenly Bree knew, and her heart dropped to the floor. "The trust," she said dully. "You want her land."

"It's not *hers,*" he said tightly. "It's been in my family for a hundred years. It never should have been sold. We've fought for it, died for it—" Catching himself, he relaxed his clenched hands. "So. The land will be mine in three days, when the banks reopen. After that, I can either divorce her quickly with a nice settlement, or..."

"Or?"

His eyes met hers coldly. "Or I can seduce her, make her fall in love with me and destroy her pitiful little heart. I can force her to be my wife forever, and you will never see her again. It is your choice."

Bree flinched, even as her heart pounded with fear. "How do I know this isn't all some lie? It might just be some sick joke, some game in the battle between you and your brother—"

Taking the cell phone away from her, he dialed a number, then pressed the phone back against Bree's ear. She heard her little sister's voice.

"Hello?"

Bree gripped the phone. "Josie," she gasped. "Where are you?"

"I'm so sorry, Bree," her sister whispered. "The poker game was all my fault. I was trying to save you. That's why I married him...."

"But where are you?" Bree cried.

Kasimir yanked the phone away. As he disconnected the call, Bree went for him, her hands outstretched. He pushed her away easily, tucking the phone in his tuxedo jacket pocket.

"Tell me where she is," she cried. "Or—or I'll kill you!"

"You're scaring me," he drawled.

"Then..." Bree had already threatened to kill him. What could be more frightening than that? She lifted her chin furiously. "I'll tell Vladimir!"

Kasimir's expression was cold. "Go. Tell him."

She was flabbergasted at his casual tone. "But he will destroy you!"

"He's tried to destroy me for years," he said scornfully, "and

I only grow stronger." He moved closer. "And you are wrong, Miss Dalton," he said softly, "if you think his desire for you will make him sacrifice anything for you or your family. He cares for you because you please him in bed, and he values that pleasure. But given the choice between helping you or himself, he will not hesitate."

Was Kasimir right? She licked her lips, barely hearing the music from the nearby ballroom. With a deep breath, she lifted her hand to her necklace. She felt its rough weight around her throat.

"Vladimir cares for me," she whispered.

"Because he gave you my great-grandmother's necklace?" His brother lifted a dark eyebrow. "He sold that once, you know. And he will sell you, if it ever gives him any advantage."

"You're wrong."

"Try him and see," Kasimir suggested silkily. "Go to him. Explain how Josie agreed to marry me and give me every acre of the land. He will say her predicament is her own fault, for being foolish enough to seek me as her ally. Vladimir is not a man who excuses mistakes. He punishes them." His brother narrowed his eyes. "He will not lift a finger to save her."

Bree trembled in her blue silk ball gown. Was it true?

Vladimir had cut Kasimir out of his life completely, cheating him out of hundreds of millions of dollars, just because of a few angry, drunken words to a reporter. He'd forced Bree to live as his mistress even when she'd begged him for her freedom—all because of a one-card wager. "You made the bet," he'd said. "Now you will honor it." Thinking of how he'd just abandoned her on the dance floor when she'd told him something he apparently didn't want to hear—that she loved him—Bree's heart lifted to her throat.

Would he treat Josie any more mercifully?

"She will never grow up," she remembered his hard voice saying. "She will always be helpless and weak, unless you allow her to face the consequences of her own actions."

"What do you want me to do?" she whispered.

Kasimir's eyes glittered. "You will help take back what should have been mine." Pulling an envelope from his pocket, he handed it to her. "Make him sign this."

"What is it?"

"A deed that transfers control of his company to me."

Bree stared down at the paper. "I hereby renounce all shares in Xendzov Mining OAO," it read, "giving them freely and in perpetuity to my brother...."

She looked up, openmouthed. "He will never sign it."

"You are a clever girl, with a flair for trickery and deceit." Kasimir tilted his head. "For your sister's sake, you will make him sign. Even if it causes you a small twinge of grief." He walked slowly around her. "Your lies caused *me* a great deal of grief ten years ago. I am glad to finally see you and my brother suffer—together. I could not have it planned better."

Bree's heart gave a sickening thud.

"It was you," she breathed. "You're the one who arranged for us to be taken to Hawaii. You're the one who bribed Greg Hudson to hire us."

Kasimir smiled. "My brother was stuck there, bored out of his mind, attending the same poker game each week. I knew he had a weakness for you. I hoped seeing you would cause him pain." Kasimir snorted. "Instead, you created an opportunity for justice I never could have imagined. You insinuated yourself into his life. Like a disease."

"Even if his signature is obtained through trickery," she said desperately, "it will never stand up in court."

"Then you have nothing to worry about, do you?" he said coolly. "Bring the signed document to my house in Marrakech within three days."

"And if I fail?"

He looked straight into her eyes, like an enemy looking over the barrel of a gun. "Then you'll never see your sister again. She'll disappear into the Sahara. And be mine. Forever."

Bree shook her head with a weak laugh. "You're joking."

"I am a madman. Ask my brother. He knows." Kasimir looked at her blue silk ball gown. "Your sister was frantic about you. She came to me, begging for help. She was willing to do anything to save you, even sacrifice her own soul." His lips twisted into a sneer. "And for the last two hours I've watched you, drinking champagne, dancing in his arms, giggling like a whore." She flinched as he growled, "So much for Josie's *sacrifice*."

Bree sucked in her breath, lifting her gaze. "You like her, don't you?" she said slowly. "I can see it in your eyes. I can hear it in your voice. You don't want to hurt her."

Kasimir glared at her, gritting his teeth. "What I *want* is revenge. And I will have it." Turning away, he said over his shoulder coldly, "You have three days."

CHAPTER NINE

WITH a low curse, Vladimir shoved the short fat man out of the palace, into the dark, deserted garden.

"What the hell are you doing in St. Petersburg?" he demanded.

"I'm allowed to visit here, if I want. You don't own this city, Xendzov," Greg Hudson brayed in response, shivering in his badly fitting tuxedo. "It doesn't *belong* to you!"

"Wrong," Vladimir replied coldly, shoving him again. Moments before, in the middle of Bree's innocent, tearful declaration, he'd seen Greg Hudson skulking near the buffet table. Vladimir had been overwhelmed by Bree's three simple words. He hadn't known how to react to them.

Seeing Greg Hudson, he'd known exactly what to do.

Fury had filled him at the sight of the man who'd insulted her, offering money to be *on her list*. He'd dragged him out of the ballroom, wanting to knock him to the ground and kick him repeatedly in his soft belly until he learned to respect women. Especially Vladimir's woman. "You will leave this city and never come back."

Hudson quivered like a rabbit. "Think you're something big, do you, Mr. Hoity-Toity Prince? You have no idea how you've been played!"

Ignoring him, Vladimir lifted his fist. "Were you following her?"

The man flinched. "No! I swear! I just happened to be in

town—" he looked up slyly "—to see your brother. The other prince."

Vladimir slowly lowered his fist. "You know Kasimir?"

"He owes me money."

"For what?"

The man looked smug.

Grabbing him with one hand, Vladimir lifted his other fist and thundered, "For what?"

"He offered me a lot of money to hire those Dalton girls. And a bonus if I could arrange for you to meet the older one. By accident."

Vladimir's body turned hot, then cold. His hand tightened on the man's lapel.

"If you ever disrespect Miss Dalton again," he said evenly, "if you so much as mention her name or look at her picture in the newspaper, you will regret it for the rest of your short life." He gave him a hard stare. "Do we understand each other?"

"Y-yes," the man stammered. "I never meant any harm."

Vladimir let him go, and Hudson fell back into the snow. Leaping up again with a gasp, he fled into the night, slipping on ice in his haste, leaping over a snowdrift as he called wildly for his driver.

Relaxing his clenched fists, Vladimir exhaled.

Slowly, he turned back toward the palace. But he felt numb, as frozen as if he'd fallen asleep in the white snow. He looked out at the fields in the moonlight. So soft. So beautiful. So mysterious.

So treacherous.

Breanna's beautiful face appeared in his mind. Was it possible…could it be that meeting her had been more than a co-incidence? That it had been a plan cooked up by Bree and Kasimir, to finally get their revenge for his treatment of them ten years ago?

Was he a gullible fool falling for the same woman's lies—twice?

If Kasimir hired Hudson, Vladimir told himself harshly, *Bree didn't know.*

Or did she? Against his will, a gray shadow of suspicion filled his soul.

As he entered the ballroom and walked through the crowds, his feet dragged. He had no idea what to do. What to say to her.

"I love you," Bree had said. His heart beat with the rhythm of her words. "And what I need to know is, can you ever love me?"

How could she love him? Bree was too smart for that. He'd warned her that he would never love her. Told her it was impossible. He wanted to make her happy, yes. He'd bought her clothes, spent time with her, gotten rid of the men who'd threatened her and Josie. But what had that cost him, really? Nothing.

No matter what she seemed to think, there was no shred of goodness in Vladimir's soul. He would never risk or sacrifice anything that truly mattered.

All he had to offer was sex and money—and though Bree seemed to very much enjoy the sex, she didn't care about money. So what could she possibly see to love in his black soul?

He'd kept her against her will. Stolen her freedom for his own selfish pleasure. She should hate him. Instead, she'd offered him everything. Not just her body, but her soul. Her warmth, her tenderness and adoration, her honest heart.

If it really was honest.

No. He wouldn't think that. It was Kasimir who'd arranged their meeting, not Bree. But why? What could possibly be his goal?

Vladimir pushed through the crowd, his pulse throbbing in his throat. He had to find Breanna. He hungered to feel her in his arms, to know she was real. To look into her eyes and see that she wasn't—couldn't be—allied with his brother against him. Vladimir needed her. That was as good as love, wasn't it?

She deserves a man who can love her back with a whole, trusting heart. The thought whispered unbidden in his mind.

Not the careless, shallow affection you can give her, the shadowy half love of a scarred, selfish soul.

She's mine, he told the voice angrily.

So you'll keep her as your prisoner forever, taking her body every night without ever returning her love? Until you see the adoration in her eyes fade to anger, then bewildered hurt, and finally dull, numb despair?

Vladimir closed his eyes. He couldn't let that happen. Not to Breanna. He couldn't feed on her youth and energy, like a vampire draining love and life from her body.

If he couldn't love her, he had to let her go.

But damn it. *How could he?*

He sucked in his breath when he saw her across the ballroom, like a modern-day Grace Kelly, willowy, blonde, impossibly beautiful in her strapless, pale blue ball gown. But her shoulders drooped. She stood alone by the dance floor. Shame shot through him. He could only imagine what she was thinking, after the way he'd left her.

Grabbing two flutes of champagne, he came up behind her, then touched her on the shoulder. "Breanna…"

She jumped, turning to face him. Her eyes were wide, her cheeks pale. "Oh. It's you."

"Who were you expecting?"

She tried to smile, but her expression looked all wrong. "A handsome prince."

He wondered if she'd seen that little weasel Greg Hudson, in spite of his effort to get the man out of the ballroom quickly. "Did someone…bother you?"

"Bother me?" She tossed her head with forced bravado. "You know I can take care of myself."

"Tell me what's wrong," he said quietly.

She took a deep breath, then lifted stricken eyes to his. "You just…ran away so fast from me on the dance floor, I thought you'd be halfway to Berlin by now."

Ah. He suddenly knew why she was upset. "Um. Right."

The collar of his shirt felt tight. "Sorry I left like that. I was... thirsty." That sounded ridiculous. He pushed a champagne flute into her hand. "I got you something to drink."

Vladimir waited for her forehead to crease in disbelief, for her to demand why he'd really run off the instant she'd told him she loved him. For her to challenge and goad him into telling her the truth.

But she didn't. Her fingers closed around the stem of the crystal flute, but her thoughts seemed a million miles away.

"Hey." He touched her cheek lightly, and she lifted startled eyes. "Are you angry with me?"

Her lips parted, then she shook her head.

"No," she whispered. "Why would I be?"

Putting the flute to her lips, she tilted back her head and gulped down the expensive champagne like water.

For a long, awkward moment, Vladimir just stood there, pretending nothing was wrong. They didn't speak or touch or even look at each other as, all around them, people drunkenly, joyously celebrated the New Year. Finally, Vladimir could bear it no longer.

"I don't blame you for being angry." Taking the empty glass from her hand, he deposited it on the tray of a passing waiter, along with his own untouched champagne. He took her hand in his. "But Bree," he said slowly. "You have to know how I feel...."

With a sudden intake of breath, she looked up, her hazel eyes luminous. "It's my sister. She needs my help."

Her *sister?* He'd been raking himself over the coals, hating himself for hurting her, and all this time she'd been thinking about that hapless sister of hers?

He exhaled. "You need to stop worrying about her. My men will soon track her down. In the meantime, she's a full-grown woman. Treating her like a child, following her around to fix her slightest problem, you'll make her believe she's useless and incompetent. And she will be."

"But what if, this time, she really needs my help?" Bree's beautiful face grew paler. She searched his gaze with an intensity he didn't understand. "What if she's done something—something that might destroy her life forever—and I'm the only one who can save her?"

Irritated, he set his jaw. "Like you saved her from the hundred thousand dollars she lost at the poker game? When you risked yourself, offering your body to strangers, to save her from the consequences of her actions?"

Her voice was very small. "Yes."

Narrowing his eyes, Vladimir shook his head. "If she didn't learn from that, she never will."

"But—"

"There is no *but,*" he said harshly. "She is twenty-two years old. She must learn to make her own choices, and live with them."

Bree's shoulders were rigid. She fell silent, turning away as she wiped her eyes. On the dance floor, people were still swaying to the music, toasting the New Year with champagne and kisses. But somehow, he wasn't quite sure how, the mood between him and Bree had utterly changed. And not for the better.

"I'm sorry," she said in a low voice, not looking at him. "I can't just abandon the people I love the instant they make a mistake. I'm not *you,*" she said tightly.

Feeling the sting she no doubt intended, he said in a low voice, "My brother made his own choice to get out of the company."

"Because you made him feel worthless for a single mistake. When all he did was tell you the truth about yours."

"Falling in love with a woman who was deceiving me," he said, watching her.

"Yes," she whispered. She shook her head. "No wonder he hates you."

"He intends to destroy me," Vladimir said shortly. "But not if I ruin him first."

Her expression became bleak. "Neither of you will ever give up, will you? No matter who gets hurt."

There was no way she was working with Kasimir, Vladimir thought. *No way.* He exhaled. "Forget it." He gave her a crooked smile. "Sibling relationships should be my last topic of advice to anyone, clearly. Or relationships of any kind. What do I know about loving anyone?"

But his attempt at an olive branch failed miserably. Her eyes looked sadder still. She glanced down. "I'm tired."

"All right," he said in a low voice. "Let's go home."

As soon as we get back to the palace, I'll seduce her, he told himself. They would get everything sorted out in bed.

But once they arrived there, Bree was even more distant, colder than he'd ever seen her. Colder than he'd ever imagined she could be.

She didn't fight with him. She just withdrew. She moved away when he tried to pull her in his arms. "I want to go to bed."

"Great," he murmured. "I'll come with you."

"No." She practically ran up the stairs, then looked down from the top landing, a vision in a blue gown, like a princess. Like a queen. "Tonight, I sleep alone."

Her voice wasn't defiant. It wasn't even angry. It was inexpressibly weary.

He frowned, suddenly puzzled. None of this made sense, but he knew one thing: somehow, some way, he had screwed up. "Bree," he murmured, "what you said to me, back on the dance floor—"

"Forget about it." She cut him off and drew a deep breath, her hands tightening at her sides. "It doesn't matter. Not anymore."

But it did matter. He knew that from the way his heart seemed about to explode in his chest. But he couldn't let himself feel this. He couldn't...

Anger rushed through him, and he grabbed at it with both

hands. Climbing the stairs, he faced her. "You can't keep me out of our bed, Bree. Not tonight. Not ever."

She looked at him coldly.

"Try it, then, and see what happens, Your *Highness*."

Turning on her heel, she left him. And if Vladimir had had any hope that he might be able to warm her up, as he climbed naked into bed beside her ten minutes later, those hopes were soon dashed. Bree lay on the other side of the large bed, pretending to be asleep, creating a distance between them so clear that the space between them on the mattress might have been filled with rabid guard dogs and rusty barbed wire.

Their romantic, magical night hadn't exactly gone as planned. Lying in bed, Vladimir tucked his hands behind his head and stared at the shadows on the ceiling. The reason for her coldness was all too clear. She'd said she loved him, and he hadn't said it back.

But he couldn't say it. He didn't feel it. He didn't *want* to feel it.

There. There it was.

He didn't want to love her.

He'd done it once. He'd given her everything, believed in her, defied his brother and all the world for her sake. And he'd only proved himself a fool. He would never let himself feel that way again. He would never give his whole heart to anyone.

Especially not Breanna. No matter how much he admired her, or how much he cared. He wouldn't let her have the power to crush his heart ever again.

But as a gray dawn broke over the first day of the New Year, Vladimir looked down at Breanna beside him in bed, listening to her steady, even breathing as she slept. He saw trails of dried tears on her skin.

Tomorrow was her birthday, he remembered. She would be twenty-nine years old. She'd saved herself for him for ten years. She'd been brave enough to give herself to him completely, holding nothing back.

I love you. Her words haunted him. *Even when I hated you, I loved you. You have always been the only man for me. And what I need to know is—can you ever love me?*

Instinctively, his hands pulled her sleeping body closer. He breathed in the vanilla-and-lavender scent of her hair.

Could he continue to use her beautiful body in bed, keeping her prisoner to his pleasure, watching as her love for him soon turned to hatred, then numb despair?

He had no choice.

Sitting up, Vladimir leaned his head against the headboard, feeling bleak.

If he couldn't love her, he had to let her go.

Bree woke up with a gasp of panic and fear.

Seeing she was alone in bed, she fell back against the pillow with a sob. Within three days, she would have to betray someone she loved. Who would it be?

Josie?

Vladimir?

She felt sick with grief and guilt and fury. Numbly showering and getting dressed, she went down downstairs, where she spoke in terse monosyllables when Vladimir greeted her, wishing her a cheery Happy New Year. She kept her distance from the man she loved, sitting as far as possible from him at the long table as they ate the elaborate holiday breakfast prepared by the chef. She stopped all of Vladimir's attempts at conversation and just generally made herself unpleasant. But having him close, looking into his handsome, trusting face, was like poison to her.

For some reason, he was bending over backward to try to be nice to her, which made her feel even worse. But by late afternoon, her rudeness had managed to push him to the limit. With a muttered, inaudible curse, he stomped off to work in his home office.

And Bree exhaled, her heart pounding and blood roaring through her ears.

What should she do?

She had to save her little sister. There was no question. Whatever it took to save Josie, she would do. Immediately.

Except...

Betray the man she loved? Could she really steal Vladimir's company, his life's work, the only thing he truly cared about—and give it to his brother?

Bree's mind whirled back and forth in such panic that her body trembled and her knees were weak beneath the strain.

The clock was ticking.

"You have three days," Kasimir Xendzov had told her. Less than that now. She looked at the clock. Her hands shook, desperate to take action. But what action?

She could contact the police. True, they were in Russia and Josie was...anywhere in the world. But they could contact Interpol, the American Embassy, something!

But while Bree was trawling through layers of international bureaucracy and jurisdictional red tape, Josie would be gone, never to resurface.

I can seduce her, make her fall in love with me and destroy her pitiful little heart, Prince Kasimir had said. *I can force her to be my wife forever, and you will never see her again.*

Bree paced across the morning room, stopping to claw her hand through her tangled hair. She felt like crying. She didn't know what to do.

Tell Vladimir everything, her heart begged. *Throw yourself on his mercy and ask for help.*

Right, she thought with a lump in her throat. Since Vladimir was such a merciful man.

But still, three times that afternoon, she went down the hallway of the palace to the door of his study. Three times she raised her hand to knock, wanting to confess everything. But each time, something stopped her.

His own words.

She is twenty-two years old, he'd said harshly. *She must learn to make her own choices, and live with them.*

And each time, Bree put her hand down without knocking. What if Vladimir said Josie had brought this on herself, by seeking Kasimir's help?

If Bree told him everything, and he refused to help her, she would lose her chance to get him to sign Kasimir's document. And all hope for Josie would be gone. Her baby sister would be left terrified and alone, somewhere in the Sahara. Bree would never see her again.

Vladimir doesn't even love you, a voice argued.

But I love him. She swallowed. *He deserves my loyalty.*

And what about your little sister, whom you've always protected? What does she deserve?

Bree covered her face with her hands. She was stuck, frozen, equally unable to betray either of them. And time was running out.

If only fate could make the decision for her…

"Breanna." She jumped when she heard Vladimir's voice behind her. "I'm sorry if I've neglected you today." He put his arms around her, nuzzling her neck. His voice was humble, as if he thought he was to blame for their estrangement. "I should work tonight. Paperwork for the new merger has piled up, and it all needs my signature by tomorrow."

Twisting her head, Bree looked back at him, her heart breaking. He'd just told her exactly how to get Kasimir's document signed. Was it fate?

"But let it wait until tomorrow." Smiling down at her, he kissed the top of her head. "Shall we have dinner?"

But by the end of the night, Vladimir's smile had turned to bewilderment. They slept in the same bed, a million miles apart. When Bree woke up alone the next morning, January 2, she realized two things.

Today was her birthday. She was twenty-nine years old.

And the whole meaning of her life came down to this one choice. Which of the people she loved would she betray?

Sitting up in bed, she looked at the gilded clock over the marble fireplace. Over half the time since Kasimir's ultimatum was gone, and she'd done nothing. She'd neither tried to trick Vladimir into signing the dreadful contract, nor confessed the truth and begged him for help. For the past day and a half, since midnight on New Year's Eve, she'd always felt one breath away from crying. So she'd pushed him away, to keep him from seeing into her soul. In response to Vladimir's innocent question yesterday, asking what she wanted for her birthday, she had answered so rudely that she blushed to remember it now.

She couldn't tell him what she really wanted for her birthday.

Freedom from this terrible choice.

Bree's knees trembled as she slowly climbed out of bed and fell blearily into the shower. She got dressed in a black button-down shirt and dark jeans. She combed out her long, wet hair. She pulled it back in a severe ponytail.

Cold, she told herself as she slowly pulled on her black stiletto boots. *My heart is cold. I am an iceberg. I feel nothing.*

Tucking the document Kasimir had given her beneath her black shirt, she went down the wide, sweeping stairs in Vladimir's eighteenth-century palace, as if she were going to her death.

After so many gray, snowy days, brilliant sunshine was pouring in through the tall windows, leaving patterns of golden light on the marble floor. She'd been happy here, she realized. In spite of everything. She'd loved him.

Looking back now, Bree saw it had been enough. They'd been happy. Why hadn't she appreciated that happiness? Why had she fretted, worried, groused about Vladimir's one major flaw—that he didn't want her to ever leave him? What kind of stupid flaw was that? Why hadn't she just fallen to her knees in gratitude for all the blessings she'd had—so unappreciated then, and now so swiftly gone?

Creeping softly to the open door of his study, she peeked inside. Empty. Holding her breath, keeping her mind absolutely blank, she swiftly walked inside and stuck the page in the middle of the pile of papers she'd seen him working through yesterday. She would distract him today, and if luck was on her side, he would sign it without reading it. She felt confident he wouldn't suspect her.

He trusted her now.

As Bree left the study on shaking legs, she hated herself with every beat of her heart.

Perhaps having his company stolen wouldn't hurt him too badly, she tried to tell herself. Hadn't Vladimir insinuated that it had become a burden? "Money is just a way to keep score," he'd said. Perhaps he would someday understand, and forgive her.

But even now, Bree knew she was lying to herself. Even if he was able to accept losing Xendzov Mining—even if he started over and built a successful new company, as Kasimir had—she was making herself his enemy for the rest of his life. The fact that she'd done it to once again save her sister would not gain her any points, either. He would despise her. Forever. Everything between them, every good memory, would be lost.

Bree walked heavily down the gilded hall, past the arched windows. She heard the sharp tap of her stiletto boots against the marble floor. Brilliant January sunlight reflected off the white snow and sparkling Gulf of Finland. She looked out the windows, and saw sun as warm as his touch. Sky as blue as his eyes.

Suddenly even walking felt like too much of an effort. She stopped, staring at the floor, her heart in her throat.

"Breanna. You're awake."

Blinking fast, she looked up. Vladimir was coming down the hall toward her, looking impossibly handsome in a white button-down shirt and black slacks. An ache filled her throat as she looked into the perfect face of the only man she'd ever loved. The man she was about to lose forever.

"I have something for you. A birthday present."

Her voice was hoarse. "You shouldn't have."

He gave her a crooked grin. "You can't already hate it. You don't even know what it is yet."

The warmth of Vladimir's grin lit up his whole face, making his soul shine through his eyes, making him look like the boy she'd known. Like everything she'd ever wanted.

Swallowing, she looked down at her stiletto boots. "I'm just not in much of a party mood."

He took her hand. She felt his palm against hers, felt his fingers brush against her own as he pulled her gently down the hall. "Come see."

He led her into a high-ceilinged room centered around a glossy black grand piano. The conservatory had a wall of windows overlooking the sea. Antique Louis XIV chairs flanked the marble fireplace, and expensive paintings covered the walls, along with shelves of first-edition books.

"I know you said you didn't want a fur coat," Vladimir said. "But if you're going to live in St. Petersburg, you need some Russian fur to keep you warm...."

Bree saw a lumpy white fur stole on the pale blue couch beside the window. With an intake of breath, she cried, "Vladimir, I told you—"

He gave her a crooked half grin. "Just go look."

Hesitantly, Bree walked toward the blue couch. She got closer, and the lump of white fur suddenly moved, causing her to jump back with a surprised little squeak. From the pile of fur, a shaggy white head lifted.

She saw black eyes, a pink tongue and a wagging tail. Vladimir lifted the puppy into her arms.

"She's an Ovcharka. A Russian sheepdog." Lowering his head, he kissed her softly. "Happy birthday, Breanna."

With a little bark, the white puppy wiggled her tiny furry

body with joy, warm and soft in Bree's arms. Cuddling the dog close, she looked up at Vladimir's smiling face, and felt a bullet pierce her throat.

She burst into tears.

"Bree, what is it?" He bent over her, his handsome face astonished and worried. "You seemed sad about the dog you'd lost long ago, so I thought… But I see I've made a mistake." He clawed back his dark hair. "It was a stupid idea."

"No," she choked out. She tried to wipe her tears off her cheek with her shoulder. "It was a wonderful idea," she whispered. "The best in the world."

"Then why are you crying?" he said, bewildered.

Trying to choke back her tears, she buried her face in the dog's soft, warm fur. "Because I love her." Looking up, she whispered, with her heart in her throat, "And I love you."

He grinned, clearly relieved. "What will you name her?"

Heartbreak. She stared at him for a long moment, then looked at the windows. "Snowy."

"Snowy, huh? Did you put a lot of thought into that?" But the teasing grin slid from his face when she gave him no answering smile. He cleared his throat. "Well, I have one more surprise for you. But you'll have to wait until dinner to get it."

As the day wore on, Bree's heart broke a little more with each hour. They played with the puppy, then had a delicious late lunch with champagne. Afterward, the palace staff rolled in a giant, lilac-frosted cake on a cart.

"Chocolate cake," Vladimir said happily. "With lavender frosting."

"Is this my big surprise?" she asked, dreading further kindness.

"No. And don't ask me about it. You won't get it out of me. Even if you use your feminine wiles."

He said it as if he were rather hoping she would try. It had been two nights since they'd made love. It felt like a lifetime.

The heat in his eyes made her cheeks go hot, along with the rest of her body. Trembling, she pretended not to notice.

The servants sang Happy Birthday to her in cheerful, slightly off-key English, led by Vladimir's low, smooth baritone. He lit the two wax candles on the cake—one shaped like a 2, the other a 9.

He nudged her with his shoulder. "Make a wish."

Leaning toward the flickering candles, Bree closed her eyes, wondering what she'd done to deserve this fresh hell. And knowing it wasn't what she'd done, but what she was about to do.

She took a deep breath, her wish a silent prayer: *I wish I didn't have to hurt you.*

She blew out the candles, and everyone applauded.

As the staff departed, after giving Bree their well wishes in a mixture of English and Russian, Vladimir took her in his arms.

"Do you want to know about your other gift?" he said softly.

She gulped. "I thought you weren't going to tell me."

"If you kiss me, I might change my mind."

But she backed away. "I'm not really in a kissing mood, either," she mumbled.

From the corner of her eye, she saw the stiffness of his posture, and felt his hurt. "Very well," he said finally. "It is your special day. You don't have to do anything you don't want to do."

He paused. She didn't move. His hands tightened at his sides.

"So I'll just tell you what the big surprise is, shall I?" he said. "I've bought you a hotel. The Hale Ka'nani Resort."

She looked up with a gasp. "What?"

"You dreamed of someday running a small hotel." He gave her a crooked smile. "I bought you one."

"But the Hale Ka'nani isn't *small!* It must have cost millions of dollars!"

"Two hundred million, actually."

"What?"

"Don't worry." His lips lifted in a smile. "I got a good deal."

"Are you out of your mind?"

"It's an investment. In you."

Tears filled her eyes. "Why would you do something so stupid?"

"Because…" he said softly, reaching a hand toward her cheek "…with your brilliant strategic mind, Bree, I've always known you were born to rule an empire."

Trembling, fighting tears, she stumbled back from his touch.

"I need to take Snowy for a walk," she blurted out, and, picking up the puppy, she fled to the white, snow-covered lawn outside. Once there, Bree dawdled, taking as long as she could, until her cheeks and nose felt numb from the cold and even the puppy was whimpering to go back to the warmth inside. It was past dusk when she finally returned to the conservatory, her feet heavy, her heart full of dread.

To her surprise, the room was empty. The puppy flopped down on a rug near the warm fire, and Bree frowned. "Where is he?" she said aloud.

The puppy answered with a stretch and a yawn, clearly intending to have a long winter's nap.

Bree went down the hall, passing various rooms. Then she saw Vladimir. In the study. At his desk. Signing papers.

Shock and horror went through her like lightning.

"What are you doing?" she breathed.

"There you are." His voice was cold, and he didn't bother to look up. He seemed distant—and how could she blame him? "I will join you for a late dinner after I finish this."

He was signing the papers by rote, with rapid speed, as if his mind was on something else. She saw Kasimir's contract peeking out beneath the next paper. "Stop!"

"I got your message loud and clear, Bree." He pushed the

op paper aside. "You don't want anything from me. You can't even bear to look at me—"

As he reached, unseeing, for Kasimir's contract, Bree suddenly knew.

She couldn't let him sign it. She couldn't betray him.

She *couldn't*.

With a choked gasp, Bree flung herself across his study and blocked him the only way she knew how. Shoving his chair back, she threw her leg over him, straddling him, separating him physically from his desk. Tangling her hands in his hair, pressing her body against his, she leaned forward and kissed him.

At first he froze. For one dreadful instant she thought he would push her away. Then a sound like a low sigh came from the back of his throat, and his powerful arms wrapped around her. His lips melted roughly against hers.

The pen in his hand dropped to the floor. The pile of papers on his desk was forgotten.

Holding her against his chest, Vladimir rose and, in a savage movement, swept the papers off his desk. Pressing her back against the polished oak, he looked down at her with eyes so full of emotion that her heart caught in her throat.

"Now, Bree," he said hoarsely, as he lowered his mouth to hers. "I need you now."

CHAPTER TEN

VLADIMIR had never felt such fire.

Bree had never initiated lovemaking before. The heat of her passion, in contrast to her earlier ice, burned through his body, incinerating his soul. Moments before, he'd felt dark and angry, rebuffed in all his efforts to show he cared, to make her birthday special, and to compensate for those three little words he could not say.

But now, as they desperately ripped off each other's clothes on his desk, as they kissed and suckled and licked, he felt her soft body move and sway beneath him, pulling him deeper, deeper. And suddenly those same unthinkable, forbidden three words rose in his heart, like sunlight bursting through a dark cloud.

Could he...? Did he...?

Bree moved, rolling him beneath her on the desk. Her silken thighs wrapped around his hips. He looked up at her expressive face, at her breasts swaying like music. A glowing sunset through the study's window washed her pale shoulders red, the color of a ruby.

The color of his heart.

With a gasp, she impaled herself upon him, pulling him deep inside her. As he filled her completely, for the first time in ten years everything was clear.

He loved her.

He'd been afraid to see it. He'd tried to deny it, to ignore it,

He'd buried himself in work, in sex, in dangerous sports. But e could not deny it any longer.

He loved her. The truth was he'd given her his heart long go. When he thought she'd betrayed him, his heart had simply rozen, like an arctic sea. But from the moment he'd seen her gain, across the poker table at the Hale Ka'nani, his heart had egun to thaw. Feeling the sting of her cold rejection today had aught him that he still felt pain. He still had a beating heart.

A heart that loved her.

Whatever the cost. Whatever the risk.

His love for her was absolute. He could not change it.

He wanted to go back in time and be the generous, trusting 1an he'd once been. He wanted to be the man who deserved 3reanna Dalton.

When she gasped with pleasure, he tilted back his head nd the first hoarse cry escaped his throat. Their joy built to-ether, until he could no longer tell where his voice ended and ers began.

With a final cry, she collapsed in his arms. He held her ghtly, both of them still sprawled on his desk. As he stroked er naked back, his heart pounded in his chest. He wanted to lurt out the words. But words were cheap. He would show er, the only way he knew how. He would do what terrified im most.

"I'm letting you go, Breanna," he said quietly. "I'm setting ou free."

For a moment, he thought she hadn't heard. Then she lifted er head to look into his eyes. He'd thought she would be happy. nstead, she looked stricken, almost gutted.

Vladimir frowned.

"Don't you understand?" Reaching up, he caressed her heek, tucking wild tendrils of sweaty blond hair behind her ar. "You're no longer my property. You're free."

"Why?" she choked out. "Why now?"

He smiled despite the lump in his throat. "Because…" Cupping her face with both his hands, he looked straight into he eyes. "I'm in love with you, Breanna."

Pulling back, she gasped, as if his words had caused he mortal injury.

He sat up on the desk beside her. "It took me ten years t realize what I should have admitted to myself long ago. I neve stopped loving you. And I never will."

Blinking fast, she looked away.

"But what if I don't deserve your love?" she whispere "What if I've done things that…"

"It doesn't matter." Gently, he turned her to face him "Somehow, in spite of all my flaws, you decided to love me. was too much of a coward to do the same." Lifting her hand t his lips, he kissed her skin fervently, then looked at her wit tears in his eyes. "Until now."

She sucked in her breath.

"Whatever you do," he said quietly, searching her gaze "for the rest of your life, I will love you. For the rest of mine

Bree started to speak, then shook her head as silent tea spilled down her cheeks.

Was she so amazed, then, that he could return her love The thought of that shamed him, reminding him how selfis he'd been. Pulling her back into his arms, he held her. Whe she claimed she was too tired to eat dinner, he took her to be He held her through the night as she cried herself to sleep. H didn't understand her tears. But as Vladimir stroked her ha and naked back, he vowed that he would never give her an reason to cry again. Ever.

His heart was irrevocably hers. But she was free.

Would she choose to stay with him? Or would she go?

Shortly before midnight, when Breanna finally slept, Vlad mir realized he had to prepare for the worst. Pulling on a rob he quietly left their bedroom and went downstairs to his o fice. Turning on his computer by habit, he looked for his ce phone. He'd order the jet to be available in the morning, t

ke her wherever she wanted to go. Then he prayed he could
onvince her to stay....

His foot slid on the mess of papers scattered across the
oor. In the dim glow of light from the computer screen, the
rst words on the page of a contract he'd never noticed before
aught his eye. Bending over, he picked it up.

I hereby renounce all shares in Xendzov Mining OAO...

His heart stopped in his chest. Hand shaking, he turned on
lamp, thrusting the paper beneath the light.

...giving them freely and in perpetuity to my brother, Ka-
mir.

He read it again. Then again.

This contract had been slyly slipped into the pile of papers
n his desk. And with sickening certainty Vladimir knew how
had gotten there. Only one person could have done it.

He closed his eyes. When he'd first seen Bree in Hawaii,
e'd assumed she was there to con someone. Later he'd con-
inced himself that meeting her at that poker game had been
ild, pure coincidence. Even when he'd discovered from Greg
udson that Kasimir had deliberately tried to plot that meeting,
e'd convinced himself that Breanna, at least, was innocent.

Exhaling, he crushed the paper against his chest.

But his first instincts had been right all along. She'd been
Honolulu for a con. And just like ten years ago, Vladimir
ad been her mark.

As he opened his eyes, the dark shadows of his study were
leak. All color had been drained from the world, leaving only
ray.

Bree and his brother had to be working together. After Vlad-
nir had started attending private poker games in Honolulu,
hile recuperating from his racing accident, Kasimir had ar-
anged for Bree to get a job there. His brother must have known
ll along that she was the poison Vladimir could not resist.
he poker game, the wager, the whole affair had been a setup
om start to finish.

All so that Bree could infiltrate his house and infiltrate his soul.

All so that Vladimir would sign this document.

His hands shook as he looked down at the contract.

His brother had baited his hook well. And so had she.

Bree had tricked him, the same way she'd done ten years ago. And Vladimir was so stupid that instead of being on his guard, he'd been fooled even worse than before. He thought of how he tried to please her, giving her his great-grandmother's peridot, buying her a puppy, buying her a hotel, and worst of all, declaring his love—when all the time, all he was to her...was a job.

He leaned back wearily in his desk chair. Just hours before, the purpose and meaning of his life had seemed so clear. So bright and full of promise. He'd felt young again, young and fearless. For that one shining moment, he'd been exactly the man he'd always wanted to be.

Rising to his feet, Vladimir poured himself a glass of vodka over ice. Going to the window, he swirled the tumbler, watching the prisms of the ice gleam in the scattered moonlight.

He could still destroy her.

Destroy Breanna? The thought made him choke out a low sob and claw back his hair.

Was there any way he could be wrong? Any way she could be innocent?

All the evidence pointed against her. It was obvious she was guilty. He looked down at the contract on his desk.

But should he believe the proof of his eyes?

Or the proof of his heart?

Standing alone in the shadows of his study, Vladimir drank the vodka in one gulp and put the glass down softly on a table.

Loving her had brought him to life again. Going back to the window, he opened it and leaned against the sill. He took a deep breath of the cold air, smelling the frozen sea, hearing the plaintive cry of distant, unseen birds. Midnight in Russia, in January, was frozen and white, gray and dead.

But still, he knew spring would come.

He took another deep breath. Everything had changed for him. And yet nothing had.

He loved her. And he always would.

Vladimir looked back down at the unsigned contract. In a sudden movement, he leaned over the polished wood of his desk where, hours ago, he'd made love to her, the woman he loved. Where he'd looked into her beautiful face and told her his love for her would last forever.

Slowly he reached for an expensive ballpoint pen. He looked down, reading for the tenth time the contract that would forever give his billion-dollar company to his brother.

And then, with a jagged scrawl, Vladimir signed his name.

The warm sunlight on Bree's face woke her from a vivid dream. She'd been standing with Vladimir on a beach in Hawaii, the surf rushing against their bare feet, the warm wind filled with the scent of flowers as they spoke their wedding vows.

Vladimir's eyes looked blue as the sea. *I, Vladimir, take you, Breanna, to be my wife....*

Smiling to herself, still drowsing, Bree reached out her arm. But his side of the bed was empty.

With a gasp, she sat up.

Last night, she'd thrown herself at Vladimir because she'd been physically unable to let him sign away his company to his brother. But she still didn't know what to do. She couldn't betray him. Or her sister.

I'm in love with you, Breanna. I never stopped loving you. And I never will.

She trembled, blinking back tears.

He loved her.

But even before he'd spoken the words, she should have known. He'd shown her his love a hundred times over, with each gift more precious than the last. Bree looked down at Snowy, curled up in a ball at the foot of her bed. Vladimir dreamed bigger things for her than she dared dream for herself, buying her a Hawaiian resort to support her dream of running a small bed-and-breakfast. And last night, he'd set her free. He'd sacrificed his own needs for hers.

Bree took a deep breath, setting her jaw.

She was going to tell him everything.

Pulling on a T-shirt and jeans, she went downstairs, her whole body shaking with fear. She tried not to think of Josie, or the risk she was taking. When Bree told him her sister was in danger, he wouldn't coldly reply that Josie should face the consequences of her own actions. Would he? He would help Bree save her.

But if he didn't...

Oh, God. She couldn't even think of it.

Going down the hallway, she looked in his office. It was empty. Her cheeks grew hot as she saw the desk where they'd made love so passionately last night. Then she stiffened. With an intake of breath, she rushed into the room and rifled quickly through the documents now stacked neatly on his desk, intending to destroy the contract before Vladimir ever saw it.

Then she gasped. Lifting the page, she stared at his scrawled signature.

He'd done it.

He must have had no idea what he was signing. But he'd transferred his company to his younger brother.

Bree closed her eyes, holding the paper to her chest. Why had he finally decided to love her now, of all times? It had taken Vladimir ten years to trust her again. It would take a single act for her to wipe that trust off the earth forever.

But what if this was a sign? What if this was the universe telling her what to do?

Midnight tonight was the deadline to save her sister, and Bree held in her hands the golden ticket. And unlike Vladimir's mercy, it was guaranteed. She could exchange it for Josie, then return to Russia and beg for Vladimir's forgiveness. After all,

f anyone was going to be thrown on his mercy, shouldn't it be
Bree herself, not her helpless younger sister?

*Even if I give Kasimir this contract, it'll never stand in any
court,* she told herself. Vladimir was powerful, well connected.
He would be fine.

Even if he had enemies aplenty who would rejoice to see
his downfall....

I'm in love with you, Breanna. She whimpered as she remembered the dark midnight of Vladimir's eyes, the hoarse
rasp of his voice. *I never stopped loving you.*

With a choked sob, she ran upstairs. Not letting herself
look at the mussed-up sheets of the bed where he'd held her
last night as she wept, she packed up her duffel bag, tucking
the paper beneath her passport.

"Are you leaving?"

Looking up with an intake of breath, she saw Vladimir in
the doorway, wearing a black button-down shirt and black
trousers. His face was half-hidden in the shadow.

She swallowed. "Yes." She turned away. "You set me free.
So I'm going." *Forgive me. I can't take the chance.*

He exhaled, and came closer. When she clearly saw his face,
she nearly staggered back, shocked at the luminous pain in his
eyes. Then she blinked, and it was gone.

"I have a plane waiting to take you wherever you want to
go," he said.

"Just like that?"

"Just like that."

"You knew I would leave?"

"Yes." Lifting his gaze to hers, he whispered, "But I hoped
you wouldn't. I hoped you could—love me—enough."

Her heart was slamming against her chest. She wanted to
sob, to throw her arms around him, to pull out the contract and
rip it up in front of his eyes. "Perhaps I'll come back."

"Perhaps," he said, but his lips twisted. "And Snowy? Are
you leaving her behind?"

"Of course not," Bree said, shocked. "I wouldn't abandon her!"

"No," he replied quietly. "I know that. You wouldn't abandon anyone you truly loved."

Bree swallowed. "Vladimir, I told you the truth. I do love you. But I—"

"You don't have to explain." His eyes met hers. "Just be happy, Bree. That's all I want. All I've ever wanted."

"Your great-grandmother's necklace is on the nightstand," she said in a small voice.

"That was a gift." Picking up the necklace, he held it out to her. "Take it."

She shook her head. "That belongs to...to your future wife."

Coming up behind her, he said softly, "It belongs to you."

He put the necklace around her neck. She felt the cool, hard stone against her skin, and grief crashed over her like a wave. Closing her eyes, she sagged back against him. He wrapped his arms around her, cradling her against his chest for a single moment.

Then he let her go.

"I will always love you, Breanna," he said in a low voice. He turned away. "Goodbye."

Vladimir left their bedroom without looking back. She wanted to chase after him. She wanted to fall at his knees weeping and begging for his forgiveness.

But she couldn't. She had the signed contract. Fate had made the decision for her.

It won't stand up in court, she told herself again, her teeth chattering. *After Josie's safe, I'll come back. I will somehow make him forgive me....*

Bree had no memory of collecting Snowy and her duffel bag. But somehow, twenty minutes later, they were in the back of the limo, driving away from the palace. Her puppy sat in her lap, whining as she looked through the window at Vladimir's palace, then plaintively up at her mistress.

As Bree looked back at the fairy-tale palace, snow sparkled on Vladimir's wide fields and on the forest of bare, black trees around the palace of blue and gold. And she realized she was weeping, pressing her hand against the necklace at her throat.

Bree felt something prick her finger. Looking down, she saw the peridot's sharp edge had pricked her skin. A Russian prince had once sent his beloved wife and child into the safety of exile, with this necklace as their only memento of him, before he'd died alone in Siberia, in ultimate sacrifice.

A sob rose to Bree's lips. As Vladimir had sacrificed...

Her eyes widened. With an intake of breath, she looked back at the palace.

You knew I would leave?

Yes. His eyes had seared hers, straight through her soul. *But I hoped you wouldn't. I hoped you could—love me—enough.*

What had Vladimir sacrificed for her?

Was it possible...that he *knew?*

"Stop," she cried to the driver. "Turn around! Go back!"

The puppy barked madly, turning circles in her lap as the limo stopped, struggling to turn around on the long, slender road surrounded by snow.

Bree didn't care if the signed contract had miraculously fallen into her lap. She didn't care what the universe might be trying to tell her. *The choice was still hers.*

All this time, she'd thought she had to choose between the two people she loved. She didn't.

She just had to choose herself.

Ten years ago, loving Vladimir had changed her. He'd given her a second chance at life. He'd shown her she could be something besides a poker-playing con artist with a flexible conscience. He'd made her want to be *more.* To be honest and true, not just when it was convenient, but always.

This was the woman she was born to be.

And she would never be anything else ever again. Not for any price.

Before the limo stopped in the courtyard, Bree had thrown open the door, leaving her duffel bag and valuables behind as she leaped headlong into the snow. Her puppy bounded beside her, barking frantically as Bree ran straight back to the only answer her heart had ever wanted.

She found him in his study, standing by the window that overlooked the sea.

"Vladimir," she cried.

Slowly he turned, his handsome face like granite. It was only when she came closer that she saw the tears sparkling in his eyes.

He wasn't made of ice. He was flesh and blood. And letting her go had ripped him to the bone.

Choking back a sob, she threw herself into his arms. She jumped up, hugging him even with her legs. Startled, he caught her, holding against him.

"Are you really here?" he breathed, stroking her hair, as if he thought she was a dream. "You were free. You had the signed contract. Why did you return?"

Bree slowly slid down his body, her eyes wide. "You knew."

Blinking fast, Vladimir nodded.

"Why did you do it?" she said. "Why would you set me free when you knew you'd lose everything?"

His phone rang from his pocket, but he ignored it. He cupped her face, tracing his thumbs against her trembling mouth. "Because I knew I'd already lost everything, if you walked out my door." He shook his head. "I had to know. If you really loved me. Or if you...didn't."

"And what did you decide?" she whispered through numb lips.

"I decided it didn't matter." He looked straight into her eyes. "I meant what I said. Whatever you do, I will love you, Breanna. For the rest of my life."

She burst into tears, pressing her face against his chest. "I'm sorry," she sobbed as her tears soaked his shirt. "I was wrong to think I could ever betray you."

He stroked her hair gently. "Did my brother promise you money to pay off your old debts? Is that why you agreed to help him?"

"*Help* him?" Drawing back, Bree looked at Vladimir. "I had no idea he was behind us getting jobs in Hawaii. Not until he threatened me!"

Vladimir's hand grew still. "He threatened you?"

"At the New Year's Eve ball."

He sucked in his breath. "Kasimir was there?"

"He found me on the dance floor when I was alone. Right after I told you I loved you—when you took off...."

"*That* was why you've been acting so distant?" Vladimir looked at her, his expression fierce. "What did he say to you?"

A lump rose in her throat.

"He's married Josie," she whispered. "He's holding her hostage."

"What?" Vladimir cried.

"He wanted to get back your family's land, and it was the only way to break the trust. Josie agreed to marry him, because she thought it was the only way to save me."

"From what?" he demanded.

"From you." With a bitter laugh, Bree wiped her eyes. "Funny, isn't it?"

His face filled with cold rage. His phone started ringing again. He didn't move a muscle to answer. "Hilarious."

"He said if I ever wanted to see her again, I had to bring the signed contract to his house in Marrakech before midnight tonight."

Vladimir looked ready to commit murder. "Why didn't you tell me?"

"I'm sorry," Bree said miserably. "I was afraid you'd say it was Josie's own fault, and that she should face the consequences."

He scowled. "She's just a kid. I never meant she should—" He broke off with a curse as, for the third time in five minutes, his phone started ringing again. He snatched it up angrily. "What the hell do you want?"

Then Vladimir froze.

"Kasimir," he said quietly. "About time."

Stricken, Bree held her breath, staring up at him.

His eyes narrowed. "She already told me. Your plan to turn us against each other didn't work." He listened, then paced three steps. "I am willing to make the trade."

Bree covered her mouth with her hands, realizing that Vladimir was offering to give up his billion-dollar company to save her baby sister. Then he scowled.

"Kasimir, don't be a fool! You can still—"

Vladimir stopped, then pulled the phone from his ear, staring at it in shock.

"What happened?" Bree said anxiously. "What did he say? Is he willing to make the trade?"

"No," Vladimir said, sounding dazed. "He said he no longer has any intention of divorcing her. He told me I could keep my stupid company."

Her mouth dropped open. "He said that?"

"His exact words." Vladimir's lips twisted. "It seems he cares about keeping her more than hurting me."

Bree took a deep breath. She could still hear Kasimir's cold words. *What I want is revenge. And I will have it.* "I'm not so sure...."

Then she remembered the anger in his blue eyes.

So much for Josie's sacrifice, he'd accused her bitterly.

Bree had wondered about that then. It seemed even more certain now. She licked her lips. "Is it possible...he *could* care for her?"

"I don't know about that. But he won't hurt her. My brother had—has—a good heart."

"How can you say that, after how he's tried to destroy you?"

Vladimir's jaw tightened.

"Perhaps he had a good cause," he admitted in a low vo. Shaking his head, he continued, "But your sister is in no da ger. Kasimir hates me, and perhaps you. But he has no quar rel with her."

"If I could only be absolutely sure—"

"She is safe," Vladimir said simply. "I would stake my life on it. And the fact that he actually wants to stay married to her…" He slowly smiled. "It's interesting. Very interesting."

His phone rang abruptly in his hand, and he put it to his ear. "Hello?"

Kasimir? Bree mouthed.

He shook his head at her, his hand tightening on the phone. "Lefèvre, at last. Give me some good news." He listened. And then a smile lifted his handsome face. Seeing that smile, Bree's heart soared. She suddenly knew everything was going to be all right.

He hung up. "My investigator has found her."

Bree gave a joyful sob. "Where is she?"

"Safe." His smile widened. "And very close."

Bree started to turn. "We should go to her—"

Vladimir grabbed her by the wrist. "First things first," he growled. "I want to do this before anything else comes between us." And before her amazed eyes, he fell to one knee.

"I don't have a ring," he said quietly, "because I didn't let myself hope this could happen." Quirking a dark eyebrow, he gave her a cheeky grin. "And I think I'd better let you pick out your own ring, in any case."

She held her breath.

His darkly handsome face grew serious. Vulnerable.

"Will you marry me?" he whispered.

Marry him? Bree's heart galloped. Vladimir wanted her to be his wife, the mother of his children—just like she'd dreamed?

He swallowed, and his stark blue eyes became uncertain.

ll you have me, Breanna?" Reaching up, he gripped her
ds in his own. "Will you be mine?"

Tears rose to her eyes.

"I am yours already. Don't you remember?" The corners
of her trembling lips tugged upwards. "You own me, heart
and soul."

He exhaled in a rush. "Does that mean you'll be my wife?"

"Yes." Tears streamed unchecked down her cheeks as she
pulled on his hands, lifting him to his feet. "With all my heart."

Vladimir cupped her cheek. "I belong to you," he vowed.
"Now and forever."

As their white Russian puppy leaped and barked in happy
circles around their feet, he wrapped Bree in his arms. Lowering his head, he kissed her with the passion and adoration
that promised a lifetime. And she knew, come what may, that
he would always love her, because she'd been brave enough
to love herself.

"Never play with your heart, kiddo," her father had once
told her. "Only a sucker plays with his heart. Even if you win,
you lose."

But as Bree looked up into the face of the man she loved,
the man she would soon wed, the man who would bring Josie
safely home—she suddenly knew her father was wrong. Because when the chips were down, love was the only thing worth
a risk. The only thing worth gambling for.

Playing with all your heart…was the *only* way to win.

* * * * *

LET'S TALK
Romance

For exclusive extracts, competitions
and special offers, find us online:

 facebook.com/millsandboon

@MillsandBoon

@MillsandBoonUK

Get in touch on 01413 063232

For all the latest titles coming soon, visit
millsandboon.co.uk/nextmonth

MILLS & BOON

THE HEART OF ROMANCE

A ROMANCE FOR EVERY READER

MODERN

Prepare to be swept off your feet by sophisticated, sexy and seductive heroes, in some of the world's most glamourous and romantic locations, where power and passion collide.

HISTORICAL

Escape with historical heroes from time gone by. Whether your passion is for wicked Regency Rakes, muscled Vikings or rugged Highlanders, awak the romance of the past.

MEDICAL

Set your pulse racing with dedicated, delectable doctors in the high-pressure world of medicine, where emotions run high and passion, comfort an love are the best medicine.

True Love

Celebrate true love with tender stories of heartfelt romance, from the rush of falling in love to the joy a new baby can bring, and a focus on the emotional heart of a relationship.

Desire

Indulge in secrets and scandal, intense drama and plenty of sizzling hot action with powerful and passionate heroes who have it all: wealth, status, good looks…everything but the right woman.

HEROES

Experience all the excitement of a gripping thriller, with an intense romance at its heart. Resourceful, true-to-life women and strong, fearless me face danger and desire - a killer combination!

To see which titles are coming soon, please visit

millsandboon.co.uk/nextmonth

JOIN US ON SOCIAL MEDIA!

Stay up to date with our latest releases, author news and gossip, special offers and discounts, and all the behind-the-scenes action from Mills & Boon...

 millsandboon

 millsandboonuk

millsandboon

It might just be true love...